NIGHT AND DAY

IRIS JOHANSEN

St. Martin's Paperbacks

NIGHT AND DAY

Copyright © 2016 by IJ Development, Inc.
Excerpt from *No Easy Target* copyright © 2017 by IJ Development, Inc.

For information address St. Martin's Press, 175 Fifth Avenue, New York, NY 10010.

ISBN: 978-1-250-07590-1

Our books may be purchased in bulk for promotional, educational, or business use. Please contact your local bookseller or the Macmillan Corporate and Premium Sales Department at 1-800-221-7945, ext. 5442, or by e-mail at MacmillanSpecialMarkets@macmillan.com.

Printed in the United States of America

St. Martin's Press hardcover edition / July 2016
St. Martin's Paperbacks edition / March 2017

St. Martin's Paperbacks are published by St. Martin's Press, 175 Fifth Avenue, New York, NY 10010.

10 9 8 7 6 5 4 3 2 1

ALSO BY IRIS JOHANSEN

PRAISE FOR IRIS JOHANSEN'S EVE DUNCAN NOVELS

SHADOW PLAY

"Johansen delivers a no-holds-barred mystery that maintains suspense throughout and boasts a cast of multifaceted characters."
                                   —*Publishers Weekly*

"Thrilling, emotional, and downright riveting certainly sum up this incredible tale!"   —*RT Book Reviews*

"Eve Duncan novels by Johansen are so good that, supernatural or not, readers and fans remain completely engaged."   —*Suspense Magazine*

"The suspense of every page is enough to keep readers hooked in all night long."   —*San Francisco Book Review*

YOUR NEXT BREATH

"Delivering gut-wrenching emotion and spine-tingling suspense is what Johansen does best, and when you add in a touch of the supernatural . . . you get the perfect storm of a thriller! Johansen never disappoints."
                          —*RT Book Reviews* (4½ stars)

"Gripping . . . Iris Johansen's talent in character development, impeccable plotting, and remarkable depiction is nonpareil."   —*Reader to Reader*

SILENCING EVE

"Johansen brings her tautly paced trilogy to a pulse-pounding conclusion."   —*Booklist*

CHAPTER
1

GAELKAR, SCOTLAND

I don't like to lose, Eve. I did very well, but I don't like partial victories."

The woman's voice drifted back from the cockpit of the helicopter to where Cara was lying in the rear.

So hard, Cara thought dazedly through the thickness of the chloroform clouding her mind. The woman's voice was so hard and full of venom, and it was all aimed at Eve. Cara had heard that voice before as she had floated in and out of consciousness during the last minutes after Eve had come and talked to her, comforted her as she lay in the woods. The woman's voice had been hard and ugly then, too. But Cara couldn't remember exactly what she had said.

She had to protect Eve. It was all Cara's fault that Eve was here and had to face those terrible people. She should have known Eve would come after her. Just the fact that Cara was only eleven would guarantee that Eve would try to save her. Eve spent her life trying to protect children and punish the people who hurt them. But Eve hadn't been able to save Cara. She could hazily remember shots and explosions and that woman's hard voice giving orders to everyone around her. Giving orders to Eve . . .

She had to help her. Help Eve.

Cara tried to move, but her muscles seemed weighted. She tried to open her eyes. The second time she made it. She was still on the floor of the helicopter, where she had been shoved only minutes before. Why was she there?

It didn't matter. She had to get to Eve.

There was something bad happening . . .

Keep your eyes open.

Help Eve.

That hard, vicious voice again. "I want it all. I think I need to do something to impress you with that."

A shot.

"*No,*" Eve screamed.

Terror seared through Cara.

Eve shot! Eve screaming!

Eve dying as Cara's sister had died, as her friend Elena had died.

Not again. Please, not again. Not Eve.

But the woman was laughing. "Let's get out of here, Nikolai. I believe that Eve Duncan has learned a lesson she'll remember."

Maybe that meant Eve wasn't dead, Cara thought. Maybe she could still save her. But the helicopter was lifting, she realized in a panic. She had to get them to land, to go back so that she could help Eve.

Once more she tried to move. Weak. So weak.

She managed to turn over and look around her. Find something to hurt them, to make them go back.

What was she thinking? She was only eleven, just a kid. How could she make anyone do anything?

How could she not do it? Eve was hurt, maybe dying. She had to help her.

Find something . . .

There was a flashlight and a tool chest on the opposite side of the helicopter. Maybe there was something she could use inside that chest. She started to crawl toward it. She had to go very slowly. Her arms seemed to be working now, but her legs were still weak. She finally reached the tool chest and reached out to flip open the lid.

"I thought I heard something back here. What are you doing?"

Cara froze. Then she turned her head to look at the woman standing several feet away.

Dark eyes, with lustrous dark hair in a single braid and a face that was as beautiful as any movie star's. She wasn't smiling and her eyes were narrowed on Cara. "Or maybe I can guess what you're doing. You may have been with Eve Duncan too long. What has she said to you? Has she completely destroyed your faith in me, Cara?"

It was the same voice that had spoken to Eve with such ugliness, but now this woman's voice was no longer hard, Cara realized in confusion. It was soft, silky, and full of both sadness and affection.

"Eve . . ." Cara's voice sounded hoarse, slurred even to her. "You . . . hurt . . . Eve."

She shook her head. "Nonsense. Of course, I didn't. Even though she hurt me more than you can imagine." She knelt down beside Cara and took her hand. "But that's all over. I'll make you understand, Cara. After all we've gone through, we're together now." She touched her cheek with a gentle finger. "What a pretty little girl you are. I believe you look a little like me. What do you think?"

Cara gazed at her in bewilderment. "Why should I look—"

"Because it's perfectly natural that you should, silly." She was laughing, her beautiful face brimming with warmth and humor. "Because I'm Natalie Castino. Because I'm your mother, Cara."

LOCH GAELKAR
TWO HOURS LATER

"Are you okay, Eve?" Jane MacGuire was walking toward her down the south bank of the lake. "I saw Joe up on the road with the local police getting rid of the last of the IEDs. I expected him to be with you."

"What was he going to do? Hold my hand?" Eve shook her head. "You've been doing your share of that, Jane. I'm not the one Natalie shot. It was Joe, and he was lucky it was only a flesh wound. I believe she was only trying to show me that she could reach out and hurt us whenever she wished. Give the guy a break."

"You mean give you a break," Jane said quietly. "I know that you don't want us hovering over you. But having Natalie snatch Cara like that had to be a traumatic wound in itself. Did you tell Joe to go and get rid of those booby traps?"

"I suggested it might be the thing to do so that everyone will have access to the lake. As soon as MacDuff is out of the hospital, I know he'll be back here hunting for that treasure chest." Her lips twisted. "And Joe needed to have something to do until we know something about Cara. He called his contact, Burbank, at Scotland Yard, and put him on tracking down that helicopter Natalie Castino used to take Cara. But it may take time. You know Joe would be going straight after Natalie Castino on his own if he wasn't kept busy. Joe's not the most patient person."

"Neither are you." Jane shook her head as she looked at Eve. She had been Eve's adopted daughter since she was ten years old, and she knew her strength. Eve Duncan had become one of the foremost forensic sculptors in the world after her seven-year-old daughter, Bonnie, had been taken and died. She had given closure to hundreds of families who had lost their children over the years, and she didn't deserve to have to face this threat to Cara. Eve had originally only wanted to help and shelter the child who had known only fear and deadly risk. But Jane knew that had changed. Eve had grown to love Cara, and she didn't need this heartache and trauma. Particularly not at this point in her life. "It's been a rough day. How do you feel?"

"Angry, scared, panicky." Her lips twisted. "How do you expect me to feel? That bitch Natalie Castino has Cara, and I don't know what she's doing to her."

"I meant physically."

Eve glanced at her. "Oh, for heaven's sake. Fine. Just fine. There's no way I'd have a miscarriage. Do you think I'd let Natalie do that to me?"

"No, you're tough. Just checking. It's been one hell of a day." She looked up at the road, where Joe Quinn was working. "I'm certain that Joe asked the same thing."

"Of course he did."

"And that's why he's up there disarming IEDs."

"He wanted to do it. He's got those police experts helping. And he's got this water-blade gadget that makes it fairly safe. It's not as if I—" She broke off. "I wish I had something as valuable to do. I hate this waiting."

"I know you do." She took her arm. "Come on, let's get a cup of coffee. I believe we both need it." She guided her down the steep slope toward the camp area, where their living and work tents were set up beside the lake. "It can't be too much longer." She took the coffeepot simmering on the campfire and poured Eve a cup of coffee. "Scotland Yard and Interpol have all kinds of high-end satellite stuff. All they have to do is locate one helicopter." She handed Eve the cup, then poured one for herself. "And a child is involved. That always makes a difference."

"It didn't make a difference to Natalie Castino." Eve sat down by the fire and cradled her cup in her hands. "You'd think I wouldn't be so shocked. It's not as if I haven't run across all kinds of monsters who didn't think a child was important enough to care whether they lived or died."

"But none like Natalie Castino," Jane said quietly as she sat down across from her. "She appears to be one of a kind."

Eve nodded jerkily. "She's clever and manipulative and a complete sociopath. I don't think Cara would have a chance if Natalie decided to focus all that poison on her."

"I'm not so sure," Jane said. "Cara may only be eleven years old, but she's smart and she's wary and she's been on the run since she was a child of three. She may be more able to deal with her mother than you'd think."

"Natalie Castino has been responsible for three deaths today." Eve shuddered. "I watched her shoot Ramon Franco in the heart because she just thought he might be a problem for her later."

"I don't think the world will miss Franco," Jane said dryly. "He was a killer for Alfredo Salazar's drug cartel and nasty as they come. And Joe actually took out Salazar by planting IEDs on that hill where you met with him and Natalie."

"Because Natalie set Salazar up to die on that hill," Eve said. "Just as she set up the ambush on her husband

in Mexico City so that she could frame her lover, Salazar, for his death. It was all Natalie."

"I wasn't defending her," Jane said. "I was just point-
ing out that ever since Cara came into your life, you've
been dealing with a pretty rough group of scumbags. It's
a wonder you've survived them."

"It wasn't Cara's fault. She was a victim."

Jane knew that was true. She was saying all the wrong
things. Cara deserved a chance for a normal life after
years of running, and Eve hadn't even known Cara was
involved at the beginning of the nightmare. She had
told Jane she had been sent the skull of a nine-year-old
girl to reconstruct by a sheriff in northern California. She
had done the reconstruction and become involved with
that skull in a very personal way. It was clear someone
had not wanted that child's skull to be reconstructed or
her body to be identified. After Eve had sent off the reconstruction to the sheriff who had requested her help,
the FedEx driver who had picked it up had been murdered and the reconstruction stolen. Eve had been upset
and angry, and she and Joe had gone out to California to
find out who that child was and who had killed her. After a heartrending, painful search, they discovered that
the little girl was Jenny Castino, the daughter of Juan
Castino and his wife, Natalie. Castino was the head of a
drug cartel in Mexico City, and his daughter had been
kidnapped, together with her sister, Cara, and Elena, their
nanny, over eight years before. Jenny had been killed
shortly after they had been kidnapped, but Cara had escaped and was still alive and on the run. The hired killer,
Walsh, who had murdered Jenny, was committed to finding Cara and killing her to protect himself from the possibility of anyone's finding out he was responsible for the
crimes. Eve and Joe had stopped him, killed him, and

saved Cara. But the nightmare hadn't ended. Salazar, who had hired Walsh, had gone on the hunt himself. Which was why Eve and Cara had ended up in the Highlands of Scotland, hiding.

And why Natalie Castino had suddenly emerged as the real monster of the piece.

"It's still hard for me to believe a mother would kill her own children," Jane said. "I can't get my head around it."

"Everyone has trouble with it," Eve said. "Maternal love dominates every family and, when it doesn't exist, it turns that family upside down. Joe said that even Detective Manez, who suspected Natalie wasn't a grieving mother, wouldn't commit her because he didn't want to believe it. It's a crime against the helpless from the person who should be dedicated to caring for them."

"You've seen it before?"

"Only a couple times in my entire career. The courts declared both women insane." She shook her head. "I told you, it's hard to prove, hard to believe." Her lips thinned. "Natalie isn't insane though she'd accept that loophole if she had to do it. She's a sociopath, and that's even more frightening. She'll do anything she wants to do unless there's a danger to her in doing it."

"And she wanted to kill Jenny and Cara. You told me that she played the affectionate mother before they were kidnapped."

"She did, but they were in her way somehow. Her husband wanted sons and was toying with mistresses who might give them to him. She was probably afraid she'd be displaced. She liked being queen of all she surveyed. Juan Castino was the most powerful cartel boss in Mexico City, and everyone was afraid to cross him. She liked that power. Once the children were out of the picture, she would have been a bereaved mother, and her husband would have hesitated to set her aside. She was the daughter of a Russian Mafia boss, Sergai Kaskov, and he would not have been pleased. Castino would have found himself dangling headless from one of the bridges down there."

"And no one suspected her of having anything to do with the kidnapping of the children?"

"She seduced and manipulated Alfredo Salazar into hiring Walsh to do the actual kidnapping . . . and killing. He was the head of a rival cartel, who hated Castino anyway."

"Terrible," Jane murmured. "I knew some of this, but no details about Natalie Castino. Only the fact that Joe wasn't sure that Natalie was what she seemed to be and neither were you. No wonder you're frightened for Cara. Natalie Castino has to be totally ruthless."

"But we have a wild card. When Natalie found out that we might have found Cira's treasure, she lit up like the Fourth of July. She might have even moved up her plans about killing her husband and Salazar to make an adjustment that would suit her." Her hands were trembling as she lifted her cup to her lips. "She wants money and power, and Cira's gold could give it to her. We've just got to use that wild card to get Cara back."

"I'm sure it's not as if it hasn't been used before for less worthy purposes," Jane said. All through the many centuries since the eruption of Vesuvius had destroyed Herculaneum, that fabulous chest of coins had been a lure that had drawn everyone who had heard about it, she thought. But it had all centered around Cira, the young actress who had been born a slave, and who had taken the gold with her when she had escaped the raging volcano. She had schemed and fought to keep that treasure for herself and her family even to the extent of fleeing to the wilds of Scotland and establishing the MacDuff dynasty here at Gaelkar. "We'll find a way."

Eve looked down at the huge lake, with its eternal mist hovering over the entire north bank. "What do you think the chances are that it's really down there?"

"Sometimes I think that it is, sometimes I just don't know. That chest of coins has been missing for centuries, and you know that Cira has been a mystery I've never been able to solve."

"You know MacDuff would argue with you," Eve said dryly. "He's convinced that you have some kind of ancestral connection or something with Cira and that you can lead him to that treasure."

"Because I had those dreams about Cira when I was seventeen? That doesn't prove anything." But it had meant a great deal to Jane while she was going through that chaotic period. Those dreams had been so real, they had dominated her thoughts and her life. And when she had been driven to do in-depth research and found that Cira had actually existed, they had led her to MacDuff, the Laird of MacDuff's Run. "I don't dream about Cira any longer."

"Except that one dream that led us all here," Eve said. "You may not be sure that chest is out there somewhere lost in that mist, but MacDuff believes it."

"He's grasping at straws because no one has even gotten close to finding Cira's gold." She smiled. "But maybe Cira is ready to release her secrets. And I couldn't think of anyone more worth her doing it for than Cara."

"Neither can I." Eve moistened her lips. "I hardly knew Cara when all this began. I felt sorry for her. I wanted to help her. But then I got to know her. She was brave and honest and sometimes a kid, but most of the time more mature than she should be." Her voice was unsteady. "She wanted to help me. She wanted to take care of Jock Gavin. One of the last things she asked about was Jock."

"He was her friend. She didn't have any friends," Jane said. "And because she'd lost so much, she didn't want to lose either of you."

"I don't want to lose her, either," Eve said. "I . . . care about her, Jane. I won't let her be taken from us."

"I know you won't." She frowned as a thought occurred to her. "But Cara isn't going to let Natalie Castino hurt you, either. That may be a problem. I've gotten to know Cara. She'd fight for you, Eve. And that might mean she'd piss off Natalie Castino. Is that possible?"

"God only knows," Eve said wearily. "It depends on how Natalie handles her and what she wants from her. Cara hasn't seen her mother since she was three years old. I know that Elena, who raised her and took her on the run when her sister was killed, told her it wasn't safe for her to go back to Mexico to her parents. But it wasn't because Elena suspected Natalie. It was because the cartel situation was so deadly there that she thought it wouldn't be safe for her. They had no idea who was behind the kidnapping of the girls. Elena thought it might be Salazar, who was a rival cartel boss. He was an enemy of Castino and wanted to hurt him by taking and killing his children. We didn't suspect Natalie ourselves until Joe recently found out Natalie and Salazar were lovers."

"But you didn't tell Cara?"

"It didn't seem the time to tell her that it was her mother who had probably murdered her sister," Eve said bitterly. "How do you tell a child something like that? She was safe with me. I thought I could keep her that way. And she was having enough to face at the time."

Jane was silent. But now Cara was going to have to

face that truth and make her own judgments . . . and mistakes.

"I know." Eve was reading her expression. "Hindsight, Jane. I should have prepared her. I left her alone and vulnerable. I just have to trust her and hope for the best."

Eleven years old, Jane wanted to tell Eve. Cara was only eleven years old, and she was up against a woman Eve had called a monster. She didn't say it. "Cara's very smart. She'll get through this. We just have to—"

"Burbank just called me." Joe Quinn was striding down the slope toward the campfire. "They've located Natalie's helicopter. They think it's heading for Liverpool. Natalie will probably be switching to a private jet there. Let's go."

Eve jumped to her feet. "Can't Scotland Yard intercept them? After all, it's a kidnapping."

"It would be difficult. Proof. Family rights. Natalie is her mother." Joe took Eve's elbow and headed toward the road. "It's probably going to have to be us."

Jane felt powerless. "What can I do to help?" Jane called after them. "Should I come along?"

"No, stay here and hold everything together," Joe said over his shoulder. "The local police aren't pleased at those booby traps on the road. They're asking a lot of questions I don't have time to answer. The first thing that came to their mind was terrorists. They're going to ask a lot more if they find out we've blown up the top of one of those scenic hills, and there may be bodies to deal with."

"How are you going to get to Liverpool in time?"

"I parked the helicopter about seven miles from here when I arrived in that heavy fog. We'll grab one of the cars and drive there and hop on it. Try to cover for us, Jane."

"I'll do what I can." She gazed after them as they hurried up the slope toward the road. "But I'd rather be with you. Be careful, Eve . . ."

Be careful . . .

The time for being careful was over if they could manage to reach Liverpool in time, Eve thought, as she waved back at Jane in response and turned to Joe. "What are our chances?"

"Natalie's pilot is bound to reach there before we do," he said curtly. "They have a big head start. But they may not be able to pick up a private jet right away. Burbank said they'd checked the rental companies, and there was no advance rental to Natalie or any Russian company or entity. We have a chance of getting there before they find one to rent."

"That's not like Natalie." Eve frowned. "She planned everything else out to the last detail. Why would she slip up there?"

"Maybe it wasn't up to her." Joe's brows rose as he glanced at her. "You're very sure. You seem to be on the same wavelength as Natalie Castino."

"Heaven help me if I am," Eve said. "There's no way I'd want to have any bond or similarity with Natalie Castino."

"But you believe you know how she thinks."

"Yes." She and Natalie had only shared phone calls and one traumatic meeting that had ended with Natalie's shooting Joe and giving him that flesh wound before taking Cara. But there was no doubt that Eve knew the woman in a very real and terrifying way. "And she knows how I think." Her lips tightened. "Though she believes I'm a sentimental fool and will try to use it against me to get her hands on that chest of coins she wants so desperately."

"Which she won't be able to do if we can stop her at Liverpool. Then we can—" He stopped short as they reached the road. "Shit."

Eve's eyes flew to his face and then followed his gaze to a black limo that had parked a good distance down the road behind the yellow tape put up by the local police. A man in a brown suit and graying hair had gotten out of the car and was walking down the slope toward the camp. "What is it? Who is he?"

"Agent Jason Toller. Justice Department. Bad timing."

Worse than bad timing, Eve thought. Joe had told her that Agent Toller had been investigating Jenny Castino's death after he'd received a tip the skeleton found in California was the daughter of drug czar Juan Castino. He'd not been pleased that Joe and Eve had taken Cara, Castino's other daughter, and hidden her away from both the Mexican and U.S. governments. So displeased that he'd threatened to toss Joe into jail for interfering with an international immigration case if he got in the way of his investigation. He would definitely consider Joe's leaving the U.S. and rushing here to help Eve and Cara as getting in his way.

"We don't have time to make excuses or try to talk him out of anything." Eve added with frustration, "And, dammit, we can't have him chasing after us."

"And what do you suggest?" Joe asked. "He's not a bad guy, just a hard-ass. I'd really prefer not to shoot him."

"No choice. You go and try to stop Natalie." She turned on her heel and started back down the slope. "I'm not going to let him grill Jane when she doesn't have any idea what's happening. I'll try to delay him myself. Hurry. Get out of sight and on the road."

He started up the slope. "I may get to Liverpool too late, you know."

"And you might not. Call me, Joe."

He didn't answer.

When she looked back, he was gone.

And Toller was heading toward Jane, who was still standing by the campfire.

Eve increased her pace as she glanced over her shoulder.

No sign of Joe. Good.

Jane was always careful and discreet, but Eve hadn't mentioned Joe's trouble with Toller to her. Still, there was no way Jane would say anything, and in a few minutes, Eve would be there.

And hopefully Joe would be halfway to that helicopter he'd parked several miles away.

She wanted to be with him. She wanted to be there when he tried to stop Natalie. As she had told Joe, she *knew* her. If Natalie panicked, Eve might be able to talk to her, deal with her.

And keep Cara safe.

But she had made the right decision, she realized reluctantly. Toller was far more likely to be antagonistic and interfere with Joe than with her.

And Joe could fly the helicopter.

Trust Joe.

And pray he got there in time.

"Here you are, Eve." Jane smiled and turned to her as Eve reached her. "I was just telling this gentleman I had no idea where you'd disappeared. He was looking for either you or Joe." She gestured. "Agent Jason Toller with the Justice Department."

"Well, here I am," Eve said. "And I'm sure Joe is somewhere about."

"Exactly where, Ms. Duncan?" Toller asked.

"I saw him down by the lake several minutes ago," Jane said quickly. "I think it's something to do with our Cara, Eve."

"*Our* Cara?" Toller repeated sourly. "You do know, Ms. MacGuire, that Cara Castino has been held illegally by Joe Quinn and Eve Duncan and that your knowledge makes you an accomplice?"

"She knows no such thing," Eve said bluntly. "Jane only knows that Cara is going to live with Joe and me on a trial basis before we commit to adopting her. I brought her on this trip to the Highlands so that Cara could get to know Jane. I'm sure you're aware that Jane is my adopted daughter."

"Yes, I'm aware of everything about Ms. MacGuire," Toller said curtly. "Including the fact that she's friends with John MacDuff, Lord of MacDuff's Run, who organized a hunt for a lost family treasure that included her and a few other intimate friends of the earl. Let's see, they were Jock Gavin and a Seth Caleb . . . It's very convenient that you suddenly felt the urge for a family reunion and joined them. Particularly since the hunt was to take place in the wilds of the Highlands." He looked at the surrounding rugged hills that plunged down to the large crystal blue lake. "A very good hiding place, wouldn't you say? I might have to have a talk with MacDuff."

"You will *not*," Eve said. "MacDuff is presently in the hospital, as you probably know. He was injured during the hunt and had to be airlifted out of here. You won't bother him or Jane or anyone else to try to get information from Joe or me." She turned to Jane. "Will you excuse us, Jane?"

"Are you sure?" Jane was gazing at Toller. "Stop worrying about me, Eve. If he's trying to intimidate me, he's not succeeding."

"I know that. I just don't like for you to have to fight my fight."

Jane smiled. "It's always my pleasure." She turned and walked toward the lake. "If you need me, call."

"Very loyal," Toller said. "But she should be intimidated. She's involved herself in a tangle that's of concern to our government."

"Back off," Eve said. "You'd have a hell of a time proving Jane was doing anything but being a good daughter and extending hospitality to me and Cara. As far as questioning MacDuff, you're in his country, and he has more influence here and in London than you'd ever dream. He's a war hero and something of a folk hero, too. You'd find yourself very unwelcome if you push him." She added, "But that was probably a bluff. Joe said you were smart and efficient and wanted to avoid international incidents. You wouldn't go up against MacDuff."

He was silent, staring at her. He shrugged. "No, I wouldn't."

"Then why did you try to bluff me?"

"Because I'm pissed off that Quinn made a fool of my agents and skipped out of the country. By doing it, he also made a fool of me. I warned him against that. I could tolerate his hiding you and the kid away. I knew we'd find you eventually. But I warned him that I'd toss him into jail if he made a move that would hurt my investigation. He did it anyway."

"To save Cara's life, to save my life."

"I have no proof of that. And he made me scramble to find him. But not too hard, he wasn't covering his tracks when he decided to go to you. He was just in a hurry. Which let me piece together a little of what was happening with you." His lips tightened. "Very little. There are too many blanks. MacDuff is in the hospital with broken bones, but they examined him for internal injuries that might have occurred from a blast. Would you like to tell me what happened to him?"

"Not unless you prove to me that it would help Cara."

"And those local policemen on the road up there brought in an explosives expert to disarm IEDs. Same answer?"

"Same answer." She paused. "But aren't you curious why someone would be so determined to kill an eleven-year-old girl that they'd plant IEDs to keep her from escaping?"

"All the more reason why you should turn her over to us to keep her safe."

"And you'd turn her over to Child Services and start negotiating with the Mexican government to return her to her loving parents. Isn't that right?"

"That's the law."

"And someone would be worried that she knew too much, had seen too much, and she could end up dead. Joe and I aren't going to risk that."

"You have no choice unless you intend to stay on the run."

"We'll find a way."

"Look, I told Quinn that, good as his intentions were, Cara Castino is a Mexican citizen who could cause us boundless red tape and years of diplomatic problems if we let her stay in the U.S. She'd be the focus of all kinds of activists on both sides of the border."

"He told me," Eve said coldly. "Screw your red tape. We're not sending her back to Mexico. She'd be surrounded by the worst elements if we did. The Mexican citizen who was her loving father was Juan Castino, a drug dealer who was high up on the Mexican government's list of killers and criminal kingpins. You'll notice I say 'was.' We were informed that Castino was

killed early this morning. I assume you heard the same
thing?"

"I did. But I'd be curious to know your source. The
story hasn't been released to the press yet. I've been told
the coalition of cartels down there is in a turmoil. The
word is that Salazar, one of his rivals in the drug trade,
took out Castino because he was afraid Castino had
found out that he was responsible for his children's kidnapping eight years ago." His gaze narrowed on her face.
"You wouldn't know anything about that?"

"I know that with Castino dead, Cara is safer, and your
red tape has dwindled enormously."

"Not necessarily." Toller smiled. "Castino's wife,
Natalie, is still alive, and I'm sure that the members of
his cartel will support her claim for her lost child. On
the other hand, Salazar will probably be denying any
knowledge of either the kidnapping or the killing of
Castino."

"I don't agree," Eve said. "I don't think you have to
worry about Salazar."

Toller's gaze narrowed on her face. "And why is that?"

Eve had a fleeting memory of Salazar's dead body torn
and broken by the blast Joe had set at the top of the hill
not more than an hour's walking distance from here. She
forced herself to keep her gaze on Toller and not glance
at that hill. "You told me yourself, the cartels are in turmoil. If Salazar is guilty of Castino's assassination, then
it would be smart of him to keep a low profile." She
paused. "But I would look closer to home than Salazar,
Toller."

He stiffened. "What are you talking about?"

She shouldn't say this. It wouldn't do any good until
they could gather evidence. She should let it go right now.

To hell with letting it go.

Tell him and let it simmer.

"Natalie Castino."

"What?" He shook his head in disbelief. "I know you're reaching because you don't want Cara to return to Mexico, but there's no suspicion that Natalie Castino is involved in her husband's murder."

"There's suspicion," she said grimly. "Joe, me, and Detective Manez with the Mexican police. Don't believe Joe and me, but check with Manez."

"And does Manez have proof?"

"No one has proof. Natalie Castino is very careful about leaving evidence about. She pays attention, and she makes sure that she dots every i."

"I understand she isn't even in Mexico at the present time. She's visiting her father in Moscow."

"That's the story." She couldn't risk telling him much more. The situation was too volatile, and anything, even a call from this agent from the Justice Department, might cause repercussions with Natalie that involved Cara. "Or it might be a fairy tale. Why don't you find out?"

He was silent a moment, gazing at her. "Because my job isn't to investigate Castino's death. It's to keep our government out of a knock-down drag-out fight for custody of a child that would be bad politically no matter how it turned out."

"Why do you think that she'd arouse such a hullabaloo? She's just a kid."

"This kid." He reached in his jacket pocket and pulled out a wallet and flipped it open to the photo section. "A kid with that face. Big trouble."

She glanced down at the photo. Cara. Winged brows, pointed chin, hazel eyes looking out of the picture with the intensity and wistfulness Eve knew so well. A face to touch the heart.

"And I hear the kid plays the violin, too," Toller said as he took back the wallet and put it back in his pocket.

"Her teachers reported that she's a phenomenal talent. Put it all together, and she's an activist's dream."

"Put it all together, and she's a sweet, remarkable child who deserves the good life she's never had," Eve said. "Don't try to take it away from her, Toller."

"I'm just doing my job." He shrugged. "And the lifestyle she'll be exposed to in Mexico City may not be pristine, but she'll have a mother to care for her." He held up his hand as she opened her lips to protest. "Which she hasn't had for the last eight years. And I'm not buying that Natalie Castino killed her husband. They seem to have had an ideal marriage. What's the motive?"

"What's the motive everyone is laying at Salazar's door?"

He went still. "My God. Her own kids? You expect me to believe she was the one who—No way."

"I don't expect you to believe anything. I'm just throwing the truth out there and hoping it will take root." She looked him in the eye. "And hoping that you'll let Joe and me keep trying to save Cara. Because if you don't, if you interfere, you may be responsible for getting Cara killed. You have that photo. How are you going to feel when you pull it out and look at it on the day you hear Cara has been murdered?"

He was silent for a moment, then gave a low whistle. "You're a very passionate woman. And very convincing, Ms. Duncan."

"And did I convince you?"

"You've convinced me that I'd better stop listening to you and do my job." His gaze was still on her face. "No hard feelings. I had great respect for you before I came here. I have even more respect for you now." His glance shifted away from her to the lake, then to the road. "Would you care to tell me what the hell has been going on here?"

What would he say if she told him that Salazar and
Natalie had tracked Cara and her down, and they'd had
to fight for their lives in the last twenty-four hours? That
MacDuff had been injured in a blast that could have
killed him. That they were all still fighting to survive
since Natalie had taken Cara. She was tempted to do
it. She was tired of fighting, and maybe he would believe her.

Too much risk.

"No, I wouldn't. You're an investigator, so investigate.
If you can manage to get clearance from MacDuff, who
owns this property. Which I very much doubt."

His expression hardened. "I see. Then are you going
to tell me where I can find Joe Quinn, or do I start looking for him?"

"You start looking for him." She went over to the
campfire and poured herself a cup of coffee. "Would you
like a cup of coffee, first? This mist that hovers over
the lake may be chock-full of atmosphere, but it can be
chilly."

"No, thank you. It's kind of like eating in the house
of the enemy."

"What a medieval thought. I wouldn't hold it against
you." She took a sip of coffee. "Until you actually prove
yourself an enemy."

"And then you'd remember?"

She nodded. "Just as you'd remember. Every single
time you look at that photo."

He smiled. "I shouldn't have shown you that photo.
You're going to use it against me, aren't you?"

"Of course. I'm fighting for a life, you're fighting for
red tape." She threw the rest of her coffee into the fire. It
hissed as the liquid hit the burning wood. "I'll use everything I can against you. So will Joe." She glanced at
him. "Where are you going to look for him?"

He tilted his head, thinking about it. "I'm not quite sure," he murmured. His gaze went to the fog-covered lake. "That entire north bank seems completely impenetrable. Interesting. I heard stories about it from my driver, who grew up in this area. Is it true that the mist never vanishes from it? That there are all kinds of legends that the mist hides either the beginning or the end of the world?"

"It's true enough."

"Pure nonsense, of course. Still, it would be an excellent place for a man to hide, wouldn't it?"

"If you think so." She wasn't going to discourage him from searching for Joe in that mist. He'd find out soon enough how futile it was, but it would give Joe more time. "Is that where you're going to look for him?"

He shook his head.

"Then where?"

He smiled. "The place where you came from when I first saw you. I'll go back up to that road."

Shit. She tried to keep her face expressionless. "Really? Why?"

"Because it's close. If I had a woman like you, I'd stay as close to her as possible. I have an idea Quinn feels the same way."

"Really? Yet he's been in Atlanta, and I've been here since I've had to hide Cara away."

"Then it must have been driving him crazy." He turned and headed back across the bank. "I'll have to ask him about that . . ."

Eve's fists clenched as she watched him stride up the slope. Had she given Joe enough time? It would take Toller only minutes to question the police on the road and determine that Joe had taken a car and left the property. After that, he would have to decide where Joe had gone. If Toller had traced him here, he must know that he'd rented a helicopter. The next step would be to go after him and try to reach him before he boarded the aircraft.

She didn't doubt he'd work it out. Toller was very sharp. She just hoped Joe wouldn't be there when Toller located the helicopter.

She just hoped she'd given him enough time.

CHAPTER
2

"Did you hear me, Cara?" The woman who had called herself Natalie Castino was no longer smiling as she looked down at Cara. "I'm your mother. Why don't you say something?"

Cara couldn't say anything. Her throat was tight, and her heart was beating so hard that she was having trouble breathing. And she didn't know what to say, she was too confused to think. Mother? What was happening?

"Talk to me," the woman demanded. "That damn drug should be wearing off by now. You were able to crawl across the helicopter to this tool chest."

The drug. The chloroform. The woman knew about it. Cara might be able to use it to keep from answering. "Sleepy . . ." She closed her eyes. "Tired . . ."

Silence. Then the woman spoke and it was no longer harsh or impatient. "Of course you are," she said gently. "You've been through a horrible experience. Do you remember being captured by those terrible men? Probably not, they kept you drugged all the time that they had you." Her hand touched Cara's cheek. "But you're safe now. I took care of that. I paid the ransom they asked for you. Your grandfather helped me with that, and we're going to see him now to show him that you're safe and well. Do you remember your grandfather? You only visited him once. You were so young, Cara."

Grandfather . . .

She had a vague memory of a face, a smile . . .

"You probably don't remember." Natalie paused. "But it would be kind of you to pretend that you do when you see him since he's done so much for us."

Lie. She wanted her to lie? Cara must have said the word because she was answered immediately.

"Not lie. Pretend. There's a difference. We have to make sure that your grandfather knows how grateful we are that he saved you from those men who would have killed you as they killed your sister."

Jenny. Killed Jenny.

Sorrow. Fear.

She evidently didn't say that out loud because the woman was still speaking. "But I was the one who really saved you, Cara."

"Eve . . ."

"No, she just got in the way. She could have gotten you killed. She was never your friend. You can't think about her again." Her voice hardened. "You must believe me, Cara. I'm your mother. You have to forget all those people who told you lies. Did anyone tell you lies about me? Did they talk about me at all? Answer me."

"No . . ."

"You're sure?"

"I'm . . . sure."

"Open your eyes and look at me. I have to be certain."

Cara's lids slowly lifted.

That beautiful face above her was tense, her dark eyes glittering. "No one talked about me?"

"No . . ."

The tension disappeared, and she smiled. "Of course they didn't. What could they say? But there are so many liars in this world. I'm glad we're going to have a fresh start." She gently reached up and closed Cara's lids. "Rest now. You've gone through so much with those terrible people. I'm so glad I was able to get you away from them. Now we're going to land this helicopter very soon and transfer to a plane that will take us to your grandfather. He lives in Moscow. I don't suppose you remember that either?"

She didn't remember it.

But she knew that Moscow was far away, and the thought sent panic surging though her.

Far away from Eve and Joe.

Far away from Jock.

Jock.

Her friend who was closer to her than anyone but Eve.

Whose smile was as beautiful as a concerto.

Who might need her, and she wouldn't be there for him.

"No!"

"Was that an answer or a protest?" The voice of the woman who called herself her mother was suddenly sharp. "Because if it was a protest, we have a problem."

"Jock," she whispered. "I can't go away. He's my friend, and he might need me. Is Jock all right?"

"I don't know any Jock." Her forehead was creased with a frown. "I suppose he's okay. But it doesn't matter. You don't have any real friends back there. And you'll do what I say. A child always has to obey her mother. I guess you haven't learned that because of the horrible things that have happened to you. But I'm sure that it won't take you long. You're my daughter, so you have to be very smart. Now do you understand the rules?"

Cara didn't understand anything. She was confused, and what her mother was telling her only made her more bewildered. She had to wait until her head cleared before she could think.

Her mother?

That single statement was the most bewildering of all, and this woman appeared to slip back and forth from hardness to loving gentleness in the space of seconds. Could she believe her? And, if she believed that she was her mother, could she believe anything else she said?

She knew she had lied when she said Eve was not her friend. She thought that she might have hurt Eve before the helicopter had taken off.

Think. What else did she remember before that sentence that had jarred her out of the haze caused by the chloroform?

Eve looking down at her. "Cara." Her hand gently brushing back Cara's hair from her face. "Cara, it's Eve. Can you hear me?"

She heard her but it was from far away.

"Eve?" Cara whispered. She forced her lids to remain open. She had to tell her . . . "So . . . sorry. Jock?"

"He's fine. So are you. Everything's going to be okay."

She wanted to believe her. But she had to tell her to run, that this was a terrible place. "No . . . Sorry . . ."

Then the haze had closed in again.

But it had exploded only minutes later. Screams. Smoke. Rocks flying. Eve holding her tight, keeping her safe.

The woman's voice. "She's alive, Eve?"

"Yes."

"Then she might stay that way if you cooperate."

The feel of the vibrating floor of the helicopter as she was shoved through the door.

Eve's voice saying desperately, "Let her go, Natalie. Don't take her."

"Answer me, Cara," Natalie said impatiently.

The woman had said she loved her. How many times had Cara wistfully thought how nice it would be to have someone who would say those words? But this woman was a stranger, and she had been taught not to trust strangers. She was beautiful, but Cara had seen that bad was not always ugly.

"I'm getting angry with you. You don't want me angry, Cara. I'm asking you one more time. Do you understand the rules?"

Don't fight her. Not now.

Rest. Think. Remember.

Then fight her if she had to do it.

She kept her eyes closed. "I understand the . . . rules." She added unsteadily, "Mother . . ."

LIVERPOOL

Joe called Eve as he was landing at Liverpool. "We could have been lucky. I checked while I was ten minutes out, and there were no international rentals scheduled to leave here for the next two hours. And none departed in the last three. Natalie might be spinning her wheels trying to set up a flight."

"And she might not even be there," Eve said. "She might have fooled Burbank."

"Think positive." He jumped out of the helicopter. "She could be here, waiting at the terminal, setting up a flight."

"I hope. We were lucky once today when Toller missed you. I'm afraid to count on another break."

So was Joe. But it could happen. "I'll call you back. I'm going to call and check again if—" He stopped as he watched a Learjet start down the runway. A jet with a company name in bold Russian script on the side.

"Son of a bitch."

"What's wrong?"

"She didn't hire a private jet from here. Her father sent one to pick her up." He was running across the tarmac, trying to think of a way to stop it. He couldn't see the pilot in the cockpit, but he could see his passenger sitting beside him.

And she could see him.

Natalie Castino was smiling at him and nodding.

Then she lifted one expressive finger and yawned.

Joe's hands clenched into fists as he watched the jet take off.

"Joe," Eve said.

He drew a deep breath and lifted the phone to his ear again. "We've lost her. She's gone."

Eve was silent. "No way anyone will stop the plane?"

"You know the answer."

"Yes. God, I'm scared, Joe."

"So am I. But now the ball's in her court. We have to deal with it."

"And what do we do next? I'm not going to wait for her to contact us."

Joe remembered that last mocking gesture. "Hell, no. We go after her."

"She's gone." Eve turned to Jane after she hung up the phone. "Probably heading for Moscow and her loving father."

Jane hesitated, then asked, "And we're sure that she took Cara with her?"

"You're thinking that she might have killed Cara before she even reached Liverpool to get rid of the last possible witness." Eve had been trying not to think of that risk. "We're not sure of anything. Joe saw Natalie and the pilot, not Cara. But when she left here, she took the trouble to be sure Cara was on that helicopter. She wouldn't have done that if she hadn't had a reason. She knows that I care about Cara." She smiled bitterly. "She doesn't understand it, but she accepts it as a weapon. Therefore, she thinks Cara can be bait, and she'll use her. I managed to convince Natalie that we either have Cira's treasure or can find it. Now she's sure she's destined to have it."

Jane made a face. "Oh, then all we have to do is find Cira's treasure that has been lost for centuries and swap it for Cara?"

Eve shook her head. "I said she'd use Cara for bait, I didn't say she'd go through with the deal. Cara will always be a threat to Natalie as long as she's alive. She'll always be afraid that Cara will remember something that someone told her or something she saw the night she was kidnapped."

"So no matter what happens, Cara is going to be a victim?"

"No," Eve said fiercely. "We won't let that happen. We just have to play for time until we figure a way to get her away from Natalie."

"Play for time with Natalie?" Jane asked skeptically. "She may not be your only problem. What about Jock?"

Jock Gavin.

Eve had been trying to keep from thinking about MacDuff's best friend, Jock, who had formed a powerful bond with Cara during the time she'd been here in the

Highlands. It had been one of those strange, rare attach-
ments that perhaps come along only once in a lifetime.
The child, older than her years, who had been friendless
and on the run all her life. The young man who had fought
his way from the depths of guilt and despair and was
probably still fighting. No wonder they seemed to fulfill
each other in spite of the difference in age and background. Jock had taken Cara under his wing, and he
couldn't have been a more supportive friend or big brother.
And Cara was just as passionately protective of Jock. In
fact, she had been captured by Salazar that night because
she had followed Jock into the hills because she was worried about him.

"Jock," Jane repeated softly. "He thinks that he's responsible for Cara's being taken. Do you really think he's
going to wait and be patient until you work out a plan?
You had to keep him from exploding and killing more
of Salazar's men than he did when he was tracking them
after they'd taken Cara. He's not going to be either cool
or sane when it's about Cara."

Eve knew that, and it was something she was going to
have to face right away. "Have you heard from Jock? Is
he still at the hospital with MacDuff?"

"No, I haven't heard from him. I didn't expect to hear
from him. I just thought when he was sure MacDuff was
okay that he'd just disappear." Jane shook her head. "Jock
is good at disappearing. Remember?"

Yes, Eve remembered all the stories about Jock, and
some of them were chilling. He had run away from home
at fifteen to see the world, and the world he had seen had
almost destroyed him. He had become the victim of
Thomas Reilly, a criminal who was experimenting with
new drugs and mind control. Reilly's goal was to develop
the perfect superassassin, and Jock had become his prize
pupil. She could only imagine the torment when Jock had

realized what he had become. She did know that MacDuff had taken him from an asylum after several attempts at suicide. Jane and MacDuff had brought him back from an almost catatonic state to normalcy, and now there appeared to be no more caring and charismatic person on earth than Jock Gavin.

Until he'd learned that MacDuff had been hurt and Cara had been taken.

"Maybe he's still at the hospital," Eve said. "If he is, I've got to talk to him."

Jane was reaching for her phone. "I'll call him. If he's there, I'll ask him to wait. If he's not, I'll ask to talk to MacDuff and have him call him to come back to the hospital. He'll pay attention to MacDuff." She was dialing the number. "He loves him."

"Should we bother MacDuff now?"

"Yes, MacDuff feels the same way about Jock. He knows how close he always is to the edge. He's not going to let him fall over." She spoke into the phone. "Jock, are you still at the hospital? Good. Stay there. Eve's on her way." She hung up. "We didn't have to involve MacDuff."

"But you would have done it."

"It was only a phone call. It wasn't going to hurt MacDuff, and Jock is worth it." She looked her in the eye. "And you think Jock's worth it, too, don't you? You're very protective of Cara, and with all you know about Jock, I was a little surprised that you weren't worried when they became so close."

She shrugged. "It was the shining."

"What?"

"Something Cara said to me once. She wouldn't believe that Jock was bad, had ever really been bad. She said that no one could shine inside like he does and be anything but good." She smiled. "What could I say? When I look at him, I see the shining, too."

"You're not mistaking that for the fact that he's probably the best-looking individual to walk God's earth?" Jane asked teasingly.

"No way."

Jane's smile vanished. "I see it, too. From the first time I met him, when he was still almost a basket case," Jane said. "But he doesn't see it in himself. That monster, Reilly, almost destroyed him."

"Then we've got to make sure that Jock doesn't complete the job himself." She started up the slope toward the road. "Cara would never forgive us."

"She wouldn't believe us," Jane said. "She thinks the sun rises and sets on him."

"Maybe it does, for her. She's never really had a friend. Then Jock came along with his smile and his shining, and his promise that he'd always keep her safe. That's pretty strong stuff."

"We've just got to make sure he keeps that promise. If he doesn't, it could destroy both of them." She shook her head impatiently as she instinctively increased her pace. "I can't think of that right now. I just have to concentrate on one thing at a time. And the first thing is keeping Jock from striking out like a bird of prey before we're ready for him to do it."

SOUTH GLASGOW UNIVERSITY HOSPITAL
GLASGOW, SCOTLAND

"I wasn't going to stay when Jane called me." Jock turned away from looking out the window when Eve walked into the waiting room. His tone was brimming with leashed violence. "I need to get out of here, Eve."

"But you did stay. So you must have had a reason."

She went over to the beverage machine and got a cup of tea. "And that reason was probably that you thought that it was the sensible thing to do." She took a sip of tea. "Or that you thought I might have information to give you. I'm opting for the latter. You haven't been behaving with any great degree of sense, you're pure instinct, right now."

"Instinct isn't always bad."

"I agree, but without control, it can become dangerous." She turned to look at him. His face was totally without expression. She took another sip of tea to buy herself more time. "You've been down that road before, Jock." Her gaze traveled from his head to his feet. "You look like hell. You need a shower and some rest." It was a lie. It was impossible for Jock to look bad. Jane had been right, he was one of the handsomest men Eve had ever seen, with his shock of fair hair and silver-gray eyes and that face that Cara had said was more beautiful than a concerto. But if there was a shining about him today, it was like the sharpness of a stiletto. "Couldn't you at least get a nap?"

"Couldn't you?" Jock said. "When was the last time you slept, Eve?"

She couldn't remember. It had been a horrendous, nerve-shredding time after Salazar had gotten hold of Cara. "Touché," she said wearily. "And I probably look as bad as you do."

"What the hell difference does that make?" His voice was suddenly savage, and he was across the room, his hands grasping her shoulders. "Why are you talking about showers and naps? Why did you come? What do you want to tell me?"

His grip was hurting her, and she opened her mouth to tell him to let her go. Then, as she met his eyes, she closed it again. His jaw was locked and his eyes glittering.

He was scared, she realized, terrified. She said gently, "It's okay, Jock."

"No, it's not. Nothing is okay right now. Is she alive?"

"As far as we know." His hands tightened again, and she said, "We think so. And, if you'll stop trying to break my shoulders, I'll tell you what I do know."

"Tell me." His hands fell away from her, and he stepped back. "So that I can get the hell out of here and find out for myself."

"Joe followed Natalie Castino to Liverpool, and he saw her leaving in a Russian jet. He's checking, but he thinks it was sent by her father, Sergai Kaskov, and that she's probably on her way to Moscow now."

"And Cara?"

"Joe didn't see her, but he assumed she was in the plane."

"Assumed?"

"He got there too late for anything else. They were going down the runway. What was he supposed to do? He couldn't have stopped them."

"I would have stopped them."

And it was possible that with the depth of lethal skills Jock possessed, he might actually have been able to do it, Eve thought wearily. "And then you might have killed Cara along with everyone else on that plane. Is that what you want?"

"I should have been there."

She was tired of it. "But you weren't. Joe was there, and he used his best judgment. And it was damn good judgment. So don't give me should-have-been, Jock. Just get a cup of tea and sit down and let me talk to you about how we're going to deal with this."

He stood looking at her for a moment, then turned and crossed to the beverage machine. "You don't know anything more?"

"Why? So that you can feel free to walk out of here?" She dropped down in a chair. "That's not going to happen. I know you're hurting, but so are the rest of us."

"None of the rest of you caused Cara to be on that hill where Salazar's man took her." He sat down across from her. "Aye, I'm hurting and angry, but I also have to make it right. So I'd say I have slightly more invested in getting her back."

"No, you don't. I don't consider guilt weighs in any heavier than love." She leaned back in her chair. "But I'm not going to argue with you about it. I'm just going to tell you that Joe has called Burbank at Scotland Yard and asked him to touch base with any contacts in Moscow and verify that Cara actually arrived there safely. Burbank turned it over to a Dima Palik, who he claims is very knowledgeable. We should know what the situation is soon."

"And then?"

"We determine what the safest way would be to get Cara away from Moscow . . . and Natalie Castino."

"I'll determine that."

"No, you won't. I know you're accustomed to going solo, Jock. That's not going to happen there." She took a sip of tea. "Sergai Kaskov is the head of one of the largest Mafia families in Moscow, and he's supposed to love his daughter."

"So?"

"So if you go in and grab Cara away from her mother, he's going to take it as a personal insult and will go after you with mega manpower and guns blazing."

He just looked at her.

"And you may not be worried about yourself, but Cara could be caught in the cross fire. I won't have that, Jock."

There was a flicker of expression. "Do you think I would?"

"No, but it could happen if you're not careful."

He shook his head. "I've been taught in a hard school to be careful. I don't make mistakes."

"I don't want Cara to be your first one." She paused. "Neither do you."

He didn't speak for a moment. "God, no." He drew a deep breath. "What do you want from me?"

"What I've wanted since Cara was taken by Natalie Castino. Do I want your help? Of course, I do. I just want for us all to work together to get her away from Natalie. I don't want to take a chance on anyone's being over-powered and causing us to lose her."

"It's never happened to me. I won't lose her."

"Jock."

He got to his feet and strode over to the window and stood looking down at the street. "I can't sit still and wait for something to happen," he said jerkily. "I'm going to Moscow as soon as you tell me where they're holding her."

It sounded like a partial victory. "And then what?"

"I do what I always did. Analyze the situation, then take care of it. I know Moscow. I've worked there before."

"You did?"

"You're surprised?" His lips twisted. "I wouldn't have been considered adequate for the duties for which I was trained if I was confined to a single area or city. I know how to operate in most cities in Europe and the U.S. Would you like to know the easiest and safest way to make a kill in Venice? Or maybe how to avoid the police in—"

"No, I don't want to hear any of that." She hadn't meant to broach any of those memories when she was trying to move him away from thinking about that life. Besides, the thought of what he must have gone through hurt her. "I just asked a question."

"But you really didn't want to know the answer. If you do, ask Jane. She managed to sit through most of it one night when I was on the verge of going crazy. She even asked for more. A catharsis, she called it." He shrugged. "I called it salvation."

"I won't ask Jane," Eve said quietly. "But if you need someone to talk to when this is over, I'll be there for you."

"Will you?" He tilted his head. "But I'm not hunting for salvation anymore, Eve. I don't lay my sins on people who care about me. I've been burden enough to them. At some point, you just have to face it alone."

"Cara wouldn't like that. She didn't want you to be alone."

He flinched. "That was one of the last things she texted me. She ran after me because she didn't want me to be out there alone searching for the men who had tried to kill MacDuff."

"She always wanted to take care of you. I thought it was strange. She was just a kid."

"Yeah, just a kid." His eyes were glittering with moisture. "Which just goes to show what a poor specimen I am if she thought she could take better care of me than I did of her."

"She made a mistake, too. She should never have run after you. But, if you want to take a lesson from any of this, it should be that she thought it was wrong for you to be alone." She paused. "Don't make that mistake again, Jock."

He was silent. She could see the conflict struggling in his expression.

"Jock?"

"I'll wait," he said harshly. "I'll analyze her situation, and if she's not in any immediate danger, I won't move. But not long, Eve. If you don't show me that you have a plan that will be safer for her, I'm going to get her away from that bitch."

She drew a deep breath of relief. It wasn't total commitment, but it would have to do. "We're not going to be dragging our feet. I'm just as worried as you about Natalie Castino."

"I'm not worried," he said grimly. "I just want to kill her. When I caught up with those bastards, I saw them give Cara chloroform a couple times to keep her under. I almost stepped in and took her away from them then. If you don't know what you're doing with chloroform, you can kill someone. But Salazar's goon, Franco, was being careful. Natalie Castino wasn't worried at all, she was laughing and joking." He looked back at Eve. "You told me to wait then. I shouldn't have listened. If I'd taken the risk, Natalie Castino wouldn't have managed to get away with Cara. I'm giving you one more chance. But if I see anything like that again, all bets are off."

"I can understand that." She finished her tea and rose to her feet. She just hoped there wouldn't be anything in Moscow to trigger Jock. It must have been agony for him to watch that being done to Cara. "But, as you say, it would have been a risk. And I can't see Natalie keeping her drugged at her father's place. It would be hard to explain." She threw her cup in the waste disposal. "Will you call me and tell me what you learn when you get to Moscow?"

He nodded slowly. "I'll do everything right. Until it's not right any longer." He turned toward the door. "But I'm leaving right away. I'll go say good-bye to MacDuff."

"I need to see him, too. Will you wait until I finish talking to him before you go in to see him?"

"Why not?" He suddenly smiled. "Are you going to read him the riot act, too? Remember, the Laird is a sick man."

"I believe he can defend himself." She smiled back at him. "Or he can call on you."

"Aye, he can always do that." He still stood staring at her. "Did I truly hurt you? I didn't mean to do that."

She had almost forgotten that she'd accused him of almost breaking her shoulders. "Yes, you hurt me. And I know you didn't mean to do it. We're all going through a bad time. It's going to get better." She met his eyes. "I promise, Jock."

"Then I'll believe you." His smile brightened, lighting his face with that warmth and radiance that Cara called the shining. "And if it does, you might be able to convince me that night is day and day is night. I'll look forward to that, too."

"I don't have to convince you. It's a fact." She headed for the door. "You just have to look at the right side of the world."

"Eve."

She looked over her shoulder.

He was no longer smiling. "I'm sorry I gave you a hard time. Not that I probably won't do it again. Take care of yourself. I've never seen you look this tired."

"I always take care of myself. It's just been a nightmare day." She gave him a wave and walked down the hall toward MacDuff's room. Jock was right, she was totally exhausted and had to focus to think what she had to say to MacDuff. She should probably have gone back to Gaelkar to rest and done this tomorrow.

She was here now. Who knew what tomorrow would bring?

She opened MacDuff's door and poked her head in and saw him lying in bed across the room. She could hardly see him for the dozens of bouquets heaped all around the room. "Hi, MacDuff, I hear you're better. Is it all right if I come in and talk?"

He scowled. "Did you bring flowers?"

"Nary a one."

"Thank God. Come in. And when you leave, take some of these flowers with you and dump them outside."

She came toward him. "That's unkind. It's clear that everyone loves and respects you and would prefer that you don't leave them to go to the heavenly gates."

"All these flowers remind me of a funeral home," he said grimly. "Aye, they should love and respect me. I'm completely extraordinary. But they should spend their money on something more productive."

"Balloons? Teddy bears?"

"What's wrong with you? From what Jock told me, this isn't the time for levity."

"I agree." She made a face. "I think I'm a little light-headed."

"Are you?" MacDuff gazed at her searchingly. "Jock said that you almost succeeded in getting Cara back before Natalie Castino managed to escape with her. It must have been quite a brouhaha. I would have liked to have been there. But you look as if it drained you."

"Almost is the key word." She shook her head. "And may I remind you that we were wondering if you'd even survive, MacDuff. How are you?"

"Tired of this hospital and flowers and wanting to get back in control of my life." His eyes were still narrowed on her. "How are you? Any news of Cara?"

"Not yet. We think she's on her way to Moscow." She paused. "But I *will* hear from Natalie. She as much as told me that she wanted to strike a bargain for Cira's gold."

"Really? A little premature, isn't she? We haven't found it yet."

"She believes we will. She thinks it's her destiny to have it."

"She's wrong. It's my destiny, Eve." He smiled. "My ancestor. My family. My gold."

"I know that, MacDuff. That's why I'm here," she said wearily. "I need your help. I'm not asking you to do anything that would jeopardize your opportunity to find and keep that chest of coins. I just want you to play the game for a little while."

"And that involves?"

"Continuing to search for Cira's gold, perhaps pretending to find it." She hesitated. "If you do find it, be willing to offer to trade it for Cara. Offer, not actually go through with it."

He was silent. "If Natalie is as clever as you think, that might be a risk. I could lose what I've been searching for since I was a boy."

"You won't lose it. Joe and I won't let you. That would be more dangerous for Cara."

He nodded. "I can see that." He suddenly smiled. "But perhaps Jock and I could improvise a little. It would be far more satisfactory to let her have it, then take it back. It would soothe my broken bones and damaged pride."

"You may not have Jock. That's another thing I wanted to discuss. He's leaving for Moscow, and I'm trying to keep him from getting himself and Cara killed before we put plans in motion. He's promised to give me a little time, but I don't know how long that will turn out to be."

"I don't either," MacDuff said soberly. "The child means something to him. Jock has a great heart, but he's very guarded these days. Cara managed to slip under his defenses."

She had slipped under all their defenses, Eve thought. Full of wistfulness and warmth and music, Cara had quietly moved in and become part of them. At first, she and Joe had thought they were only being kind and helping her. She wasn't sure at what point she had realized that kindness had become love.

"You, too?" MacDuff said, his gaze on her face. "Then we'd better do something about it, hadn't we?" He straightened in the bed. "And I can't do anything in this damn hospital. Is Jock still here?"

"Yes, not for long."

"It will be long enough. Send him in, and I'll tell him to get me out of here."

"The hospital staff may not listen to him. You're an influential man, and they won't want to take chances."

"Jock will take care of it." He added wryly, "In case you haven't noticed, Jock is a combination of sheer charisma and lethal determination. If one doesn't work, the other will. I'll be out of here in a few hours."

"And then what?"

"I keep Jock with me for as long as possible. It won't be very long. I'll tell him I need him to take me back to Gaelkar before he takes off."

"Gaelkar?"

"Where else would I go? I have a treasure to find." He smiled. "But you'll have to give me Jane to help me."

"You know Jane will make up her own mind."

"Oh, well, I'll handle it." He made a shooing motion. "I'm beginning to feel as if I can handle anything. Ah, control, it's a magical thing. Go get Jock."

She turned to leave.

"I'll make sure Jock checks in with me occasionally, Eve," he said quietly. "And sometimes he listens to me."

"I know he does. Thank you, MacDuff."

"You're welcome, Eve. Now go get some rest so you'll be ready when you hear the game is about to start."

Arrogant, mocking, controlling. He was all of those things. But no one was a stronger, more intelligent ally than MacDuff.

If she wasn't so tired, she'd be feeling both grateful and hopeful.

But she was that tired, almost numb, and she could only nod and leave the hospital room.

Jock was out in the hall, and she was glad she didn't have to go down to the waiting room to get him.

"He wants to see you."

He frowned. "Is he okay?"

"Fine. Quintessential MacDuff." She walked away from him and down the hall. She was having trouble putting one foot in front of the other.

Exhaustion.

Lethargy.

Normal after what she'd been through last night and today.

And was this dizziness normal, too?

She stopped short in the hall before she reached the elevator.

Not good.

None of this was good, and she wouldn't make it worse by trying to tough it out.

She turned and started toward the nurse's station.

Breathe deep, one step in front of the other.

She reached the desk.

The young, red-haired nurse looked up inquiringly. "Yes?"

"I'm not feeling well. Exhaustion. A little disoriented." She handed the woman her phone. "Would you please dial Jane MacGuire and ask her to come and pick me up? Tell her not to panic. Not to call Joe. It's not serious."

The nurse frowned. "Certainly. Why don't you sit down on that bench over there while you wait for her? I'll be with you as soon as I finish. Perhaps we should take you down to ER and have them look you over."

"Not what I have in mind." She sank down on the

bench and leaned her head back against the wall. "Does this hospital have OB-GYN offices on the premises?"

"Yes, several. In the south wing. You're pregnant?"

"Oh, yes." She closed her eyes. The dizziness was increasing. "About six weeks. Though I could barely tell it until today. But I believe my child is complaining of bad treatment in the only way it has of getting through to me. Could you call one of those doctors and get me down there as soon as you can?"

"What's wrong? What are you doing here?" Jane demanded as she strode into the examining room of Dr. Gil Rampfel an hour and a half later. "That nurse scared me to death." She crossed to the table where Eve was lying and took her hand. "Did you lose the baby?"

"No." Eve smiled. "I told you not to panic. I'm just being careful. I didn't like the fact that I was so exhausted today. You know I'm usually as strong as a horse."

"You don't usually go through a physically and emotionally draining twenty-four hours that would have taken down a SEAL," she said curtly. "And I have a right to panic. You don't call for help, Eve. You're too damn independent. I don't remember a time when you called me and asked—It's usually the other way around."

Eve shook her head. "I don't have the right to be independent right now. Because it might be the baby who is calling for help. I told Joe that when I was pregnant with Bonnie, I felt stronger than ever in my life, that I could lift mountains. I feel like that with this child, too. But today I had the strange feeling that I was being told that I have to obey the limits, that we have to work through this together. The two of us." She squeezed Jane's hand. "So I called my best friend to come and escort us back to camp. I'm sure that the baby approves of my choice."

"Not Joe?"

"Joe is busy trying to save Cara." She shrugged. "And you know how he would have reacted if I'd had the nurse call him with that message."

"Chaos. Possibly a nervous breakdown."

"Something like that. I have to be careful about stressing him out. He'd want to put me on bed rest. This child will be our child, but right now it's mine."

"Bed rest?" She stiffened. "Was that a possibility? What did this Dr. Rampfel tell you?"

"After extensive tests, he said that I'm extremely healthy, that the baby appears to be doing well." She paused. "After renewing my prenatal vitamins, he told me that I'd obviously overdone it, and I'm not to do it again. Eight hours' sleep every night. Eat a healthy diet. Don't worry about anything."

Jane shook her head. "Good advice. Wrong time."

"I'll do what I can." She smiled. "And I'll discuss it with the baby and explain that I might need a little help now and then. And that I'm sure Cara will be worth it in the long run."

"That goes without saying." Jane smiled back at her. "The two of us," she repeated Eve's words. "It sounds as if you've actually formed a partnership."

"Oh, we have." She sat up and swung her legs to the floor. "And right now I'm not at all sure who is the dominant partner. But I'm sure I'm going to find out soon. This child is changing, growing, becoming . . ." She shook her head. "I don't know. Is it that I don't remember when Bonnie was in the womb? I thought I remembered everything about her. All the wonder, all the love. But I didn't remember this . . . excitement. It's . . . different."

"Every child is different," Jane said as she helped Eve to her feet. "Or so I've been told. I guess we'll find out. So what's next?"

"We get out of here. I'll call Joe when we get back to camp and see what he's learned. Then I force myself to take a nap as commanded by all and sundry."

"Sounds like a plan." She headed for the door. "Stay here while I check you out of here with the receptionist."

"I'll go with you." She held up her hand. "I'm fine now. All I've done for the past couple hours is to lie here and be poked and prodded."

"Not exactly relaxing," Jane said dryly.

"It felt that way. Maybe because I had a little help from my friend." She touched her abdomen. "I saw its heartbeat, Jane. It was . . . awesome."

Jane gazed at her luminous expression, and said gently, "I imagine it was, Eve. Well, I'm glad that you're feeling better, whatever the reason. When you left the camp earlier, you were pretty ragged."

She nodded. "I was depressed, and it was hard to see where we were going and what we were going to do. I was just trying to do what I could to keep the damage to a minimum."

"And that's changed?"

"It's changed." She headed for the door. "Somewhere along the way, I picked up something called hope."

"A gift from your silent partner?"

"How would I know? Maybe. Yeah, I think so. That's what babies are all about, aren't they?" She opened the door. "Hope."

CHAPTER
3

MOSCOW

Cara could see the immense stone house surrounded by high, wrought-iron fences in the distance as they came down the hill. It looked like a mansion or a castle but not like the ones she'd seen in Scotland.

"It's beautiful, isn't it?" Natalie glanced at her. "I grew up here. Aren't you lucky that you'll be living here for a while?"

"It's very nice," Cara said politely. She didn't look at her, but the strong vanilla scent of Natalie's perfume surrounded her in the closeness of the backseat. Her mother had changed clothes at the airport before the driver of the Rolls-Royce sent by her father had picked them up. She was wearing a cream-colored silk dress and bronze high heels, and Cara knew with part of her mind that she was beautiful. But for some reason, she couldn't accept that beauty as fact. There was something wrong, like a fine piece of music with half the notes missing.

Yes, that was it. Something in her mother was terribly missing.

"It's more than nice," Natalie said. "What's wrong with you? It's a finer house than the one I lived in with your father in Mexico City. You lived there, too, when you were younger. I thought when I married him that I wanted something more modern and colorful, but I realize now that this house is so much grander. It radiates power, and nothing is more important. I just didn't realize it when I married Juan and left here."

"I don't remember that house in Mexico City."

"No, of course you don't. Poor child. What a life you've had these last years. It will be all better now."

Cara didn't answer.

And Natalie didn't like it. "You haven't said more than a few words since you woke up in that helicopter. I believe you're being rude to me."

"I don't mean to be rude. I don't know what to say. I'm confused. All of this is very strange." More than strange, Cara thought. She had tried to sort out her feelings and truth from lies on the long flight from Liverpool to Moscow. But she hadn't gotten further than the few conclusions she had drawn after that first conversation she'd had with Natalie. Not really conclusions. But she was being bombarded by impressions every moment she was with Natalie Castino. "And I don't know why I'm here."

"You're here because I wish you to be here. You're my daughter, and you do as I tell you to do." She was gazing at Cara coldly. "From what I understand, you could have saved me from a good deal of heartache if you'd not willingly gone along with that traitor, Elena, after your sister was killed. Now you need to make it up to me."

"Elena wasn't a traitor. She raised me, tried to help me."

"She was a servant who should have brought you home to me."

"She died trying to save me," Cara whispered.

Natalie shook her head. "All lies, Cara. I'm the only one you can trust."

"No, that's not true. I can trust Eve."

Anger flickered over Natalie's face. "I've told you that she meant you harm. We won't talk about her."

"I have to talk about her." She asked the question she'd been wanting to ask since the moment she had first roused in the helicopter. "There was a shot. I heard it. Did you hurt Eve?"

"I told you I didn't. How many times do I have to—" She drew a deep breath. "Very well, I was planning on having a discussion with you anyway before I let you meet my father. I won't discuss Eve at the moment. I'll save that for a time after you've proved you can be obedient and loyal to me."

"Why was there a shot? Did you hurt her?"

Natalie's hand whipped across Cara's face.

Stinging pain.

The blow was so hard, Cara's neck snapped back.

Shock and pain made her dizzy for an instant.

"I said we won't discuss that." Natalie leaned back in the seat. "Now you need to listen carefully. I want your meeting with my father to go well. I'll speak Russian to explain to my father how I ransomed you and even killed a few of the terrible men who were holding you hostage. Since you speak no Russian, you will just nod and agree when I finish. Do you understand?"

Cara couldn't let it go. Just talking about Eve was making Natalie angry, and that frightened her. She couldn't tell what was lies and truth. But maybe if she watched her, studied her, she'd be able to learn. She said slowly, expecting to be struck at every word, "Did you hurt Eve?"

"I did *not*. Good God, what do I have to do to you to make you shut up about it? I have plans for Eve. It would be stupid to get rid of her now. But I might find another way and see if I can arrange to hurt your precious Eve if you don't do as I wish. You will smile at my father and not be rude or cause me to be angry with you. Your grandfather is a very important man. More important than your father ever dreamed of being."

"Elena said my father was a killer and a drug dealer. That was one of the reasons she was afraid to take me back to him. Is that what you mean by being important? Is that what my grandfather does, too?"

"Elena was a fool. In the end, it doesn't matter what people do. It's all about the power. And my father has more power than you can imagine." She paused. "He can hurt people that get in his way, that get in *my* way. I don't want you to cause him to be displeased with me, or I might persuade him to do that."

She was talking about Eve. Cara felt a chill go through her. Natalie was smiling, her face beautiful and her expression serene. Yet Cara knew that she would do what she threatened.

"Ah, you do understand," Natalie said. "I thought it wouldn't take you long. You're my daughter, after all."

"I understand." She looked away from her. "I won't do anything to make him be angry with you."

"He's never angry with me. I never permit that to happen. I just don't want a disturbance. Just follow my lead and protect me. Always protect me, Cara. Then we'll have no problems." She paused. "And neither will any of the people you thought were your friends."

Eve, again. Perhaps Jock, too. Cara felt a ripple of panic. The threat was there, hovering on the horizon. She had to get to Eve, take care of her. It was Eve she had to protect. "If I do what you want, will you let me leave here?"

"Why would you want to do that? I'm sure that after we get to know each other, you won't want to leave." They were going through the iron gates now and gliding up the long driveway toward the house. "It's a new life for us, Cara. Just do everything I say and it will be a good one . . ."

A tall, heavyset man with iron gray hair and wearing a charcoal-colored suit was coming out the front door. His features were rugged, his nose looked as if it had been broken at one time and his eyes were a cool blue. But he was smiling as the limousine slid to a stop in front of him. "Natalie!"

"Daddy." She jumped out of the car and into his arms. She was saying something in Russian, her voice broken, and Cara could see tears in her eyes. She held her father close for a long moment before she stepped back. "And this is my little girl." She nodded at Cara and held out her hand. "Our little girl. She's been through such a bad time, but she's home now. Cara . . ."

Cara got out of the car. "How do you do, sir?" she said stiltedly.

"No Russian," Natalie said. "She's forgotten anything she knew before those beasts took her away from me. Another reason why I was glad I was forced to kill Salazar." She drew closer to him. "Did Nikolai call and tell you that he saw me kill that—"

"He told me." He reached up and stroked her cheek. "You should have arranged it so that I could do that for you."

"I was going to do it. It didn't work out." Then she was speaking in Russian again, and Cara stood there watching his face as she told him whatever story she had concocted.

He had little expression, but he continued to stroke her face and hold her.

He loved her, she thought suddenly. She didn't know if he believed her, but he did love her. And if he loved her, he might do anything she wanted him to do.

Eve.

Natalie was turning to Cara. "Tell your grandfather how grateful you are that he gave the money to save you."

Say the words. Do what she wanted. "I'm very grateful, sir."

"So formal." His English was faintly accented, but he was smiling at her. "I know this seems strange to you, but I'm very glad you're here. And I know a good deal about you. When your mother called me and told me you were safe and on your way, I phoned one of my men in the U.S. I told him to send me a report about you and everything you've been doing. I may be a stranger to you. But you're no stranger to me."

What could she say to that? "It's nice that you were interested, sir."

"That formality again. You used to call me grandfather."

"Grandfather," she repeated. Don't be rude. Don't make him angry. Because that would make her angry. She couldn't do that until she had a way to get out of here, get to Eve.

"Don't be upset with her. Everything must be so strange to her. I've told her to call me Natalie for a little while," her mother said. "She told me it's hard for her to think of me as her mother since I'm so young." She smiled. "But we'll get there, won't we, Cara?"

Another lie. Was it because she didn't like the idea of being a mother? The lies were building, growing, and giving Cara a picture. "Yes, we'll get there . . . Natalie." She added, "You do look more like a movie star."

"How sweet." She smiled brilliantly. "All I want is to look like your friend . . . and then later . . ." She turned to her father. "Let's go inside. I want to tell you everything. You heard about poor Juan? Salazar killed him before he turned Cara over to me. Salazar was afraid that Juan would go after him after he released Cara for the ransom."

"Castino should have gone after him before," Kaskov said harshly. "I would have known who took my granddaughters."

"But Juan isn't as clever as you, Daddy." Tears were brimming in her eyes. "I found that out too late for my girls. But he was good to me, and I have to remember that about him."

"You remember that. All I'll remember is that he made you suffer hell when the girls were taken. It was only a matter of time until I stepped in and took over." He turned back to Cara. "You're looking at me with those big eyes. I'm only telling the truth. Your mother put up with too much because she was desperate to find you. Sometimes it's better to just cut your losses and let the chips fall. Do you understand?"

Cara nodded. "I think so. You're telling me that it's not bad that my father is dead because Natalie is better off without him. I don't know if you're right or not because I don't even remember him."

Kaskov stared at her in surprise. Then he threw back his head and laughed. "Exactly. At your age, Natalie would have been kinder and sad about the necessity of disposing of him. But I do like your frankness, Cara."

"Do you?" Natalie's smile was forced. "It's good that you're getting along so well." She whisked Cara inside the door. "But now we have to get her something to eat, and I have to get on the phone and order her some clothes. I wasn't able to take anything when I took her away from those bastards." She shuddered. "Did I tell you that they kept her chloroformed? I'm not sure what she'll remember clearly."

"Chloroform." Kaskov frowned. "My granddaughter? No, you didn't tell me." His expression hardened. "You told me about Salazar and Franco. Was there anyone else? I believe we may need a cleanup crew to pay a visit to Gaelkar."

"It was such a terrible time," she whispered. "I was so afraid that we couldn't get Cara out alive. Everything was a blur." She looked at Cara. "I believe there were a few others. I think I heard about a woman who was involved. I'll try to remember her name."

Eve. Cara's heart skipped a beat. She was setting Eve up in case she decided that Cara had to be punished.

"Cara, do you remember hearing a woman's voice?" Natalie asked.

"No," Cara said hoarsely.

"But then you were under chloroform most of the time." She sighed. "I guess it's up to me to come up with the truth." She turned to her father. "I'm still so afraid for Cara. What if there is someone still out there who might hurt her? Could we put her in that apartment in the gatehouse? That way, she'd be surrounded by your men patrolling the grounds. And you'll make sure she's well guarded?"

"Of course." His expression softened. "Nothing will happen to her while we're wrapping this up." He kissed her cheek. "And get yourself some new clothes when you're ordering Cara's wardrobe. It's colder here than you're accustomed to these days. You never did like the cold."

"Thank you." She squeezed his arm. "You're so good to me. It's so wonderful to be home with you." She looked pointedly at Cara. "And I'm sure that Cara feels the same way and will do everything she can to stay out of your way and not be a bother."

Kaskov smiled. "What good is a granddaughter if she's scurrying around trying to stay out of my way?" He released Natalie and walked over to Cara. "One of the things I found out about you when I asked for a report was that you play the violin. Are you good or just competent?"

She didn't look at Natalie. She didn't know where this was going, but it could do no harm not to be a complete puppet. "I'm very good," she said quietly.

"I thought you might be." He met her gaze. "It's a talent that runs in my mother's family. I grew up in Siberia, and the only thing of beauty in my life was her music. She was a violinist, too. You were only three when you came here for the summer, and I remember the expression on your face when you'd sit and listen to your sister, Jenny, when she was playing the piano."

"It was Jenny who had the talent," Natalie said quickly. "I told you how she entertained all my friends in Mexico City."

"Music runs in the family." He didn't look at Natalie. "I told you that when I paid for music lessons for Jenny. Cara was too young, or I would have insisted on having her taught, too." He smiled. "But you found your way anyway, didn't you? Why a violin? Why not piano, like your sister."

"I was always having to move. I could take it with me." She smiled back at him. "And it didn't matter. The music is always there."

He nodded. "Yes, that's what I tried to tell Natalie. I could give her everything else, but she didn't understand that if all the rest is taken away, she could still have the music." He shrugged. "She was too impatient to practice."

"I may still try if it will make you happy," Natalie said.

"You have a daughter, and that just may be enough to make me happy without your bothering." He touched Cara's hair. "Will you play for me?"

She nodded. "I don't have my violin. It's back at the camp at Gaelkar."

"I'll take care of that. After dinner tonight?"

She nodded again. "You know about the music. What do you play?"

"Nothing."

She looked at him, puzzled. "Why not?"

He held out his hands. Four fingers on both hands were broken and terribly misformed. "One of the guards at the work camp in Siberia decided that I had been disrespectful. So I decided my life had to go in another direction."

"I'm sorry," she whispered. She couldn't imagine anything more terrible. The music stifled, never to be able to free it.

"I see that you are." His hand lightly brushed her cheek. "And that you understand more than anyone else could." His smile faded. "Except my son, Alex. He had the music in his soul. He played the piano and I thought I'd send him to the conservatory when he got tired of playing at my 'other direction.'"

"He betrayed you," Natalie said. "It broke my heart, but Alex did betray you, Daddy."

"He claimed he didn't," Kaskov said sadly. "But there was proof, and there were the rules. I couldn't spare my son when I spared no one else. It would have toppled me." He looked back at Cara. "But it was lonely not having anyone else who really understood. I'm glad you're here, Cara."

"And that's enough of all this sad talk," Natalie said.

"If you're set on having her play for you, she has to get settled, then get a little rest." She gave him a kiss on the cheek. "We'll see you at dinner. I'll take Cara over to the gatehouse. Will you send Ivan Sabak to be her personal guard? I remember him as being very competent."

His brows rose. "I thought perhaps Nikolai. Sabak's one of my best men. You think the threat is that serious?"

"How do I know? I'm only a woman. But I'd feel better about it." She smiled. "Please?"

"Whatever." He turned away. "I'll send Sabak. Now get out of here. I have phone calls to make." He glanced back at Cara. "Welcome to my home, Cara."

"Thank you. I'll see you at dinner."

Natalie almost shoved Cara out the door and onto the driveway. "I didn't like the way you handled those questions, Cara." She was walking quickly, her high heels clicking on the stones. "You were far too pushy, and you made me look less than I am."

"I didn't say anything about you. He did. And I only told the truth."

"It's a truth I prefer to avoid at present." She didn't speak for a few moments, then burst out, "That damn music. I should have known it would get in the way. It always did. That's why I didn't tell him about it myself."

"It's sad about his hands."

"It's *not* sad. He's far more powerful now than he would ever have been as some piddling musician."

Cara turned and stared at her. Natalie truly didn't understand, and she could see how that would have hurt her father.

"Stop looking at me," she said sharply. "That's how Alex would always look at me. And then he'd exchange glances with my father, and I knew that they were closing me out. No one closes me out."

"I'm sure that they didn't mean to do that. Your father seems to love you very much."

"Of course he does. I make sure of that. And every move that Alex made, I was able to block him. Except for that damn music. I knew I had to do something." She drew a deep breath. "But that's all over now. My father hardly remembers him any longer except when something happens as it did today."

I knew I had to do something.

What had she done to make sure that Alex would not take any of her father's attention?

Cara was beginning to believe that she knew.

"Then I guess you don't want me to play for him tonight?"

"It doesn't matter whether I want it or not. Since he's found out that you play, you'll have to do it." She shrugged. "And I may be able to use it. I'll have to see." They had reached the gatehouse, and she turned to face Cara. "But I want you to know that you'll not use it against me. I won't permit it. The minute you do, I'll take whatever you value away from you."

Eve. She no longer had to even threaten. Cara knew the threat was there. "I didn't even know how your father felt about the music. How could I be planning to use it?"

"You're my daughter." She opened the door. "There's something you inherited besides that damn music. Do you think I can't see it? Just don't think you'll be better at it than me."

She meant that Cara was like her. It had never occurred to her while she had been watching, studying her mother, to find ways to get away, to help Eve. But if the music, the wonder, could be inherited, maybe she was right. Maybe the evil that she was beginning to sense in her mother could also be part of Cara.

And could the music survive if that turned out to be so?

Please God, let it not be true.

LOCH GAELKAR

"No, I won't make a statement," Jane firmly told the young police detective who had come down the slope to question her. "I don't know what happened or why there were IEDs on that road, Detective Hastings. Perhaps it was terrorists. It sounds like it, doesn't it? The Laird is such a powerful man, and terrorists would love to take him down. Remember how Prince Harry had to be protected when he was in Afghanistan? I was so glad when he got out of there safely. And I believe that one of the Laird's caretakers said that he saw a couple foreign-looking men wandering around the property. Of course, we wouldn't want to profile anyone, would we?"

"You appear to know more than you claim you do. Why not make a statement, and we'll see if something else comes to the forefront?"

"I'm just a member of the Laird's hunting expedition. Talk to him. I wouldn't want to step on his toes." She looked him in the eye. "Would you?"

The young man looked distinctly uncomfortable. "I see your point. But my superiors want answers, and I'm supposed to bring—"

"Then tell your superiors to come out and question MacDuff themselves. I've just received a call from him telling me that he's leaving the hospital and coming back to the camp. You won't want to disturb him today, but tomorrow might be okay." She added quickly, "But, of course, no one speaks for the Laird. You'll have to call him."

"I'll tell my captain to do that." Now that he had an out, he was eager to pass the buck. "MacDuff will probably be happier talking to him. Good day, Ms. Mac-Guire." He was quickly moving up the slope. "Thank you."

"You're welcome," Seth Caleb murmured from behind Jane. "Well done. He didn't even know he'd been handled, Jane."

"I just wanted to be rid of him. He was only doing his job." Jane turned to face him. Caleb was dressed in jeans, boots, and an olive-colored sweater that were all stained or torn. But he still managed to look totally pulled together and confident. His dark hair, with that single thread of white, was gleaming in the sunlight. She knew he hadn't slept any more than the rest of them, but he was charged, his dark eyes glittering and restless in that fascinating face. "What would you have done?"

"What do you think?" His expression was suddenly mischievous. "Push him in the lake?" He paused. "Suck his blood?"

He was mocking her, and she wasn't in the mood. "Stop that. You may have that weird blood thing. But you do *not* suck blood."

"How do you know?"

"Caleb."

"Okay. You're right." His eyes were twinkling as he added, "Not in this century." When she didn't smile, he shook his head. "Your sense of humor is definitely lacking today, Jane." His smile faded. "And I don't think it's because you've heard anything bad about Cara. But I could be wrong though that seldom happens."

"No, Joe hasn't heard from Palik, Burbank's contact in Moscow, yet. We're expecting his call any minute. I hope that if it's bad news, he doesn't hear for an hour or so. I want Eve to get a little more sleep."

"I hear you went to pick her up at the hospital."

"How did you hear?"

He didn't answer directly. "You know I keep watch over you."

It was a lovely sentiment, there was even a song written about it. But there was nothing sentimental about the way Caleb said it. It was hot, dark, and purely sexual.

"Not entirely." His gaze was on her face, reading her expression. "It's to my ultimate best interest to keep you safe."

She felt the familiar tingle of heat and fought to push it away. She was tired and worried, and he should not be able to stir her like this. But it never seemed to matter when she was around Caleb. The chemistry was too intense. All the more reason to reject it.

He shook his head. "Stop trying to read something into an innocent comment." He smiled. "Innocent. Bad choice of words when connected with me. Let's go back to square one where you'll feel safer. Why did you go pick Eve up? Was she ill?"

She was glad for the escape. She was too stressed to deal with him right now. "No, she was just being careful. She was too tired, and she didn't want to take a chance with the baby." Caleb was the only one besides Jane and Joe who knew Eve was pregnant, and it was a relief not to have to be careful about talking about it. "The doctor wants her to get lots of rest, and there's not much chance of that." She made a face. "Maybe I'll take her phone and get Joe's message myself."

"Eve wouldn't thank you. She'd be pissed off." His gaze was still on her face. "And when will you get some sleep? You've been giving orders and holding down the fort all day."

"I'll sleep when we know Cara is safe." She looked at him. "Like you, Caleb."

"You believe I wouldn't be able to sleep? What a surprise. When you always tell me how heartless I am."

"Not heartless. You feel a great deal. I just don't know how you process it." She changed the subject. "What have you been doing since I saw you this morning?"

"All kinds of useful and illegal things. Are you sure you want to hear about them?"

"No, but this concerns Eve and Joe. I have to know what's going on."

"Yes, that would make a difference." He smiled. "Quinn and I looked the situation on the hill over, and we decided there was a definite problem concerning body disposal. Since he was off to chase down Natalie Castino, I volunteered to take care of it."

"Body disposal?"

"You remember that Quinn was very efficient at setting up that booby trap on the top of the hill. It killed not only Salazar but four of his hired goons. And then there was Franco, whom Natalie killed. All very deserving of their fate. But there are always questions from the police when they find bodies they didn't kill themselves." He smiled. "As you said, it's their job. So we decided to take the burden off their workload and eliminate the questions."

"And how did you do that?"

"I rounded up a few of the Laird's men and asked them to help me clean up the area." He shook his head. "Bombs leave such a mess, don't they?"

"And what did you do with this 'mess'?"

"Did you hear a helicopter about a half hour ago?"

"Yes, I thought it was a police helicopter."

"No, it belonged to a friend who owed me a favor. He landed up on the hill and we loaded up Salazar and his cohorts. My friend is going to drop the remains over the North Sea. Protein for the fishes." He looked at her inquiringly. "Now, do you feel sick or indignant?"

"No, I don't like death, but if anyone deserved it, Sala-zar did. And I don't see why Eve or Joe or anyone else should get in trouble for doing what was right."

"Excellent. I thought that would be your attitude. Are you going to praise me for my efforts? I did such a good job. Of course, if I'd had Jock's help, it might have gone smoother. He was taught all the tricks. But on the whole, I feel comfortable with the job."

"Why should I praise you? It's obvious that you have no need of anyone else's approval." She added, "And I'd just as soon that you don't involve Jock. We're trying to keep him away from memories of those 'tricks.'"

"It's not going to work," he said. "It will probably al-ways be with him. But you can hope that this business with Cara won't cause a meltdown."

"That was one of the reasons Eve went to the hospital to speak to Jock and MacDuff. She's trying to contain the situation."

"And did she succeed?"

She shook her head. "She didn't get very far, but she's hoping for the best. He's heading for Moscow as soon as he drops MacDuff off here. She said something needs to happen fast. He has to know Cara is okay." She tilted her head and gazed at him appraisingly. "It might not be a bad idea if you went with him and kept an eye on him."

"On the contrary, it would be a very bad idea. I limit my stakeouts to you, Jane. I have no interest in watching over Jock." He gazed around the camp, then to the mist-covered lake. "And I have a hunch that you may be busy enough to keep me occupied. Natalie Castino wants Cira's gold, and you'll be in the center of anything going on where that's concerned. So Jock can take care of both Cara and his eternal soul himself. I'll make sure that I have a good time right here."

"And you're certain I'll be staying here?"

"Oh, yes. You've had dreams about your little actress friend, Cira, since you were seventeen. You *know* her, she might even be your ancestress according to MacDuff. She's led you here, to this lake. You're not going anywhere until you find out why."

"MacDuff is the one who led me here. He's been harassing me for years to come on his blasted treasure hunt."

"And in the end, you said yes." He smiled faintly. "Was it to MacDuff or to Cira?"

Jane didn't know. Caleb was right, she might have used MacDuff as an excuse to go on this final adventure and find out the end of Cira's story. "It doesn't matter, does it? I'm here, and it's not really about Cira right now. It's about that little girl Natalie is using as a pawn."

"It matters. Everything you think and do matters to me." He shrugged. "But I imagine we might be able to combine agendas." He turned. "And now I'm going to my tent and clean up a bit. Today's work was satisfying, but I'm not ready for civilized company. Though I'm sure that MacDuff and Jock would forgive me and approve." He glanced up the slope toward the road. "And that may be them now. The way those policemen are bowing and scraping to someone in that car that just arrived is a good sign the Laird is on the property." He was moving across the campground. "By all means, go and save them from MacDuff's wrath. They're only going to annoy him."

Jane turned and looked at the car Caleb had spoken about. It was MacDuff. He was getting out of the car and ignoring everyone as he headed toward the slope. But Jock Gavin wasn't ignoring them as he cleaved his way through the crowd to reach MacDuff. She didn't know what he was saying to them, but the officers hurriedly faded back. Then Jock was beside MacDuff. He didn't touch him, but he was discreetly hovering as MacDuff made his way down the slope. Like a guardian angel, she thought. Not in any way insulting his strength or independence, just there for him.

Guardian angel. Considering the problem they were having with Jock, the term had a bitter irony.

But that Detective Hastings she had talked to before Caleb had arrived was now at the edge of the road and looked as if he was going take advantage of the opportunity to follow MacDuff and Jock.

No!

She ran forward to meet them. "Welcome back, Mac-Duff." She stared with deliberate meaning up at Detective Hastings. "You're looking well, but I know you need your rest. But that's okay, no one would think of bothering you now. Let's get you to your tent and settled."

The detective froze, then nodded resignedly. He turned and strode away.

"Hello, Jane." MacDuff was smiling at her. "Are you, by any chance, trying to protect me?"

"No, I'm trying to protect Jock." She nodded to Jock. "I don't think he's in any mood to be patient if anyone tries to get in your way before he has you safely tucked into your tent."

"You're right," Jock said. "So let's get MacDuff settled. Has Eve heard anything from Quinn?"

"Not yet."

Jock muttered a curse.

"Not what he wanted to hear," MacDuff said. "Not what I wanted to hear, either."

"I'm certain we'll hear soon," Jane said. She hoped she was right. Surely Joe should have heard something by now. "Let's get you to somewhere you can be comfortable."

"The two of you will not behave as if I were an

invalid. I have no intention of being cosseted," MacDuff said sourly. "I have a couple broken bones in my arm, and I feel as if I've been run through a concrete mixer. But I can function, and I won't allow you to humiliate me by treating me as if I can't."

"Suit yourself." Jane looked at Jock. "But I'm not letting you go until MacDuff is in his tent and settled."

"You think you can stop me?" he asked softly.

"I think MacDuff will stop you. He's pale. He walked down that slope as if he was balancing on eggshells. You know what's best for him. Do it."

He met her eyes, slowly nodded, and turned to Mac-Duff. "Aye, you're not at your best, MacDuff. I think we'll give it another day before you take over and start running things." He gestured toward the tents. "Let's go and get a drink and let Jane have her way."

MacDuff opened his lips to speak, then closed them again. "I could use a whiskey." He started toward his tent. "And Jane usually has her way. It has to be those Cira genes."

"Whatever," Jane said as she headed for the campfire. "I'll go get you a bowl of soup and some tea. And, if the medication they gave you at the hospital can't be mixed with alcohol, forget about that drink."

CHAPTER
4

MacDuff had finished his soup *and* his whiskey when Eve hurried into the tent. Her hair was rumpled and her shirt wrinkled. "There you are, Jane. I was looking for you." She glanced at MacDuff and Jock. "Good to see you back, MacDuff." She turned back to Jane. "I woke up, and I couldn't find my phone. Do you have it?"

"Oh, shit." Jane reached for her phone. "No, I don't." She dialed a number and said through her teeth, "Caleb, I'm at MacDuff's tent. So is Eve. Get over here."

"What's happening?" Eve ran a hand through her hair. "Caleb?"

"Yes, Caleb." Jane whirled on Caleb as he came into the tent. "Did you go into Eve's tent and take her phone?"

"Of course." He pulled her phone out of his pocket. "You said she needed to sleep." He handed the phone to Eve. "You were even wondering if you should monitor it yourself."

"And you told me she'd be pissed off. Not that I would have done it anyway."

"I know. You're too honorable, and you wouldn't want to upset someone you love." He turned to Eve. "I was right? You are pissed off?"

"I'm furious," Eve said curtly. "Invasion of privacy. Not to mention that Joe might have needed to get in touch with me."

Caleb glanced at Jane. "Then I gave you excellent advice, didn't I?"

"And then immediately went out and did it yourself."

"You were worried. You said Eve needed sleep. You wanted it done. I had nothing to lose. No one expects me to be honorable." He turned to Eve. "And I would have bitten the bullet and gone back to wake you if Joe had called. I knew it was important."

"He didn't call?" Jock asked.

Caleb shook his head. "But he's sent two texts in the last hour with updates. He said he'd call you if he knew something."

"You read the texts?"

"I had to make certain that there wasn't anything in them that you should know about." He glanced at MacDuff. "Could I have a whiskey, MacDuff? Or do you think they'd take that as a reward for bad behavior?"

"I believe that's a good call," MacDuff said dryly.

Caleb turned to Jane. "Eve had an extra hour's sleep, and I interfered with nothing that she won't hear from Quinn when he knows himself. I believe I'm golden."

"I believe you're impossible." She turned to Eve. "If I had anything to do with this, I apologize."

"You didn't." Eve was still glowering as she went through her texts, then shook her head when she finished. "And he's right. Joe just wanted me to know that Burbank had received a message from his contact at the airport but nothing definitive. The second was that the plane had landed but no one had deboarded yet."

"And you would have been in agony waiting for word," Caleb said. "I saved you that."

"Just as I am now," Eve said. "And I have a right to decide whether I want to accept that or not. It's my life, Caleb. If you ever do anything like this again, I will—" Her phone rang, and she jumped to access it. "Joe?"

"Yes, Burbank got through to his contact, Dima Palik."

Jock stepped forward. "I have to *know*, Eve. Put it on speaker."

Eve put it on speaker. "Cara. Did he actually see Cara? Was Cara with Natalie?"

"Yes, thank God."

Eve went limp with relief. "Of course, she was. We knew that Natalie wanted to use her." But she had still been terrified that Natalie could have changed her mind or had just been teasing Eve, raising her hopes only to dash them. The only certainty about Natalie was that there was no certainty. "Why did it take so long for Burbank's contact to verify that she had Cara?"

"Evidently Palik is the slow, careful type. Palik is one of the most knowledgeable freelance informants in Moscow. He doesn't only work for Burbank, but he does regard him as a valuable asset. He wanted to be sure he was earning his money. So he not only observed, he took pictures. And when Kaskov sent a car for Natalie and Cara, he followed it and took photos of the meeting with Kaskov. I'm sending them to you." He paused. "It doesn't look too bad, Eve. Judge for yourself. She may be okay until we can get her out of there."

"I hope you're right," she said unsteadily. If Joe said it didn't look bad, then Cara was probably safe enough right now. "I guess we should be grateful that Natalie didn't drop her out over the Alps or something. A part of me was thinking that just might happen."

"I know. But now we know she's alive, and we have a location. Palik is investigating to try to find out whatever else he can."

"He'd better do it quickly. Natalie is impatient. She's not going to wait long before she decides to contact me. And right now, we have nothing with which to bargain."

"Kaskov," Jock said. "If she's with Kaskov, I have to know about him. What have you found out, Quinn?"

"Smart enough to stay on top of the Mafia hierarchy all these years. Wields a hell of a lot of power in Moscow politics through bribery and intimidation. He has strict rules for all his men, and it's a death sentence if he's not obeyed. He's principally into drugs and contract killing. Evidently, he likes to pretend he's no hood but a patron of the arts because he has season tickets and gives contributions to both the Bolshoi and Moscow Music Conservatory. No women in residence. He keeps a mistress, who's a singer in the opera, in an apartment in downtown Moscow. Evidently, Natalie is the only person for whom he has any affection. That's all I know right now."

"That's enough to start. I'll find out the rest myself. Thanks."

"It's enough to cause me to shudder." Eve changed the subject. "When can I see you, Joe? Are you coming here, or should I come to you? Toller may be lurking around here."

"I'll take care of that," MacDuff said. "This area is officially closed while we undertake the exploration of the north bank. No one permitted in without my consent. Your Toller can spin his wheels at the nearest village."

"Then I'll come there," Joe said. "Are you okay, Eve?"

"Fine. Well, maybe not fine. But better than before I

heard about Cara. I'll be glad to see you. Hurry." She hung up. He was on his way. She was going to see him, touch him.

Her phone pinged as the photos began to arrive.

"May I?" Jock took the phone and began to flip rapidly through them. She could see the lines of tension gradually leave his face as he looked at Cara. Then he handed Eve's phone back to her. "They're playing a game with her. At least, Natalie is doing that. I don't know about Kaskov. Maybe not. I'll have to see."

Eve was looking at the photos. Natalie's beautiful, smiling face. Kaskov was smiling, too, but his expression was intent. Cara was the only one not smiling. "What game?" she whispered.

"Whatever it is, Cara's not in the mix." He took the phone and enlarged Cara's face and figure in the photo. "Look at her. The tension in her shoulders, the wariness in her expression."

"Fear?"

"Maybe a little, mostly confusion and watchfulness."

"Watchfulness." She moistened her lips. "I have to admit I'm relieved. I hope you're right. Natalie is very plausible. I was afraid that she'd spin Cara a story, and she'd believe it."

"No, that didn't happen." His lips tightened grimly as he enlarged Cara's face in the photo. "When they put her on that helicopter, was her face bruised or damaged in any way?"

"No."

"Well, it was when she arrived at Kaskov's mansion." He pointed to the bruise on Cara's cheek. "Someone hurt her. She had reason to be watchful and not cause a problem for Natalie."

"Then she's not as safe as Joe hoped." Eve shook her head. "*Damn.*"

"She will be safe." Jock turned toward the door. "I'll be in touch, Eve. But you'd better do something fast. I'm not going to let that happen to her again."

The next moment, he was gone.

"Moscow?" Caleb murmured.

"Moscow," Eve said, looking down at the photo of Cara. She looked fragile and vulnerable but there was also that wariness that Jock had seen. Eve had been so happy to see her alive that that was all that she had noticed. But now she could see the quiet alertness, the slight tightness about her lips. The girl was being hunted again, and she knew it. And if she knew it, then her mother hadn't been able to fool her or use her . . . yet.

No, she had to believe that Cara would be smart enough to keep Natalie from doing anything to hurt her now that she knew what kind of woman she was.

"Eve?" Jane was standing next to her.

"I'm okay. She'll be okay, too. She's been hunted all her life. She'll do what she has to do and come through fine."

She looked down at the bruise on Cara's cheek again. Such a delicate cheek. Such a brutal bruise.

God help her, she was almost glad Jock was on his way to Moscow.

"Move over." Joe was kneeling beside her in the darkness of the tent. "Thank God you don't have a sleeping bag. I need to hold you."

"Me, too." She turned over and slid into his arms. He was naked, and she ran her hands caressingly over his shoulders. "And thank MacDuff. He has all the latest equipment, but he said that sleeping bags can be smothering if you don't need them. He likes bedrolls. Besides, we have the tents."

"I'm beginning to appreciate MacDuff more every

minute." He buried his face in her hair. "It's been too long."

It seemed that way to her, too. She hadn't been able to hold him like this since she'd been forced to go into hiding with Cara. She knew it had been necessary for Cara's safety for them to have that ocean separating them, but it had seemed as if she'd left a part of herself behind. This part, the important part.

Warmth, strength, love. She cuddled closer. "You should tell him that you approve his choice. I think he's feeling the lack of control right now."

"Hell, he almost got blown up a few days ago."

"It doesn't matter." She kissed his throat. "He's got this male thing about running the world. Sound familiar?"

"And you don't?"

"Just my corner of it. And right now I'd just as soon devote my attention to that corner."

He was silent a moment. "I can't send you home. It wouldn't be safe. We can't tell what Natalie is going to do or how you'll figure in it. I need to keep you close."

"For heaven's sake, I wasn't suggesting that I opt out. I know that's not possible until we get Cara back. That comment just came out of the blue. Maybe my nesting instinct is raising its head again." She got up on one elbow and looked down at him. "What do you think? Can't you see me wearing a cutesy apron and cleaning and learning to cook?"

He chuckled. "Heaven help us. It would blow my mind. But I'm not worried. Once you get back to the cottage, I won't be able to tear you away from your reconstructions."

She knew that was true. "Yet there will have to be checks and balances. Lately, that's been brought to my attention."

He stiffened. "Why? Are you okay?

"I'd tell you if I wasn't. I have to take care of this baby." She kissed his shoulder. "Or the baby will take care of me. Or something . . ."

"What?"

"Nothing. I've just been feeling really close to the baby. I know it's too early to actually feel . . . but it's as if the baby wants me to know that . . ." She shook her head. "I don't know what it wants me to know. But I think I'm going to find out. Am I making any sense?"

"Here and there," he said thickly. "But it's all good."

"I think you're being patronizing to me."

"No way. I wouldn't dare. The two of you might gang up on me. Anything else to share?"

"Just that I've changed my mind about not wanting to know if the baby is a girl or boy. Remember I told you that I didn't want to know?"

"Yes, why the change of heart?"

"The baby is so real to me now. It's . . . magic. It's almost as if I can read its thoughts. But I have to know more, I have to know *everything*."

"I'm afraid you'll have to wait awhile. It's a little early for the usual tests, isn't it?"

"Yes, but that's okay. I just wanted to tell you that I wanted to know. I didn't want to catch you by surprise."

"You're confusing me, Eve."

"I think that because I want to know, I *will* know soon, Joe. I think the baby will want me to have what I want in this."

He stared at her for a long moment and then smiled. "Why not? I want to give you everything you want. It must run in the family." He kissed her gently. "You will tell me if the baby comes through for you?"

"Now that did sound definitely patronizing. Not that I blame you. You'd have to be in my place to understand it."

"That would be very unusual and disorienting. I'll just stand by and let you work it out."

"I'm doing that. But it helps that you're with me now and trying to take care of our child." She paused. "Just as we have to take care of Cara. Jock left for Moscow right after you called, Joe."

"I thought he would. That doesn't have to be bad."

"I know. He saw things in those pictures of Cara that I didn't see. Did you notice that bruise on her cheek?"

"No."

"Neither did I. He's so closely attuned to her that it constantly surprises me. They almost read each other's minds. That could be a good thing if he has to try to get her out."

"And he didn't blow up when he saw that bruise?"

"He just said it couldn't happen again." She went back into his arms. "And it can't, Joe," she whispered. "She's been through so much . . ."

"Shh." He was holding her tighter. "Let it go. Tomorrow we'll know more about where she is and how to get to her. Tonight she'll be fine. Just let me hold you and take it all away."

Take away all the pain and worry and sorrow. Give her love and safety and a pleasure that was always so intense that it took her breath away. That's what Joe had done for her all their years together. How lucky she was that she had found him. How lucky she was that she had never lost him. She pulled his head down and kissed him long and slow. "I love you, Joe Quinn." She pulled off her nightshirt and came on top of him. Her breasts were readying the instant they touched the hard muscles of his chest. "And I think tonight I have to give back a little to you." Her legs tightened on his hips. "Or maybe not so little . . ."

KASKOV ESTATE
MOSCOW

"Now don't be pushy with your grandfather," Natalie said as she walked with Cara down the driveway toward the mansion from the gatehouse. "Just play fifteen minutes or so for him, then I'll send you back to the gatehouse. I don't want him to become bored with you."

Cara didn't answer.

"But perhaps he won't want you to play that long. He doesn't appreciate amateurs. You sounded conceited when you told him that you were good. He might be disappointed."

"I didn't mean to be conceited. I just answered his question." She looked straight ahead. "I can't really tell what's bad or good when I'm playing. It's just . . . the music. But that's what people have told me."

"Have they? How interesting." She opened the front door. "But we've already discussed how many people lie." Her face lit with glowing affection as she saw Kaskov coming across the foyer. "Here we are, Daddy." She moved toward him and kissed his cheek. "I went to get Cara so that we could talk. I know the gatehouse is safer, but I was already missing her." She pushed Cara forward. "Tell your grandfather how much you like the gatehouse. She said that the mansion overwhelms her a little."

"She'll get used to it later." Kaskov came forward, and his brows rose as his eyes traveled over Cara's black ballet slippers, simple navy blue skirt, and white-silk blouse. "Not what I would have thought you'd have chosen for her, Natalie. Your taste runs more to designer lace and satin."

"It's what she wanted. She said that she doesn't like to draw attention to herself. And she's a trifle gangly, so anything fancier would have been wasted on her."

Lie on top of lie. Cara was becoming accustomed to it now.

"She's not gangly." Kaskov tilted his head. "But that outfit will be fine. There's a certain elegance to it. Why don't you like to draw attention to yourself, Cara?"

"Clothes don't matter. Sometimes they just get in the way."

Kaskov laughed. "Do you hear that, Natalie? Are you sure that she's your daughter?"

"Poor child. She's probably never had anything nice. No wonder she feels out of place."

"Well, I have something that she might consider 'nice.' " He took Cara's hand and drew her through the foyer to the living room. "It's there on the couch. I bought it this afternoon."

He'd already taken the violin out of the case and set it upright against the silk cushions of the couch, framing it. "What do you think of it?"

She went slowly across the room, her gaze on the violin.

The wood had a deep, burnished luster that seemed to glow under the lights . . .

"It's . . . wonderful." She reached out and touched it. "Italian? How old is it?"

"How old do you think it is?"

"I saw one that looked like this in a book Elena gave me."

"How old, Cara?"

She moistened her lips. "Over two hundred years?"

"And who made it?"

She was afraid to say it. "Amati?"

He chuckled. "Very good."

She touched the violin again. "And you want me to play it?"

"I demand that you play it. I didn't go to all this trouble to have you sit and look at it."

"What's all this about, Daddy?" Natalie asked. "You gave her a two-hundred-year-old violin? Aren't they worth a lot of money?"

"Only the exceptional ones."

"Is this exceptional?"

"Is it exceptional, Cara?"

"Oh, yes." She could hardly get out the words. "I heard a concert on PBS, and the sound . . . I'd have to play it, but I . . ." She looked at him. "And I don't think you'd buy it if it wasn't as good as the one I heard."

"I've never heard of that violin," Natalie said. "It's not like it's a Stradivarius, is it?"

"No, I might save that for later."

"Daddy, how much is it worth?" she asked impatiently.

"It was a bargain. One point four million."

"What?" Her eyes widened. "For an instrument for a child? It's ridiculous."

"It might be, but I didn't want to waste my time listening to her playing an inferior instrument." He looked at Cara. "But she's right, if you only deserve an inferior instrument, that's what I'll give you. If you show me you come close to deserving this one, then I'll allow you to keep it."

"Ridiculous," Natalie said through her teeth.

"Are you feeling the pressure?" Kaskov asked Cara. "Sweaty palms?"

She shook her head. "I don't care if you take it away if I can play it just once. I never thought I'd ever be able to do that."

He stared at her for a moment. "Interesting. Then why don't you sit down and play it?"

"Daddy."

He didn't look at her. "And you sit down, too, Natalie. I'm looking forward to this."

Cara was no longer listening to Natalie. She was only

conscious of the violin and the music she knew was there waiting for her.

She slowly picked up the violin and tucked it beneath her chin.

"Aren't you going to ask me what I want?" Kaskov asked.

"You're Russian. You'll want the Tchaikovsky."

She began to play.

The sound . . .

The feel of the strings . . .

The release, the wildness, the beauty.

The music.

She didn't know how long she played. It was pure joy that she didn't want to let go.

She went from Tchaikovsky to Vivaldi to Mendelssohn in a fever to keep the music whirling, touching, surrounding.

"Enough, Cara." She was suddenly aware of Natalie's hand on her shoulder. "You must be exhausted. I need to take you back to the gatehouse and see that you get to bed." Her voice was gentle, but the fingers digging into Cara's shoulder were not. "And you've taken enough of your grandfather's time for one evening. Give him back the violin."

Cara shook her head to clear it. She took a deep breath and got to her feet. "I'm not tired." She could still feel the music singing in her veins. She crossed the room to Kaskov's chair. "Thank you, sir." She held out the violin. "It was wonderful."

"Yes, it was," he said softly. He made no motion to take the instrument. "But there's always room for improvement. Though at the moment I can't see how. I believe you'd better keep that violin and see if you can surprise me."

Her eyes widened. "I can keep it?" Her hand tightened on the violin. "You're not joking?"

"I'm not known for my humor. And I never joke about money or music."

"It's too much, Daddy," Natalie said. "I didn't bring her here for you to spoil her."

"I disagree. It may not be enough." He was gazing at Cara. "And I'm not going to spoil her. I'll make her work for it. Every time I send for her, I'll expect her to come running with that violin and play for me. Is that a deal, Cara?"

"Yes, sir." She was looking down at the violin in disbelief. "Is it really mine?"

"I think it has to be." He turned to Natalie. "You never disappoint me. I thought her sister, Jenny, was remarkable, but you've brought me another extraordinary gift." He kissed her cheek. "Now take her back to the gatehouse and tuck her in."

"Yes, Daddy." She turned to Cara. "Pack up that violin, and let's get out of here."

"Right away." There was something in Natalie's tone that made Cara hurry to the couch and place the violin quickly in its case. It was clear that Natalie was annoyed, and it would be hard to ignore it now that Cara was no longer involved in the music. All she wanted to do was to get back to the gatehouse with this incredible gift and be alone so that she could play it again. "Thank you. Good night, sir."

"I've just given you a present that you appear to be very pleased with and yet you can't seem to remember to call me grandfather."

She smiled tentatively. "It just seems . . . disrespectful. You don't really know me. And I'm not sure you would want to if it wasn't for the music."

"Very perceptive." He smiled crookedly. "And I don't

know either. We'll have to test it and see what comes of it. Until then, you may call me sir."

She nodded and hurried toward the door.

She was only a few yards down the driveway when Natalie caught up with her. "That was quite an exhibition," she said tightly. "I might as well not have been in the room."

"I didn't ask to play for him."

"No, you didn't. And you didn't ask him to give you that ridiculously expensive violin, but somehow you got him to do it."

"I had no idea he'd give me an Amati. It took my breath away."

"My father never stints himself when music is involved. I should have remembered and tried to circumvent it."

"I could give it back."

"No, you can't. He'd blame me. We had a few other battles over his gifts to my brother, and it would make him remember them. He mustn't do that."

"Then I can keep the violin?"

"I have no choice. But don't think you've won." Her eyes were straight ahead, and her tone was ice-cold. "You'll learn that in the final battle, I always win."

"I didn't try to win anything." She was suddenly afraid. She had been attempting to pacify Natalie since she had arrived here, but everything kept going wrong.

It mustn't go wrong. She didn't know what plans Natalie had for Eve, but she was afraid for her. And the more she thought about those scraps of conversation that she remembered, she knew that somehow she was involved.

She had to get away from here.

She couldn't let Natalie use her to hurt Eve.

"Maybe you could tell your father I'm homesick, and you want to take me back to the U.S. Then he wouldn't—"

"Shut up!" Natalie suddenly exploded. "It's all your fault. That damn music. Who cares anything about it? Did you hear him thank me for providing him with you because he'd found a new pet to amuse him? It's all he cares about. Your sister, Jenny, and now you. And he doted on my brother, Alex. I'd do everything I could, but I still couldn't come out on top. I was only important if he wasn't around." She added harshly, "So I had to make sure he wasn't around."

Cara didn't want to hear this. They were close to the gatehouse and she instinctively started to hurry. Don't listen. Get away from her. Because she had a terrible idea that she knew how Natalie had solved her problem with her brother. "Your father seems to love you. I'm sure he loved you more than your brother."

"You don't know anything. That stupid music. Even after Alex was dead, my father wouldn't give up on it."

"Jenny?" Cara whispered.

"And now you." Her voice was shaking with rage. "Does he think I'm some kind of broodmare to spit out children to give him some kind of twisted satisfaction because of that prick who messed up his hands? In a way, he was like my husband, who was trying to make me give him a son. I am *not* a broodmare. Why couldn't they see that I was the important one?"

They were only a few feet from the gatehouse. Don't let Natalie say too much. She might already have said more than was safe for Cara.

"He'll probably get bored with hearing me play." She opened the door. "He might make me give the violin back in a day or two."

"I doubt it," she said curtly. "But I may have to cut this visit short. I wanted to make sure he was going to be in my corner, but you're spoiling everything." She followed her into the gatehouse. "But you will do everything I say, and you will not cause me any more trouble."

"Just tell me what to do," Cara said quietly.

"Oh, I will. First, I want you to meet someone." She went to the French doors leading to the small garden. "Ivan!"

"Yes." A tall, muscular, dark-haired man was at the door within seconds. "You need me?"

Dead eyes, Cara thought. He had a broad Slavic face but his dark eyes were totally without expression.

"This is Ivan Sabak, Cara," Natalie said. "He's your personal bodyguard while you're here. I'm sure that you've seen more of my father's men moving around the estate, but Ivan is special. He knows my father will be very upset if you take it into your head to leave here. There is nothing he will not do to prevent it. Even if he's forced to hurt you, though I'm sure that you wouldn't make him do that." She smiled at Ivan. "Isn't that right, Ivan?"

"If that's what you want," Ivan said. "I have no instructions from your father."

"Now you do. He wants you to take your orders from me." Natalie turned to leave. "I'll see you tomorrow, Cara. Take care of that violin." She opened the door. "I'm considering it a loan."

The door closed behind her.

Cara glanced at Ivan, but he'd disappeared back into the garden.

She was alone. Relief was surging through her. No Natalie. No Kaskov. No Ivan with his dead eyes. She shot the bolt on the door.

What was she doing? She was bolting herself into this gatehouse with Ivan, who was probably a more immediate danger than Natalie or her father. It didn't matter. That bolt was more symbolic than practical. She wanted to close out all the pressures, confusion, and threats, subtle and otherwise. She turned and flew up the stairs to her bedroom on the second floor. It was a nice enough room, with carved cherry furniture and its own bath and balcony.

And she could lock that door, too.

She leaned back against the door, her pulse pounding, breathing hard. She didn't feel much safer. She went out on the balcony and looked down at the small rose garden below. Was Ivan down there somewhere? No, he'd come in from the back garden. But there was still no way she could climb down and escape. She could see three men in jeans and casual jackets within a few yards of the garden.

And what could she do if she did get away from the estate? No money. No plans.

Then she would work on getting both. But it wouldn't be tonight. She'd go to bed and try to sleep.

But she wouldn't sleep anytime soon. She was too on edge from that last conversation with Natalie. She was learning more about her all the time and every word revealed—

She wouldn't think about Natalie. She turned and put her case on the bed and took out her violin.

Her violin. It *was* hers for the time being. Natalie and Kaskov couldn't take it away from her. She had made it hers when she was playing tonight. It was part of her, just as the music was part of her. She stroked the smooth rosewood. It felt warm to her, alive . . .

No, only she could bring it to life.

And she would.

She didn't have to climb down that balcony to escape. She could rid herself of Natalie and Ivan and Kaskov and the threats and terrible revelations that were all around her.

She only had to release the magic . . .

MOSCOW
TWO DAYS LATER

Jock looked down at the map on the table. "How many guards on the grounds, Palik?"

"Seven. Sometimes eight if Kaskov has a special job. I've heard stories that it was an armed camp when he was negotiating with the Chinese over drug distribution. But usually he—" He stopped as he saw Jock's expression. "But you're not interested in the Chinese. Sorry. You can count on eight. I don't believe he'll think it necessary to bring in extra firepower. But he did assign Ivan Sabak to her."

"And who is he?"

"Kaskov's principal enforcer."

"Weapons?"

"Knives. Hands. Doesn't care much for guns."

Neither did Jock. "Why did he put her in the gatehouse?"

Palik shrugged. "It's easy to guard. Hard to extract anyone. Was he expecting someone to come and get her?"

"Maybe not. But Natalie Castino would have known it was a possibility."

"And you're the cavalry?"

"You might say that."

"I just want you to know that if you expect me to join in any attack on Kaskov's estate, you're mistaken. I collect information and that's all. I could put you in touch with a few good men, but it will cost you. No one wants to go up against Kaskov. They have a tendency to end up dead after being painfully dismembered."

"I'll tell you if I need help. It's not likely." He was gazing down at the map, memorizing the layout of both the mansion and the gatehouse. "Which is her room?"

Palik pointed to the third room on the second floor. "You'd have to go through Ivan to get to her."

That was the least of Jock's concern. "Once I get her away from the estate, can you get me a plane and transport out of the country?"

"Not out of Moscow. Once Kaskov lets his dogs out, there won't be anyone who won't be on the hunt for you. No one is going to rent you a plane or any other kind of wheels. They'd know they'd be dead within twenty-four hours."

"I see." But he didn't like it. If Kaskov had that kind of power, then Eve was right. Unless he could figure a safe way to get Cara out of the country, then there was a real danger that she could be caught in a cross fire. He couldn't risk it.

"Maybe you could broker a deal?" Palik suggested.

That's what Natalie Castino was trying to do, and he might have to have Eve stall her until he could put together a plan.

Another delay.

He deliberately smothered the rage that was tearing through him. Now was the time for cool thinking and planning and gathering information that would make those plans work. He turned away from the table. "Take me to Kaskov's estate. I want to see it."

"Don't you want to take the map?"

"No, I've got it." He headed for the door. "I'll remember."

"You will? I could—"

"I just want to see the place. Take me there. After that, I'll be on my own."

He shook his head. "I can't say that I envy you. What are they paying you to do a job like this?"

Cara sitting on the stone wall at Gaelkar playing her violin.

Cara looking up at him with tears in her eyes and saying good-bye when Eve had told her she had to go on the run again.

Cara running after him through the forest because she didn't want him to face Salazar alone.

"Enough." He headed for the door. "They're paying me more than enough."

CHAPTER
5

Jock lowered the infrared binoculars and settled himself more comfortably on the branch of the oak tree fifty yards outside the gates of Kaskov's mansion. It was going to be a long night. Palik had done a good job. The buildings and layout of the estate were exactly as Palik had drawn them. It was Kaskov's guards who might be the problem. You could never predict how they would react, when they would take breaks, if one was sharper or lazier than another. But you could make a good guess if you watched long enough.

And once he knew which way they would jump, he could take them down.

He lifted the binoculars to his eyes again and focused on the gatehouse itself. He'd positioned himself so that he would be able to see the balcony of Cara's room. The French doors were closed, but he knew she was there. He'd heard her playing when Palik had dropped him off an hour earlier. Just a thread of sound in the darkness, but it was unmistakable.

She wasn't playing now, and he hoped she was asleep. She probably needed sleep. He didn't know what she had been going through, but she had to be bewildered and uncertain and frightened at this abrupt change in her life. But at least that bitch, Natalie Castino, had seen that she was given something familiar in the form of that violin she had been playing. A bribe? Perhaps. Eve had said that she was manipulative and clever. But he couldn't see Cara taking a bribe if she knew—What the hell was he thinking? Cara was just a kid and trying to function in a strange and frightening situation. But she couldn't function if she didn't know what the situation really was.

And he wasn't going to be able to get her out of here when the time came if he didn't have her prepared and ready to move fast.

Which meant he was going to have to do more than just watch and plan in the next few days.

His phone vibrated in his pocket, and he took it out and glanced at the ID.

Eve. She'd been more patient than he'd thought she'd be. Palik had called Joe Quinn when Jock had arrived two days ago to tell him he'd arrived. She'd tried to call Jock twice, but he'd not been ready to talk to anyone while he'd been studying the situation as Palik had presented it to him.

He answered this call. "Hello, Eve. How's MacDuff?"

"MacDuff is going at warp speed," she said impatiently. "You knew he would be as soon as he was on his feet and halfway healed. I didn't call to give you a report on MacDuff. Dammit, it's been two days, Jock."

"I was busy."

"Don't tell me that. Have you seen Cara?"

"No, but I heard her. Someone gave her a violin. I assume it was her mother."

"What? Why would she do that?"

"I think I'll have to find out. It's not safe for me not to know how she feels about Natalie. It could present difficulties." He paused. "And there are difficulties enough as it is. I may have trouble getting her out of Moscow when I take her out of that gatehouse. I'm working on it now."

"Where are you working on it? Where are you now, Jock?"

"Close to her." His gaze went to the balcony. "She's asleep now. She's safe, Eve. I'm watching her."

Eve drew a shaky breath. "If you ever do this again to me, I'll come after you, Jock. You answer me when I call you."

"Palik was in touch with Burbank."

"Palik isn't you. I didn't have to worry about Palik's going ballistic and turning Kaskov's estate into a battle zone."

He smiled. "No, you didn't have to worry about that. And you don't have to worry about my doing that, either. It will have to be handled quietly, with no firepower, until Cara is out of the danger area."

Silence. "You're already getting ready to do it, aren't you?"

"Getting ready." He looked down at the ground some sixty feet below him. "But things are a bit in the air right now. You may still have a chance to divert me if you can show me that there's a safer way to get her out. Have you heard from Natalie Castino yet?"

"No. And I've tried to call her, but she doesn't answer either. I've been going crazy between the two of you."

"I answered your call. I didn't have anything to say until now. I was making contact with some previous acquaintances from my shady past and probing their thoughts on the matter of a safe extraction. Unfortunately, their views were the same as Palik's. So I knew it was up to me."

"The hell it is."

"Find me a safer way, Eve," he repeated. "And I'll do anything you say. Maybe Natalie wasn't ready to talk to you either. But she might be getting impatient now. Unless she's changed her mind and thinks being Daddy's little girl will be enough for her. In that case, there's not going to be any safe way of getting Cara out of there if she's using her to cement relations." He added coldly, "And I won't leave her here, Eve. She's not going to be a pawn for Kaskov or his daughter. Pawns are much too easy to be thrown away in fits of rage."

"Don't do anything. I'll find a way to contact Natalie. Look, MacDuff and Joe are setting up infrared lights on the north bank of the lake to try to pierce that thick mist. If they work, then we'll be able to go after Cira's gold soon. It's what Natalie wants, and that will give us leverage."

"Fine. But I'll continue to make my preparations until you give me a reason to stop. I hope you do, Eve." He hung up.

He could understand Eve's impatience and worry and, in a remote way, even sympathize. But it was very remote, and he would not let it touch him. Eve belonged to that other life, the one that had too many rules and morals to let him be what he had to be. He couldn't save Cara if he let that life control him. So close Eve out, close all of them out. Go back to the control he'd learned from Reilly so long ago.

He leaned forward on the branch and lifted the binoculars again. He concentrated on the sentry closest to the east side of the gatehouse. Watching him move, look-ing for weakness . . . getting ready for the kill.

"He's cold as ice," Eve said jerkily as she turned to Jane after hanging up the phone. "I'd rather he be angry or something. Then I could talk to him, persuade him. Or you could talk to him. You know him better than any-body but MacDuff."

Jane nodded. "We knew this might be coming. I was hoping that the situation he found there might be a little more promising."

"Cara is alive. No one is hurting her right now. That has to be promise enough."

"As long as that continues, I don't believe Jock will make any quick moves," Jane said. "And he told you that he's not ready yet. He gave us warning and a chance."

"I don't know why we haven't heard from Natalie yet," Eve said in frustration. She turned and moved out of the tent to stand looking out at the lake. Joe, MacDuff, Caleb, and several of MacDuff's men had disappeared into that massive fogbank a few hours before with that lab equipment she'd told Jock about. She could only hope that they would be successful. "She wanted that treasure. She was almost salivating."

"Maybe she's just giving us a chance to find it," Jane said quietly as she came to stand beside her. "You told her we'd found the treasure to set up a trap. It worked because you and Cara were part of that bait. Otherwise, she would have demanded proof that you'd found it. She may still want it, but she'll be more cautious now."

Jane was right, Eve thought wearily. The bait might not have been strong enough to make Natalie commit to giving up Cara without proof. She might want a guaran-tee, something tangible that would tempt her over the edge. She was safe in her father's palatial home and had all the time in the world to make certain that Eve had what she wanted.

And what she wanted could be somewhere out in that mist hovering over the north bank of the lake.

"I don't see any kind of light in that mist. Do you think those gadgets will work?" Eve asked.

"Maybe. If she wants them to work."

Eve turned to look at her in surprise. "Jane? Is that a break in the wall of skepticism you've built around Cira?"

Jane shrugged. "The skepticism is still there, but I'm tired of closing my mind to Cira. I'm just accepting whatever comes along." She smiled faintly. "And maybe what comes along will give us a clue how to lure Natalie into giving Cara back to us."

"In the meantime, I'll try to reach Natalie and at least set up a dialogue with her." Eve moved down the bank and sat down on the grass. "She's got to answer sometime."

It was Eve Duncan calling again, Natalie saw with satisfaction as she looked down at her phone. She felt a surge of power as she sat there gazing at the phone and not answering.

Natalie found it strange that the woman wanted Cara enough to humiliate herself by calling repeatedly. Soft. So soft. But then, it was what she should have expected of someone who spent her life trying to put skulls back together and sending them back to their parents. Weird. Very weird.

But that softness might still be of use to Natalie. She moved across the conservatory to look into the living room, where Cara was still playing.

She felt the familiar surge of rage as she looked at her father sitting listening, totally absorbed, his gaze on Cara. He hadn't even noticed when Natalie had left the room and wandered into the conservatory. It had been like that ever since she had arrived here over a week ago. She wasn't going to be able to stand it for much longer.

She had wanted to consolidate her position before she made any moves. She still had the money her father had given her to "ransom" Cara. But she would go through that in less than a year; and then she would be dependent on her father again.

And she couldn't stand the thought of Cara's taking all his attention, all the spotlight that should belong to her. The mere thought sent rage tearing through her. It was intolerable. She still needed her father's power in the background, but she would not be put in a position where she would have to beg him for funds.

So it might be time to explore the possibility of another source of income.

And explore the possibility of getting rid of Cara sooner than she had planned.

How to do it?

She would think of something . . .

LOCH GAELKAR

"Did it work?" Jane moved toward MacDuff as she saw him emerge from the mist of the north bank. She didn't really have to ask. MacDuff's expression was not happy.

He shrugged. "Yes and no. We got a limited amount of mist clearance during the first part of the trip, but once we reached that cluster of big boulders toward the middle, it was as bad as it always was."

"Why?"

"How do I know? Who has any idea what's going on in that mist? I actually thought we might have the answer." His lips tightened. "But I'll find that answer, even if it means roping ourselves together and—"

"What good would that do? You still wouldn't be able to see. You'd just be stumbling around in that mist."

"We might stumble onto that something that we've been looking for." He turned away from her and strode toward his tent. "In the meantime, I'm going to get a drink, then call the lab where I got those lamps and ask if they have any suggestions."

She watched him until he disappeared into his tent. She was disappointed, too. Not only did MacDuff deserve to find his treasure, but Eve needed Cira's gold to offer as bait to get Cara back.

Or was she disappointed? She had felt sympathy but also a tiny bit of relief. Which just showed how conflicted she was on this subject of Cira. Maybe she actually didn't want the place where Cira had buried her son to be disturbed. Or maybe she wanted to be the one to find it herself.

She turned and looked back at the mist over Cira's lake that never vanished.

Is that what you want, too, Cira?

No answer of course. She was being totally unreasonable, and she should dismiss the mystical and embrace the practical as she usually did.

But it made no sense that the lights would work so far and no farther. She wanted to see it for herself.

She moved across the bank and into the mist.

Not too bad. They had set poles with the infrared lamps at twenty-foot intervals, and she could dimly make out shapes and shrubs. Nothing clear. But, when combined with her flashlight it was like walking in a regular fog, not that impenetrable mist.

Until she came to the cluster of boulders. MacDuff had set up a pole lamp there also, but it was as if it wasn't there. The mist wrapped itself around the light and smothered it, only permitting a weak gleam that could be seen no more than a foot away.

Amazing.

And exciting.

She stood looking at the darkness beyond the rocks.

Mist.

The sound of water lapping against the bank.

But Jane could not see the water.

Or the trees or rocks or anything but the blinding mist.

"What are you doing here?"

She stiffened and turned to see Caleb behind her. "I wanted to see for myself. MacDuff told me that gadget seemed to work on the first mile or so of the north bank, but after you passed that group of boulders, it failed. It didn't make sense to me that it would do that."

He smiled. "So you went to see if we'd done something wrong? Or did you want to know if Cira had erected some kind of ghostly barrier?"

"It didn't make sense to me," she repeated. "Don't make anything of it but curiosity, Caleb."

"I'll try to resist the temptation, but it's difficult for me. Temptations of all varieties are difficult for me. Are you ready to go back now?" He shined the beam of flashlight ahead into the mist. "It gets thicker from here on, and you won't be able to see anything at all within a few feet, even with a flashlight. I wouldn't want you to slip and fall into the lake."

"I can swim."

"But I'd feel bound to jump in after you, and that would make you feel annoyed if it turned out that I saved you."

"Extremely annoyed." She shined her own flashlight on the mist ahead. It was oddly alluring, calling, beckoning to her. She wasn't sure if she would have gone on if Caleb hadn't shown up. Perhaps. Perhaps not. She wasn't even certain why she had felt compelled to come here after she had talked to MacDuff. "But I won't risk your throwing that in my face for the rest of my life." She turned and started back toward the south end of the lake. "You followed me, didn't you?"

"Yes, I don't like the idea of losing you to Cira. I prefer to monitor the situation." He was walking behind her, and his voice was drifting toward her, around her out of the mist. "You've been upset for the last few days, and I thought that it wouldn't hurt to see what you were doing."

"Of course I've been upset. That doesn't mean I'd do anything stupid or irrational. Eve and I have both been stressed and on edge."

"But Eve has a support group that you don't have. She has you and Quinn and maybe that child she's carrying."

"And I have her. She would never shut me out."

"But you wouldn't let her know that you need her. You're being too careful to make sure that she has as little trauma as possible. Isn't that true?"

"I'm doing fine. Why should I bother her when she has all this to—I'm not talking about this to you, Caleb."

"Very well. I only wanted you to know that if you cared to release a little of that stored-up pressure I'm sensing, I'm available."

She glanced over her shoulder at him in disbelief.

He chuckled, his dark eyes twinkling. "Oh, the sex, too. That goes without saying. But I wasn't referring to that. Aren't you surprised?"

"Stunned."

"It's good for you. You have all these preconceived ideas about me, and I need to give you a fresh perspective on me occasionally. No, there are all kinds of pressure assaulting you right now, and I thought you might want to talk about it."

"Talk?"

He chuckled. "You see? Those preconceived ideas again. Do you suppose that sex is on your mind as much as it is on mine, or you wouldn't read it into my every word?"

He was coming too close to the truth. She quickly veered away. "Why do you think I'm experiencing any more pressure than anyone else in this camp? We're all after the same thing, finding a way to get Cara back."

"But with you it's all tied to Cira and the treasure and balancing what you want for MacDuff with what you need for Eve."

"I can handle it."

"Without a doubt. But would it hurt to let me shoulder a little of the load you're carrying?" He added softly, "You persist in shutting me out, and I accept it. I can work on that. But I see an opportunity for myself with what's happening here at this lake."

"Opportunity?"

"To show you that I can be of value in a way other than in your bed. Wouldn't that be different and interesting?"

"Why would you want to do that?"

"You'll have to figure that out for yourself. I'm just offering my services. With no price tag involved."

"What services?"

"Whatever you require." He looked out at the mist. "But whatever it is, I believe it will probably happen here. Don't you?"

She followed his gaze.

Mist.

Swirling.

Beckoning.

She was finding that she desperately wanted to follow that beckoning where anything could happen, any truth exist. "How would I know?"

"Then we'll find out together. Nothing permanent. Only for this moment, this day, this week. Whatever. Would it be so bad to have someone by your side to help a little when you need it? To have someone completely devoted to you and no one else?"

It was as alluring as what was waiting out there in the mist. "You paint a lovely picture, Caleb. But you always were a spellbinder."

"Right. So listen and go along with me. But I need a little help. Tell me about Cira."

"What?"

"Oh, I know all about your dreams about Cira and the obsession you've had with her since you were seventeen. Since that was such a big part of your life, I made sure I was familiar with it. But what I don't know are the details of the dream you had about Cira and this lake. I'm sure you told MacDuff all about it, or he wouldn't have pulled up stakes and sent us down here to the lake. And Eve would know. " He grimaced. "But as usual, I was shut out. But I may need to know, Jane. Tell me why the hell we're stumbling around in this mist."

"There wasn't any reason for you to know. It was only a dream, Caleb. MacDuff grabbed onto it because he thinks I have some kind of connection with Cira. Or because he's just desperate to find that chest of coins."

"I want to know," Caleb said. "Tell me."

She was silent, staring at him.

"Why are you hesitating? It was only a dream. Or was it too personal for you, Jane? Heaven forbid you share anything that means something to you."

And he was entirely too perceptive. "It was only a dream." She stared into the mist. "I don't mind telling you about it. The only thing that shook me afterward was that when I came here with Eve, it was as if I'd been here before . . ."

"With Cira."

"Yes, with Cira . . ."

"Are you sure you want to do this, Cira?" Antonio moved to stand behind her. He put his hands gently on her shoulders, and whispered in her ear. "You don't have to say farewell to him here. We can go back to the castle and have the priest give the Gods' blessings and bury him near us."

"No." She looked down at the small casket she'd had the carpenters craft with such care. "I want it to be here by the lake. Marcus liked it here." She could feel the tears sting her eyes. "He told me someday he was going to go into that mist and bring me gifts of gold and jewels fit for a queen. I told him not to be foolish, that I had all the riches I could possibly want already." She looked over her shoulder at Antonio. "It's true, you know. This is a hard, wild land, but we've made it our own. I have everything I ever dreamed about in those days when I was a slave in Herculaneum. I have a husband I love who gave me five strong sons and two daughters who may be even stronger."

"You would think that." He kissed her temple. "You did not feel love for me when you were going through those birth pains."

"It just seemed unfair that a woman has to bear all that pain. But I can see why the Gods didn't trust having children to men. We do it so much better."

"Whatever you say, love."

She could feel his tears on her temple and knew he would not argue with her at this moment. He was feeling her pain at the loss of Marcus as well as his own. Marcus, eight years old, beautiful as the sun, who had been ravaged by the fever and fallen into darkness.

She couldn't stand here, looking down at that small

*casket any longer. It was time to say farewell and send
her son to take his final journey.*

*She stepped away from Antonio and gazed into the
mist. "We're lucky, you know. To have had him this long,
to have him the only one of our children that the Gods
wanted with them."*

"It doesn't seem lucky to me."

*"No. At first, I wanted to rage and beat my head on
the stones. But then I started to think of Marcus, and I
was still angry, but there's a kind of comfort in knowing
that he'll be here where he wanted to be. I can ride down
here and imagine him running out of the mist and telling me how he'd just been hiding and playing in the caves
and had great adventures to tell me." The tears were
running down her cheeks. "And now I believe we'd better go take him into that mist so that he can begin those
adventures. Then we can go back to the castle and tell
our other children that they must stop grieving and start
living. Does that not sound like a good plan?"*

*"A fine plan," Antonio said thickly as he touched her
damp cheek. "A magnificent plan, my own Cira . . ."*

The softness of Caleb's handkerchief was on Jane's
cheek.

"What are you doing?" She tried to back away from
him.

"Be still. You're crying." He dabbed at the tears. "And
I know this is the closest to comfort you'll allow me
to go."

"Stupid," she said unsteadily. "I'm behaving very
stupidly. But don't you dare laugh at me."

"I wouldn't think of it." He handed her the handkerchief. "You've given me a gift, and that would be ungra-
cious."

She wiped her eyes again. "What gift?"

"You've shared Cira and her world with me."

"Only a dream."

"Not to you. And not to me now."

She shook her head and started back through the mist toward the camp. "And what did you learn from it?"

"Details, emotions, how you feel, perhaps what you'll react to when you're wandering around in this mist. All valuable stuff."

"I don't see it."

He smiled. "But you don't have to see it. For once, all you have to do is trust that I do. And that I'll be there to help you sort it out when the time comes."

"That's not the way I do things."

He laughed. "I know. But sometime you might think about it now and then. I'm sure when we're out of this mist that you'll try to forget that your moment of weakness ever happened. But it did, Jane, and I made tremendous gains."

She was already out of the mist, and she looked back at him, still wreathed in the pale gray haze and smiling at her.

"You're fooling yourself. I didn't have a moment of weakness. It was only a dream . . ."

MOSCOW
THREE DAYS LATER

Natalie Castino was smiling up at Ivan and was talking to him in a low voice. She had picked a pink rose from a bush by the garden wall and tucked it into her glossy dark hair.

Jock didn't like it. It was the third night that Natalie had strolled down from the mansion to the gatehouse this week. She had a perfectly good excuse to do that. A mother visiting her daughter. But there had been no visit to Cara. She had spent thirty to forty minutes in the garden talking to Ivan Sabak. Then she had gone back to the mansion.

And Ivan had stood there watching her with a smile on his face until she entered the house.

Seduction?

A business proposal?

Or both?

Natalie was capable of combining any number of attractive lures to get what she wanted.

But what could she want from Ivan that she couldn't get from her father? The answer had to be that she needed to deceive Kaskov and manipulate her present situation, and Ivan might have a role in her doing that.

And Ivan had been chosen as the guard for Cara, and therefore that manipulation had to involve her.

No, Jock didn't like it one bit.

TWO DAYS LATER

She was so tired tonight, Cara thought as she opened the front door and entered the gatehouse. Tired and on edge and a little bit afraid. She was usually charged, brimming with the excitement of the music when she came back from the mansion. Not tonight. At first the magic had been there, but then it had dwindled, then ebbed away entirely as she had caught Natalie staring at her from across the room.

Impatience. Rage. Hatred.

Hatred?

The realization had shocked her.

Why would Natalie hate her?

She knew that her mother was constantly annoyed with her, but she hadn't realized the annoyance and anger had become stronger, that it had blossomed into this ugliness.

What was it about Cara that would cause Natalie to find something in her to hate?

She had finished the concerto and said good night to Kaskov, but she had wanted to run away, and she had been afraid Natalie would notice. She had said that Cara must never make her look bad in front of her grandfather, and she was afraid that shock and fear were visible to anyone looking at her.

She leaned back against the door.

I need you, Eve. I don't understand this, I don't understand her. I don't know what to do.

But she was thousands of miles away from Eve. Thousands of miles away from Jock. They might not even know where she was.

So she had to face this alone. Stop being a baby about it.

She was lucky. She had the music. She'd find a way to get away from here that wouldn't hurt Eve. It was only a matter of watching and waiting for an opportunity.

She started up the steps. Go to bed. Maybe she wouldn't play tonight as she usually did. Maybe she'd just bury her face in the covers and try to forget that expression on Natalie's face. But if she did that, the hatred would stay with her, and Natalie would win.

Let the music take it away. Then let it bring thoughts of Eve and Jock and that wonderful misty lake that was magic, too. Don't let her win. Don't let her hurt—

A hand was clamped hard over mouth!

She instinctively kicked back and struck a kneecap.

"Ouch." It was a soft breath of sound. "Give me a break. I may need that kneecap."

Jock.

She tore his hand away from her mouth. "Jock!" She threw herself into his arms and held him tight. "Jock."

She couldn't seem to say anything else. "I didn't—I can't—" She buried her head in his chest. "You're here."

"And evidently very welcome." His voice was unsteady. "And you're a little inarticulate. That's okay. I'm not doing so well myself."

"I wasn't sure anyone knew—Is Eve okay? Natalie kept telling me that she was, but she lies. She lies so much that I can't—There was a shot. Is she okay?"

"Eve is fine, except for worrying about you." He was pulling her into her bedroom. "I need to talk to you. I've checked this room, and there aren't any bugs, but I think the bathroom is safer. Your guard, Ivan, stays mostly in the other garden, but he patrols below your balcony every once in a while."

"I didn't know that." She had thought she had that small amount of privacy. "How did you know?"

"Because I had to." He was pulling her into the bathroom and closing the door. He crossed the small room and turned on the shower. "Sound barrier. And he's used to your coming in and taking a shower before you settle down with your violin. He'll expect it."

"Will he? I don't care what Ivan expects. Turn on the light. I want to see you." She didn't wait for him to do it. She switched on the overhead light herself.

Jock. He was dressed in a black turtleneck sweater and jeans, and his fair hair shone under the light. He was smiling at her, and that smile was as radiant as always. She couldn't stop looking at him. It seemed like a century had passed since she had seen him that night in MacDuff's tent. "I'm . . . sorry. I'm so sorry. I've been wanting to tell you that since Franco caught me. I was so afraid that he'd find you, too. And it would have been my fault. I tried to warn you."

"Shh. I know." He was there beside her, looking down at her. "Stay. You typed in STAY on your phone."

"But was it too late?"

"Not for me. Only for you."

"That's good. I was so worried, and I couldn't find out anything. Natalie didn't seem to know about you, and she could have been lying about Eve." She closed her eyes and drew a deep breath. "I'm talking too much, aren't I?" She opened her eyes and felt the tears stinging. "It's just that I haven't been around anyone who—And there are so many things I don't know." She reached and touched his arm. "And I've missed you, Jock."

"Hey, I've missed you, too." His voice was soft as he brushed a kiss across the tip of her nose. "And I'd probably be babbling as much as you are, but I've had an advantage. I wasn't in the dark and surrounded by strangers. I knew where you were, knew I could reach out and take you if I had to do it."

"Then why didn't you do it?" She shook her head. "No, I shouldn't have said that. It's bad here. It's all pretty and smooth on the surface, but it's bad. I wouldn't have wanted you to come after me. That Ivan man in the garden has dead eyes. And Kaskov seems all right with me, but then he turns away, and his face changes, and I know that he—"

"Hush." Jock's fingers touched her lips. "I'll tell you everything, and you can tell me everything. But not in this rush that's tearing me apart. And maybe not all right now. There are things you have to know." He dropped down on the white-tile floor and pulled her down beside him. "First, are you okay? Has anyone hurt you? I haven't seen anything. But I have to be sure."

She shook her head impatiently. What did that matter? "Natalie, one time. She didn't like it because I kept asking about Eve. But no one else."

"Kaskov?"

"No, he treats me . . . like a kind of pet. He loves the

music, and he's proud that someone in his family can play. I think he thinks of it as his own—" She tried to put into words the thought she had never consciously formed. "He thinks the music comes from him, that it belongs to him."

"That could be a problem."

She took his hand. He felt so good. Strong. Warm. Safe. Nothing else was important right now. "I don't care."

"But have either Kaskov or Natalie threatened you?"

She tried to think. "Not Kaskov. Natalie said something to Ivan once about how I wasn't to be allowed to leave here. I think she meant—" She stopped. She didn't want to think about what that meant. That moment tonight when she had realized how Natalie felt about her seemed far away. Jock was here. Whatever was wrong, they could make right together. "And I don't know why she would want to keep me here anyway. She doesn't like me to be here. She pretends when she's with her father, but she'd like it better if I wasn't around."

"Would she?" Jock drew her close so that she was leaning against his shoulder and couldn't see his face. "You're sure about that?"

"Yes." She rushed on, "But we don't have to worry about that now. We'll be able to leave here. I was just worried about Eve. She kept saying things about Eve, and I thought there was some way that she'd be able to hurt her if I didn't do what she wanted. She can't do that, right?"

"No, she can't do that." His hand was gently stroking her hair. "She can't hurt Eve. She can't hurt you. I won't let her do it."

"That's good. I was so—" She suddenly stiffened as the realization hit her. "No, that's not good. You shouldn't be here. I told you, it's bad here. You have to go away, Jock."

"No, I don't. That's not going to happen."

There was something in his tone that frightened her. "Jock?" She tried to lift her head from his shoulder so that she could look at him, but his hand was suddenly firm, holding her still. And that frightened her more. "Jock!" She was struggling. Pushing him away. "What are—"

Then she saw his face.

Still beautiful as a concerto, gray eyes still with that unforgettable shimmer.

But hard, so hard, his lips tight, the cheeks more hollow than when she had seen him last at Gaelkar.

"What's wrong?" she whispered.

"You," he said jerkily. "You're what's wrong, Cara. And I can't pretend that it's not. God knows, I've tried. I wanted to pretend that I could be just your kindly big brother who is going to whisk you out of here on a magic carpet. The big brother works fine, but there's nothing kind about me, and I have no magic carpet. I am what I am. And right now, you're not going to like what I am."

"No, I'll always like you. I'll always love you. Stop talking like that. You're my friend. I never really had a friend before I met you." She could feel the tears sting her eyes. "So you have to stop scaring me like this. Do you hear me?"

He was silent. "I hear you. But you'll have to remember that I did warn you." He suddenly smiled. "But for now, we'll pretend that I'm not who I am and that there is a magic carpet." He took her hand. "I'm going to have trouble getting you back to Eve. I don't anticipate a problem here, but Kaskov is a powerhouse. He has informants and connections in every walk of life. It will be difficult getting you out of the city. Hell, it may be difficult getting you out of Russia."

"I don't have to go right away." She found herself

clinging to his hand. "You don't have to help me. Maybe I could—"

"Be quiet. Why do you think I came to Moscow?" he said roughly as he cupped her face in his two hands. "Of course I'm going to help you. I just want you to see the big picture. It could be important. You said you were in the dark. You're not going to be that way any longer."

"Okay." She drew a deep, shaky breath. "But I really would like it if you wouldn't keep telling me not to talk. Do you know how much I've missed talking to you?"

"Oh, shit." He kissed her forehead and let her go. "You always manage to lay me low. May I point out that usually when you've been speaking tonight, it's brought on an emotional meltdown? Besides, I don't know how much more time we have. You've had an awfully long shower. Usually you're in and out. You always want to get to your violin."

She smiled. It was all right now. He was Jock again. "How do you know that?"

"I've been watching you." He grinned as her eyes widened. "Not in the shower, silly. I've just been keeping an eye on what's going on here. I have a stakeout position outside the gates. I can see your balcony and most of the grounds surrounding the gatehouse. I can't see or hear what's going on in the mansion, but I don't see that as a drawback. Except that I can't hear you play for Kaskov."

She made a face. "Natalie wishes that she couldn't. She doesn't like it when I play for her father." Her expression clouded. "No, she hates it."

"Really. Peculiar."

"No." She was silent, thinking. "I . . . think she thinks of the music as a weapon, and anyone who has it is the enemy." She shook her head to clear it. "Tonight it was bothering me . . . I felt as if she—" She smiled, and said, "But I'm not going to think of her right now. She's like a poison that spoils things. I'm not going to let her spoil your being here." She got up on her knees, and said eagerly, "If you could see the balcony, could you hear me play? Wasn't it wonderful?"

His lips quirked. "You're always wonderful."

"No, I mean the violin. Kaskov gave me an Amati. It's like playing—" There were no words. "Didn't it sound fantastic?"

"I was more aware of the artist and the music than the instrument. I'll pay more attention the next time." His smile faded. "And there will be a next time. I can't take you now. I promised Eve that I'd let her try to negotiate a deal with Natalie that would be safer for you. If she can't do it, then we go for it."

Disappointment.

No, it would be better to wait, she told herself. Then Jock wouldn't be in danger. And she wouldn't have to see that look on his face that had so frightened her. "It's okay. Eve is smart, she'll find a way." Her hands tightened on his. "And it's okay for me here. I have that violin, and no one touches me. They just talk and listen and leave me pretty much alone. It will be better now. I'll know that you're out there, close to me. It won't be dangerous for you? You'll stay near me?"

"I'll be near you. And I'll know what you're doing every minute."

"You . . . couldn't come back and see me, could you?" She rushed on, "That was a stupid question. Forget it. I know better. I wouldn't let you do that. You shouldn't be here now."

"No, I shouldn't. And I won't take the risk again until I have to come and get you. I just didn't want you to think that you were alone in this. Every day I'd watch you walk up the driveway to that mansion, and before you'd go in the door, you'd straighten your shoulders as if preparing yourself. That's why I wanted to make sure that no one was hurting you." He touched her cheek. "And I know there are other ways to hurt you than that bruise Natalie gave you. I had to be certain." He added, "Besides, I had to tell you that when I do come for you, you'll have to be ready. We'll be moving fast. No questions. No arguments. Understand?"

She nodded. "That's not new to me. Should I tell you how many times Elena and I had to leave a place and go on the run when she thought Salazar was close?"

"No, don't do that. I've had enough tonight. Just be ready when I come for you." He rose in one fluid motion and pulled her to her feet. "And if you feel that there's any threat to you, any threat at all, go out on the balcony and put your violin case on that little table out there. You'll remember that?"

"Of course I'll remember." She paused. "You think that you'll have to come after me, don't you?"

"I hope I won't. I just don't like how things are shaping up. Nothing I can put my finger on." He turned off the shower. "Give it seven minutes, then start playing your violin. That's the usual time it takes you to dress and settle for the night." He opened the door. "By that time, I'll be out beyond the gates."

"You'll be safe? How can you do that?"

"Very carefully." He smiled at her. "I've been trained to fade in and out where I please. It's a part of me that you wouldn't like one bit, Cara."

"I like *all* of you." She launched herself at him and held him for a minute before she backed away. "And if it keeps you safe, I like that, too. How will I know if you made it out the gates?"

He was heading for the staircase. "You'd know if I didn't." He looked over his shoulder as he reached the stairs. He stopped, his eyes meeting her own. "I told you once that from now on I'd keep you safe, that you'd never have to look over your shoulder or be afraid again. I broke that promise," he said hoarsely. "Trust me. I'll never break it again."

Before she could answer, he was gone.

She stood there, looking after him. Pain. That moment, he had been in pain. He should have stayed and let her talk to him. Maybe she could have helped. There was so much pain stored inside Jock. She had sensed it since the first moment she had met him.

Later.

Now she had to do what he had told her to do. She looked at the clock. Seven minutes. Four minutes had already passed. She went to the stairs and picked up the violin case she had dropped when Jock had surprised her. She opened it and took out the violin. He had said that by the time she started to play the violin, he'd be outside the gates.

That she'd hear if he'd been caught.

She closed her eyes. Dear God, don't let it happen.

Five minutes had passed.

Two minutes to go.

She walked toward the balcony.

One minute.

She opened the balcony doors.

Seven minutes.

Safe!

She lifted the violin.

Do you hear me, Jock? You left too soon. But maybe you didn't.

Tchaikovsky. Jock always liked the Tchaikovsky.

Let it flow. Let it sing.

Joy. Triumph. Thanksgiving.

She started to play.

CHAPTER
6

"MacDuff is *not* pleased," Jane murmured to Eve as she watched Caleb, Joe, and MacDuff disappear into the mist for the third time that day. "He's accustomed to getting his own way, and he can't understand why that damn mist won't cooperate. He was on the phone until the wee hours last night, trying to find a lab that would give him what he needed."

"Did he get it?"

"He got a promise that they'd send out a prototype of a new runway light that the airlines are experimenting with that they say is at least forty percent more efficient. But they can't get it here for another couple days."

"Not good," Eve said. "Particularly since they can't guarantee that will work either. No wonder he's baffled. That first light should have done the trick. There's no reason why it didn't."

Jane nodded. "That's what I told him." She studied

Eve's expression. "But you don't seem too upset. You're almost . . . serene."

"Only on the surface." She shook her head. "Not entirely true. Yes, I'm worried about how slow the hunt is going. And it's driving me crazy that I'm out of touch with Natalie. It's been a waiting game for all of us. But at least I know that Jock is keeping watch on Cara, and there's no indication that he's near explosion level." She shrugged. "As for serenity, the baby and I have come to an agreement."

"What?"

"I won't become overwrought without due cause, and I'll get a little help to smooth everything down and make sure we're both on an even keel."

"Interesting." Jane smiled. "And how did this agreement come about? I don't believe verbal would enter into it."

"No, it's just a kind of knowing. But there's no doubt that the link is there." She made a face. "And I realize that it sounds very weird. It sounds that way to Joe, too. Though he does try not to let me see it. I can't help how it sounds, it's the way I feel."

"Did you ever feel that way before Bonnie was born?"

"No. I felt love and worry and wondered what I could do to help her. But there was no actual link until she was born. Who knows? Maybe because I'm older now, and have seen more, I can recognize the signs the baby is trying to show me."

"Whatever. I do like the idea that you're feeling calm and happy."

"Not happy. Not until we get Cara back." She sighed. "Which reminds me that I have to call Natalie again so that she can ignore it. I'm getting very frustrated and not at all serene about Natalie." She moved out of the tent. "Think good thoughts, Jane."

"That's difficult when applied to Natalie Castino," Jane said dryly.

Eve knew exactly what she meant. Just the thought of the arrogance and venom that was Natalie's trademark caused a ripple of rage and disgust to go through her.

And then it was gone, and there was only hope and sunlight and the promise of something brighter to come.

She looked down at her abdomen and shook her head.

You do that entirely too well. You do know I'm not going to let you con me once we get past this rough patch? Not that I don't enjoy it. But there appears to be a little too much control involved.

The sunlight remained firmly in place, and was there . . . laughter?

Accept it. She needed all the sunlight and laughter she could garner dealing with Natalie.

She sighed and took out her phone.

And it rang before she could dial.

Natalie Castino.

She gazed at it in bemusement.

Very good. If this is your idea of hope, forget I was a bit snippy with you.

She accessed the call. "Did you get tired of not answering my calls, Natalie?"

"I've told you that I like to be in control. You should have expected that I wouldn't be too eager to talk to you. What do you want, Eve?"

"Cara."

"Not possible. Why would I give up my dear child after I've been all these years without her?"

"Because you don't give a damn about Cara. You conspired with Salazar to murder both Cara and Jenny."

"How can you say that?" she asked mockingly. "And more to the point, how can you prove that? Everyone knows how devastated I was when they disappeared. And now, after my tragic loss of Jenny, I have Cara back in my arms. Her grandfather is ecstatic to have her here. How could I possibly take her away from him?"

"You tell me, Natalie," Eve said. "When you left Gaelkar so abruptly, you mentioned that you might be amenable to a deal. You liked the idea of Cira's gold."

"It did catch my imagination. But I'm not certain that my father would approve of any deal concerning Cara. It's so like human trafficking, isn't it?"

"And your father has never been involved in anything like that, has he?" Eve said sarcastically. "Nor drugs, nor murder, nor prostitution. I'm sure he'd be shocked at the idea."

"Not shocked. But he's fond of Cara. He might be annoyed enough to strike back at anyone who decided to take her from him."

"You're talking about Kaskov, not yourself."

"Well, my feelings are known by everyone. I've told you that no matter how much you want my daughter, I'd have to refuse unless you can prove that Cara would be happier with you."

"And what would be the proof?"

"That you'd actually give up that fantastic treasure to prove how much she means to you. Now that would indicate true affection."

"I'd say that it would. Can we make a deal?"

"I'm thinking about it. It's possible if we do it right away. I'd hate for my father to become more attached to her than he is already. I really believe a clean break is best, don't you?"

"And what do you consider would be 'right away'?"

"Within the week. Perhaps the next few days. Providing you really do have Cira's gold in your possession."

"I have it. Where can we meet for an exchange?"

"I'll choose the place after you prove that you have it.

You were much too vague when you offered a trade before. I was dealing with too many problems at the time, or I would have pinned you down then."

"Yes, the killing of both a husband and a lover in one day could have caused a bit of stress."

She ignored the accusation. "At any rate, I must have proof that the treasure exists and that you have it. Is that understood?"

"And how am I to do that?"

"But that's up to you, Eve. You're the one who is so desperate to steal my little girl away. I'm only seeking proof you can give her a good home."

"It may take more than a few days."

"Don't push it." Natalie's voice was suddenly hard. "I want it to happen now. Two days, tops. I'm not happy with my present situation, and I believe that Cara's absence might improve it a great deal. One way or another." Her tone changed, became almost sweet. "Perhaps I'll send her to school or something of that nature. It's just that a child on her own can be so threatened in the big world. I'm hesitating to do that to her again."

And Eve was feeling a shiver run through her. It was as close as Natalie had ever come to actually coming out with a threat over the phone. It just went to show both her determination and her utter ruthlessness. "Then I'll try to see that you have your proof right away."

"I'm sure you will. You're so clever, it won't be any problem for you." She hung up.

And Eve let out the breath she hadn't known she'd been holding.

Two days.

They didn't have Cira's gold and, since they couldn't break through that blasted mist, the possibility that they'd have it by then was almost nil.

And Eve had been able to tell that Natalie was not only

impatient, she could be on the verge of something violent.

Don't think about it. Stave off the thought that Natalie had cold-bloodedly tried to kill her girls eight years
ago and succeeded with Jenny.

Concentrate only on how they could get the prize that
Natalie had demanded.

Proof.

"Proof," Eve repeated. "Maybe I can find a way to stall
the actual exchange of the chest for Cara, but Natalie's
not going to play the game if we can't furnish her proof
that it's worth her while." She'd gathered MacDuff, Joe,
Caleb, and Jane together in MacDuff's tent as soon as the
men had returned from the north bank to try to brain-
storm some way out. "What are our chances, MacDuff?"

MacDuff shook his head. "I'll try to get the lab to up
the delivery time on those lights, but I can't guarantee
they'll even work, Eve. It might be trial and error for
weeks."

"We don't have weeks," Eve said unsteadily. "We have
two days." She looked at Joe. "I don't want to turn Jock
loose, if we don't have to do it. But Natalie sounded . . ."
She shook her head. "She's so damn volatile. There's no
telling what she's going to do."

"If it comes to that, I'll head for Moscow, too," Joe
said. "Between Jock and me, we'll be able to get her out."

"We could try going around the north bank without
those fancy lights," Jane said quietly. "It wouldn't hurt
to try it the way Cira and her family did all those centuries ago. Maybe that's the way it should be."

"And you're just aching to do that, aren't you?" Caleb's eyes were narrowed on Jane's face. "I could tell that
you were tempted to go on the other day."

"Yes, I was." She looked him in the eye. "And now I have a reason."

"Not a good enough one," Caleb said roughly. "We don't know what's around that bend in the lake, and we can't see hazards. For all we know, there could be a sudden drop-off, or a whirlpool, or quicksand."

"Or there could be nothing at all," Jane said. "Except a cave with the remains of a child who died all those centuries ago." She paused. "Or a chest with Cira's gold. That we need desperately right now."

"Not good enough," Caleb repeated. He smiled recklessly. "Not when we have another option. So stop trying to find an excuse to risk your neck to find answers. We'll do that later."

"I'm curious to know what that other option is," Eve said. "I'm having trouble thinking of one that's acceptable."

"The proof," Caleb said. "Natalie wants proof that we have the treasure. Who said it has to be authentic? We'll lie to her."

"She's not stupid, Caleb," Eve said. "She wants that treasure, but she's not going to go for the bait if she thinks there's any question that we don't have it."

"But we'll give her proof." Caleb smiled. "What would be proof that we have it? A handful of the coins themselves. We send them to her to show our good faith."

"And where do we get these coins?" Joe asked.

"I have no idea yet. That's up to MacDuff." Caleb turned to MacDuff. "You've done extensive research all your adult life about Cira and that chest of coins you've been hunting for. You must have a fairly good idea about the probable age and denominations of the coins that are in that chest."

"There's no way of being certain," MacDuff said.

"I said probable," Caleb said. "And Natalie can't be certain either. But she won't be fooled unless she can check and verify that there is an excellent chance of the coins' being authentic. That means that the coins have to be rare enough so that they'll pass muster."

"And be of the right age and national origin," MacDuff said dryly. "You're not asking much."

"You must have run across collectors who have what we need."

"And if the coins are that rare, we don't have a chance in hell of prying them loose from a collector. They can be fanatic."

"But that's my job," Caleb said. "I'm exceptionally good at prying. All you have to do is the research to send me in the right direction. But I imagine it has to be done quickly. Eve will be nervous until she gets the coins in her hands."

"Extremely nervous," Eve said dryly. "And maybe even more nervous about how you're going to do this."

"But not so nervous that you'd be willing to send Quinn and Jock into the mouth of the dragon instead." Caleb shrugged. "We all have our own priorities." He glanced at Jane. "I find I have an aversion at the idea of Jane's tripping through that mist. I don't like the unknown when it's connected to her. Strange, when I enjoy it for myself."

"Will it work?" Joe asked MacDuff. "Can you locate coins that could fool her?"

"I have a few ideas." MacDuff was frowning. "I'll have to do some research, as Caleb said. But however you look at it, getting them away from any of those collectors will be a major headache." He grimaced. "And if force is involved, possibly fatal."

"Then you'd better get to it," Caleb said as he turned

to leave the tent. "Let me know when you find the prime candidate. I'll be down by the lake." He raised a brow and glanced at Jane as he said melodramatically, "Would you like to come and hold my hand? Who knows what I'm going to face in the days ahead."

"I would not."

"You're annoyed. And all because I wouldn't let you go flying after your Cira . . ." He left the tent.

And she wanted to run after him and yell at him, shake him.

"It's not a bad idea, Jane," Joe said quietly. "If it works, it's safer for Cara."

Jane realized that, but it didn't help. "But not safer for Caleb. Not that he cares. He's probably been looking for some trouble to get into."

"I'll go with him if it looks as if there's a possibility of difficulty," Joe said.

"With Caleb, there's always a possibility of difficulty. He thrives on it," she said jerkily. "And sometimes I think he concocts it."

"Come on, let's go down to the campfire and have a cup of coffee." Eve took Jane's arm. "We'll leave MacDuff to his research. Maybe Caleb won't get what he's looking for." She was leading her toward the door. "Maybe the collector MacDuff chooses as our prime candidate will be a little, white-haired college professor with wire spectacles and a generous disposition."

Two hours later, Jane marched down to the lake, where Caleb was lolling lazily beneath a pine tree and gazing out at the distant mountains. And that very indolence irritated her even more than she was already.

She tossed the sheet of paper down on his stomach. "Your collector. And you'll be happy to know that he's not a little white-haired college professor with wire-rimmed glasses. And he certainly doesn't have a generous nature."

"Am I supposed to know what you're talking about?" he asked mildly as he sat up. "And did you come out to hold my hand?"

"No, I've been waiting for MacDuff to finish researching so that I could bring it down myself and tell you what an idiot you are."

"I always appreciate your attention, no matter what the motivation." He glanced down at the paper. "Derek Helmberg. Munich, Germany. That's not bad. At least it's not in the middle of Africa. I was thinking that it might be."

"Not bad? He not only smuggles antiquities, he's a gunrunner. He also dabbles in human trafficking and computer hacking. According to that résumé you have in front of you, the only passion he has other than the acquisition of money is his coin collection, which he keeps at his estate in Munich."

"He has the correct coins?"

"Yes, MacDuff thinks that he even has a few that he's liberated from historical libraries that are virtually unknown on the market. Perfect." She paused. "Except that collection is guarded by several of Helmberg's goons, and you have an excellent chance of being killed. But that's perfect for you, too."

"Ah, that's why you're so angry with me. You think I'll get killed; and then what would you do? No one to fight or abuse. And all those possibilities looming on our horizon disappearing . . ."

"I'm angry with you because you're taking chances, and it's stupid for you to—Even if Joe goes with you, it's still a risk."

"I won't take Quinn with me." He held up his hand.

"I won't need him. What I'll do requires Helmberg and me, and anyone else will get in the way. It's not that I don't think Quinn would be of value getting us in and out of the estate. But there is a risk, and Eve may need him more than I do." He smiled. "You should be on board with that, Jane. Eve needs a father for that child. I can't keep him out of whatever action goes down in the future, but I can do this."

How was she supposed to argue with that?

"He'll want to go along."

"Then I'll leave now, and you can tell him how stubborn and difficult I was about having company. You'll be very good at that."

"Yes, I will."

He got to his feet. "And while I'm gone, you'll think how brave and self-sacrificing I am, and you'll worry and remember all the good things I am and none of the bad."

"No, I won't. I wouldn't give you that satisfaction when you're probably only doing this to manipulate me."

He chuckled. "We'll see who is right." He started to turn away. "Good-bye, Jane."

"Wait."

She couldn't let him leave like this.

He looked over his shoulder.

"Maybe I do want to hold your hand."

He smiled and came back to her and took both her hands in his own. "Thank you," he said softly. "I'll remember this when I'm fighting the dragons and being disgustingly heroic."

"You'll only remember that you got your way." She looked up at him. "How are you going to get those coins from Helmberg?"

"The usual way, shock and intimidation. Even someone who has a fanatical obsession can be persuaded that he'd rather stay alive to collect again."

"You're going to do that . . . blood thing?"

"The ability to control blood flow is what I do best. I'd be foolish not to use it as a weapon if necessary." He lifted her wrist to his lips. "Though I much prefer to use it this way."

Heat. Her arm was tingling, hot. Her pulse pounding in her throat. Her breasts were swelling, her breath coming in pants. She wanted to step closer, brush against him, take more of him.

She jerked her arm away and stepped back. She was still panting. "Not fair, Caleb."

"Very fair. I picked a time when I could derive pleasure, then walk away and not be tempted to carry it further. That's almost noble." He was walking up the slope toward the road. "And it took your mind off the less pleasant aspects of my talent that was causing your imagination to run riot. I'll see you soon, Jane."

When would she see him?

She could feel her eyes sting. Her hands clenched into fists at her sides as she watched him walk up the slope.

He stopped when he reached the road and turned back toward her. A mischievous smile lit his face as he gave a half bow and blew her a kiss.

Asshole.

It was almost as if he'd read her mind because he threw back his head and laughed.

Then he turned and headed for his car, parked down the road.

MOSCOW

Ivan Sabak was ready, Natalie thought, as she strolled slowly down the driveway toward the gatehouse. She had been preparing the way for the last several days, but she'd had to be cautious. Sabak was afraid of her father, and that had to be overcome. She needed complete compliance from him if she was going to succeed.

But she would get what she needed. She always did.

She saw him coming toward the garden gate as she approached. He was eager. She could see the faint tension in his muscles. Yes, he was ready.

She smiled at him. "Hello, Ivan. I couldn't wait to get to you tonight."

He frowned. "You didn't come last night."

"It was so difficult. My father . . . You know how he is. And I didn't want to get you in trouble."

"I can handle Kaskov."

"Of course you can. I just didn't want you to have to do it." She came closer to him. "I know how strong and smart you are. My father would never have assigned you to guard my daughter if he didn't know it, too. Did you know I asked him to do that because I knew you were the best and most clever man he had?" She sighed. "Being a mother to a child like Cara is so difficult. Sometimes I think he likes her more than he does me. I feel so alone. I know it's only a matter of time before he sends me away." She took a step closer to let him feel her warmth, catch her scent. "I think I'm going to need someone to be there for me when that happens. Will you be that person, Ivan? Will you help me?"

He stiffened.

He wasn't ready for commitment yet, she thought. But now he knew it was coming. He would become accustomed to the idea once he found it was to his advantage.

"I have some money. I can get more, much more. But I need someone to protect it, protect me." She took his hand and put it on her breast. "I want it to be you," she whispered. "I'm a woman who needs a man, and what a man you are, Ivan." She moved closer. "Let me show you how much I need you."

His hand closed brutally on her breast. "Are you playing with me?"

"Let's go inside the house. The couch in the living room." Her tongue moved on his lower lip. "Let me show you . . ."

He started to drag her toward the French doors leading to the living room, then stopped. "The kid. She might hear us."

Let him get a hint of the way it was going to go. "I don't care." She rubbed slowly, sensuously, against him. "She's not important. *You're* important. She's just getting in our way . . ."

MUNICH, GERMANY

One guard at the road leading up to the house.

One guard who was patrolling the grounds and patio area.

Another guard in the massive garage where he kept his collection of antique cars.

Helmberg was evidently a collector of a number of objects besides antique coins, Caleb thought after he had disposed of the guard patrolling the grounds. He moved across the patio toward the French doors that led to the library, where a light was burning.

The door was unlocked. Why not, when the grounds were so well protected? Caleb could see Helmberg sitting in a leather easy chair before the fire with a brandy in his hand. His gray hair was perfectly barbered, as was his Van Dyke beard, and he wore a black designer smoking jacket. He was relaxed, comfortable, a king enjoying his kingdom.

Time to invade the kingdom.

He silently opened the door, but there must have been a gust of wind because Helmberg started to turn his head.

Caleb went into top speed, across the room in seconds.

"Who the hell—" Helmberg didn't get the rest of sentence out before Caleb reached his chair.

Caleb's hands were around his throat. "We can do this easy or hard, Helmberg. Your choice."

"I'll kill—" He gasped as Caleb's grip tightened. "You won't get away with this."

"But I will. You'll see that I do." He looked down into his eyes. "You'll do everything I want you to do, or you won't live through the night. I'm tempted to just end it now, but there are reasons why I don't want a stir to ripple out from our little meeting."

"Someone will come. You won't get off the property."

"Then I'd better get down to business, hadn't I? Your coin collection. Go to the safe and get it for me."

He stiffened. "The hell I will."

"You're going to experience pain in your left temple. It won't be excruciating, just a demonstration to show you what could be on the horizon."

Helmberg screamed!

"Should I do it again?"

"What—is—this?" Helmberg gasped. "Are you some CIA interrogator or something?"

"Oh, no, just a common thief. But I do want what I want. Get me the coins."

He moistened his lips. "I don't keep the collection here. It's at my safe-deposit box."

"Wrong answer."

Helmberg screamed again. His face contorted with pain.

"You wouldn't have that collection anywhere you couldn't see it, touch it. Collectors have a passion, and they have to have it satisfied. It's probably tucked behind that Rembrandt painting. Now go to the safe and get me the coins."

"Very well. Let me go."

Caleb released him and stepped back.

Helmberg got up and moved toward the wall behind the desk. As he reached the desk, he dove for the carved ivory box on the corner. He knocked it off the desk and a Luger fell out of it. He followed the gun to the floor and grabbed it.

"At last, something interesting," Caleb said. "I was getting really bored."

"Sit down." Helmberg got to his knees and pointed the pistol at him. "We're going to have a little talk."

"I don't believe I have the time. But I applaud your initiative." He shook his head regretfully. "No, you really have to drop that weapon. I need those coins."

"You fool. I'm going to kill you. But first I want to know who you are and who sent you. I won't—" He threw back his head and groaned. "What—" He looked down at his hand holding the gun. It was swollen twice the normal size, and his finger on the trigger was bleeding, gushing blood, around the nail.

"I think you'd better drop the gun," Caleb said. "If you don't, your hand is going to explode. I judge in about two minutes."

Helmberg almost threw the gun away from him.

"Good. Now go to the safe and get me what I want."

"I can't use my hand."

"You can use it. Very clumsily, but you can use it. But it's still swelling and will continue to do so until you open the safe."

Helmberg staggered to the picture and swung it back to reveal the safe. He stood looking at it. "I could pay you a lot of money. Don't take the coins."

"Open it. You won't be able to do it in another minute. It would be difficult without a right hand."

Helmberg hurriedly spun the combination and opened the safe.

"Now take out the containers and put them on the desk, so I can examine them."

Helmberg took out the two velvet boxes and placed them on the desk. "Do you even know what you're looking for?"

"Am I an expert?" He shook his head. "But I have a description of a few of the coins in your collection that are very valuable. I just have to make sure that they're all here." He looked through the first box, then opened the second. He gave a low whistle. "This one wasn't on my list and by the way you have it displayed, I'd wager that it's the star of your collection."

"Don't take it," Helmberg said hoarsely. "I'll give you anything."

Caleb shook his head. "I'm afraid that you'll have to give up coin collecting. Your car collection with have to suffice."

"I'll come after you. You won't get away with this. Who the hell are you?"

"You won't come after me. You won't mention anything to do with this night to anyone. As far as anyone knows, your collection is still intact." He moved toward Helmberg until he was only inches away. He stared into his eyes. "Do you know how much it hurts when your organs explode? First, I'd do the lungs before I went for the heart. Pressure. Excruciating pressure. The blood controls everything, you know. Let's have a little preview. Are you starting to feel it?"

Helmberg's hands were clutching his chest, his face scarlet as he struggled to breathe. "Don't—" he gasped. "Hurts."

"Just a little more. I want you to remember."

"No." Tears were running down Helmberg's cheeks. "Please . . ."

"I'll lessen it, but the pain won't go away until an hour after I leave here. You'll stay there on the floor and won't call for help. If you try to move, the pain will increase, and it may affect your heart."

His eyes were bulging. "I . . . won't move."

Caleb knelt beside him on the floor and took out his phone and tossed it across the room. "And you'll pretend I never paid you a visit. If I hear that you've said one word, then I'll come back. And you'll find out how much it hurts to die very slowly. I can stretch it out a long, long time, Helmberg. I would kill you now, but I don't want any suspicion surrounding anyone who is a known collector."

"I don't know . . . what you mean."

"You don't have to know. You just have to do what I tell you."

Helmberg screamed and clutched his chest.

"Oops." Caleb got to his feet. "Sometimes my feelings get away from me. You might remember that."

"Who—are—you."

"Names aren't important." He shrugged. "But at the moment, I'm one of the good guys."

"No." Helmberg was still cradling his chest. "You're . . . a monster."

"I've been called that, too." Caleb gathered up the two boxes and headed for the door. "But then I'm sure so have you, Helmberg."

Then he was outside the door and drawing a deep breath of the cool night air. Not a bad evening. Not as satisfactory as it might have been. He really didn't like Helmberg. Maybe he'd have a reason to pay him another visit.

Oh, well, forget Helmberg. Even if being one of the good guys was a bit boring, Jane would be pleased, and that was always paramount. He moved quickly across the manicured grass toward the gates and his rental car parked beyond them. He should be at Gaelkar within the next three hours . . .

"You got it?" Eve was looking down at the two boxes Caleb had just placed on MacDuff's desk. "Any trouble?"

"No, he was surprisingly obliging," Caleb said. "He agreed to everything I asked of him."

"And is he still alive?" Joe asked dryly.

"Of course. We wouldn't want any rumors circulating around that a well-known coin collector had been killed. He agreed that coin collecting was no longer for him. He's looking at other hobbies."

"And he won't come after you?" Jane asked.

"I doubt it. Though I've been wrong before." He glanced at MacDuff, who was going through the coins. "I checked before I left his library, and all the coins you mentioned were there. And one more coin in that second box. He was really hurting when I took that one."

MacDuff opened the box. "Good God." He carefully took out the coin and examined it. "If I didn't know where that Greek drachma was at this minute, I'd think this was it."

"Drachma?" Eve asked.

"It's a silver coin minted in Sicily during the fifth century B.C. So far only twelve have been found, and they're either in private collections or museums. One was auctioned off fairly recently. But this one might be even more valuable. It was minted two years earlier."

"What was the auction value on that drachma?" Eve asked.

"Two million pounds."

"What?" Joe gave a low whistle. "No wonder Helmberg was in agony about losing it."

"Well, actually it was kind of a combined effect," Caleb murmured.

"I imagine it was," Jane said as she stepped closer to the table to look at the chariot with four horses on one side of the coin. "It's beautiful, true artistry. It doesn't look that ancient."

"We can be sure it was if Helmberg had it in his possession. He wouldn't have bothered with it otherwise," Joe said. He looked at MacDuff. "So do these coins look like the real thing?"

"They *are* the real thing," MacDuff said. "And they look like what they are. They were all minted in the years before the eruption of the volcano at Herculaneum in 79 A.D. So the time factor is correct. They came from the nations that were in existence then and whose money could have ended up in Cira's treasure chest."

Jane picked up the drachma from the box. "I wonder if there is one of these in her chest . . ."

"What do you think?" Caleb asked.

"I believe there's a good chance. Cira was very canny about money." She put the coin down again. "We'll have to wait and see."

"In the meantime, we have Natalie's proof," Eve said. She could feel the excitement begin to build within her. She had been afraid to let herself think about it while Caleb was gone. "What should we send her? Three coins? Four?"

"As little as possible," Joe said. "It pisses me off to give her anything."

"Four," Eve said. She picked up the drachma. "And this has to be one of them."

"Ouch," Jane said. "Are you sure?"

"I'm sure," Eve said. "Because of the date, it's a coin that's never been found as far as anyone knows. That's important. And we want to stun her. Dazzle her with the thought that there might be more of those coins in the chest. We won't even display it as if it was of any importance. We'll put that coin and the three others we choose together in a leather pouch. Then we'll deliver it to Natalie and let her discover it herself. She might even think that we just tossed it in there and didn't realize the value. It would encourage the vision of a treasure just waiting to be found by her."

"I see what you mean," Jane said. Then she wrinkled her nose. "I just hate giving her anything that valuable."

"We can always take it back," Caleb said. "Just say the word. I've been growing attached to it."

"Later," Eve said. "Right now, I just want to get it into her hands and have her set up an exchange." She sat down at the stool in front of the desk. "And pick out the other three coins . . ."

CHAPTER
7

Done." Eve sat back on her stool and looked down at the three coins she'd chosen an hour later. Two were gold and minted in Macedonia. The other was a silver denarius and minted in Rome. "I think they're all plausible choices. Rome during that period was conquering the entire world and bringing back treasure and tribute. Any of these coins could have ended up in Cira's stash." She dropped the coins in the leather pouch before she stood up and arched her back to ease it. "Now I've just got to call Natalie and set up a way to get them to her."

"Give it another hour." Joe took her hand. "Come on. Get some air and a cup of coffee before you get stressed out again by talking to Natalie."

She wasn't going to argue with him. It had been a day of strain and nervous exhaustion while they had waited for word from Caleb. She needed a little time to unwind. She grabbed the pouch with the coins and let Joe lead her from the tent.

Five minutes later, she was sitting in front of the fire and staring into the flames. "I drink a lot of coffee. I wonder if that's bad for the baby? Maybe I should look it up on the Web."

"Later. You need it right now." He grinned. "Besides, wouldn't the baby tell you?"

"Stop being a smart-ass. It's possible, but maybe it's supposed to be in my domain."

"Then I'll Google it and tell both of you." He looked at her across the fire. "You shouldn't even be here. You should be at home, going to classes, and visiting the doctor."

"Joe, during Cira's time, she probably rode her horse until the day she had the baby and squatted in one of those horrible medieval chairs to give birth." She smiled. "I'm doing fine if all I have to do is worry about how much coffee to drink."

"I'll Google it," he repeated. He moved around the fire and dropped down beside her. "And you're not sleeping well, either." He drew her close. "That can't be good."

"Cara." She leaned against him. "But we're getting through it. The coins will help. At least, we're on our way."

"Yeah." His lips brushed her temple. "I should have gone with Caleb."

"He appeared to do fine without you. I'm glad you didn't. I didn't have to worry about you." She looked at him. "Is that bothering you? You didn't go with Jock. You didn't go with Caleb. You've been stuck here with me instead of doing what you do best?"

"Not stuck."

"Isn't it? You were restless as hell while Caleb was gone." She grimaced. "But then so was I. Forget it, I guess I'm having guilt feelings because I haven't seen any way to get to Cara." She put her coffee cup on the ground. "And now it's time I gave Natalie a call and told her that she has her proof. That should make both of us feel better."

"I could call her for you."

"No, you couldn't. She's made this between the two of us." She took out her phone. "But if you're available for a little TLC after I finish, I'd appreciate it." She was quickly dialing the number. "She always makes me feel . . . dirty."

"Always available. Always here for you."

He was smiling at her, and she felt a rush of warmth go through her as she looked at him. Always. What a wonderful word.

Natalie was picking up the call. "I was expecting to hear from you before this," she said curtly. "Why are you stalling? Either you have proof or you don't. If you don't, I'll have to make other plans."

"You gave me two days." Eve realized she sounded defensive. The immediate attack had thrown her off guard. And that last sentence was a definite threat against Cara. "And you have to realize that I'm not in sole control of Cira's gold. MacDuff was hard to convince."

"But you convinced him, didn't you?" Natalie asked with dulcet sweetness. "Because you're so soft and caring. Do you sleep with him? You'd find him much more compliant if you did. Money is important, but sex is always the clincher with a man."

"No, I don't sleep with him," Eve said, trying to keep control of her temper. "But MacDuff is a good man, and he's willing to negotiate to get Cara back for me."

"Negotiate? I want it all." She paused. "If I find that you haven't lied to me. Where's your proof, Eve?"

"I have it in my hand right now." She looked down at the leather pouch. "Where do you want me to send it?"

Silence. "You really have it?"

"I told you I did. Take a look at it, then call me and

we'll deal. It will be a small package. Where do you want me to send it?"

She thought for a moment. "Don't send it directly to me. Send it overnight to a post-office box in Moscow in care of Ivan Sabak." She rattled off an address. "Did you get it?"

"I got it," Eve said. "You must trust this Sabak if you're willing to involve him."

"I don't trust anyone. But I can control him. Just as you should be able to control MacDuff and everyone else around you." She paused. "What's going to be in that package?"

"I prefer to surprise you."

"Tell me."

"Let me know when you want to deal." Eve hung up.

"Who is Ivan Sabak?" Joe asked.

"I have no idea." She reached for her pen and scrawled down the address Natalie had given her. "Probably someone Natalie recruited to use to do her dirty work. She's lacking in backup at the moment. She's like a black widow spider killing off all her mates. She got rid of Salazar, Franco, and her dear husband before she hopped on that helicopter and took off with Cara. Now she needs reinforcements." She shuddered. "I'm sure he's competent in all the lethal arts." She straightened her shoulders and tried to shake off the fear and depression the thought brought. "But let her try to control this Sabak to her heart's content. Our job is to get these coins into Natalie's hands as soon as possible and try to set up an exchange. Let's head for Glasgow and try to find the quickest overnight service available from there." She got to her feet. "And then call Jock and let him know what's happening and check on this Sabak."

"Ivan Sabak?" Jock repeated. "Yes, I know who he is. He's Kaskov's most competent goon and has an impressive record of kills. He's also acting as Cara's guard at the gatehouse." He paused. "And in the past few days has become Natalie's sex partner."

"Cara's guard," Eve said. "I don't like that, Jock."

"Neither do I," he said grimly. "No one has more access to Cara than Sabak. And now the chances are he's no longer working for Kaskov but his daughter."

"But it could be that her having influence with Sabak would make it easier for her to arrange for Cara to leave the estate if she'll agree to a deal."

"And do you really think she's going to do that?"

"It could happen. If it was worth her while to do it." Eve added wearily, "But that's what this is all about, to make her think it's worth her while. Do I trust her not to hurt Cara? No, she'll do whatever she thinks will give her long-term protection. And that would be for Cara to just disappear in a way that would not incriminate Natalie with the law or her father. But if she can't arrange that, then she may just give us a chance to snatch Cara while she's trying to snatch that chest of coins."

"I'm glad that you realize that this may be a long shot."

"I've always known that. But if we can get Natalie to remove Cara from beneath her father's protection, then you won't have to do it. It will solve the biggest problem you've been worrying about. Getting her out of Moscow itself. Isn't that true?"

He was silent. "Aye, it's true." He added brusquely, "Very well, we'll give your coins a chance to do their magic. And I'll be at the post-office box in Moscow when they pick them up and watch reactions."

"It might work, Jock," Eve said. "If it does, it's safer for Cara."

"You've told me that before. And I agree . . . if it works. Good-bye, Eve." He hung up.

Eve was still not sure that she could trust him not to

act on his own, Jock thought as he stared out into the darkness. She had a right to her doubts. Watching Cara go through this had strained his self-discipline to the max. There were times when he was on the verge of breaking. Every night, he went over the best possible kill cycles for the guards. Someday would he just stop planning and do it? So easy. It would be so easy . . .

Music.

Cara was on her balcony, playing her violin.

It was the Tchaikovsky. Ever since he had gone to Cara that night, she had played that concerto first when she got back to the gatehouse in the evening. She was trying to reach out, to tell him she was fine, and everything was all right.

It was *not* all right.

Not when Natalie was seducing Cara's guard in the same house where she was keeping her daughter prisoner. Not when Jock knew that could be a prelude to Cara's death.

He felt the rage start to spiral within him, the heat building. Crush it. Ice it.

But that was dangerous, too, if he wanted to go along with Eve's wishes for the time being.

Because when the ice came, so did the killing.

PETROVA STREET
MOSCOW

"Eve Duncan told the truth," Ivan Sabak said as he handed Natalie the box when he got back in the car after retrieving it from the post-office box. "It's very small. We have to hope what's inside is big enough to be important to us."

Us. Natalie had wanted him to feel involved, and this

was a sign that Ivan was heading in the right direction. "Eve isn't a fool. She wouldn't go to this trouble if she didn't believe that I'd be satisfied with the result." She was tearing into the box as she spoke. "It has to be—" She broke off as she saw the leather pouch. "And she may be right. Last night I was going over in my mind the possibilities of what she could send me, and this was close to the top of the list." She opened the pouch and carefully poured the coins into her palm. "*Yes.*"

"Not much treasure. Four coins," Sabak said. "And they don't look very valuable. Old. Very old."

"That's what they're supposed to look like," she said impatiently. "But I have to make sure they're old enough and could be genuine. And that she's not trying to slip something over on me."

"And how are you going to do that?"

"When I decided she might possibly be going to give me a sample of the coins, I made an appointment at the university with Feodor Dostkey for this afternoon. He's a professor of ancient history and an expert at numismatics. He'll be able to tell me what I need to know." She reached for her phone. "I'll confirm it with him now, then we'll be on our way to the university."

"You said you didn't want anyone to know about this."

"And he won't know about it after I get his report." She put the pouch in her handbag. "I'll sit in his office while he makes his examination and tells me what I need to know. I've made the appointment at the end of his school day, and he should be on his way to his home after that." She looked at Ivan. "I can't be involved. I'll walk down to the cab stand two blocks from the university and go home from there."

His gaze narrowed on her face. "What are you telling me to do?"

She smiled brilliantly at him. "What you're so wonderfully good at, Ivan. But it has to look like an accident, and neither one of us must be implicated." She put her hand on his inner thigh and rubbed it slowly, sensuously. "Can you do that for me? For us?"

He nodded. "If you're certain that it has to be done. Kaskov wouldn't like me to be involved in the killing of a professor. It could bring out all kinds of flak from the local government. He's always told me that we have to stay under the radar."

"Then you have to be good enough to be sure we are." She leaned back in the seat. "I can hardly wait until I get back to the gatehouse tonight and can tell you what happened." She smiled. "And, if it's good news, then we'll celebrate. Shall I tell you how?"

"No." He started the car. "I'll make you show me. Again and again and again."

"I can't tell you how grateful I am for your time. Thank you, Professor Dostkey." Natalie shook his hand as she opened the door of his office to leave. "My brother will be so happy that you verified what he thought that he'd found on that farm in Estonia." She tucked the report he'd given her into her handbag. "Evidently it's a find that happens only once in a lifetime."

"At least, as far as the drachma is concerned." Dostkey frowned. "But you shouldn't be walking around with that coin. Wouldn't you like me to put it in my safe until you can arrange security?"

"How kind you are. But no one knows I have it but you." She shook her head. "And I'm completely bewildered that it's so valuable. I'm sure no one but an expert like you would know how much I have to lose in that little pouch. Again, thank you, Professor."

"It's been a pleasure."

He stood watching her as she walked down the hall and out of the building.

Natalie could feel the heat flush her cheeks as she hurried down the walkway toward the street.

Two million dollars. Or perhaps more. The professor hadn't been certain what it would bring at auction.

That much money for one little coin. It seemed impossible. The other coins had also been valuable, but that drachma was the prize.

She couldn't believe Eve would have known the value and still sent it to her with the other coins. How many other coins of equal value were in that chest?

Excitement was soaring through her, making her breathless at the possibilities revealed in that small pouch. She had to play it cool. She *had* to have that chest. It would give her everything she wanted in life. Money, power, and, most of all, freedom. No more having to plead and use tears or sex to get what she wanted. All her life she'd had men telling her what she had to do, what she had to be, to make them happy. What about what made her happy? *She* was the one who was important. And that chest full of gold would guarantee that everyone knew it. She would never have to be anyone's wife or lover or daughter ever again.

But she could not let her father know what she was doing, or he might either confiscate the chest or try to keep her from using Cara to get it. Either would be possible.

So make a plan that would get her everything she wanted and not hurt her in any way.

She could do it.

But Cara, alive, would always be a threat to her. She could not turn her over to Eve no matter what sleight of hand she had to perform. So that added to the complexity of her problem.

Natalie *had* to have that treasure chest.

Cara *had* to die.

And Eve Duncan would have to be destroyed before either of those goals could be met.

Now concentrate, plan, make it happen.

"Natalie took the pouch to an expert at the university," Jock told Eve when he called her. "She just left his office, and she was practically walking on air. I believe she definitely took the bait."

"Who wouldn't? It was multimillion-dollar bait," Eve said dryly. "And we made sure it had potential to dazzle. Now we have to see what ploy she'll concoct to get her hands on it. I'll give her a day to call me, then I'll call her and see if I can push it."

"I imagine she can do a lot of damage in a day," Jock said. "I'd push it before that."

"One day," Eve said. "I know you're impatient, and so am I. I just can't let her know she has all the control."

"She doesn't," Jock said coldly. "I have the control. Just give me the word."

"One day." She hung up.

Jock watched Natalie's taxi turn onto the road leading to Kaskov's mansion as he kept a safe distance behind her.

On the surface, Eve's lure had been successful and had the potential to give them a chance to safely extricate Cara. Beneath the surface, Jock could see all kinds of jagged rocks in the waters ahead.

And he'd better make sure he knew the sharpness of those rocks and the depth of those waters before Cara was overwhelmed by them.

Eve didn't have to wait for twenty-four hours. Natalie Castino called her six hours later.

"I wasn't expecting such a prompt response," Eve said. "You received the package?"

"I received it. At first, I was hesitant about accepting those coins as proof, but they appear to be authentic. At least, it was a good-faith effort. And I decided that you wouldn't risk Cara to try to fool me."

A good-faith effort of two million dollars, Eve thought dryly. Evidently Natalie had decided not to indicate that she knew the value in hopes that Eve did not. "No, I wouldn't take that chance. And the coins couldn't be more authentic. Have them checked if you don't believe me."

"I'm sure I will, that would be the intelligent thing to do," Natalie said. "I just wanted you to know that I'm leaning toward the deal. But I have to make arrangements. As I said, my father is very fond of Cara. I'd have to have a reason to take her away from here."

"Then find a reason," Eve said. "I'm having trouble keeping MacDuff in line. If I don't close this deal soon, he may back out. Right now, he's talking about a fifty-fifty split."

"No." Natalie voice was sharp. "I want it all. If you can't handle MacDuff, leave him to me."

"That's easy to say. He doesn't care anything about Cara. Why should he give up a fortune to save her? You have to make arrangements to let me take Cara right away."

"I'll work on it," Natalie said curtly. "I'll phone you when I set it up." She hung up.

Eve turned to Joe. "She's hungry. I can hear it in her voice. And she's so eager that she called me too soon. She wants that chest so much that she forgot to play it cool."

"That's good." Joe took her in his arms. "That will make her move faster. And maybe make more mistakes."

Or perhaps be more reckless . . . and ruthless. Her

arms slid around him, and she held him closer. "It's beginning, Joe," she whispered. "She's coming closer. It's starting . . ."

It was starting.

Eve stared into the darkness of the tent two hours later, remembering those words. Why couldn't she shake this tension and uneasiness? Almost a foreboding. It wasn't as if things were going wrong. That phone call from Natalie had indicated weakness, not strength. She had taken the bait, and now all they had to do was to find a way to snap the trap.

And hope Cara was not caught in those lethal jaws.

She stiffened at the thought. Her heart was pounding, and she felt suddenly suffocated. She had to get out of here.

She carefully moved Joe's arm from around her and slipped from beneath the covers. Then she grabbed a sweater to slip over her nightshirt and almost ran from the tent.

She drew a few deep breaths of the cool night air before she walked down toward the bank of the lake. That was better. The lake, with its eternal mists, was soothing in itself. She dropped to the ground once she reached the bank, and even the chill of the grass on her bare legs felt good. She linked her arms around her knees and gazed out at the water.

Had Cira sat here on this bank all those centuries ago, waiting for her Marcus to come to her after playing in the mist? Somehow, she thought that she might have, and it gave Eve a feeling of continuity with that woman from Herculaneum who was dominating all their lives right now.

No offense, Cira. I'd much rather you dominate my every thought than Natalie Castino.

She touched her stomach.

And I think the baby gets far more upset when I'm having to deal with her. You don't cause me sleepless nights.

"You're right, Mama. You shouldn't be having sleepless nights. We're both a little worried about that."

Bonnie!

She turned in shock to look where Bonnie was sitting beneath the oak tree a few yards away. Bonnie, still seven years old as she had been the day she had been taken and killed all those long years ago. Still dressed in her jeans and Bugs Bunny T-shirt, the moonlight casting a shimmer on her curly red hair. Still with that beloved smile that had been Eve's salvation when somehow she'd been permitted to come back on occasion and visit her. "It's been a long time. I was getting scared that it might be forever."

"Never forever. Not for us." Her smile widened. "And I thought that you should have a little break from me. A lot of changes are happening to you. Good changes."

"Did you have anything do with that?"

"Who, me?" She laughed. "I can suggest, but I don't have much clout. I guess it was just your turn. You've been doing good for people for a long time, and you needed something fresh and good in your own life."

"The baby."

"And Cara. That was why Jenny was sent to you. To prepare you for Cara."

"Well, I've not been doing so good for Cara," Eve said jerkily.

"Better than anyone else could do, and you'll just keep trying until you bring her home."

"Yes I will." She paused. "I love the baby. I love Cara. But I still miss you. I'll always miss you. No one can re-

place you. So don't think you're doing what's best for me by walking away. You have to stick around."

"Yes, ma'am." Bonnie chuckled. "Maybe not quite so much. You're going to be busy, and so will I. But that's good, too. Purpose is always good."

"Is that why you came tonight? You wanted to tell me that you were going to ration your time with me? I don't like that."

"No, that's not why I came. And ration isn't the way I'd put it. I'll always be there for you, Mama. So stop frowning."

Eve made a face. "I know. I know. Who's the kid in this relationship? But I haven't had your experience in the great beyond. I don't have patience."

"You won't miss me as much as you think." She paused before she said softly, "You're going to experience something extraordinary with him. He'll be a constant challenge."

Eve went still. "He?"

"That's why I'm here tonight. You wanted to know, and he's not capable yet of making it clear to you. So he told me to come instead."

"He?" She repeated again. "Are you saying what I think you are?"

"Your child is a boy," Bonnie said quietly. "And he thinks his name is Michael, but he's leaving that up to you."

"A boy . . ." She couldn't quite take it in. "You're sure?"

"Well, he's sure," Bonnie said. "And he was most insistent on giving you what you wanted to know. So I believe you can trust him."

"A boy." She moistened her lips. "I have to get used to it. I had you, then Jane. It will be . . . different."

"He would be different regardless. I told you, he's extraordinary."

"So are you. So is Jane."

"No, not like him." Bonnie leaned back against the tree. "You'll see soon, once he gets a little older."

"I don't know what you mean."

"He'll make sure you know. How do you think that he was able to bring me into this? It's not at all usual, Mama."

She frowned. "What are you saying?"

"I'm saying that he's very strong, very loving, very protective even at this age. He has a . . . force. Extraordinary."

She shouldn't have been surprised. She had felt that strength. But she was surprised and bewildered and just a little intimidated. "You keep using that word. I'm not sure exactly what that will mean to me."

"Why, you'll match him. You're extraordinary, too. And, everything he is, will be for you, Mama." She smiled. "I like that. Now tell me his name."

"He's already told you. Michael. It's a perfectly good name, and there must be some reason why he thinks it belongs to him." She touched her stomach. "It's okay with me. Michael . . ."

Was there a stirring, perhaps a warmth, or was that pure imagination?

"I don't know either," Bonnie said. "Maybe Michael will tell you once you're down the road a little farther. By that time I'll be out of it for a while." Her smile faded. "Unless something happens to bring me back. He's worried, Mama."

"What about?" Eve was instantly alarmed. "The doctor said he was doing fine."

"I don't know. He's just worried. He wants you to be careful."

"Of course I'll be careful. I have to make sure nothing happens to him."

"I've scared you," Bonnie said. *"I didn't want to do that. But that was the other reason why I came tonight. I had to make certain that you knew he was worried. He can't get to you yet."* She wrinkled her nose. *"Though heaven knows he's trying."*

"Point taken. I'm worried about him, too. And Cara. And Jane. And Joe. You're on my list, too. Though that may be a little silly considering your circumstance."

"Silly. But very loving. I'm doing fine where I am, Mama."

"Good." She looked at her, seeing all the brightness and the love and the laughter that had been with her in life and was still there now. It brought to Eve both a feeling of thanksgiving and infinite hope. *"Then if you've done your duty, could we just sit here and look out at the lake and be together?"*

"I'd like that." Bonnie suddenly giggled. *"If Michael has no complaints. I told you how protective he was."*

"Then it's time that he realizes that there are some areas where he can't interfere. We have to start this relationship as we mean to continue."

"I told you that you could match him." She looked out at the mist-laden lake. *"You think a lot about this lake, don't you?"*

"Not as much as Jane does, but, yes, as soon as Jane told me about her dream of Cira and her child, I couldn't help but identify. Her child, Marcus, died." She looked at Bonnie. *"My child died. I wondered if perhaps Cira might have been given a special dispensation as I was."*

"I don't know, Mama. I know that Cira was a very special person. I know she's still special. I know this place is special. I was glad you came here. It seemed a good place for you to get to know Michael."

"We won't be here that long. Once we get Cara back, we'll be going back to Atlanta. I have to work to do." She smiled. "And a child to be born."

"It will be time enough. As I said, it's a special place." Eve looked out into the mist. "Magic?"

"Maybe. There's magic all around us if we look hard enough. If we want it badly enough."

"The only magic I want is a healthy child and the safety of the people I love."

"And that may be the most complicated magic of all," Bonnie said. "That's what Cira wanted, but she had to compromise."

"Shh. Don't say that. Not when I don't know what's ahead of me," Eve said. "We're going to think positive, young lady. No compromises. Just magic."

Bonnie smiled and nodded. "Just magic, Mama . . ."

The sky was lightening to pearl gray when Eve left the lake and went back to her tent. Bonnie had stayed with her a long time as if she sensed how bewildered and on edge Eve was tonight. There had been no talk of Natalie Castino or the danger that was threatening. They had just been together, and there had been only love and mists and the knowledge that love never really faded or vanished.

Just like the mists, she thought, as she quietly went into the tent. The mists that no one knew how to pierce or vanquish, that had continued on through the centuries from the time of Cira to this small group who were trying so desperately to find their way to what lay beyond.

Joe was still asleep, one arm thrown behind his head, his cheek buried in the pillow.

She shrugged out of her sweater and tossed it aside. Then she slid into bed and pulled his arm down and around her. He stirred and half opened his eyes. "Eve?"

"Shh. Go back to sleep. It's not even dawn yet."

"Okay." His eyes started to close, then flicked open. "No, something's . . . wrong. Your legs feel cold. Is everything okay?"

She should have known Joe would realize any type of discrepancy connected to her. "I went outside for a while, but I'm back now."

"But everything's okay?"

"Fine. Everything's wonderful, Joe," she whispered as she cuddled closer. "We have a son." Her lips pressed against his warm, naked shoulder. "And his name is Michael . . ."

CHAPTER
8

"Where's Cara, Natalie?" Kaskov frowned as he came into the living room from his study. "I sent for her thirty minutes ago."

"I told her I'd let her know when to come," Natalie said. "I need to talk to you, Daddy."

"Can't it wait?" he asked impatiently.

He was brushing her aside again because of Cara. Natalie tried to smother her anger. It just showed how right she was to escalate the move to get rid of the threat. "I won't be long. I know how much you enjoy our little girl." She put her hand on his arm. "I just wanted to talk to you when Cara wasn't around. I didn't want to bring up that horror she went through again when she seems to be healing so nicely." She paused. "Do you remember I told you that I thought there was a woman involved in the group that was holding Cara for ransom? Well, I received a phone call today from that woman." She shuddered. "It was terrible. She was so angry. She threatened me. She said she was Alfredo Salazar's lover, and she knew that I had killed him to save Cara. She said that the money I had paid for Cara wasn't enough, and I had to be punished. That both Cara and I were going to die because of what I'd done to Salazar." She let her voice quiver. "Daddy, I can't let Cara—"

"Wait a minute," Kaskov interrupted. "What woman?"

"Her name is Eve Duncan, and she's some kind of artsy sculptor or something." Tears were brimming in her eyes. "I wouldn't be afraid of her except she might be able to persuade Salazar's cartel to go after Cara again and kill her this time."

"That won't happen," Kaskov said grimly. "She gets near either one of you, and she's dead."

"I knew you'd say that." She slid her arms around him. "And it may be just a horrible bluff, but I had to tell you about it. I have to know more about her in case it's not a bluff." She looked up at him and allowed the tears to fall. "Would it be all right if I use that man, Peter Jadlow, that you hire to investigate everybody, to run a check on Duncan? Just to put my mind at rest?"

"Do you have to ask? I'll call Jadlow right away."

"No, you've done so much already for Cara and me. I'll call him and get the report. I just wanted your permission." Her voice was shaking. "I didn't want to bother you, Daddy. You're so busy, and you have that trip to Beijing in a few days."

"I'll tell Ivan Sabak to double your guards while I'm gone."

"That will be a great comfort." She kissed his cheek. "This nightmare keeps going on and on, doesn't it? But maybe this is just some hysterical woman who wants to frighten me and doesn't have the power to do anything."

"I don't care how much power she thinks she has. I don't like the fact that she feels free to threaten you.

You're my daughter, and it's an insult to me that she believes I'm unable to take care of you." His voice was harsh. "When I come back from Beijing, I'll take care of this business once and for all."

"Whatever you decide, Daddy." She smiled as she backed away from him. "Just letting me have Jadlow so that I'll know what we're up against will make me feel better. You always told me that knowledge was power. If he comes up with anything troubling, I'll be sure to let you know."

She had what she wanted. Time to move away from demands and requests and give him something he wanted. Even though what he wanted was a festering sore these days. She picked up her phone and started dialing. "Now, I'll call our Cara and get her to run up here right away. Why don't you sit down, and I'll get you a drink while you're waiting?" She spoke into the phone, "Cara, your grandfather wants you. Come at once." She hung up and went over to the bar across the room. "Isn't it nice, that you can snap your fingers, and Cara will be here playing for you? I'm so glad that I could give that to you. It makes me feel that I'm paying back some of the wonderful things you've done for me."

"Does it?" His gaze was narrowed on her across the room. "Sometimes I've felt that you resented it."

She must have slipped up somewhere, revealed too much. Think fast. "Not resented it," she said gently. "It's just that listening to Cara playing reminds me of Jenny and how much you loved listening to her playing the piano when I brought the girls to you before." She turned and started back across the room to him. "And that brings back the thought that my Jenny is dead, and that breaks my heart." She gave him his drink. "I'm sure that you can understand. You understand everything about me."

"Yes." He lifted his drink to his lips. "I thought I did.

But I'm still learning. I look at Cara, and sometimes I see you in her. Sometimes my mother, sometimes I see myself."

"As long as you're pleased with her. After all, she's my gift to you. Enjoy her."

"Oh, I do." He lifted his glass to her. "I couldn't be more pleased with my gift." He sat up eagerly, his head tilting. "I hear her in the foyer." He called, "I'm in the mood for the Vivaldi tonight, Cara. Come in and get started."

He was through with her, Natalie realized bitterly. But at least she'd managed to slide past that sticky spot. She forced a smile as she faded into the background as Cara came into the room. "Yes, by all means, entertain him, Cara. He's been very kind to me tonight." She could see Cara's shoulders stiffen and the wariness in her expression. Good. She wanted her to be afraid. How would she react if she knew that Natalie had been talking to her father about Cara's precious Eve Duncan?

Not yet. Eve was a weapon she could hold over Cara, and so far it had worked very well. Just a hint made Cara surprisingly meek and cooperative at the very threat of harm to Duncan. If she knew the threat was growing and about to become reality, it might boomerang.

Cara was still looking at her, her eyes wide and wary.

The child knew how she felt about her, Natalie realized suddenly. The girl had annoyed her so much that, many times, Natalie had not even tried to hide her feelings. Oh, well, she still had the control over her, and it would be a relief not to have to pretend except in the presence of her father. "Come along, Cara." She moved toward the door. "Do what your grandfather asks while I get you a glass of lemonade to drink during your breaks."

She stopped just outside the door and drew a deep breath as Cara started to play.

She had been very effective, and it had been a fairly successful evening so far. It had been imperative that she know everything possible about Eve Duncan, and she would have that advantage in a day or so after she received Jadlow's report. It was going to be very tricky manipulating a way to get the treasure without surrendering Cara. It was going to be even more difficult to frame Eve Duncan for Cara's death and convince her father that she had done it.

But she had started to set up the scenario tonight, and she would build on it and adjust as she went along.

It would all come together.

But it should probably be done while her father was in Beijing, so she could work freely to accomplish her ends. Three days. She had three days to prepare; and then it had to all go like clockwork.

She headed down the hall toward the kitchen to ask a servant for Cara's lemonade. The music followed her, and she could imagine her father sitting there, held captive as he watched Cara.

Tick-tock, Cara. Enjoy every minute of all that attention he's giving you. Your clock is definitely ticking.

"You were magnificent." Natalie bent over Ivan and rubbed her naked body catlike over him. "So much pleasure . . ." She licked his shoulder. "Did I please you?"

"You know you did." He was panting, his breath coming in gasps. "I've never known—where did you learn that?"

"My husband wanted me schooled in the things he considered most important. He sent me to a bordello in Istanbul for a month. I consented because I considered it almost as important as he did." Her teeth sank teasingly into his flesh. "And you agree, don't you? You like everything I do to you?"

"You know I do." He looked at her. "But nothing is free with you. What do I have to pay?"

"I've told you I have a few problems. But it would be foolish of me to expect you to help solve them because I have sex with you. Though that would be a pleasant part of it for both of us."

"You promised me money," he said roughly. "A fortune in gold. I killed that professor for you. Kaskov thinks I belong to him, and he'd have me killed if he knew what I was doing. You know there are the rules."

Of course she knew about the rules. She had used them herself on occasion. Those inflexible rules that Kaskov demanded all his men obey when he brought them into his syndicate. First among them was total loyalty to him in exchange for remaining alive and earning fees far higher than anyone else in any of the Russian Mafias. "I believe you've already made your choice, haven't you?"

He didn't answer directly. "Then when do I get the gold?"

"Soon. We'll go get it together." She sat up on the couch. It was time to hit him with it, get him used to the idea of the task for which she'd been preparing him. "But there's one thing that you'll have to do for me . . . My problem involves my daughter."

"You want me to kill her." He shrugged. "I knew it was coming. You were dropping hints from the first time you let me have you. Do I have to do it? Kaskov isn't going to like it." He grimaced. "But what am I worrying about? I broke the rules. I'm a dead man anyway when Kaskov finds out. When do you want it done?"

"I'll let you know." It had been easier than she had thought it would be. He hadn't even asked her why she wanted it done. It had always amazed her that even hardened criminals often had hesitations with killing children. It appeared that Sabak had no problems with any kind of slaughter as long as he was rewarded with sex and money. It was no wonder that he occupied a high place in her father's organization. She had chosen well. "I just wanted to let you know that it was going to happen, so you wouldn't be surprised. My father is going to Beijing for some kind of meeting in three days. It won't be until then or later. I'll ask him to let you stay here and protect Cara."

"The gold," he reminded her. "If I'm going to risk my neck, I want the gold."

"You'll have it." His persistence was annoying her. She might have to rethink her long-term relationship with Ivan if he wasn't as malleable as she'd hoped. But that was down the road, and there were always twists and turns available to her if she chose to find them. But now it was time to make him forget everything but the fact that she had the talent to make him dizzy with erotic pleasure. "And you'll have me, Ivan." She moved back over him, her hands sliding, playing, on his body. "And before I leave you tonight, I'll make you tell me you want me more than you do that gold . . ."

LOCH GAELKAR

"No word from Natalie yet?" Jane looked up as Eve came out of her tent the next morning. "It's been two days. I thought she was supposed to be so eager."

"That's what I thought." Eve sat down and poured a cup of tea from the pot over the campfire. "I've been on pins and needles since yesterday. I've been wondering if something is going wrong. I called Jock, and he said that Cara is still okay." She wrinkled her nose. "And that Natalie is spending a good amount of time humping Sabak. That's not what I wanted to hear. She kept Salazar under her thumb for years by becoming his lover. She was the one who first talked him into kidnapping Jenny and Cara."

"I know. You told me." Jane reached over and squeezed Eve's arm. "She's got to call soon. Hang in there."

"Tell that to Cara. She's the one who's the pawn in this game. I can only imagine what she's going through." She took a sip of tea. "And Jock said that she was worrying about us. It's damnable that she's—"

"How is Michael doing?" Jane interrupted.

Eve glanced at her in surprise. "Are you trying to distract me by any chance?"

"Yes, there's no use dwelling on the negative when you have something so positive on the horizon. I'm sure your son would agree with me."

"I'm sure he would. I have the feeling that he tries to distract me, too." She looked at Jane over the rim of her cup. "You accepted the fact that I told you that my baby was going to be a boy without batting an eye. You're not just trying to soothe me? You're a very reasonable, practical person, and we both know I won't be able to have a medical confirmation for a few weeks."

"Screw medical confirmations." Jane smiled. "You told me that it was a boy, and I believe you. Some things you just have to take on faith." Her smile faded. "As I take you on faith. As I take Bonnie on faith." She paused. "Do you know that for a long time I thought Bonnie was a figment of your imagination? I even pretended I didn't know that you thought the spirit of your little girl was visiting you. It was okay with me that you were having hallucinations if it brought you some measure of peace and happiness. Anything that made you happy was worth it. So much for my practicality and dedication to reality." Her lips twisted. "I had to grow up and learn that reality isn't necessarily truth. And experience the same kind of horrible trauma you did to realize that it's not the soul that dies. When I fell in love with Trevor, he was everything I wanted a man to be: gentle, kind, loving. Then, when he was killed protecting me, I thought my life was over. I *wanted* it to be over. When I realized I couldn't let that happen, I prayed that Trevor would come back to me as Bonnie does to you, but he chose not to do it. Maybe he thought that was best for me." She took a sip of her tea. "But you *do* have your Bonnie, and I believe that with my whole heart. If she tells you that Michael wanted you to know you're going to have a son, then it will happen."

"Trevor loved you," Eve said gently. "You're young, and you have a wonderful life ahead of you. He didn't want you to stop living because he did. I don't know how I got so lucky that I got to keep my Bonnie with me."

Jane smiled. "Maybe because it was in the cards that Michael would need an intermediary. He seems to be a very demanding presence even now. I hope he approves of me as a big sister."

"There's no question of that. I chose you, didn't I?"

"We chose each other," Jane said softly. "I was probably every bit as demanding as Michael. I wasn't going to let you—"

"I just talked to Palik." Joe had come out of the tent and was striding toward them. "And I'll bet you're going to hear from Natalie anytime now. Palik just got word that Kaskov is leaving for Beijing tomorrow to meet with some Chinese narcotic distributors. She's probably waiting to make sure he's out of the picture before she makes her move."

"It would make sense," Eve said. "One less force for her to have to deal with if Kaskov is gone." She just hoped she'd hear soon. She had once compared Natalie to a black widow spider, and she could imagine her plotting, planning, weaving her web. The longer it took her, the more dangerous and intricate the trap. It had taken her entirely too long to get back to Eve this time. She made a face. "Who knows? She might decide to wait until her sleazebag father has left Moscow to make contact."

"I doubt it. Time will be at a premium then. She'll want to have plans in place." He bent and kissed her. "Let me know. I'm going to the north bank to try out the new lights MacDuff received last night."

"I will." She watched him walk down the bank and disappear into the mist. "Joe is becoming almost as obsessed with breaking through that mist as MacDuff. I should have known that he'd be caught up in the fever. It's too much of a challenge."

"For all of us," Jane said quietly, her gaze on the mist.

"I've noticed that you've been spending quite a bit of time there, too." Eve was gazing curiously at her. "And I don't believe that you're helping those men rig those poles with those super-duper lights."

Jane shook her head. "But I watch them do it sometimes. Most of the time I just walk or sit and look out at the mist."

"Why?"

She shrugged. "I don't know. I guess I feel . . . comfortable there."

"In blinding fog, on a bank where you can't see what's land or water?"

"I said I didn't know. And you can tell land from water. You only have to listen and feel all the textures of grass and earth and leaves. It's all there waiting for you."

"You do realize that sounds a little strange."

She nodded. "But then this entire hunt for Cira's treasure has been bizarre, hasn't it? Let's face it, this current hunt through the mist may be strange, but look at what preceded it. As I said, we've all been caught. It could be that's what Cira wanted." She smiled, and she got to her feet. "And, after that equally bizarre remark, I believe I'll follow Joe into the mist and think about Cira and her son and wonder what she has in store for us." Her smile became mischievous. "And you called me reasonable and practical? That should show you how far I've gone beyond the pale." She waved and sauntered down the bank.

Eve watched her disappear from view. It was true that emotions and conflict had dominated all their lives recently, but there had also been growth and healing and love. Jane had started to put the tragedy of Trevor's death behind her and was beginning to live again. She was changing and questioning with every passing day. Eve could not know what Cara was going through right now, but she had found the friend of a lifetime in Jock, and a home and love with Eve and Joe. As for Eve, she had a son who cared enough to send her a message of comfort by Bonnie, the beloved.

*Not so bad, Michael. We can get through this as long as we remember—*She had a sudden thought. *Did you have anything to do with all this sweetness and light I'm feeling all of a sudden?*

Warmth. Mischief. Humor.

That's no answer. I'm clearly going to have to watch out for you.

But what a wonderful gift to have the knowledge that he was here with her, even if he was trying to control her thought processes to keep her happy.

We'll have a discussion about this later. I have a right to—

Her phone rang, jarring her out of the warmth that was Michael.

Natalie. Like ice water being thrown on her, freezing out everything else.

"I thought you were going to arrange an exchange

soon," Eve said when she picked up the call. "I told you I was having trouble holding off MacDuff from—"

"It wasn't convenient. I decided I didn't have to rush to make it easier for you. Not after I read the dossier on you that one of Daddy's employees put together."

"Dossier?" Eve repeated warily.

"You don't like that, do you? Well, I felt it was necessary to know you very well, Eve. I needed to know everything about you that could affect me in any way. We had such a brief acquaintance that I was uneasy. I felt I had a good grasp on your character, but I had to be sure."

"How clever of you."

"I *am* clever. All the men in my life have underestimated me, but I don't believe you did."

"And what did you find out of any value about me?"

"That you're smart and strong and stubborn. But you also have faults. You're soft, very soft. I knew that, of course. Your attitude toward Cara is amazingly weak and without reason. I couldn't see why anyone that strong would allow herself to give up so much to keep a child you scarcely know alive." Her tone was completely without inflection. "After all, she has no real value to you."

"She has a value. But you wouldn't understand."

"I hope not. Because I'm not in the least soft, nor will I ever be."

"That's no surprise. And how did reading your report on me help you to plan the exchange? Did it make you trust me?"

"Oh, no, that would have been a total disappointment. I fully believe that you would cheat me of my gold if you could. Because you think I'm bad, and so it would be morally right to do it. You appear to be all into morally right. Though you've tottered on the edge of legally right a few times. Surprising, since your lover is a detective. But you're so emotional about keeping Cara alive that there's no way that you'd risk her life to keep that treasure." She paused. "And you're so strong that you'll find a way to get around MacDuff's stubborn insistence on keeping part of my gold. You won't allow him to get in the way of saving Cara. So you see, I know you very well now. I can block any move you make that's not to my advantage."

"You've referred to Cira's treasure as 'my gold' a couple times in this conversation. You're already considering it's yours, but it won't be yours until you tell me how I can get Cara back."

"I was getting to that. Day after tomorrow is good for me. You'll deliver the chest to Drostkey Park at the carousel at 4 P.M."

"Is that Moscow? I thought you might want to make the exchange here in Scotland."

"Why? I want to hold all the cards. Drostkey Park. Don't worry, you'll actually see her on that carousel. After I check the contents of the chest, I'll have Cara brought to you. Does that sound reasonable?"

"It depends on the circumstances. You could have the park packed with Kaskov's men."

"No, I'm trying to leave my father out of this transaction. It could prove awkward for me. That's why I set the exchange up in a park that caters to children. Though I admit it does have a Catherine the Great theme that appealed to me. But I can tell him that Cara was intrigued by the music on the carousel. But even if my father's not involved, you can be certain that I'll still be very secure. And I'm sure that Detective Quinn will make it as safe as possible for you." She paused. "Because you *must* be there for the exchange, Eve. That's part of the deal."

"I won't object. I want to be there."

"Good. Then we're in agreement. I'll see you day after tomorrow."

Eve's hand was shaking as she pressed the disconnect.

Day after tomorrow.

It had to be some kind of trap, either for them, or Cara, or both.

But there had to be a way of springing the trap before it caught them. Or maybe turning the trap against Natalie. They'd have to work until they found that way.

Drostkey Park.

Day after tomorrow.

Cira's treasure chest . . .

She'd already started preparing the contents of that chest, but now it was necessary to make sure it would pass at least a cursory inspection.

And how to be certain Cara would be safe while all this was going on?

She started to dial Joe.

"Day after tomorrow," Joe repeated. "It's not much time to complete setting up, but we'll make it do." He and Jane had only been back at camp for thirty minutes, but he was already thinking, making plans, looking for ways and means. "The first thing we need is a complete plan of Drostkey Park and that carousel area. The second thing is a way to extricate Cara if Natalie decides that what we're offering her is bogus."

"Which it is," Jane said. "But it's not likely she'd risk an extended examination of the contents of the chest we show her while she's in a public place. She'll know that we may want to take any opportunity to snatch Cara away."

"Not we, Jane," Eve said quietly. "You're not going to be there."

"The hell I'm not," Jane said. "I won't let you go into that park to face that Medusa without me. I can help, dammit."

"Yes, you can. But not in that park." Eve had known this would be coming, and she had already marshaled her arguments. "Look, Natalie knows all about me now. And she thinks I'm very soft. She also knows about you and how I feel about you. The first thing she'd do if she felt threatened or suspicious would be to try to take out someone I love. I won't provide her with a target that could hurt not only you but me." She paused. "And maybe Cara."

"But I want to—" She stopped as she met Eve's eyes. "Okay, I won't go into the park. How close can I get, and what can I do to help?"

"We'll work it out." She smiled. "But there's something you can do even before we head for Russia. We're going to need an authentic-looking chest in which to put Cira's 'treasure.' She held up a finger. "One. In order for it to logically withstand the wear and tear of centuries, it will probably have to be of metal of some sort. Two. A false bottom so that we don't have to completely fill it with coins. We're going to have enough trouble getting sufficient coins to fool Natalie into releasing Cara. Three. It has to look aged and absolutely genuine. You're a phenomenal artist. Can you do all that?"

"Of course I can do it," Jane said curtly. "I'll head for Edinburgh right away. I don't work in metal, but I can pull in a couple of my friends who work in mixed media and metal. I can do the rest. It won't be easy to do it in the time frame you've given me, but I'll have it ready for you." She frowned. "But you're not going to be able to transport a chest like that without comment. We'll build a wood chest to put it in."

"Fine," Joe said. "But I guarantee we're not going to be going through customs. We'll be sliding in and out of Moscow with lightning speed."

"We hope," Eve said.

"I'm still going with you." Jane's jaw set. "Find me something to do."

"You can be the getaway driver," Joe said with a grimace. "That's far enough away to keep Eve comfortable, and it may turn out to be a key position."

"You don't think Natalie will go through with the exchange?"

"She may do it. She wants Cira's gold very much," Eve said. "I hope she does. She may let us have Cara, then go after her later when she feels safer." She shook her head. "But she *will* go after her. She's always felt she had to protect herself from anyone's finding out that she'd arranged for the kidnapping and killing of Jenny and Cara. That won't change."

"It might," Joe said. "It could change in Drostkey Park."

"No, Joe." She knew what he was saying. "It's not about Natalie. It's about getting Cara away from her and bringing her home."

He shrugged. "We don't know how things will go down. I'm just saying that I wouldn't hesitate to take her out of the picture if things don't go as we hope." He turned to go to the tent. "But we'll pretend that all will go as we intend it to. I'm going to set up transport and get those maps of Drostkey Park."

"Drostkey Park," Jock repeated slowly. "It's a strange place to set up an exchange. You do realize that it might be bogus, Eve."

"Of course, I do. But it's the best opportunity we'll have. It gets Cara outside those gates of Kaskov's estate and away from most of his men. It's a public place, and it would be hard to stage anything . . . violent."

"No, it wouldn't. You can kill anywhere, anytime. You just have to make preparations."

"We're making our own preparations. Cara is going to be in that park, and we're going to take her," Eve said grimly. "Joe arranged for us to fly into Cadzav Airport on the south side of Moscow. It's a small airport used by smugglers and drug dealers who pay the government to look the other way. After we have Cara, we'll be on that plane within thirty minutes."

"If you're allowed to get out of Drostkey Park."

"Joe will be making plans to make sure we do."

"You trust Quinn implicitly. I'm impressed."

"Of course I trust him." She paused. "I don't expect you to trust him. You don't really trust anyone, Jock. But he won't let anything happen to Cara. I want you to know that."

"I know that Quinn is very good, but he has one fault in a situation like this."

"And what is that?"

"He's not willing to make necessary sacrifices to get the job done."

"I don't know what you mean."

"Think about it. It will come to you." He added, "But you didn't only call to tell me that you'd arranged your exchange and tell me the details. You want something from me."

"I want you not to make any move that would spoil the exchange."

"And what else?"

"I want you to be in that park watching to make sure that Cara is safe."

He laughed. "You know very well I'll be there. No question."

"And the exchange?"

"I've never objected to anything that would keep Cara safer than I could."

"That's not an answer."

"I'll let you have your chance. But I'll prepare for it not to be a success."

"Fair enough."

"And you have to prepare for it, too." His voice was steel hard. "You want me in that park to watch and keep her safe while those negotiations are going on. If I do see something I don't like, I'll act on it. I'll act fast and hard, and you may not know what's happening. But if something, anything, goes down that doesn't seem right, or you don't understand, you don't question. You and Quinn get out of that park and head toward the airport."

"Not without Cara."

"Dammit, I'll *have* Cara." He tempered the harshness of his voice. "And if Cara sees you're in trouble, I'll have a hell of a time getting her away. You know how she is."

Eve did know. But what he suggested was completely against her nature. "I don't think I can do—"

"Then let Natalie keep Cara and see how long she lives," he said harshly. Then he was silent for an instant, struggling for control. "You trust Quinn. This time you have to trust me, too. You do what I tell you to do, and I'll keep her alive. Promise me. No judgment calls. If something doesn't seem right, it's me trying to make it right. You and Quinn get out of that park."

She didn't answer.

"I'll *never* let her die. I'll never let anyone hurt her. Promise me."

She was silent. Then she said, "I promise. Though I'm going to have problems with Joe. He's not into blind trust."

"And neither are you." He paused. "Thank you."

"And maybe neither of us will have to commit to it." She moistened her lips. "I hope not."

"So do I," Jock said. "But in my world, happily ever after never happens. Particularly with scum like Natalie and her new lover. I'm a bit stressed with dealing with them long-distance at the moment. I want to be up close and personal."

His voice was ice-cold now, and after the passion that had gone before, it came as a shock to Eve. "I suppose that it's been difficult watching them with Cara."

"You could say that." The ice was gone, and his words were jerky. "She's clean and brave and filled with music. And she's surrounded by dirt and blood and ugliness and trying not to let it touch her. But it *does* touch her, I watch it touch her. And it *kills* me." He drew a deep breath. "And it may kill a hell of a lot more before this is over."

She had thought she realized what Jock was going through, but she'd had no real idea. "It's going to be over soon, Jock. Two days."

"Two days," he repeated. "I'll check out Drostkey Park and call Quinn and tell him if there's anything he should know. He's already got diagrams and maps of the park?"

"Yes, he's studying them now."

"And I'll be doing the same thing. And I'll talk to Palik and see if he's heard anything else that I should know. He has his ear to the ground."

"Joe's been talking to Palik, too." There was something she had to say to him. "I know that you think that I've been getting in your way, Jock. It's not because I didn't believe that you weren't doing everything you could for Cara. I just want you to know I'm grateful to you for caring, for watching over her. And I do trust you."

"I *do* care. So keep trusting me. You won't be sorry." He hung up.

Eve couldn't doubt how he felt about Cara, but those last words held a passion and commitment that unsettled her. But no more than that promise he'd wrested from her.

It was too vague, yet he wanted her to act on just a feeling that something was not as it should be.

How on earth was she going to explain that to Joe?

Never mind. She would do it somehow. Maybe everything would go down just as it should, and there would be no need to blindly trust Jock.

But, though her world wasn't like Jock's, where happily ever afters never came, they came so infrequently that they couldn't be counted on.

Best to make very sure Joe knew that she'd been sincere in her promise to Jock. She braced herself and turned to go find him.

"What do you think?" Jane took the tarp off the bronze chest and took a step back. "Does it look ancient enough? I spent hours sanding and staining it. And those carved emblems were a nightmare to do. That one in the center of the lid was common in Herculaneum. It's the best I could do, Eve."

"It's wonderful. It looks fantastic." Her finger gently traced the emblems. "And, yes, it appears very ancient. How did you choose those emblems?"

"It just came to me. They were . . . right." She opened the lid. "The interior looks old, too, but not as ancient as the exterior. And you have your false bottom, but the interior is so dark and cracked, it's not easily visible."

"That's exactly what I wanted."

"So now we have to fill it with coins? How's that going to happen? I notice you didn't send Caleb out to rob any more collectors."

"Not necessary. MacDuff is finding what we need on the Internet. Even ancient coins aren't exorbitantly expensive as long as they're not in the collectable category like that drachma. What we'll do is spread those other coins that Caleb took from Helmsberg on the top of the other coins in case Natalie checks closely or has an expert there to check for her. We'll also throw in some silver drachmas that don't have the same value as the one she had appraised. She'll recognize those and hopefully think they're of similar value. I believe it will work." She made a face. "But we didn't want to have to fill up that chest. Hence the false bottom."

"I can see that would have been a problem." Jane shook her head. "It's an amazing plan."

"I don't know about amazing." Eve wearily rubbed the back of her neck. "We just had to make do. We needed coins. We needed a chest." She smiled. "So I asked for a little help from my friends. And they came through for me. Thank you, Jane."

"No problem. It was . . . interesting. Like dipping my toes into Cira's world."

"Well, you did a wonderful job of dipping." She turned away and headed for her tent. "And now I'm going to tear Joe away from studying those maps of the park and drag him out to take a look at this chest."

Jane watched her walk away before she turned back to the chest. She had done a good job on it. It had gone lightning fast and, as she had told Eve, it was as if she had known every moment what stroke, what carving to make on that bronze surface. She reached down and gently touched the hawk emblem on the lid.

"Would it have been too much trouble to let me know where you'd gone?" Caleb asked as he came to stand beside her. "One minute you were here, and the next you were off to Edinburgh. Not courteous, Jane."

"I was in a hurry. There wasn't much time." Why was she making excuses? "And I don't have to account for either my time or presence to you, Caleb."

"But you did." He was smiling. "And now I feel vindicated. But you're lucky I didn't follow you to Edinburgh and impose my unwelcome presence on your artistic friends. If I'd truly felt slighted, I would have done that."

"And we would have ignored you as you deserved. As I said, there wasn't much time. I was lucky to get the chest done on Eve's schedule."

"And did a superb job." He gazed appraisingly at the chest. "I couldn't tell the difference if I were Natalie Castino."

"But any expert with time to examine it in detail would be able to tell it's a phony. We just have to hope she doesn't bring in that expert."

"Yes." His gaze had lifted to her face. "But it didn't feel like a phony to you when you were doing it, did it? You weren't just stroking that emblem, it was more like a caress."

"I'm . . . proud of my work." When he didn't say anything, she said curtly, "And stop making something out of nothing, Caleb."

"I wouldn't think of it. Not when that something is already there in full force." He tilted his head. "Your Cira is getting to you, isn't she? I've been watching you in the mist while we've been working with those lights. You're liking it there, you're beginning to feel at home."

"You shouldn't be watching me when you should be helping MacDuff."

"But you're always my first concern. We both know that. Besides, I like the idea that I'm sharing Cira with you in my small way."

She frowned. "What?"

"Trevor was always there with you when you were searching for information about those dreams of Cira you were having. From the time you were a girl of seventeen." His smile was suddenly reckless. "But you're not seventeen any longer, and now I'm the one who is here. I think Cira might have been curious and interested enough to approve of me. What do you think?"

Jane had never thought of Caleb in connection with

Cira. But Cira would have been fascinated by Caleb. She would have regarded him as a challenge, and she had always been both sensual and passionate in her life and relationships. No one could say that Caleb wasn't both of those things.

Caleb was gazing at her quizzically. "You're not answering."

And she wasn't going to lie to him. He would be able to tell that she wasn't telling the truth, and it would only amuse him. "If I were to guess, I'd say that you were right. Cira would find you interesting enough to spend some time with you. But she was always sensible and realistic about her relationships." She met his eyes. "You'd never have been able to hold her. You'd only have been a one-night stand."

"Really?" His voice was soft as dark velvet. So were his eyes holding her own. "Now that really is a challenge. Because one-night stands can sometimes be so powerful that they can cause a fever that can blur all that realistic nonsense you attribute to her."

She knew that they were no longer talking about Cira. She forced her herself to pull her gaze away. "I believe I'm a better student of Cira's character than you, Caleb. And I don't know how this entire conversation started anyway."

"Cira's chest." He glanced down at the bronze chest again. "And you'll recall the other nuances when you're by yourself and not on the defensive." He looked up at her and smiled. "And now that I've stated my protest regarding your lack of consideration in keeping me in the dark, I'll have to leave you and get on my way. I'm sure I'll see you in Moscow."

She stiffened. "You're going with us?"

"Not with you. I'm taking my own plane to have on hand if needed. You may have tried to shut me out, but

Quinn recognizes how valuable I can be. MacDuff stays here, but there's no reason why I can't join in the fun."

"Fun? Natalie will make sure that no one has fun from any of this."

"All the more reason for me to go." His smile faded. "Did you really think that I wasn't going to be there if you went with Eve?"

"I didn't think about it one way or the other."

"Then it's time you started. I'm starting to lose my sense of humor about fighting those walls you're putting up against me." His dark eyes were glittering in his suddenly taut face. "You don't want me to do that, Jane."

He turned on his heel and strode away from her.

Jane tried not to stare after him. He had managed to both shake and arouse her. And that last warning had caused a bolt of sheer uneasiness mixed with a strange excitement at the coming battle.

Battle? That would have been Cira's take on Jane's relationship with Caleb. A battle and a constant challenge.

She drew a long breath. This was no time to be thinking about battles and challenges when they had a major battle on the horizon that could mean life or death.

She could see Joe and Eve coming toward her, and she waved to them. "Come and see Cira's chest, Joe. I think she'd be proud of it."

CHAPTER
9

Children playing.

Dogs being walked.

Mothers chatting with other mothers as they watched their children.

The carousel turning slowly as the music played.

Everything going on here now should be precisely as it would be tomorrow when Eve met Natalie for the exchange, Jock thought.

He had already timed the exact minutes the carousel would take to make its revolution, but he did it one more time in case of a mechanical discrepancy. Natalie had mentioned that Cara would be on that carousel, and that made it of utmost importance. Jock had taken two hours to make every aspect of that carousel familiar to him.

Now it was time to check out the park itself.

He started to pace off the carousel from the other features he had noticed. He had already memorized every detail of the outbuildings and the landscaping, but there was nothing better than on-site inspection.

The carousel . . .

Center of Natalie's plan?

Why?

How?

Explore . . .

KASKOV'S GATEHOUSE
MOSCOW

Cara tucked her violin back in its case and carefully fastened the metal snaps. She didn't set it on the floor but left it on the bed. She might want to play again tonight. She was very restless. As usual, the music had been there for her tonight, but it had been difficult for her to begin. Afterward, it had been fine, beautiful.

But everything was different. Kaskov had left on some trip, and she hadn't had to play for him. So she had been in the gatehouse all day and evening. And she hadn't seen Natalie at all today. Not that her absence had upset Cara. She knew that anything that Natalie said to her was probably lies and pretense anyway. And Cara didn't have to pretend in return if she didn't have to deal with either Natalie or Kaskov.

But the hours alone had seemed very long. And she'd had time to think of Eve . . . and Jock.

Jock.

Had he heard her play for him tonight?

Of course he'd heard her. He'd told her he'd always be there for her, and she believed him.

It was just hard not to see him, talk to him. It had seemed a long time since he'd come to her that night. She had thought of him every—

"Hush. Not a word."

Her gaze flew to the staircase.

Jock!

She flew across the room and into his arms. "I was just thinking of you. It seemed like such a long—" He was covering her mouth with his hand. She drew a shaky breath, then whispered, "Are you going to take me with you tonight? Give me just a minute. I'll change out of my pajamas and be ready."

He shook his head. "Not tonight. I just wanted to tell you what was happening, so you won't be frightened." He was whisking her into the bathroom and shutting the door. "Natalie didn't come to the gatehouse tonight, so Sabak is still in the garden. There's less chance that he'll hear us in here."

"I know. I hear them all the time when they're downstairs in the living room."

"Do you?"

"Yes, they do all that sex stuff. It's pretty noisy."

"And a kid shouldn't have to listen to it," he said grimly. "It's not a great introduction."

She couldn't understand why he was upset about something that didn't matter. "Why can't I go with you tonight?"

"Because tomorrow, Natalie is going to take you to Drostkey Park. She's supposed to be meeting Eve and doing an exchange of you for Cira's gold."

"No." Cara's fingers dug into his arm. "She'll hurt Eve. I *know* it, Jock."

"It's going to be in broad daylight. Joe Quinn will be there, and I'll bet he'll have backup. He won't let anything happen to her."

"You should tell them not to do it."

"It's going to happen, Cara. We just have to do it right."

She shook her head. "Can't you just take me now?"

"Eve wants it this way. I don't like it. But there are a few advantages even if it doesn't go the way she wants it to. At least it will get you away from most of Kaskov's goons here on the estate."

"Natalie will hurt Eve if she gets a chance."

"Quinn will see that she doesn't get a chance." He paused. "But if the exchange doesn't go as planned, you have to be ready for me to take you."

Her eyes widened. "You'll be there?"

"I'll be there. You won't see me unless it becomes necessary. But then we'll have to move very fast. Okay?"

"No, it's not okay." She swallowed hard. "I *hate* it. Eve could get hurt. You could get hurt."

"But we won't, and you'll be out of here." He touched her cheek. "And the rest of it won't be easy, but we'll handle it." He brushed his lips across her forehead. "Now, where's your violin?"

"What?"

"I'm taking it with me and having Palik send it out of the country."

"Why?"

"Because I'm not letting you go through all this without getting something of value out of it. You love that violin."

"But it's not really mine."

"It is now." His lips twisted. "And I don't think, even if this offer to exchange is sincere, that Natalie would send the violin with you as a farewell present."

"No, Kaskov gave it to me, but she said to consider it a loan."

"Then you've just paid off the loan. Where is it?"

"On the bed. In its case. I'm finished for the night."

He opened the bathroom door. "That's why I didn't come earlier. I wanted you to follow your usual routine as much as possible."

"Because you intended to take the violin."

"I couldn't take you. So the violin will have to do." He smiled and moved over to the violin case on the bed. "The next time you play, it will be at Loch Gaelkar."

"You're trying to make me feel better," she said unsteadily.

"It might be my mission in life. Is it working?"

"No, I'm scared. I'll feel better once I know you and Eve are safe." She moved toward him and buried her face in his chest. "But I won't let them hurt either of you. I'll find a way to—"

"Shh. You've gone through a hell of a lot. We're on the home stretch. Stop worrying about anyone but yourself." He brushed a kiss across the tip of her nose and turned toward the stairs. "See you at Drostkey Park."

The next instant, he was gone.

Seven minutes until he reached safety, he'd told her the last time he'd been here.

She went out onto the balcony. The air was bitter cold, and she remembered that Kaskov had mentioned it was supposed to snow before he'd left for the airport today. She gazed out at the forest beyond the fence. It wasn't because of the weather that she felt cold and sick to her stomach. There wouldn't be any triumphant fanfare this time when that seven minutes had passed.

Everything had changed.

Three minutes.

She stood there, tense, as the minutes passed.

Six minutes.

Tomorrow it would be Eve as well as Jock who was in danger.

Seven minutes.

No music to herald that triumph.

Only gratitude that Jock was safe and a prayer for tomorrow.

DROSTKEY PARK
3:45 P.M.

"You're sure everything is ready?" Natalie asked Sabak as she watched Cara walk ahead of them toward the large, glittering carousel several yards away. "He's in place?"

"Of course, he's in place." Sabak glanced at the refreshment stand, his gaze on the window above the awning. "I don't make mistakes." He had to raise his voice a little to be heard above the music of the carousel. "It will go off as planned."

"It's starting to snow." She looked up at the faint white dusting that was starting to fall. "Will they stop the carousel? It would be terrible if they—"

"This is nothing. It's not supposed to snow hard until later in the day. The park will want to squeeze every ruble out of those customers before they close it down."

"What about the guard to watch her?"

"Judok is freelance. He has no connection to your father. I saw to that. And neither do the guards who are going to follow us back to the mansion with the chest. Now stop questioning me."

She didn't like his attitude, but she wasn't going to challenge him at this delicate juncture. She hurried ahead as the carousel stopped. "Get on the carousel, Cara." She looked appraisingly at the horses, lions, and various other figures. Which one . . . ? "Sit down in that seat with the swans on either side."

Cara looked at her. "Do I have to do it? It's sort of silly. I haven't ridden on a carousel since I was eight."

"Yes, you have to do it." She smiled. "And, if you do as you're told, I'll have a surprise for you at the end of the ride."

Cara hesitated, then turned and got on the carousel. The next moment, she was sitting down on the swan seat.

Natalie could see Sabak talking on the phone, his gaze on Cara.

It was good to see that Sabak was being careful. She smiled maliciously. It was clear that Cara was now set up for her great surprise.

And Natalie had to get across the lush, manicured grounds to that red-awning-covered enclosure she'd rented to prepare for her own reward. She had chosen this place well, she thought with satisfaction. Glittering carousels and these scarlet awnings that looked like ermine-trimmed velvet, children's carriage rides with coaches painted gold. All this nonsense meant to honor an empress who had lived in dishonor since the Revolution. Natalie didn't care. She liked the idea of playing empress. It seemed a precursor of things to come.

Eve.

She tensed as she saw Eve coming through the ornate, carved gates across the park.

But where was the chest?

Then she saw the medium-sized wooden box on the wheeled cart that was being guided by Joe Quinn. She relaxed, for a moment she had been worried. But Eve would never have taken a chance like that. Soft, she thought again with contempt.

Natalie had reached the awning, and she sat down and waited for them to approach her. It made her feel like the pictures she'd seen of Catherine the Great as she'd waited for tribute to be brought to her. Yes, this sort of treatment was what she wanted.

And this treatment was what she was going to get . . .

"Dear God, she looks arrogant," Eve murmured, as they walked toward Natalie. The last time she had seen Natalie Castino, she had been covered in dirt, her clothes torn. Now she was wearing a fashionable red-velvet maxiskirt and black-suede jacket, every hair in place, her gaze fixed on them with mockery. "So sure of herself. Does she have a right to be that sure of herself, Joe?"

"I had Palik check over the park, and he didn't report any of Kaskov's men but Sabak anywhere near that carousel or Natalie." He kept his gaze fixed on Natalie. "And we have four men scattered around the park that Palik hired to back us if we need them."

"But where is Jock? I don't see—" Then she forgot Jock as she saw Cara sitting in the swan seat as the slowly revolving carousel brought her into view. Dressed in a black jacket over a white blouse and pleated navy skirt, she looked thinner, older than she usually did. Her face was pale, her lips tense. "She looks scared. I want to *kill* Natalie."

"Easy." His gaze was on a muscular young man in a black-leather jacket who was standing a short distance away from Cara, holding on to one of the brass poles. "She's being watched. That's definitely not the type who'd be hanging out at a carousel."

Eve nodded. "I repeat, where's Jock?" But they were already only a few yards from Natalie, and all of her attention was focused on her smiling face. "We're here," she said curtly. "Let's get this over with, Natalie."

"You're in such a hurry," Natalie said. "I, on the other hand, want to enjoy this a little." Her gaze was on the wooden box. "And that box doesn't appear to be very interesting or promising."

"Did you expect us to transport the coins in the original chest? It would have attracted too much attention." She flipped up the lid of the wooden container. "Besides the fact that I wasn't sure it would have withstood the journey. It's a bit fragile."

Natalie's gaze was hungrily devouring the sight of the bronze chest. "I can see that." She reached out and touched the hawk emblem on the lid with one finger. "All those centuries . . . I imagine the chest may be worth a fortune, too."

And Natalie was buying the authenticity of the chest, Eve thought thankfully. First test passed. "We weren't concerned with the chest itself. It was what was inside that interested us." She looked around. "I thought you'd have an expert here to examine a few of the coins. Where is he?"

"Why, I trust you, Eve." She was lifting the lid of the bronze chest. "And I took the precaution of having the other coins you sent me appraised, and they were adequate."

Two million dollars' worth of adequate, Eve thought cynically.

"But I'll just have a look at these coins." Natalie's cheeks were flushing as she stared down at the heap of glittering gold and silver coins before her. "Beautiful . . ." She picked up one of the Greek drachmas, then reached out and picked up another. "I recognize these coins. You sent me one that was something like these."

It was the reaction for which Eve had hoped. "Did I? I don't remember." She picked up a gold coin. "These gold Roman coins look more valuable."

"Maybe." She was dipping her hand in the coins and letting them flow through her fingers. "We'll have to see, won't we?"

Natalie's motion was making Eve extremely nervous. The last thing she wanted was for Natalie to notice the false bottom on the chest. "You, not we. You've seen to it that I have nothing more to do with Cira's gold."

"Yes, I have." To Eve's relief, she was closing the lid of the chest. "But you don't care about that, do you. All you're concerned about is our dear Cara." Her gaze lifted toward the carousel. "My father is going to be so sad to part with her."

"We've given you the treasure, now have Cara brought to us."

"Presently. I want to see Cara enjoying herself one last time. You can't blame me for that, can you?"

"Yes, since it's a huge lie."

"But no one else would blame me." She gestured to Sabak to come forward and take the chest. She smiled at him as he guided the wooden box and bronze chest to a spot a few yards away. "And now that this troubling business is over, I really wish to watch Cara for a few minutes. Do you want to know why I arranged to have the exchange in broad daylight in such a public place?"

"Because it would make me feel safe?"

"Oh, no, why would I care about your feelings?"

"I forgot," Eve said sarcastically. "It's all about you."

"Of course," she said. "And my father, who has true affection for his granddaughter."

"I find that hard to believe."

"Well, he thinks he does." She pointed. "Look, she's coming around again. Such a pretty child. She looks like me."

"I don't want to look at her. I want her here with us. Keep your word, Natalie."

"But I never told you why I chose this place. It's because I'm going to tell my father that Cara was so despondent that I decided to take her out for a little treat. But I found that I'd been followed." She smiled at Eve. "By you."

"And I kidnapped her?"

She shook her head. "I've prepared the way for something more to my satisfaction." She said softly, "I'll tell Daddy that you hired an assassin to kill her because I killed your lover, Salazar."

Eve's heart stopped, then started to race. "You're crazy," she said. "No one would believe you."

"My father would believe me." She looked at her watch, then rose to her feet. "It's starting to snow a little harder and perhaps I'd better leave you and take my treasure home." She added softly, "And now you'd better have your Joe Quinn run for that carousel to try to save Cara." She turned and hurried toward the gate entrance. "Because when she comes around again, she's going to be a target."

"Joe?" Eve exchanged a panicky glance with him. "My God, she means it." She started running toward the carousel, but Joe was already ahead of her.

The cacophony of the carousel music.

The blinking lights.

The motion of the horses going up and down, up and down.

She could see the edge of the swan seat as it began to come around the corner.

"No!"

A bullet splintered the head of the swan!

"Cara!"

The carousel was still moving, bringing the swan chair in full view.

Another shot!

"Keep low," Joe said. "That was a sniper bullet from one of the outbuildings. Maybe a Remington . . ."

"She said assassin. Cara . . ."

"It's okay, Eve," Joe said over his shoulder. "Cara's not in that swan chair, thank God." He jumped up on the carousel stand and ran past the splintered chair to a crumpled heap lying on the floor by one of the brass poles.

Cara's guard, Eve realized dazedly. Dark hair. Black leather jacket . . .

And a broken neck.

"I believe that answers your question," Joe said grimly.

"Jock." He glanced at the open elaborately painted red door in the center of the carousel that allowed for maintenance. "He must have been hiding in there, just waiting for his chance."

"Where are we—" She stopped. She'd made a promise, and she had to keep it. Trust Jock. He'd saved Cara so far. But, dammit, it was so hard. "We have to get out of here. It won't be long before they find out something has gone wrong. He said that Cara would make it harder for him to save her if she thought I was still here and might be in danger. You know how protective she—" Joe wasn't moving. "Joe, I promised."

"I didn't."

"Joe."

"Shit. Okay." Joe was holding her elbow and running at top speed toward the side entrance, where Jane had parked the rental car. He glanced back over his shoulder at the turmoil going on at the carousel. "All that confusion will help us. Natalie will be expecting there to be a body on that carousel, and there's definitely a body there. Maybe they'll think that there's some kind of mistake about its being a man."

Maybe. But Eve wasn't going to bet on it. Natalie had managed to slip out of any number of tight places, and she might be able to find a way out of this one. "And, if she thinks that we've arranged ahead of time to get Cara away from them, they may take a closer look at that treasure chest. They'll let loose all the dogs if she thinks we've cheated her."

"Without a doubt."

They'd reached the rental car and Jane already had the car started. "No Cara? What happened?"

"A case of Natalie major betrayal." Joe jumped in the backseat, and Eve followed him. "Not entirely unexpected. But it's not as bad as it could be."

"You don't have Cara." Jane pulled away from the curb. "That sounds pretty bad to me."

"But neither does Natalie," Eve said. "And Cara is alive. Natalie set up a shooter to kill her and hang the blame on us. But it didn't happen. It has to be Jock who screwed up her plans."

"Jock?" Jane looked at her in the rearview mirror. "He was there?"

"He was there," Eve said firmly. "He got to Cara first. He said he'd be there, and suddenly, there was no Cara. That's proof enough for me."

"And for me," Jane said. "We'll have to wait and see what he—" She stopped as her phone rang. "Caleb." She answered the call and pressed speaker. "No, it didn't go as well as we hoped," she said before he could speak. "But Jock has Cara, and we'll go on from there."

"Then may I suggest that you get the hell out of Moscow and let *him* go on from there," Caleb said. "My Gulfstream is at Skovski Airport north of the city. I'll be waiting for you."

"No," Eve said sharply. "I'm not leaving her here."

"Look. Our Natalie will be out to get you as soon as she finds out you've cheated her. She has all the cards on her side while she's in Moscow under her father's protection. If she manages to take you captive, she'll have a way to get Jock to give her Cara back."

"I'm not too sure of that," Eve said dryly. "Jock may not think I'm worth it."

"Then there will be a brouhaha to end all brouhahas," he said. "And that's not good either. Get out of there and trust Jock."

"*Trust me,*" Jock had said.

"Maybe." She looked at Joe. "But I won't go back to Scotland. No way."

"Then I'll fly you to Helsinki," Caleb said. "Finland

is an hour or less from Moscow. And you can wait there for word from Jock."

"Joe?"

"I want you out of here," Joe said roughly. "I saw her face when she was talking to you. It was like a cat toying with a mouse. You were willing to trust Jock before. Trust him now."

She thought about it. No, that wasn't the right word. She was agonizing about it. There was no way she wanted to leave Cara in this huge city, where Natalie had all the advantages. She wanted to find her, scoop her up, and take her home.

Advantages. That was the key word. And if Natalie managed to capture Eve, then that would be another advantage for her since Cara had a fixation on taking care of Eve.

"Stay clear," Caleb said. "And then go in and save the day. That's always been my favorite game plan."

But Caleb had not seen how fragile and pale Cara had looked sitting there in her pleated skirt and wool jacket, her hands folded on her lap.

Trust me.

All right, Jock, you'll get your way, but, dammit, you'd better pull it off.

"Okay, no more than an hour by jet away from here," she said. "If Finland is really only an hour, I'll leave Moscow."

"Done," Caleb said. "Bring them to me right away, Jane. By now, Ivan Sabak will know the airport you flew into, and they'll go there first."

"And that's why you wanted to take your own plane," Jane said. "Other than that, you always like to be in control."

"But I'm not in control. Eve made the decision. I just entered a humble plea. I'll see you in twenty minutes."

DROSTKEY PARK

"Follow me," Jock whispered as he crawled behind the bushes that bordered the refreshment stand. "No noise, Cara."

He didn't need to tell her that, she thought in panic. She was too scared to utter a word. She had been terrified from the minute that Jock had come out of that maintenance closet on the carousel. She had never seen him like that. He had moved with lightning speed, and she had not realized what he was doing until the man in the black jacket had grunted and fallen to the floor. He had killed him, she had realized dazedly. Jock had killed that man as easily as she would have snapped a pencil in two. Then he had dragged her back into the maintenance closet and covered her mouth with his hand.

A shot.

Two shots.

Screams.

Jock had dragged her to the floor and pulled her to the crawl space beneath the ornate seats, trains, and carousel horses. "Let's go. There will be a crowd, but they'll be looking at the body, not at us." He rolled out from beneath the carousel to the ground.

She rolled after him.

He grabbed her hand and started to crawl behind the shrubs. Jock was right. There was a big crowd, but no one was looking at them. They were all excited and chattering and looking in curiosity and horror at that man Jock had killed.

Don't be afraid.

Don't think about that man.

Don't think how easy that kill had been for Jock.

Just follow Jock.

Trust Jock.

"We're behind the refreshment stand now, and there are stairs that lead to a storage room on the second floor. Stay here and wait. I think it's safe, but I have to be sure." Jock moved up the stairs and disappeared inside. He came out a second later and motioned for her to come.

She almost ran up the stairs. She might have been a little frightened of him, but it was nothing compared to what she had felt without him.

"This is the safest place in the park for us right now." He drew her inside and put his fingers on his lips. "The refreshment stand closes at five," he whispered. "I think the owner is probably over at the carousel seeing what all the fuss is about, but we won't take the chance. We'll just sit here and not talk until we hear him closing up for the evening. Okay?"

She nodded and curled up against the wall. It was dim in this small room that had only the one window. It smelled of plastic cups and bitter chocolate.

There was something underneath her left palm.

She looked down and lifted her hand.

A shell casing.

She felt shock ripple through her. Her gaze flew to Jock's face.

He went still. Then he put up two fingers.

Two shots.

Somewhere in this storage room there was another shell casing from a shot fired at the carousel.

Had that shot been aimed at her?

Her gaze flew to Jock's face.

He nodded slowly.

Death. Someone had wanted her to die as she sat on that seat in the swan chair.

Natalie.

She closed her eyes tightly as she started to shake.

"No!" He was suddenly next to her, holding both her

hands. His voice was low and fierce. "Don't *look* like that. I had to tell you. Because I won't ever lie to you. Now hold on to me until it gets better."

Would it ever get better?

"Look at me."

She opened her eyes and looked up, and she was held, captured, by those shimmering gray eyes. Beautiful eyes. Jock's eyes. If she just kept looking at him, all the bad things would vanish, and they would be all right.

Her hands tightened on his.

Just keep looking at him . . .

"It's okay now. I heard them closing up downstairs." He tried to release her hands, but she wouldn't let him. He stopped, and said quietly, "You'll be fine. I know you. This was bad but you're already moving forward. I can feel it."

"That's more than I can feel," she said unsteadily. "I'm sorry . . . I should have—I didn't expect—" She drew a long, quivering breath. "I shouldn't be this weak. I'll try to do better."

"For God's sake, you watched a man killed in front of your eyes. You were almost killed yourself. I'd say that you deserve a little slack." His lips tightened. "But I can't give it to you. I warned you that you had to do exactly as I told you, and we have to move fast."

"Eve. You said this was about Eve and an exchange. Is Eve all right?"

"I think she's okay. She should be if she did what I told her to do. I was a little too busy to check. I'll call her and check once we're halfway out of this." He went over to the small window and gazed down at the carousel. "The police are there now, and they'll be reconstructing the crime. That means that they'll be coming here."

"Why didn't they come before? Why was it safe then and not now?"

"When I broke the neck of that guard who was watching you, I took his gun and threw it down beside him," Jock said coolly. "Any layman would assume that he fired the shots. But the police would realize that the bullet holes were made by a sniper and from this location."

"But it was safe here for us even though you knew that the shot was fired from here?"

"We weren't hiding from the police then. We were hiding from the people who hired the sniper. And they would know that the first thing a sniper does is get as far away as possible from the scene of the crime. They might be angry with him for screwing up the job, but they wouldn't go looking for him. Which left us with a place to hide while they searched the park for us."

"The people who—" She couldn't go on and she said, "So how do we leave here?"

"The way we came in. The way the sniper got out. Beyond those ornamental bushes in the back is a gate where the owners of the refreshment stand bring in their supplies. It saves them from going through the park." He got to his feet. "Come on, time to leave. Natalie is having hysterics and playing the bereaved mother with those police detectives down there at the carousel. She'll distract them for a few minutes while we get through the gate and a block down, where I parked my rental car." He pulled her to her feet. "Ready?"

She nodded. "Ready."

Don't think. Just do what he said. She followed him toward the door and down the stairs. It was dark now, but through the falling snow, she could see that the carousel lights were still on, and the music was playing. Shouldn't they have stopped the music? A man had died, and yet the music was still—

Jock had killed that man.

Her mind veered away from that thought. Don't think about that now. Later. She would think about watching that man die before her eyes later. Now she had to make sure Jock was safe. He had saved her, and she mustn't do anything that would cause him to be in danger.

Hurry.

Get him away from this park.

Then they were past the tall hedges, and Jock was opening the gate. He motioned to her, and she followed him out onto the street.

Don't think.

Just move.

Do what Jock was telling her to do.

She was half running down the street beside him.

Don't think . . .

CHAPTER
10

Cara didn't speak again until they were in Jock's car and had driven a few miles through the city. The snow was falling harder now, cocooning them in the car, and she felt somehow safer. "What happened back there?" She was trying to keep her voice steady. "Why . . . did they want to—"

"Kill you?" he finished. "The same reason that Natalie Castino wanted you dead before. She was afraid you knew too much and would be a threat to her."

"She said she had a surprise for me." Her lips were quivering. "Isn't that . . . funny?"

"Bitch." His voice was razor-sharp and laden with fury. "No, I can't say I think that's funny. Don't think about her. She's not worth it."

But how was she not to think about her? "Did Eve give her Cira's gold?"

"No, I believe she managed to trick her."

"Good." She had a second thought. "Or not so good.

She'll be angry. She'll want to do something terrible to her."

"I don't doubt it," Jock said. "But Eve has Quinn, and she has a hell of a lot of strength on her own. I believe she could face down the devil himself."

"Herself," Cara whispered.

Jock looked at her, then nodded. "Herself."

"And she shouldn't have to face Natalie. That's my job. She did everything to save me. I can't let it happen again."

"We'll talk about it later." Jock looked straight ahead. "You're not thinking straight right now. We'll go into it once we're out of Russia, and you're safe."

"I'm thinking straight," Cara said. "Eve tried to save me. You tried to save me. It's time I did something for myself."

Jock looked at her and shook his head. "Let it go. I don't need this right now."

She nodded. "I'll let it go."

"Until you decide to resurrect it." He made a face. "I know you too well, Cara."

"I'll let it go," she repeated. "Could we call Eve now?"

"I believe that's an excellent idea. It will take your mind off things I prefer you not to dwell on."

A man in a black-leather jacket falling to the floor of the carousel, his neck at an odd angle.

"Aye," Jock said, his gaze on her face. "That and many other things." He was dialing his phone. "And you need to know that she's safe and well." He put the phone on speaker. "Eve, tell Cara where you are so that it will put her mind at ease."

"At the moment, we've just landed at Helsinki. It's only an hour from Moscow, and we can come back if you need us." Eve rushed on, "You have Cara? She's safe."

"Not as safe as you are. But she will be, once we get

out of Moscow." He looked at Cara. "Most of the roads
will be blocked, so I'll try to take her over the hills to
the north. I'll let you know when we've reached somewhere we can be picked up." He handed Cara the phone.
"Cara wants to talk to you."

"Eve?" Cara rushed on, "Be careful of Natalie. She'll
want to hurt you. I think she probably does anyway, but
she'll be so angry now."

"Did she harm you, Cara?"

"No, I'm fine. But be careful, don't do anything to
make her more angry."

"I'm afraid we're past that point of no return now," Eve
said. "And I don't care as long as you're safe. So pay attention to Jock and let him get you home to me."

"I'll pay attention. He won't let me do anything else.
Good-bye, Eve." She handed the phone back to Jock.

"I'll let you know if we need a pickup," Jock said.
"Keep in touch." He hung up and looked at Cara. "As I
told her, it's not going to be easy getting out of the city.
We're going to have to do some hiking."

She remembered what he had told Eve. "Hills?" Cara
repeated. "You believe they won't expect us to go over
the hills?"

"It's a chance we have to take. We're safer than on the
roads. We're going to tackle the area where the tourist
department built ski resorts at the edge of the city. The
mountains were too far away for them, so they built their
own winter-sport centers. A few of them were pretty
impressive, and I've zeroed in on one that's promising.
Lascovic Ski Resort. It's been closed for the last eighteen
months. A few ski runs, but they mainly took advantage of the natural hiking and sledding trails. It's near
Khimki."

"Promising?"

"You'll see. Though I'm hoping they'll think we might

have gone on the plane with Eve. But I can't take any chances. Kaskov is going to button this city down. He's had decades to bring his bribes and influence peddling to state of the art in every government bureaucracy in Moscow. I imagine your photo will be all over the place."

"Not yours? When I asked Natalie about you, she said she didn't know who you were. So maybe you'll be safe."

"I'll bet she knows who I am now," he said dryly. "Ivan Sabak will have asked quite a few questions when Natalie's plot was blown. Someone will remember seeing me at the park the day before."

Yes, someone would remember Jock. How could they not remember him?

And that would mean his danger would be even greater.

"When do we leave?"

"We're on our way. I've got a change of clothes for us and equipment in the car. It wouldn't be unusual for a brother to take his little sister on a trip up there."

"You said they might recognize you."

"Then I'll deal with it."

A man's body in a black-leather jacket falling to the floor of the carousel.

He nodded as he saw her expression. "And I'll deal with that, too. Because I have no choice. But not until we both have a chance to assess the damage."

She didn't want to deal with it. She wanted to ignore it, to block it out.

He was shaking his head. "That would mean giving you up, and I won't do that." His gaze returned to the street. "So make up your mind, you have to face it. We both have to face it. That's just the way things are. I would have liked it to have gone differently, but it didn't happen . . ."

KASKOV ESTATE
MOSCOW

"This is the man?" Natalie gazed in fury down at the photo. "Who is he?"

"We think his name is Jock Gavin. We found a few vendors at the park who had security cameras on their booths and had shots of him on the day before the exchange." Sabak said savagely, "I'd like to slice that face to pieces."

"How do you know what his name is?"

"I checked out Eve Duncan and the people who were on the MacDuff treasure hunt. Jock Gavin was one of them. He's supposed to be very good."

She looked down at the photo. "He was good enough to make a fool of you. How could you let that happen?" she asked furiously. "Not only was Cara's guard killed, but she was whisked away before your sniper could finish his job. You kept telling me you had everything covered."

"I did have everything covered. It shouldn't have happened. But I don't believe that Cara or Jock Gavin left with Duncan. Not according to my informants at the airports. They must be somewhere in the city."

"But I was still left with a dead body that had no connection with either Cara or Eve Duncan. Now I have to find a way to explain that away to my father. Do you know how difficult that's going to be?"

"At least we have the chest with the coins."

"Do we?" She strode toward the front door. "Go to the car and bring that box in here. I want to see it. Everything else has gone wrong. I want to make sure that the chest isn't another mistake." A moment later, she watched him wrestle with the heavy box and drag it into the foyer. Her nails were digging into her palms as Sabak opened the wooden box, then the bronze chest. She walked forward as his hand dipped into the coins. "It seems all right," he said. "You said there were even some other coins like that drachma."

"Like it, not necessarily of equal value." Her voice was trembling with anger. "I think she wanted me to make the comparison." She bent over the coins and began to dig through them. "I think she might have—" She stopped as her fingers touched the bottom of the chest. Pure rage seared through her, so strong that she couldn't speak for a moment. "That *bitch*." She looked down at the false bottom. "I'm going to cut her throat. She's made a fool of me. She's going to die."

"We don't have the gold?" Sabak asked.

"You fool, of course we don't." Keep control, don't alienate Sabak. She was going to need him. "And I don't believe that it's just a question of her keeping a portion of the treasure for herself. I think she did a substitution on these coins." She could feel the heat sting her cheeks as she looked down at the coins. How dare Eve Duncan make a fool of her like this? Natalie always won. She couldn't remember a time when she hadn't come out on top.

Except this time.

Except with Eve Duncan.

"What are we going to do?" Sabak said.

"We're going to get what we bargained for," Natalie said. "And we're going to teach her that she can't cheat us." She slammed the chest shut. "In the most painful way possible." She turned to face him. "You said you thought Jock Gavin and Cara were still in Moscow?"

"That's what my informant said at the airport where Eve Duncan took off. Eve Duncan, Joe Quinn, Jane Mac-Guire, and Seth Caleb. No Gavin or the kid. As soon as I heard that, I spread the word that everyone be on the lookout for them."

"And you're going to find them," she said sharply.

"We're going to find Cara, then we'll see how clever Eve thinks she is. I'll show her that she can't try to make a fool of me."

"I'll find them," Sabak said. "This may be a big city, but it's a city that Kaskov controls. I'll hear, and I'll catch them. What are you going to do?"

"I'll take these coins in to some expert and have them appraised. Just to be certain. Then I'll talk to my father and see what I can do to explain away this nightmare."

"Don't involve me," Sabak said curtly. "I'm not going to go up against Kaskov unless I have to do it."

"I won't involve you," she said sarcastically. "Even though you managed to mess up a simple job that anyone should have been able to accomplish. I'll protect you." She looked him in the eyes. "And you'll protect me, or I'll make sure that my father finds out 'accidentally' that you were the one who was careless with his granddaughter. You wouldn't like his reaction to that. He regards Cara as his little pet, and I can point in the direction of Eve Duncan, or I can point at you. Do you understand?"

His lips tightened. "Yes."

"Good. Then we won't have any problems." She smiled. "And there's no reason why we can't still enjoy ourselves."

"There's a reason."

He turned and walked out the door.

She could not remember any man's walking out on her like that, she thought furiously. She had always been in control of any relationship. Why was she having trouble controlling Sabak?

Calm down. She had obviously made mistakes. She would go to Sabak later and make it right.

And she would have to be extremely careful in his handling from now on.

But she couldn't worry about it now. She had to concentrate on handling the most important person in her
world . . . and it wasn't going to be easy.

"You're angry with me, Daddy." Her hand tightened on
her phone as she made her voice tearful. "And you have
a right to be. I was only thinking of Cara. She was so sad
because you had left her and gone off on this trip. I just
wanted to cheer her up."

"And you got her shot at, then taken by that bitch,
Duncan." His voice was grim. "What were you thinking?
You kept telling me that you were so worried about her. It
doesn't look like it, Natalie."

"How can you say that? I'm so afraid of what that
woman will do to her." Her voice was panicky. "She actually had a sniper shooting at her. That poor little girl,
just having a good time on the carousel, then—"

"But that bullet didn't hit her," he interrupted. "So it
was probably a scare tactic. She thought she could intimidate you." He added coldly, "Well, she can't intimidate me. If you get a message from Duncan wanting
money or just a general threat, turn it over to me. I'll deal
with her."

"But she wasn't talking about money before, she was
just terribly angry." Her voice lowered to a whisper. "I
think she may have taken Cara to show me she could. But
I think she intends to kill her, Daddy."

"No," he said sharply. "I won't let her do that. She took
something of mine that I valued. I'll not let her keep it.
I'm going after her."

"Thank you. I knew I could count on you. But you
may have to resign yourself that Cara is—"

"I never resign myself to anything. How do you think
I've managed to stay on top? I can't leave Beijing right
now. I'm in the middle of negotiations. But I'm going to

call Sabak and tell him to pull out all the stops. I'll make sure that no one is going to be allowed to take Cara from the city."

"I already told him that, Daddy."

"He'll pay attention to me. You're only my daughter."

Only his daughter?

She smothered the rage that phrase ignited. "That's true, but I had to do what I could. When will you be back?"

"Two days. And by that time, Sabak may have found her." He added viciously, "And skewered that bitch, Duncan, and roasted her." He hung up.

Only his daughter. Would he have spoken so disparagingly about her before Cara had come on the scene? His entire reaction to her news had that same tone. No sympathy, just impatience. She'd done something that had deprived him of Cara, and he was angry and wanted only to get her back.

No time for Natalie.

No acknowledgment of her importance in his life.

That had to be changed, altered, erased as if it had never been.

And to do that, Cara had to be tragically killed before Kaskov got back to Moscow. Then everything would magically return to where it was before.

But just in case she might have lost him permanently, she had to see about Cira's gold and her chances of retrieving triumph from failure.

And punishing Eve Duncan for making a fool of her. Her father's idea of roasting Eve had definite merit, but she could do better than that. She had only to study what could hurt her the most, then go execute it. In fact, she already had an idea in the works.

But only two days to do it, so she wouldn't have to dodge around her father's machinations on his return.

She could manage it. She just had to solidify her base and go into high speed.

And her base was Ivan Sabak, who was even more important now than she had thought before.

She went in search of him.

LASCOVIC HILLS

"We're supposed to climb that?" Cara's eyes widened as she gazed up at the rugged, snow-covered hills towering above them. She could see snakelike hiking trails, but they appeared narrow and treacherous. "There's no other way?"

"There are other ways, but none that would allow us to get to a deserted area where Eve and Joe could land a helicopter without interference. You saw how closely the highways and side roads are being watched. Twice, we just barely managed to slip by a roadblock." Jock grimaced. "It appears that Kaskov has pulled in every favor and bribe that's owed him by the Moscow police and bureaucracy as well as working the underbelly of his fellow crime buddies." He added bitterly, "He really doesn't want to let you go. You've evidently charmed him."

"Not me. It's the music." She was still looking doubtfully up at the hills. "I've never done any climbing."

"You won't have to climb to the top. Most of the trails wind around and through the hills." He pointed to a small lodge with shuttered windows, and then at two manmade ski runs a short distance away. "The trail we'll be taking goes past the lodge and ski runs up into the hills, then down the other side. Though I won't lie, it's going to be a rough trip with all this ice and snow on the trails. It just started to snow in the city, but it's been snowing up here in these hills for days."

"It will be okay. You'll be there." She had changed to

boots, warm pants, and parka at the last gas station they had passed, and now she put up the hood. "I'll try not to slow you down."

"No problem." He smiled. "As you said, I'll be there for you." He set off walking down the trail. "It's going to get dark before we start down the other side. There's supposed to be a rest house near where the trail changes. We'll stay there for the night."

"You don't have to stop for me."

"I'm stopping for both of us. I don't want to take a chance of falling off that trail in the dark."

But she couldn't imagine Jock's falling off a mountain, much less these hills, she thought. Every step was light and springy and full of barely suppressed energy. On the other hand, she had been having trouble from the first yard or so. The trail was icy, and she had to watch her every step.

He glanced over his shoulder. "All right?"

She nodded. "I'll be fine." Concentrate. Don't fall. Don't give Jock any more trouble than she had to.

But she did fall—more than once. The first time he was there, pulling her to her feet. The next time she waved him away. "I'll do it." She struggled to her feet.

"How am I supposed to be there for you if you won't let me help?"

"You're for emergencies. Not stuff like this."

His lips tightened. "You're not going to change your mind?"

She shook her head. "We're in this together. I have to do my part."

"Have it your own way." He turned and strode down the trail.

He wasn't pleased. Well, she couldn't help it. She was already feeling guilty enough without having him baby her.

Though she could have used a little coddling the next time she fell . . . and the time after. Jock waited for her, but he didn't look back or offer to help.

She fell twice more before the trail did become more rocky and easier to negotiate during the next few hours. By that time, she was very tired and was only thinking of putting one foot in front of the other.

"Okay, we're here." Jock was suddenly beside her. "Right up ahead. I thought you were going to go right past it."

The rest house. A small cabin perched beside the trail that was blessedly now leading downward. "Are you sure we should stop? I could hold—"

"I'm sure," Jock said firmly as he took her arm and guided her toward the door. "Now be quiet until I can get you inside and warm. I'm considering that an emergency, even if you don't."

It wasn't, of course, and she should argue with him. But it seemed a little thing on the big scale. She gazed around her as he opened the door. It was getting dark, and the snow had a chill, bluish tinge in the half-light. Chill. Yes, it was becoming colder, too, as night fell.

Jock pulled her inside and slammed the door. "Go sit down on that heap of blankets in the corner while I light the oil stove." He was already piling logs from a brass storage rack beside the fireplace onto the grate. In a moment, he had a blazing fire growing, and he turned to the stove. He had to clean out the interior, but in ten minutes she could feel the heat begin to pulsate through the room. He turned to face her. "Thank God you didn't decide to make a statement about this. I've had about enough."

"I wouldn't have done that. I might have gotten in your way, and that's not the point at all." She rubbed her eyes. "Are we going to eat soon? I think I'm hungry."

"I'll see what I can do." He took off his knapsack and

rummaged in the backpack. "I seem to have jerky, crackers, health bars, and some old-fashioned Spam and brie cheese. Choose."

"Cheese and crackers." She pushed her hood off. "But I have to go out and wash my hands. I'll be right back."

His lips twitched. "Such a polite, well-behaved, girl."

"Elena used to tell me that cleanliness was healthy, and we had to keep clean if we were going to be healthy enough to keep running."

"Now that was an inspiring life lesson to teach a little girl," he said dryly.

"She taught me what I had to know to keep alive," she said soberly as she opened the door. The cold air struck her sharply after the warmth of the cabin. "I don't know about inspiring."

Then she was outside, dipping her hands into the clean, icy snow. A moment later, she was hurrying back into the cabin. "It's almost completely dark out now. It was so strange that it happened that—"

"Give me your hands." Jock was there, meeting her at the door, taking her hands and rubbing them vigorously with the corner of one of the blankets she'd previously been sitting on. "This blanket isn't too clean, but you'll have to put up with it. At least, they'll be warmer now." He held her hands a moment after he'd finished. "I didn't mean to be flip. I know your Elena taught you to stay alive," he said quietly. "And I thank God every day for her." He turned away. "Now sit down and eat. You need to get some sleep. All that flopping around on the trail had to be exhausting."

"Flopping around," she repeated. "If I'd flopped, I wouldn't be this sore. I hit hard every time."

"I have no sympathy."

"Yes, you do. Or you wouldn't have gotten so mad at

me." She was eating the cheese and crackers. "It made you angry that I wouldn't let you help me."

He opened the Spam. "Did it?"

"You know it did."

"I just didn't want to have to deal with you after all of this hits home. I thought that if you didn't have such a rough trip, you'd be more likely not to be upset at the end of the day."

"I don't know what you mean. I'm fine, Jock."

He started to eat.

"I'm fine," she repeated.

"If you say so." He kept on eating.

"And I wouldn't make you deal with me even if I wasn't. I'd hate that."

"Then we won't talk about it. Just finish eating and I'll try to find us some semiclean bedding among those blankets. Providing you don't mind if I deal with that problem."

"I don't mind." She was suddenly exhausted and cold even in this warm room. "Whatever."

He looked up at her, his gaze narrowed on her face. "Aye. Whatever."

The shot splintering the beak of the wooden swan beside her.

Jock beside the man in the black-leather jacket, twisting his neck.

Jock holding up two fingers as she looked down at the shell casing.

The carousel going round and round, the music that was no music blaring.

Natalie's beautiful smile beaming down at her. "I'll have a surprise for you, Cara."

A surprise.

Death.

The carousel going round and round and round.

"Get on the carousel. I'll have a surprise."

Cold. So cold. Cold eyes. Such a cold heart.

She was shaking. She couldn't stop shaking. So cold. How could anyone be that cold?

"Stop it," Jock said roughly. "Wake up. I can't take it anymore." He was suddenly beside her, dragging her up his body to lie against him. He said between his teeth, "I *won't* take it."

He was warm in a world that was ice-cold.

She opened her eyes. "I . . . don't think . . . I was asleep."

"I was hoping that you were." He was pushing her head down to his chest. "Though, if you were, I woke you up because I evidently didn't give a damn. I was more concerned with myself than you."

"I'm glad. I was so cold . . . Jock. The whole world was cold. The carousel . . ."

He went still against her. "The carousel?"

"I have a little . . . surprise for you. She said that . . . so cold. So cold."

"I'm certain that a number of things struck you as . . . cold about the carousel."

"Yes. The whole world . . ."

"I had to kill him, Cara. I had no choice. It had to be fast and clean because I knew what was coming next. I didn't want to do it in front of you, but I'm not sorry."

He wasn't talking about Natalie, Cara realized hazily. It was the man in the black-leather jacket. "His neck . . . was funny."

"Aye." He paused. "I suppose you'll have nightmares about it. I told you once that I wasn't a good man. I didn't think I'd have to demonstrate how bad I really am. But that was a different world, wasn't it?"

Gaelkar. Mist on the lake. Mountains in the distance.

Eagles soaring high. A different world. But she shouldn't be thinking of those things right now, she realized. Because there was pain in Jock, and she should try to heal it.

"Not bad. Sad. Very sad. And shining . . ."

"You never give up, do you? I thought seeing me in the act would do it for you." His hand cradled her head. "You will give up someday, you know."

She shook her head. She was beginning to come awake, and there was something else she should say. "When Joe Quinn was trying to save Eve and me from that man who was hunting me down, I knew that Joe would probably kill him. It would be the only way to save us. Does that make Joe a bad man?"

"It's not the same thing."

"Because you think you have a wicked soul, and Joe doesn't?"

He didn't answer.

She was silent, staring into the fire. "I . . . was . . . It came as a shock when I saw you do that. I will probably always remember it. But that was because it was you, not because it was evil. Killing is always evil. I learned that a long time ago when my sister, Jenny, was killed. But she sacrificed herself for me and Elena. So if the opportunity would have been there, would I have killed to protect her?" She nodded. "I think so, Jock."

"You're a kid. You shouldn't have to be thinking about things like that," he said roughly.

"Jenny was nine. You have to protect the people you care about."

"Not like I do."

"Maybe not. Because it hurts you more than other people. And every time you kill, I'll hate it. Because I'll know how much it's hurting you. But I won't hate you, Jock. I'll never hate you. Because it would be like hating myself." She said with sudden fierceness, "And I *won't* do that. No matter what. Because I don't deserve it. Do you understand?"

"No, I don't," he said unsteadily. "Let's stop all this talk about hating yourself. You must be a bit woozy from hitting that ice so hard."

She nodded and tried to smile. "That must be it. So we should both stop being so serious. We were talking about you, not me."

"Were we?" He was silent for a moment. "That's right, the conversation is always about me. Never about you, Cara. I find that very curious."

"Not so curious. You lead a much more interesting life than I do."

"Really? Yet I'd say being chased by killers and kidnapped and being—"

"You know what I mean."

"You mean you'd like to ignore what I'm trying to get at and skip to something else. I'm not going to let you do that, Cara."

"Please let me do it." She steadied her voice. "Remember, you said you didn't want to deal with me after all of this hit home. I don't want you to have to do it either. Let's just forget about it and go to sleep."

"Too late. Talk to me. I shouldn't have said I didn't want to deal with it. I was just hurting, watching you struggling, and it made me angry."

"But you were right, I shouldn't have—"

"Talk. You were very defensive about never hating yourself. That's an odd thing for a kid like you to say. Was it because you heard someone else say that you should?"

"Listen to you." She raised herself on one elbow to look down at him. "You're all ready to go out and beat somebody up just because I said something in the wrong way."

"I don't beat people up, Cara. It's all or nothing. So convince me it should be nothing."

She stared at him in frustration. He wasn't going to give up. And she was too tired and sore and on edge to fight him any longer. She buried her face in his shoulder again. "She . . . hates me, Jock. I knew it before. One night I was playing for Kaskov, and I looked up and saw it on her face. I . . . didn't know what to do. I couldn't understand why. I knew she wanted to have me there to use in some way. That she probably didn't care for me even though she was my mother. But I didn't know about the hate. I couldn't understand what I'd done to deserve it. I thought you had to be a bad person to have someone hate you." Her voice was suddenly fierce. "I'm *not* a bad person, Jock. I didn't deserve it."

"Shh, of course you didn't." His hand was threaded in her hair. "No one could ever—"

"Don't *say* that. She *does* hate me. She tried to kill me. She was smiling and saying she had a surprise for me. And she meant she was going to kill me."

"Will you let me talk? I was going to say that no one in their right mind would ever hate you." He was silent. "I remember you said she said that to you. About the surprise. What a sick bitch. And you should know just from that bit of ugliness that she isn't in her right mind."

"Everybody who doesn't like somebody else isn't always crazy. I guess the same thing goes for hating. Natalie doesn't seem crazy. Sometimes she's smart about stuff."

"But there are some people who aren't able to—" He stopped, feeling his way. "Eve told us once that she thought Natalie was a classic sociopath. Do you know what that is?"

She shook her head.

"It's someone who has no empathy for other people

though they may pretend. They also have no conscience. If they are clever, they do everything possible to hide it and blend in with the population. Because it's all about them and getting what they want."

"Natalie." She added, "And that's crazy, too?"

"It can be. Because it leads them to do things most of us wouldn't consider doing."

"I . . . was thinking . . . that maybe Natalie . . . might . . . have done something . . . bad to her brother, Alex. I tried not to think that was true, but could she have—She wanted him out of the way." She moistened her lips. "And then something happened with Kaskov . . . and her brother was gone. Could she have hated him, too, and wanted him dead?"

"No one would be exempt. She'd believe she was the only one of any importance." He muttered a curse. "I only wanted release for you, but I seem to have opened a can of worms. I had no idea all of this was stored up inside you."

"I've been living with her. Watching her to see how I could get away and go back to Eve. Sometimes she hides things, sometimes she doesn't. I don't believe she thought I was important enough for her to try very hard." She swallowed. "And the music made her angry because she thought that it made me seem important."

"Not seem. It makes you very important to anyone but her. With or without the music, you're important, Cara. Don't ever forget it."

She was silent, then said, "You're wrong, it's the music that's important. I'm only important when I'm playing it. But I'm not a bad person." Her hand clenched on his. "I won't be like her, Jock. She said I was her daughter, and she expected me to do the things she'd do. Just because she's my mother, she thought I'd—"

"Hush." He drew her closer. "She may have given birth

to you, but you're not her daughter. You were born with your own soul, and she wasn't able to taint it. It's still as clean and wonderful as it was on that day. And it will be your soul, with your choices, for the rest of your life. Your friend, Elena, was more your mother than Natalie was." He paused. "And your sister, Jenny, gave her life for you. Do you think she would have done that if she had one bit of Natalie in her soul? That should prove it to you."

Your soul, with your choices.

She stared at him in shock.

She hadn't realized until he had spoken those words how heavy the burden had been that Natalie had thrust upon her. All the horror that Natalie had been for her, and to her, was nothing beside the fear that, somehow, Natalie could reach inside Cara and manage to change what she was. Because that would also destroy the music.

But if what Jock had said was true, it changed everything.

Freedom.

She couldn't speak, all she could do was lie there, holding him.

Your soul, with your choices.

Strength. She had never felt more strong. Or more her own person even though that strength had come from him.

"You're not talking. Am I getting through to you?"

"You're getting through to me." She raised her head and smiled at him. "Why not? Sometimes you're very smart, Jock."

"I'm glad that you realize that," he said warily. "I must have done something fairly good this time. I was afraid we had something serious to contend with."

"Nah, that shining knocked it right out." She was shifting over to her own blankets. "And I'm sorry you had to deal with all this stuff. I'll try not to bother you like that again."

"Friends should bother each other if there's a problem. And it's not as if an eleven-year-old shouldn't feel free to talk to anyone if—"

"Twelve."

"What?"

"I'm twelve now. I had a birthday after I came to Moscow. Not that I feel any older. Elena said every year was a milestone, but I never knew what that meant."

"It means that every year means something, even if we don't know what it is. And every year from now on will have a special significance for both of us."

"Because we're friends."

"Aye. Friends," he said gently. "Happy birthday, Cara. I'm sorry I didn't know you'd had a birthday. I'll be sure to give you a gift once we're somewhere civilized."

"Thank you." She closed her eyes and bunched up the blankets beneath her head to make them softer. "But you don't have to give me a gift," she said drowsily. "You already did that, Jock . . ."

CHAPTER
11

Cara was up before Jock and was adding wood to the fire when he sat up in his blankets.

"You slept well," he said quietly. "I woke a couple times and checked on you. I was afraid after that upset that you might have a problem."

"You're always afraid I'm going to have problems," she said as she sat back on her heels after stoking the flames. "I suppose that I shouldn't be surprised since I've caused so much trouble for everyone lately. You wouldn't be here if I hadn't run after you and tried to bring you back." She looked into the fire. "But I'd probably do it again. I'd just be smarter and not get caught by the bad guys."

"Eve and I discussed blame after Natalie took you, and we agreed that it was pretty well shared all around. You were just the one who paid the penalty." He shook his head. "But not again, Cara, I couldn't go through that again." He got to his feet. "Now I'm going to go out and check on the trail, then we'll have something to eat and start out. I checked the weather, and it should be clear for a while. But it's going to get progressively worse as the day goes on. But I believe we'll make it to the plateau where we can be met before the storm actually hits."

"And when will that be?"

"Four, five hours. If all goes well."

"It will go well, I know it." She stood up and followed him to the door. "So many bad things . . . it's time that something went right. You'll make them right, Jock. And I'll help." She opened the door. "And you'll let me help because friends share everything, don't they?"

"So I've heard though we both have limited experience in that area." He watched her go out in the snow and wash her face in the cold snow. "You appear to be full of optimism at the moment. Not what I expected."

She glanced at him over her shoulder. "I've been running all my life. I'm tired of being afraid and having you and other people I love having to protect me and keep me safe. There have to be things I can do not to have to rely on other people. I just have to find them."

"Very laudable. I don't know why it fills me with such uneasiness."

"I don't either." She smiled. "You would do the same thing."

"That's different."

She looked at him.

He shook his head. "Don't dive into all this independence headfirst. I realize you're all of twelve years old now, but you need to strike a balance." He started down the trail. "And don't stay out here too long in the cold. We have a long trip, and you don't want to start off with hypothermia."

"Jock."

He shrugged. "It will take a long time, if ever, that I'll

be able to look at you and not see you in the crosshairs. Accept it."

She gazed after him. So much pain and torment. She would accept it, but last night, he'd given her a new lease, and she wouldn't let that go. She'd just have to find a way to give him the same freedom.

Her hands were red and beginning to tingle, and so were her cheeks. She made a face as she turned back to the cabin. Time to go back in so that Jock wouldn't say I told you so if she got a touch of hypothermia.

"Four or five hours," Jock told Eve when he called her from the trail. "Will you be able to make it? I know you said you're within an hour of Moscow, but Caleb is going to have to do some flying below the radar to avoid leading anyone to us. You'll have to time it just right because the minute they get an unidentified aircraft on the radar, they'll start to try to pinpoint our location. The weather is going to be fairly rough for us going down the trail, but by the time we reach the plateau the full storm shouldn't have hit yet."

"We'll make it. We'll start out right away." She paused. "How is Cara doing, Jock?"

"Physically, fine, except for bumps and bruises. Mentally? She had to face some hard truths about Natalie and the concept about mother-daughter relationships when you're the daughter of a nutcase like Natalie."

"Dear God," Eve said. "And she had to learn it all herself. I didn't tell her before Natalie took her because it was never the right time. It's a wonder that she managed to survive Natalie."

"Cara's strong. She was hurt and bewildered and questioning, but she made it through."

"Because you were with her. I'm relieved you were there, Jock. I wish it had been me."

"I did okay." He paused. "But we didn't get to the point where we discussed the fact that Natalie actually was responsible for Jenny's and Elena's deaths. You might have to deal with that soon. Or maybe it will just come to her as she works her way through all this. She's bouncing back hard and fast."

"I'll do whatever I have to do." She said, "Just as you did. Caleb is on the phone telling them to ready the helicopter. We've got to leave. I'll let you know if we run into trouble on the way to you."

"Likewise." He hung up.

He looked back down at the winding trail. It wasn't snowing yet, and he'd been on worse trails. But it was a long trek and going to be rough on Cara.

Stop looking and go ahead and tackle it. Go get her, make sure she was fed, and as warmly dressed as possible and get on the road.

He turned and headed back to the rest house.

"Finish that health bar while I put out this fire," Jock said. "And then make sure your gloves are dry and so are your socks."

"You're being very careful."

"We need to move fast. I don't want anything to hold us up."

"I won't hold you up," she said quietly. "That's all over. You said there wouldn't be much more ice. I'm not used to ice. That's why I kept falling." She smiled. "I spent most of my life in California. Not much ice in California unless you're in the mountains. Elena could never afford to take me to the mountains."

"That didn't occur to me. Why didn't you mention it?"

"It didn't matter. It was still my job to stay on my feet." She checked her gloves. "I was wondering, what kind of mother did you have, Jock?"

"What?" He turned to look at her.

"You know about Natalie. I was wondering what your mother was like. Good? Bad?"

"Far better than I deserved. A mother like Natalie is rare in the scheme of things. Most of them are loving, kind, wanting the best for their children."

"That's what I'd always heard. That's why Natalie confused me." She paused. "But your mother, Jock. She couldn't be better than you deserve. Not if she was kind and loving. You deserve that."

His lips twisted. "I put her through hell. I was a wild lad who turned into the worst kind of monster imaginable after Reilly got hold of me. Through it all, she never gave up on me." He added curtly, "But I gave up on her. After MacDuff brought me back from the hell Reilly had sent me to, I never saw her again until the day she died."

"No," she said, shocked. "That wasn't right, Jock."

"Would it have been right to inflict a stranger on her? I wasn't the child she'd raised. He'd been destroyed somewhere along in the process. She kept sending me messages through MacDuff, and every now and then I'd think perhaps—But I couldn't stand her looking at me and being hurt again. So I let her get on with her life."

"You were wrong," she murmured. "It wouldn't have hurt her to see you, she would have seen the shining, too. I know it, Jock."

He shook his head. "You're daft, Cara. There is no shining. I just had to spare her as much as I could from everything I'd become."

"And it hurt you to do that. You loved her."

"Aye. But not as much as it would have been to see her pain." He rose to his feet and crossed to stand in front of her. He put up her hood and tied it under her chin. "Stop fretting. It was a long time ago." He checked her

gloves. "And I was luckier than I deserved to be to have
a mother who loved me as long as she did. Some mothers are like that. No sense. On the whole, a very peculiar
breed." He opened the door and gave her a gentle nudge.
"Now let's get down out of these hills, so that you can
see your Eve again. She was concerned that she had to
leave you to my less-than-subtle psychological probing.
I believe she wants to check you for damage."

"No, you have to be joking. She sees what I see." She
started down the trail. "What your mother would have
seen if you'd given her the chance. She would have tried
to heal you. She might have done it, Jock."

"Or I might have destroyed her." He shook his head.
"As I said, it was a long time ago . . ."

KASKOV ESTATE
MOSCOW

"I've just received word that a suspect aircraft entered
Moscow airspace thirty minutes ago." Ivan strode into
the living room. "A small, private plane or helicopter that
could be the one we're looking for." He handed Natalie
the slip of paper. "As soon as they get a closer look at it
and get an aircraft number, we'll be able to verify. If it's
Duncan, we'd have a chance of shooting it down if she
tries to land."

"Of course she'll try to land," Natalie said impatiently.
"But we don't want her taken down until after she picks
up Cara." She looked at the sheet of paper. "When will
we have an idea where she's heading?"

"Right now the aircraft is traveling north. Unless she
changes direction." He added, "We may not know until
the last minute. But I'll make a guess and position men
anyway."

"We have to find her soon," Natalie said sharply. "My father will be home tomorrow evening, then he'll be in control. We won't be able to hide anything that's been going on. The only way to salvage any of this is to make sure Cara isn't able to talk to him."

"We'll find her." Ivan shrugged. "And the aircraft will be shot down as Duncan tries to take Cara away from you and her loving grandfather, Kaskov. And you will shed tears, and Kaskov will be angry." He gazed at her coolly. "And I will have gone to a lot of trouble and still not have the gold. I want you to fix that problem, Natalie."

"Don't tell me what I must do. I can't do anything until we take care of the girl. I'll think of something." She was still staring down at the paper. "They haven't found Jock Gavin's rental car yet?"

"No, they have to be staying off the main roads. Gavin is very smart. He knows exactly what he's doing. The police haven't even had a sighting of the two of them since I gave them a description." He tapped the paper. "But this could point the way for us. It should only be a little longer . . ."

It was starting to snow harder now.

Cara could barely see anything on either side of the trail.

But she could see Jock.

She kept her eyes straight ahead, fixed on his back.

Keep close to him.

Don't make him slow down because of her.

The snow would melt, then refreeze, and she'd have that ice again. She could only hope she'd do better the second time around.

So cold. The snow was stinging her cheeks.

Put one foot in front of another.

Keep close to him.

She had to do her part.

She was strong. She could do anything if she tried hard enough.

Her own soul . . .

Keep close to him.

KASKOV ESTATE

"We've located the rental car," Ivan said. "It was half-buried behind a large snow-removal truck in a garage at a ski resort." His index finger stabbed a location on the map in front of Natalie. "Here. It's Laskovic Ski Resort in the hills near Khimki. It's been closed for repairs for the last eighteen months. One caretaker. He was the one who found the rental car."

"They're at this resort?" she asked eagerly.

"Somewhere on the property. I've sent men to search the area. We'll know soon." He smiled savagely as he stared down at the map. "I told you I'd find them." He took out his phone. "Now we check and see how close that aircraft is to those hills."

"You check." She jumped to her feet. "I'm going to drive there and make sure there aren't any slip-ups." She was calling over her shoulder as she headed out the door. "If we're this close, there's no way I'll let Duncan get her hands on Cara."

"How near, Caleb?" Eve asked, her eyes on the whirling snow driving against the windshield of the helicopter. "And is this damn snow going to stop us? It looks like it's getting heavier."

"It will be close," Caleb said. "But we'll make it, if we don't run into trouble." He added quietly, "Jock said that he thought the same thing, remember? And he wouldn't risk Cara in this weather if he wasn't pretty certain he could get her out."

"You can never be certain of the weather," Joe said. "It's always a risk."

"Still, I'd lean toward Jock," Caleb said with a smile. "He can be fairly uncanny on many levels."

"The pot calling the kettle black?"

"I don't care about kettles and pots," Eve said impatiently. "How close are we to that mountain?"

"Forty-five minutes," Caleb said. He added gently as he saw her expression, "And if Jock says that the weather will hold until we get them out, believe him." He banked the helicopter. "Now let me see if I can nudge a little more speed out of this copter so that we can hedge his bet . . ."

"They're nowhere in the resort itself," Ivan said as he came back to the car where Natalie was waiting. "And all the ski lifts are shut down. But there's a trail that leads through the hills past a plateau. It's rough country. There would be no one to see if there's a helicopter pickup. That could be a possibility."

"How good a possibility?"

"The only one we have," Ivan said flatly. "That helicopter was near here on the last sighting. I'm calling that plateau as the target." He started across the snowbanked resort entrance. "And I'm phoning to another ski resort in the hills about thirty miles from here and arranging to get several bobsleds to get us down that trail to the plateau very fast. If you want to go along, be ready when they get here. I'm not waiting for you."

Son of a bitch, she thought viciously, as she jumped out of the car. Arrogance on top of arrogance. She couldn't wait to punish him for that ugliness to her. Keep cool. Not yet.

"Of course I'll be ready," she said sweetly. "We both realize how important it is that we cooperate with each other. You're doing everything that's needed, and I appreciate it." She jammed her hands into her pockets. "After this is over, we have to work to get back on track. It was Duncan who caused all this disturbance. Everything will be fine again once we get rid of her."

"Will it?"

"Do you doubt me?"

"Yes." He was silent. "But you're a great lay, and if you show me that gold, I might get over the way you treated me."

"Oh, I do hope so. I'm only a woman, and I realize I've made mistakes." She smiled. "I'll surely try to make you happy, Ivan."

"There's the plateau," Jock said quietly.

He had turned around on the trail and was watching Cara come toward him. She had been so numb with weariness that she hadn't been aware that he had stopped.

It was over?

Relief.

The plateau was only a blur of white in the falling snow. All of that effort and pain, and she could barely see the result.

No, the result was that she had made it, that she hadn't failed Jock.

That was enough.

He was frowning and walking back to her. "Okay?"

She nodded jerkily. "Tired." She laid her head on his chest. "So tired. But I made it, didn't I? Pretty darn good for a kid from California."

He held her close. "Aye, you did. Pretty darn good. How do you feel, other than tired?"

"Strong." She nestled closer. "Though I had to start

making up my own music about halfway here to keep going. I can usually hear it, but I was having trouble."

"Imagine that."

"But I kept telling myself that I owned my own soul, and a soul has choices. I made this choice, and I was going to take it all the way." She stayed close to him a few seconds more. He felt warm and strong, and she didn't want to let that go. Then she stepped back. "When will they get here?"

"Anytime now. I received a text from Caleb that they were in the area fifteen minutes ago. I'll call and tell him that we've—" He stopped as his phone rang. "Caleb." He picked up. "I was just going to—"

"How close are you?" Caleb interrupted.

"We're on-site."

"Stay there. We'll be there within five minutes." Caleb's voice was clipped. "And hope that someone isn't there ahead of us. As we flew over that resort, it was teeming with people, a couple of police cars, two very stylish dark sedans. And several bobsleds getting set to go down the trail. I'd say they know you're there. I thought I'd warn you."

"You've warned me." Jock gazed back up the trail they'd just traveled. "Just get here and get her out. I can cover you." He hung up. "Cara, get to those rocks." He pulled Cara off the trail and toward the rocky outcroppings that bordered the trail. "Stay low. They'll be here in five minutes. There's not going to be any time after they land. The door opens, you jump for it."

"They've found us? That's what you were talking about?" Her heart was beating hard as she watched him lift his binoculars to his eyes and look back up the trail. And she'd remembered something else he'd said. "You said you'd cover us. You want me to go without you?"

He'd lowered his binoculars. "You'd just get in my

way. There are five or six men in bobsleds on that upper trail. Those sleds travel fast, anywhere from a hundred miles per hour to sometimes double that. It's going to be close." He was opening his backpack and pulling out a disassembled automatic rifle. He clipped it together quickly and efficiently. "I can take care of myself, but you'll be a bother from now on. I'm turning you over to Eve and company."

"Liar. Stop lying to me."

"I'm not lying. This is what I do. What I am." His head rose. "I hear the helicopter. Go out to the middle of the plateau and wait for them."

She stayed where she was.

"Move." He slung the weapon over his shoulder. "Or I'll carry you."

She shook her head. "Enough people have risked their lives for me. I'm not going without you. If you make me fight you, you could get me killed. And I guarantee that I'll make you hurt me."

Jock stared at her, then shook his head. "Cara."

She raised her head to look at the sky. "That helicopter sounds like it's right on top of us. You'd better get me out there." She held out her hand to him. "Take me to them, Jock."

He looked at her in frustration and muttered a curse. He grabbed her hand and half pulled her, half ran her, out to the landing helicopter. He opened the door, and Joe was there waiting.

Joe held out his hand to Cara. "Get in. Those snow vehicles will be within range in seconds."

She didn't take his hand. "Jock, first."

"Dammit." Jock dove into the helicopter, and said through his teeth, "*Get* in here, Cara."

She took Joe's hand and let him pull her into the aircraft.

The next moment, the helicopter was lifting off the plateau.

Not soon enough.

A bullet struck the rim of the door.

Jock pushed her roughly aside, unslung his rifle and positioned himself to the side of the door. "You've had your way, now let me have mine." He called to Caleb, "I'll get rid of that first snow sled. It should give you time to get away from these hills."

The helicopter was dipping, bouncing, but Jock appeared to be rock steady.

He started to shoot, the automatic weapon firing a steady stream that tore up everything in its path, then it reached the snow sled.

He destroyed it, glass, plastic, metal.

A moment later, he hit the gas tank, and the vehicle blew.

Cara could feel the shock wave, and she saw the sled explode.

"Cara."

Eve was beside her, Cara realized.

"Come and sit down, Cara," Eve said gently.

"Eve." She went into her arms as Eve held her close.

Safety. Warmth. Love.

Eve stepped back. "Come on. We need to get you buckled into a seat, Cara."

Cara nodded jerkily. "If Jock is finished with me now. Are you done, Jock?"

He turned and looked at her. "It's what I do. It's what I *am*."

"It's not true. You're angry, and you wanted to show me, but it's not true." She turned back to Eve. "I do want to sit down. I'm tired. I walked a long way." It seemed a long time ago that she had been so happy about that victory. "What about that snowstorm? Do we have to worry?"

"We have to worry." Eve pushed her down in a seat and sat down beside her. "But now that we've got you, that doesn't seem as important."

Cara knew what she meant. Risks all around them, but she was here with all the people she cared about who had become her life. All but one. "Where's Jane?"

"We dropped her off at an airport about eighty miles from here. She's going to rent a plane so that we can trade off this copter for it and make some speed getting back to Finland to pick up Caleb's Gulfstream." Eve's fingers smoothed Cara's hair back from her face. "I imagine that you're anxious to do that. It's been pretty much of a nightmare for you."

"I'm the one who caused the nightmare, Eve. I've caused you so much trouble." She looked across the copter at Jock, who was talking to Joe. "Caused him so much trouble. I'll do better from now on. I promise you."

"Hush. Now isn't the time for anything but being grateful that we're all alive and together. We'll worry about the rest later." The copter gave a jerk and lost altitude. "Oops. Along with getting to Jane and that airport safely. I believe that storm has hit us at last."

Fire!

Natalie could feel the heat of the flames from the burning pyre of the vehicle that had just blown up ahead of them. She frantically crawled through the snow, away from the wreckage. The blast had not only destroyed the vehicle in front of them but overturned their own vehicle and dumped her in the snow.

And she could see Eve's helicopter flying away from her.

Humiliation.

Fury.

It was unbearable.

"Ivan!"

She saw him talking to the men in the next vehicle, gesturing to the departing helicopter.

Instead of paying attention to her.

Another humiliation.

"Ivan!"

He gave her a casual glance and kept on talking.

She wanted to scream.

To curse that woman who had taken Cara, who had made a fool of Natalie when no one could make a fool of her. Who had stolen *her* gold and endangered her relationship with her father. Who had made her turn to that simpleton, Ivan Sabak, for help because there was no one else.

That woman, that supreme bitch.

Eve Duncan.

She *hated* her. She had hated people before but not like this. It was twisting inside her, burning like that hot metal.

Natalie sat there in the snow, ignoring everything going on around her, watching the burning of the vehicle, no longer in a hurry to race after Duncan. She knew it would be too late now. Cara's precious Eve had won.

Phoenix. The flames reminded her of that opera her father had made her attend with him years ago. Something about some silly bird being resurrected from the flames. From defeat to triumph. Death to life.

Don't rest easy, Eve. Always look behind you.

Because, when you least expect it, I'll be there.

The snow was slightly abating by the time Caleb landed the helicopter at the airport where they'd dropped Jane off.

Jane gave Cara an enormous hug and smiled at Jock. "You did it. Congratulations."

"Let's get going." Jock turned away. "We're not out of the woods yet." He strode toward the waiting jet. "We're still on their territory."

Jane's brows rose as she gazed after him. "A little tense? I guess he has a right."

"He's angry with me," Cara said. "It's not you." She hurried after Jock and caught up with him as he was boarding the plane. "I was right," she said desperately. "You were wrong. I had to do it. I can't let you take care of me forever. Not if it means losing you."

He shrugged and finished climbing the steps. "It's not the time to discuss it. Get on board. This time I'm not going to plead with you to do it. I'll leave that to Eve."

"You didn't plead with me."

"Didn't I? That's what it felt like."

She watched him walk down the aisle and sit down beside Joe and Eve.

"He'll get over it." Jane was standing beside her. "Though I admit I'm surprised. You're the one person that I thought would never be subject to Jock's anger."

"I'm changing. He doesn't like it." She dropped down in her seat, her agonized gaze still on Jock. "I didn't know it would happen like this. He helped me so much . . . what he said to me . . . it was a gift . . . but it brought other things with it. And now he's angry. It hurts . . . Jane."

"I can see that." She took Cara's hand. "And that's all I can see. It's between you and that wild Scot and always will be. You'll have to work it out for yourselves. But I'm here for you, if you need me." Caleb was starting to taxi and she buckled her seat belt and reached over and did the same for Cara. "All I can suggest is that you focus on something else. He's not your whole world any longer. I can understand how in these last days it must have seemed that way."

It still seemed that way, Cara wanted to tell her. But

she was right, there was Eve, whom she had promised to take care of and then became lost along the way. She was being selfish worrying about Jock's anger. "I never even asked Eve where we were going from here."

"Back to Gaelkar for a little while." She smiled. "MacDuff has done us some major favors and been injured in the process. He deserves to have our help in finding out whether Cira's treasure is somewhere in that mist." She added, "And Joe thinks it will be safer for you there until we find a way of getting you totally free of Natalie's clutches. Possession may be nine-tenths of the law, but Immigration may still be set on returning you to her."

"No!"

"It won't happen," Jane said quietly. "No one is going to let you go back to her. Believe me, Jock may have been your entire world over here, but we've all been fighting for you in our own ways. I think you should know about that, too."

Cara listened in stunned silence as Jane related all that had been happening that had led up to Drostkey Park. "All that trouble . . ."

"No," Jane said firmly. "All that caring. There's a difference. It's never trouble if you care enough. I think you've already discovered that truth."

She nodded slowly, still bemused. "But all my life I've had Jenny and Elena, then no one. It seems strange that you all would want to—Oh, maybe Eve, but it causes so much—"

"Trouble?" Jane finished with a smile. "You'll just have to become accustomed to the idea and the differences, Cara. I believe you've acquired an extended family."

"You, Jane?" she whispered.

"Me, Cara," she said gently. "You had a head start with me. We had the Eve connection. But you came the rest of the way on your own." She nodded at Eve. "But now we've both got to focus on that connection. She's going to need both of us."

"Of course, I'll do whatever—" Her eyes widened as she saw Jane's grave expression. "What's wrong? Is she sick?"

Jane quickly shook her head. "I didn't say that. I just said that it's time to focus on Eve." She leaned back in the seat. "Now settle down and relax. You have to be exhausted from that trip down the mountain. It would be a good idea if you could manage to nap. You don't need to do any more soul-searching than you've already done." She closed her eyes. "And forget about Jock."

Not possible. Any more than she would be able to forget everything that Jane had told her. Any more than she could forget that odd hesitance Jane had made when she had asked if Eve was sick. Her gaze flew to Eve across the aisle. She didn't look sick. She had wonderful color. But she did look tired. That was probably Cara's fault. Everything that had happened recently to her "extended family" was probably her fault.

"Cara." Jane didn't open her eyes. "Sleep."

Cara's lids shut. Rest. Find a way to repay everyone. But concentrate on Eve.

Focus on Eve.

CHAPTER
12

"I'm not in the mood for tears at the moment, Natalie," Kaskov said coldly. "I prefer answers."

"I told you what happened," Natalie said as she put her hand on his arm. "I even told you I might have a way to get her back. We're still doing everything we can to find out exactly where Duncan is keeping our little girl. I'm so glad you're home, Daddy."

He turned to Ivan Sabak. "Why did you fail to get her back? I gave you every tool I had to hunt them down. A bribe, Sabak?"

"No," Sabak said quickly. "Would I still be here if I'd betrayed you? I know the rules and the penalties."

"Then why?"

"They had someone very good on the inside, and the plan was well coordinated. But we almost intercepted."

"Not good enough. You say she's out of Russia now?"

"Scotland. But well protected by MacDuff, who has contacts in high places."

"I can get to anyone I choose. I just have to decide if it's worth it."

"Of course, it's worth it," Natalie said. "But I've been thinking that perhaps there's a way that would be less of a risk for you . . . and for Cara, naturally."

Kaskov nodded. "So you've told me." His lips twisted. "A very ugly little scheme. You have such a soft heart, it surprised me that it would occur to you."

There had been a hint of sarcasm in that remark. She ignored it. When all this was over, she'd be able to ease her father back to the point where she'd had him before. "I'm just a mother fighting for her child." She smiled unsteadily up at him. Make it convincing. It might be ugly, but that was what made it perfect. "I have it all planned. All I need is a little help from you, Daddy. Let me tell you all about it, down to the last detail . . ."

LOCH GAELKAR

"Welcome home." MacDuff smiled as he came forward to greet Cara. "You're looking remarkably well for all that Jock has told me you've gone through." He glanced at Jock, who had only nodded, then followed Jane and Caleb away from them toward the lake. "Though I can't say the same about him. Very moody at the moment. He treated you decently, I hope."

"He saved me," she said quietly. "He just didn't like the way he did it." She smiled at MacDuff. "And you're looking wonderful, sir. I was so worried about you."

"Then we've both come out of this on top." He grimaced. "Even though I was sidelined from the action because I came too close to being blown up." He turned to Eve. "Where is Quinn?"

"He went to see Agent Toller. He wanted to see if he

could budge him on letting us go back to the U.S. and retain custody of Cara. Not much hope, but we'll make the effort." She smiled. "Otherwise, you may be stuck with us for a little while. We're not letting her go."

"No problem. She hasn't gotten in my way yet." His lips tightened. "Though her mother has caused me a bit of bother. I was hoping we'd be through with her once and for all."

"We all were, but we'll take what we can get." She touched Cara's arm. "And we got Cara. That's a major triumph."

"I'm sorry that Natalie has done all those bad things," Cara said jerkily. "I'll try to make it up to you, sir."

"You're not your mother's keeper," MacDuff said. "You can hardly be blamed."

"I know that. Jock said I have my own soul, and I believe him. But if I hadn't been here, then she wouldn't have had a reason to cause you trouble. I'm sorry I was here and did that."

He inclined his head. "Then I accept your apology. We'll start over." He turned back to Eve. "And I'm just as happy that you're going to stick around and help me find Cira's treasure. I wouldn't want to have to keep Jane on task by myself, and I've always thought Jane was the key."

"Tell me something I don't know," Eve said dryly. "If it means anything to you, I believe that Jane is totally committed to helping you now, MacDuff."

"It means something. Everything that you do and say is important to Jane. And I've particularly noticed how protective she's been of you lately. If you stay, she'll stay. If you go, she'll examine her options."

Eve couldn't argue with him when Jane had insisted on coming to Moscow when she'd known Eve was going. "It's been difficult . . . The situation isn't as crucial now. We're not joined at the hip. Jane is her own person."

"Still, I believe we'll try to escalate the hunt so that Jane won't have anything 'crucial' to worry about in the near future. See you at the camp." He lifted his hand as he turned and strode down the slope toward the loch.

Eve stared after him a moment before she started down the slope with Cara beside her. "Did all that about your mother bother you?" she asked quietly. "MacDuff didn't mean anything personal toward you. As you know, he's not always the most tactful man on the planet."

"But he's a good man," Cara said. "Jock wouldn't love him if he wasn't a good man."

"Did it bother you?"

"A little, until I thought about it. Jock told me that she gave birth to me, but she wasn't really my mother. I have to believe that, Eve."

"It's the truth. Believe it."

"I will. But it takes getting used to." She looked down the slope to where Jock and Caleb were standing by the lake. "And there are all kinds of things it brings out that I never thought about. It's confusing, Eve."

"You'll work it out."

"I have to do it." She looked back up at Eve and said simply, "Because I can't live without Jock now."

Eve felt a ripple of shock. She'd been aware that the ties between Jock and Cara had been unusually strong since their first meeting, and it was clear their time together in Moscow had only strengthened that bond. "Sometimes we have to do without people we love, Cara."

She shook her head. "I won't do that. I'll find a way." Her gaze shifted back to the lake. "MacDuff was right about Jane. She won't stay if you don't. She's worried about you."

Eve's gaze flew to Cara's face. "She is?" she asked cautiously.

"You know she is," Cara said. "You're very smart, Eve. And you and Jane love each other. You'd know everything that she's feeling."

"And how do you know that she's worried." She paused. "Did she say anything?"

Cara still didn't look at her. "She said that you were going to need us. She said that we have to focus on you from now on." She moistened her lips. "It scared me. I thought maybe you were sick."

"I'm not sick, Cara."

"But would you tell me if you were? Lots of times people don't tell kids stuff like that. You don't look sick."

"I'm not sick, Cara." She put her hands on Cara's shoulders and turned her around to face her. "I feel fine. I feel great."

"Then why do you take pills?"

Eve's eyes widened. "Pills?"

"Jane told me I had to focus on you. So I focused while we were on the plane. Twice you went to the back of the plane and poured a glass of water. You had four bottles of pills. You took two each time you went back."

Eve shook her head in amazement. "Good heavens, you should train to be a detective."

"Why do you take pills if you're not sick?"

"For a perfectly good reason."

"Why? I have to take care of you. If you're sick, I have to know about it."

Eve chuckled. "Cara, stop it. I'm fine." She was rifling through her handbag and pulling out pill vials. "And, at this rate, everyone in camp is going to know just how fine I am. I was trying not to let it interfere." She put the vials in Cara's hands. "But it appears that's not going to happen."

Cara looked down at the vials. "Are you angry with me? Was I too nosy? I won't look if you don't want me to."

"Even though you think you're obligated to take care

of me?" She was smiling gently. "By all means, look. I believe Michael would want you to know."

"Michael?" Cara was looking through the vials one by one. She was frowning as she read the labels. Then she drew a deep breath of relief. "These are just vitamins."

"Not just vitamins. Read a little closer."

Cara's brow knitted as her gaze went back to the label. "Prenatal? What's that supposed to—" Her gaze flew to Eve's face. "Does that mean—"

Eve nodded.

Cara stared at her, stunned.

Eve laughed. "It's fine. It's wonderful. I'm healthy. The baby is healthy. I just take the vitamins to make sure Michael keeps on being healthy."

"Michael . . ."

"I'm going to have a little boy, Cara. His name is Michael."

"When?"

"About seven months." She touched her abdomen. "Though I believe he's going to be very impatient. He's shown the signs repeatedly of wanting his own way. Maybe he'll talk me into going along with him."

"No, you should do everything the doctor tells you to do," Cara said eagerly. "I'll help you. That's why I'm here. Jenny told me that you were going to need me. This has to be why."

Eve's smile faded. Cara had told Eve repeatedly that Jenny, Cara's sister who had given her life for her, had come to her in dreams and told her that she was to go to Eve and take care of her. Eve had never thought it would take this turn. "Cara, the reason Jenny wanted us to be together is so that we can help and support each other, to be family, not because she wanted you to be some kind of nursemaid. You are just as important to me as Michael."

She shook her head. "But why now? There has to be a reason why I came to you now. It must be because of the baby."

"We're going to have to have a few conversations about this." She looked at her quizzically. "I take it you're happy about Michael?"

Cara smiled luminously. "Oh, yes. A baby. I've never been around a baby before. I'll take good care of him, Eve."

"You're not listening, Cara. That's not the attitude you should have. That's my job, not yours."

"But there has to be a reason." She was stuffing the vitamins back in Eve's handbag. "It has to be Michael. It has to be you." She handed her the handbag. "Those vials are almost empty. You need to get some more vitamins."

"I've been a little busy. I'll get around to it now."

"Do you want me to call someone for you? Do you have a doctor here?"

"Yes, in Glasgow." She held up her hand. "I'll take care of it, Cara."

She nodded. "But you'll let me go with you?"

"I'll think about it." She shook her head as Cara started to speak. "Look, I don't like the idea of your not being where you have protection. You were almost killed in Moscow, and Natalie doesn't give up. I'm not going to put you at risk until I'm sure she can't touch you."

"What about you?" Cara said. "I think she hated you before, but now it will be different." She swallowed. "She . . . hates to lose. I could see it when she talked about her brother. And whenever she loses, someone dies. She lost to you."

"Then we'll just have to take care of each other, won't we?" She gave Cara a warm hug. "And we won't take chances."

"But I'm not enough," Cara said. "I'm just a kid. Could I tell Jock about the baby?"

"I thought you were on the outs with Jock."

"It's not about me, it's about you and Michael. You should have all the protection we can give you. Nothing else matters. May I tell Jock?"

She shook her head ruefully. "Why not? Practically everyone else knows now. So much for keeping it confidential."

"Jock . . . knows how to do things . . . that can protect you and Michael."

"Things you didn't want to let him do for you on that plateau," Eve said quietly.

"Maybe he won't have to do anything. Maybe there's something I can do instead." Her gaze met Eve's. "But we have to protect Michael, don't we?"

"That's not a question to ask me right now. I *will* protect my child, Cara."

She nodded. "And I *will* protect you . . . *and* Jock." She smiled with an effort. "You're right, it's going to be fine. You're healthy, Michael is healthy, and I'm here to take care of both of you." She started back down the slope. "And now I'm going to go talk to Jane and tell her she doesn't have to worry about not being able to tell me about the baby. I think it bothered her."

"I'm sure it did. Jane cares about you."

"Yes, she does." Cara grinned over her shoulder. "And it's not just the Eve connection. She told me so."

Eve watched Cara wave to Jane as she walked down the slope. It was good to see the two of them so close. Their backgrounds so similar and yet with stark, painful, differences. But both of them were honest and independent and loving.

Eve was lucky they had chosen to have her as their "connection."

"I thought you'd be down at the tents settling in." She turned to see Joe on the slope behind her.

"I had a slight delay. Cara decided that I had some dire disease when she saw me taking my vitamins. I had to explain . . . in detail."

"And how did she take it?"

"How you would expect her to take it. Loving, happy, excited." She grimaced. "And protective as hell, and convinced that her job in life was to take care of me and Michael. We have some attitude adjustment to work on."

"Maybe not quite yet." He took her hand as he reached her. "I kind of like the idea of everyone around you wanting to take care of you and my son." His lips twisted. "Particularly after talking to Toller."

"Not a good conversation," she guessed. "You were back entirely too soon for any progress."

"Well, I did succeed in staving off extradition, which he wanted to put in motion the minute he saw me. But that was only because one of the magistrates MacDuff has in his pocket was standing beside me."

"You couldn't convince him that Cara was in danger while she was in Moscow?"

"Natalie is still her mother, and we have no proof she tried to kill her daughters. Toller wants her returned to her mother and out of U.S. jurisdiction."

"And she'd end up dead before the day was over," Eve said hoarsely. "We can't let that happen to her after all she's been through."

"Easy." His hand tightened on hers. "We'll find a way to keep her safe. We got her back from Natalie, didn't we?"

"For the time being. Who knows what Natalie is planning?"

"I called Dima Palik while I was driving back from talking to Toller. The Kaskov camp is being remarkably silent after Natalie lost Cara and the chest of gold. Kaskov, himself, did some initial investigations, but he's not been taking any overt actions as yet."

"And what would that be?"

"He hasn't given the order to kill Ivan Sabak, which would be the usual action if he suspected him of being either a failure or betraying him. Which means that Natalie appears to be protecting Sabak and herself with utmost efficiency. And she has to have offered her father something that's appeased him in some way."

"What?" Eve murmured. "She doesn't have the gold. She wouldn't share with him anyway. All her plans were aimed at protecting herself."

"I've asked Palik to probe as much as he can. I don't like this silence."

Neither did Eve. The black widow was weaving her web, and now she appeared to have the approval of Kaskov. It was enough to cause a chill to go through her. "Cara's safe here, right?"

Joe nodded. "MacDuff doubled the guards. Security is very tight. No one's going to try to take Cara . . . or you." He paused. "But, if you'd feel better about it, I could take Jock and Caleb and we could pay another visit to Moscow. It's time this was ended anyway."

"I wouldn't feel better about it. I want you here with me, safe. It would scare me to death."

"We don't want that." He lifted her hand to his lips. "But make up your mind that it will happen, Eve. We can't let this go on much longer." He smiled. "Michael wouldn't like it. He doesn't like you upset."

"But he doesn't have your background or mind-set."

"How do you know? There are all kinds of possibilities. Reincarnation, racial memories . . . After all, he has my DNA. Maybe he also has some of the other stuff, too."

She shook her head. "Then heaven help us, Joe."

"That's what I say. You deserve everything Michael and I can give you." He kissed her hand again. "Heaven help us, Eve."

LOCH GAELKAR
THREE DAYS LATER

The Amati violin was lying on the ground in front of Cara's tent when she left it to go to breakfast that morning.

She stood looking at it for a moment before she could bring herself to go over and open the case.

Jock smiling that beautiful smile that night before Drostkey Park as he took the violin from her room at the gatehouse.

"I'm not letting you go through all this without getting something of value out of it. You love that violin."

And he had kept his word.

She swallowed hard as she gazed at the violin. She reached out and touched the beautiful, satin-smooth wood with a caressing finger.

But he hadn't bothered to give the violin to her himself this morning. He had set it outside her tent as if it were just a duty he'd had to perform. He hadn't even let her thank him.

It . . . hurt.

She'd hoped the anger would go away, but it had been days, and she'd barely seen him. She could only hope with the passing of time that he'd forgive her for not being what he wanted.

But she had to thank him in some way for not only her violin but all the other gifts he'd given her.

You have a soul. You have choices.

Even if the choices weren't the ones he wanted her to make.

There was only one way she could thank him although she knew he wouldn't acknowledge it. One way that might remind him that she wanted everything as beautiful for him as this violin was to her.

She slowly took out the violin and tucked it under her chin.

She started to play the Tchaikovsky.

LOCH GAELKAR
FIVE DAYS LATER

The mist was heavier than ever this morning, Jane thought, as she looked out at the north end of the lake. It was as if Cira had drawn all her misty robes around her as if in defiance of the work being done on the lights illuminating the shore.

What a thought, she thought ruefully as she jammed her hands into the pockets of her jacket and strode into the mist. She had been trying to ignore those vibes since Caleb had mentioned her less-than-objective attitude toward this hunt for Cira's treasure. But why should she? she thought with sudden defiance. It was more her hunt than anyone else's except MacDuff. Maybe more than MacDuff, too. After all, he hadn't been dreaming about Cira since he was seventeen. It didn't hurt anything to let herself drift along and let the possibilities . . .

"I was wondering when you'd be along." Caleb had suddenly appeared ahead of her out of the mist. "You resisted longer than I thought you would today." He came toward her. "I thought I might have to come and get you."

She stiffened. "Why would you do that? Did something happen? Have you found something?"

He tilted his head. "Do I detect a hint of disappointment?" He smiled. "Is it because you didn't find it yourself?"

"Did you find something?" she repeated.

He shook his head. "Just the opposite. This mist is so thick today that MacDuff said early this morning that we'd scrap the work and hope for a better day tomorrow." He made a face. "With appropriate obscene oaths to accompany the sentiment."

"But you couldn't resist dangling the possibility in front of me," Janc said dryly. "If you're not going to try to help put up those lights today, why are you still here?"

"Why do you think? We both know that helping MacDuff isn't high on my agenda. I'm all for seizing opportunities when they occur." He smiled recklessly. "And, since you've been cautiously avoiding giving me any opportunities, I decided Cira must be doing it for you."

She instinctively braced herself. There was something very different about him today. Caleb was always an enigma, but the recklessness she was seeing at this moment was white-hot and casting out an emotional wave that put her on her guard. "Cira? Only you would think that Cira would bother to make anything easy for you. Cira always thought everyone should take care of themselves."

"Like you do." He nodded. "According to my research, you're a good deal like Cira. Except maybe where the people you love are concerned. Then you're willing to use whomever you have to use to protect them. Was Cira like that, too, Jane?"

"Perhaps. Why are we standing here talking about Cira?"

"Because I've been thinking a good deal about her lately. I haven't had much else to do in the past few days. You've been avoiding me and, as you know, that has an unsettling effect on me. I have a tendency to be a trifle undisciplined if I become restless." He held up his hand as she opened her lips to speak. "So I decided that I had to take care of it before it came to that point."

"Take care of it?" she repeated warily.

"You see, I've been so disgustingly noble and cooperative since I've been involved with all the people who are surrounding you that it's been a constant trial to me." He took a step closer to her. "And how close have we come during that time, Jane? Did I force you? Did I do anything but make you admit that you wanted it as much as I do? I was more patient than you can imagine. You have no idea how angry I get when I see you letting a dead man stand between us. Trevor wouldn't have wanted you to do it. We both know that." His lips twisted. "And now I think you're using it as an excuse because you're still afraid of me."

"I'm not afraid of you. You flatter yourself, Caleb."

"Then are you afraid of what we'd be together?" He moved another step, his dark eyes glittering in his taut face. "Oh, yes, that could be it. It could be . . . exceptional. I've always known it . . ."

And so had she, Jane realized. Even now, when she was feeling this wary and uncertain, she could still sense the sheer magnetism that was sparking between them. "Sex is sex. Okay, the chemistry is there. But I don't want to be involved with someone who doesn't really care anything about me."

"How do you know I don't care anything about you?" he said with sudden fierceness. "With what you know about me, would you believe me if I said that my emotions are pure as the driven snow?" He shook his head. "And I wouldn't leave myself that open to you. You'll have to take the sex and the fact that I have a major obsession for you."

"I don't have to take anything I don't want to take."

"But that's why I'm here, to make sure that you want to take me."

She inhaled sharply. "Just why are you here, Caleb?"

"Waiting for you." He smiled recklessly. "I think you know. From the moment you saw me today, you knew that I'd decided, we had to move a step forward. It's not often I get the opportunity to get you alone in a place where you're so vulnerable."

"Vulnerable?"

"Yes, that's the right word. When you're out there in the camp, you're surrounded by everyone who loves you and wants the very best for you. Here, you're on your own and have to deal with me, a man who only wants the very best for myself. Or so you think." He took a step closer. "But who has no objection to sharing the wealth."

She took a step back. "What are you doing, Caleb? You're . . . different."

"No, I'm only reacting to the effects of severe restraint. You'll recall I don't behave well under those circumstances. I don't believe you've even noticed the signs that should have been very obvious." He sighed. "I've been too good, Jane. I decided I had to take a little, or I might take too much."

She stopped and stared at him. "Are you threatening me?"

"God, no. I'm just trying to strike a balance that will let me continue with this charade without doing something you'd consider unforgivable. In which case, I'd have to work twice as hard to make it at least palatable."

"You're not making sense." She moistened her lips. "I think it's time I went back to camp."

"I'm making perfect sense for me." He took a step closer, and his hand reached out to cup her throat. "It's been too long, Jane. I've played the game. I've done everything that you'd want me to do and more. I knew it was going to be a long road, but I need something to keep me steady."

Her pulse was pounding beneath his hand. She could smell the scent of him, his eyes . . . Her body was readying, tensing. She had to force herself not to move toward him. "I can't help what you need. You can't dictate to me, Caleb."

"No, but I can make you need it, too." He was close, his breath warm on her cheek as his tongue touched the pulse point in the hollow of her throat. "And that's what you're doing, isn't it? Feel your blood sting, burn, Jane?"

She did feel it, and she couldn't breathe. "Don't you do this to me, Caleb. It's not . . . fair."

"This is you. This is me. I haven't even started to let your blood flow help things along. I'm tempted not to even do it, but you fight me too hard. You fight yourself too hard." He was unbuttoning her shirt. "In many ways, I'm under a tremendous disadvantage with you, Jane."

"So you're going to force me?"

"Would I do that? I'm just going to make you very, very happy. And let you have a unique experience that you might have wanted for a long, long time." His hands were on her breasts, and she arched helplessly toward him. "And I won't use anything but what we are together until you tell me you want it."

She had to smother a gasp as sensation after sensation tingled through her. He was brushing his cheek against her breasts, and she felt the faint roughness against her nipples that was unbearably erotic. *He* was unbearably erotic. The feel of his hair against her, his hands on her stomach, moving over her.

How long had she wanted this? How long had she

wanted him, she wondered dazedly. All she knew was that she wanted him now with a desire that was overwhelming.

"It's fine." He was pulling her down to the ground. "Don't panic. It's all up to you now. Nothing's going to happen that you don't want to happen. Not easy for me . . . But I'll keep the savage at bay." His teeth were on her nipple, biting, pulling. "Do you want me to stop?"

She was on fire. Her heart pounding, exploding.

He bit down harder. "Stop?"

She arched upward with a cry, and her arms slid around him. "No, damn you."

"Then I believe we're ready to start . . ."

Madness.

Heat.

Mist.

So much mist.

The bank was damp, soft, beneath her naked body.

He was hard, muscles piston tense, moving above her, within her.

She was screaming, her hands digging into his shoulders.

"Shh." Antonio was laughing down at her. "Though it pleases me that I can still make you scream after all these years, Cira."

"Braggart." Her teeth bit his shoulder. "I suppose you are somewhat adequate."

Then she screamed again as he went deep.

Mist.

Passion.

Deep.

Madness.

Sex.

It went on and on and on.

Antonio.

No, Caleb.

Cira in the throes of her passion for her Antonio.

Caleb moving in and out in a frenzy that made Jane weak with sheer sexual exhaustion.

She didn't know how long it lasted.

The mist.

Caleb's tense face above her.

The muscles of her stomach clenching with every touch, every breath.

"Let it go, Jane."

Caleb's voice. Not Antonio's. Caleb's hands on her. "Now."

She exploded, her entire body convulsing.

She was panting.

Her entire body flushed, hot, malleable.

"It's okay." Caleb's fingers touching the tears running down her cheeks. "It's fine, Jane."

Her heart was still pounding painfully as she looked up at him. "The hell it is. You son of a bitch. What did you do to me?"

"I have no idea. I left it up to you." He moved away from her. "I started it going, then let your fantasies take charge. The mind can be so much more erotic, can't it?"

"As long as you have that blood thing going for you." She sat up and began to put on her clothes. They were both naked, and she forced herself not to look at him. He was all power and sexuality, and she remembered those gleaming muscles flexing above her. "You take advantage. Not fair, Caleb."

"No, but not unforgiveable. I amused both of us, but I didn't force you." He leaned up on one arm, watching her dress. "And I would much rather have gone for the purely physical and skipped the mind games. But I wasn't sure that wouldn't have defeated my purpose. We were at a standstill and I had to be sure that we took a few steps

254   IRIS JOHANSEN

forward." He made a face. "Besides, I just needed something, and I took what I could get."

"It will be your last chance. I'm not going to forget this."

"I don't want you to forget it." He smiled. "I want you to remember it every time you see me. I'll remember it, Jane."

She could feel her cheeks burn. He had said that on purpose, so that it would be a constant reminder. "Then I'll have to arrange not to see you, won't I?"

"Eventually. But now we're tied together with MacDuff and the hunt, and you'll have a problem avoiding me."

She pulled on her boots. "I'll manage," she said jerkily.

"Don't you want to tell me about your fantasy?" he asked softly. "Though I think I can guess. The mists. The dreams. What else could it be?"

"I don't want to talk about it."

"Cira and Antonio."

She didn't answer.

"Was it good?"

"I don't want to discuss this."

"Why not? It was my gift to you." He tilted his head, studying her. "Or did it get a little mixed up? Was it me or Antonio? In the end, which one was it?"

She got to her feet. "I'm going back to the camp. I'll do my best to avoid you from now on, Caleb."

"I know." He didn't move. "But this was just a temporary fix for me. I believe the next time I'll have to find a way to get you to give me what I want with no reservations."

She shook her head.

"Yes, I don't know why I'm obsessed with you, Jane, but I don't appear to be able to get over it. But I'm becoming impatient. How many favors have I done for you? I'm tired of playing the good guy. You want something from me, you pay the price." He met her gaze. "You understand?"

"You couldn't be more clear. But that's not likely to happen." She turned and strode back toward camp.

Mist.

Heat.

Caleb.

She involuntarily looked back over her shoulder.

He still hadn't moved. He lay there totally naked, olive skin gleaming . . . aroused.

She could feel her body tauten, her breasts swell again as she looked at him.

Antonio or Caleb?

There was no doubt that Caleb had been dominant. Yet he was right, he had given her a gift when he had let her see into the Cira-Antonio passion. Those dreams had been such a part of her life that it seemed right that she should share that most intimate bond.

But she would not be grateful. As usual, Caleb had taken every bit as much as he'd given.

Or had he?

But, at any rate, gratitude to Caleb could be extremely dangerous.

CHAPTER
13

"Joe, we've got to do something about Cara," Eve said bluntly as she walked into their tent late that afternoon. "I could see it coming, but it's now in full bloom."

"What's wrong with her?"

"She's becoming my shadow. Other than the time she's playing her violin, she's watching me like a hawk, running for everything she thinks I might need." She added with exasperation, "Remember the discussion we had about you hovering over me after we found out about the baby? She's twice as bad." She glared at him. "And stop smirking. This isn't funny."

"I realize that." His lips were twitching. "It only seems that way. May I remind you that you had no trouble putting me straight?"

"She's a child. She has nothing to do but sit here in camp and wait for that bitch of a mother to pounce on her. I've sent for schoolbooks for her, she has her violin, but she needs something else to occupy her."

"Except waiting on you hand and foot?"

"Exactly." She sighed. "I don't want to hurt her feelings but I can't have her—" She broke off, then said, "I have to go to see the doctor for a checkup and a vitamin refill tomorrow. She wants to go with me. I don't believe it's safe for her to be away from the camp."

"Just tell her no. I'll go with you; that should be enough for her."

"This is Cara. She's determined to be my guardian angel. Michael's guardian angel."

"I believe I can fill that job."

"Of course, you can." She absently brushed a kiss on his forehead. "We just have to convince her that—" She stopped. "Or maybe not, maybe I'm going at this the wrong way." She turned and strode out of the tent and up the hill toward MacDuff's tent. They had stopped early today because of the fog, and she knew that Mac-Duff was going over the measurements for the light placement for the north bank.

And she knew who was with him.

Who had been with him every day since they'd come back to Gaelkar.

She stuck her head through the entrance of the tent. "Jock, you come out here. Right now. I need you, dammit." She didn't wait, but whirled, and started walking toward the lake.

Jock caught up with her seconds later. "What's wrong? Trouble?"

"You're what's wrong. I've been trying to put on Band-Aids, and I need a tourniquet." She turned to face him. "I don't care what you think the problem is with Cara, you fix it. You've practically ignored her since you got back. Which has put me in a hell of a situation since all that love and devotion she squanders on you is being heaped on my shoulders. I can't handle it right now. I know she's just being helpful and loving, but sometimes I feel as if I can't breathe."

"What are you talking about?" He was frowning. "Do you know how lucky you are? Do you know what kind of person—"

"I know all of that," Eve interrupted. "I also know she wants to leave camp and go running to Glasgow with me on my errands. And all because she had a good friend, but he's not there for her right now." She looked him in the eye. "She leaves here, she's vulnerable. And you know how determined she can be. If she actually makes up her mind, do you think anyone can stop her?"

"You have to stop her. You can't expose her to—"

"No, *you* have to stop her. This is all your fault anyway."

"I was right, Eve, Cara has to learn that she can't control the way I—"

"Be quiet. You don't know what you're talking about. You're acting as if Cara is a grown woman. She's only twelve years old and trying her best to see her way through a hell of a lot more than any kid should have to stand."

"I know that."

"Then act as if you do. Give her a break. I think she's wanted to come to you, but she won't do it unless she thinks you need her. That's what Cara's all about. Or have you forgotten?"

"I haven't forgotten." He gave her a ghost of a smile. "Tough medicine, Eve."

"Then take it and make it right with her. I don't give a damn about what you think is right or wrong for her. Settle that later. Right now, I want peace and serenity and safety for everyone I care about. You see to it, Jock." She turned on her heel and strode back toward her tent.

What do you think, Michael? Did we make a point? I feel pretty good about it.

Warmth. Humor. Love.

And maybe a little concern?

Okay, I got a little excited. But in the long run, I think that's not so bad. Maybe you need a little rush of adrenaline now and then.

Definitely humor this time.

Joe looked up as she walked in the entrance. "You're looking . . . victorious. Problem solved?"

"No, but it's temporarily out of my hands, and I'm hoping it will head that way." She pulled him to his feet and went into his arms. She laid her head on his chest as she held him close. The strength, the beat of his heart, the love that never faltered. "But Michael thinks I got a little excited. It might be good if I took a nap. Want to join me?"

"It has to be a nap?"

"Eventually." She pulled him down to the bedroll. "But I have been preaching the values of adrenaline to your son. A demonstration might be in order . . ."

"Get out here." The next word crackled. "Now!"

Jock, Cara realized in panic. She jumped to her feet and ran out of her tent. "Are you hurt? What's wrong? How can I help—"

"I'm not hurt." He grabbed her wrist and dragged her down toward the lake. "Nothing's wrong with me except the fact that Eve tore a strip off me fifteen minutes ago. It seems you're behaving stupidly, and it's all my fault."

"I wasn't stupid. And nothing is your fault." She tugged at her wrist. "How could it be? I haven't even talked to you in days."

"That appears to be the crux of the matter." He turned to face her. "I didn't know what you were doing, and you decided that you needed to leave camp." His lips tightened, his silver-gray eyes glittering. "That's not going to happen, Cara."

"That's up to Eve. I hope she lets me go. I have to take care of her."

"You think Quinn won't do it? He was a SEAL, for God's sake."

"I thought about that, but there has to be some reason why I have to be with her. I should go wherever she goes."

"Wrong. You're not responsible for me, you're not responsible for Eve. You're only responsible for keeping yourself alive and well. End of story."

She shook her head.

He took her shoulders in his two hands and stared down at her. "Don't do that. You have to listen to me."

"Why? You're not making sense." His eyes were blazing down at her, and she couldn't stand that he was so upset with her. "Do as I say, not as I do? When we were on that plateau, you weren't thinking only about yourself. You were ready to send me and everyone else off in that helicopter to get us out of your way. It was wrong. *You* were wrong."

"I wasn't wrong. I swore to you that you'd always be safe, that you'd never have to look over your shoulder again. And I got you back from Natalie. But it didn't end there, and I had to go a step further." His hands tightened on her shoulders. "And you wouldn't *let* me. You *fought* me, and I could see you dying up there."

"I had to do it."

"The hell you did. I told you, I'm trained to handle situations like that. You should have let me do what I do."

"And I'm not trained, and I'm not smart about things like that, but maybe I could have done something. I had the right to help you, Jock." She swallowed and blinked back the tears. "Because I can't let you do those things alone and have you take all the blame and pain yourself. I won't do that anymore. I have to help. Because I couldn't stand it if anything happened to you, and I didn't."

"For God's sake, don't you dare cry," he said hoarsely. His hands were kneading her shoulders. "I'm confused enough as it is."

"I won't cry."

"Too late." He drew her close, and his hand cradled her head against his chest. "And you're lying. Now stop it."

"Okay." She stayed very still against him, afraid that he'd move away from her. "I wasn't—Well, maybe I was, but it was only because I couldn't make you understand. And I *hate* it when you're angry with me."

"I notice it didn't stop you from doing what you want to do."

"I couldn't let it matter. You said I had a soul, and it's true. I have to be what I am, not what someone else wants me to be." Her arms went around him. "Not Natalie . . ." She whispered, "And not you, Jock. Even if it hurts me."

He was silent. "Did I hurt you, Cara?"

"Yes."

He didn't speak for another moment. "You hurt me, too. Because you wouldn't let me take care of you. You hurt me and you scared me and I could see you doing it again and again and again." He pushed her back and looked down at her. "Eve said that I was stupid because I was treating you like a grown woman instead of a kid. But that's just part of the confusion. It's your fault. You keep shifting back and forth, and when I think I know who you are, you change again." He met her gaze. "So we've got a lot of adjustments to make if we want to find a way to stay together. And one of those adjustments is going to have to be that you stay safe and don't drive me crazy."

She shook her head. "But you weren't going to stay safe on that plateau. That's not fair."

He sighed. "We're obviously going to have to go into this in some depth. But I have to come out with at least a semivictory on this, Cara. I believe the only solution is to remove you from anywhere that you're exposed to threats." His lips curved in a wry grin. "Maybe I can convince Eve to send you to one of those high-security schools for CEOs' and diplomats' kids."

"I couldn't do that." But she was smiling with relief as she looked up into his face. It was going to be all right. He wasn't angry any longer. "I have to be with Eve. It's important."

"Back to square one." He was no longer smiling. "Eve isn't going to want you trailing behind her when it could be a danger to you. I certainly don't. How can I convince you that it's totally unnecessary? Do you want me to go with her?"

She hesitated. "I told her I might ask you to do that," she said. "I told her that you knew how to . . . protect people. But then you still were angry with me, and I didn't know if—I thought maybe I should go myself."

"No, you shouldn't," he said flatly. "Quinn and I can handle a few errands in Glasgow, thank you. No big deal."

She shook her head. "Very big deal. That's why I have to be sure that everything goes well for Eve. I know that she gets annoyed with me for hovering over her, but there has to be a reason, and it has to have something to do with me."

"What reason?"

"I told you that I'd had dreams about my sister, Jenny, and that she told me that I had to go to Eve and take care of her." She moistened her lips. "I never really understood. I'm only a kid. I wasn't sure what I could do to take care of someone as smart as Eve." She smiled eagerly. "But now I understand. It's Michael. I have to help take care of Michael."

"Michael?" Jock repeated blankly.

"Eve's Michael," Cara said. "She's going to have a baby, Jock. Isn't that wonderful?"

"Oh, shit." He took a step back. "Glasgow?"

"She has to get more pills and have a checkup. She was almost out of vitamins on the trip from Russia, and I—"

"Hold it." He held up his hand. "And that's why you were so insistent about going with her?"

"It has to be about Michael. I'm supposed to take care of him and Eve."

"But you were going to let me help before you decided I couldn't be trusted with—"

"I trust you. I told Eve that you . . . knew things."

"Oh, yes, I do. Which is why I was trying to persuade you to let me practice what I know." He added, "And why you're going to stay here with Caleb, Jane, and MacDuff and let Quinn and me keep Eve safe." He smiled teasingly. "I promise we'll scout Glasgow as if we're expecting a commando raid."

That beautiful, radiant smile that she had missed so desperately during these days without it.

"Will you trust me?" he asked gently.

She nodded. "I always trust you, Jock. But I'm just learning to trust myself. It's kind of confusing."

"And that's the twelve-year-old talking. Heaven knows what we'll be facing tonight or tomorrow."

"But you'll still like me?"

"I guess you could say that. Want to go for a walk by the lake? I have about thirty minutes before I have to get back to MacDuff and help him go through his paperwork. Lord, he hates to do that. And since he lost MacTavish, it's an added burden." He took her hand. "But he can just put up with it and keep an eye on you since I'll be in Glasgow tomorrow."

His hand felt hard and warm and full of affection. They had taken walks like this many times both here and at the castle. Dear heaven, she had missed those walks. She had missed everything about him. Her grip tightened instinctively around his.

He glanced down at her as he felt the pressure. "Aye," he said gently. "Me, too." He smiled. "But I was in the right, Cara. I guess I'll just have to convince you . . ."

She giggled. "Not bloody likely," she said, deliberately mocking his Scottish accent. "Do you want me to come and help you and MacDuff? I'm good with a computer and I—" She broke off. "Never mind. I should stay close to Eve in case she needs me."

"Somehow, I don't believe that Eve's in dire need of your services while she has Quinn on hand."

She giggled again. "Sex stuff? But you know, I don't think it's like it was with Natalie and Ivan. I don't know much about it, but I think it has to be different with different people, and Eve and Joe probably have the kind that's sort of . . . beautiful."

"That wouldn't surprise me. But I really don't want to discuss this with you, Cara."

"Why not? You must have done it lots and lots of times. Look at you. Anyone would want to see you without your clothes on."

He was trying to keep from laughing. "It's nice to be appreciated, but Eve would definitely consider the subject inappropriate."

"But you could probably tell me more than most people. You answer everything else I ask you."

"Trust me. Eve would definitely want you to go to her with those particular questions."

"But Joe and Eve are very private, and I don't think they'd want to share."

"Cara . . ." He gazed at her with narrowed eyes. "I believe you're teasing me a wee bit. Suppose we go and discuss it with Eve and Quinn right now?"

Cara threw back her head and laughed. "Just a wee bit. It's good to laugh with you. Everything has been so . . . grim. You've been so grim. You were never meant to be that way, Jock. Isn't it funny how talking about sex makes people—"

"—Back away so that Eve will not accuse me of taking over her duties," he finished. "But, aye, it's good to see you smile. So good that I think that I'll linger a little longer and talk and see it come again." He sat down on the bank and pulled her down beside him. "And maybe give Eve and Quinn just a bit more time without you 'hovering.'"

GLASGOW

"You're doing very well, Ms. Duncan. Everything is checking out A-OK." Dr. Rampfel smiled at her as he adjusted his glasses over his beak of a nose. "Now if you'll roll over, I'll give you your Vitamin B-12 shot, and we'll get you out of here."

"I was afraid of that." She made a face. "There's something undignified about getting a shot in the butt."

"I'll take your dignity in full consideration, but it's the best place to get to the muscle tissue." He chuckled. "Okay, I guess the muscles in the hip will do as well if I do a little adjusting." She felt him pinching the flesh of her hip, then the expected prick. Then he drew the sheet back over her. "Indignity over. You can get dressed now."

She rolled back over and sat up. "You made it almost painless to both my body *and* my dignity. I'm done?"

"You're done." He smiled at her as he nodded for his

nurse standing at the door to help her. "Unless you're interested in the sex of the child? We could run a check, but there's a doubt that we could determine it."

"Oh, I'm interested." She jumped off the table and moved behind the curtain at the end of the room. "But I don't believe that's necessary right now," she said as she quickly dressed. "I believe that boys run in Joe's family." She left the enclosure and went to the mirror over the cabinet and tidied her hair. "We'll go with that."

"Not exactly scientific."

"Good enough." She turned and shook the doctor's hand. "If we're wrong, we'll have a surprise. Thank you for everything. I'll make an appointment with the receptionist for my next visit, but I may have to cancel. We could return to Atlanta if things work out."

"I'll be happy to see you again." His eyes were twinkling as he glanced at the door. "But I'm not certain that Detective Quinn is happy to see me. I'm not accustomed to having my examination rooms go through such a thorough search."

He sounded tolerant now, but she had noticed how tense the doctor had seemed when Joe had gone into full detective mode. It was no wonder he had felt threatened. Joe could be very intimidating.

"Joe's a little protective." And she might not be encouraged to return in spite of the doctor's words, she thought ruefully. Between Joe and Jock Gavin, it had been an uneventful but definitely edgy visit. "Good-bye, Doctor. Have a nice day."

Five minutes later she had her vitamin pills, her next appointment, and was out the door and walking down the hall with Joe.

"It took long enough," Joe murmured.

"It did not," Eve said. "I'm not an expert, but I think it was fairly short. You and Jock were just on high alert.

I could see that you were making the doctor nervous. Where's Jock now?"

"Checking out the parking garage."

"And it will probably prove to be pristine clean by the time he does a sweep." She gave a profound sigh of relief as they got in the elevator. "And I'll be very glad to get back to Gaelkar. I'd just as soon be back with Michael and forget all about all these medical things."

"Did you discuss Michael?"

"A little, not really. I didn't want to burst the doctor's bubble by telling him we didn't need him. You should know that you have a lot of boys in your family history."

"Do I really? I'll have to check on that."

The elevator stopped, and the doors slid open. Jock was on the other side. "All secure." He smiled at Eve. "You, too?"

"So the doctor said. Michael couldn't be better."

"Cara will be relieved." Jock opened the passenger door of the car for her. "Since she believes she has a personal investment in your son." He got in the backseat. "Let's get back to the camp. I've been feeling a little uneasy ever since we left there this morning."

"I checked in an hour ago," Joe said quietly.

"I've been checking, too. I just don't . . . like this . . . feeling . . ."

"Is Michael okay, Eve?" Cara asked eagerly as she ran toward them across the camp. "Did you get your vitamins?"

"Yes." She smiled. "As well as a B-12 shot and an offer to tell me the sex of the baby. I'm glad you weren't along. I didn't set a good example. I had to fib a bit not to hurt Dr. Rampfel's feelings. He was edgy enough about dealing with Joe." She watched Jock and Joe striding toward MacDuff's tent. "No problems here? As soon as they stopped worrying about me, they started worrying about everyone here."

Cara shook her head. "MacDuff was a little impatient about getting back to the mist, but he'd promised Jock he'd stay close, and he tried not to show it." She grinned. "So Jane and I volunteered to help him with his paperwork and research. But I know he's going to want everyone to hit that mist now that you're back." She changed the subject. "Did you have lunch? Do you want me to cook something for you? I looked up some high-protein recipes that are supposed to be good for—"

"You're hovering," Eve said gently. "But I'll let you off easy, because I didn't have lunch. Joe wanted to get back here, and I knew I had a terrific chef just waiting to ply me with attention." She touched Cara's cheek. "Something light?"

Cara nodded eagerly. "You just go sit by the lake and rest. I'll do everything and—" She stopped. "Almost everything. Maybe we can do the dessert together?"

"Thank you. Now you've got the program. Together." But Eve did move down to the lake and sat down on the bank. Now that she was away from the hubbub of the trip and visit, she was feeling strangely depressed. She was glad to get back to this beautiful, mystical place that felt oddly homelike. She looked out at the mist hovering over the lake. Cira's mist, Cira's lake. Did you sit here sometimes and look out at the mist and think of your son, Marcus, Cira? Could you have saved him, if you'd lived with all the miracles we have today? Perhaps not, sometimes it's necessary to accept and not—

Rejection.

She inhaled sharply as that emotion struck her with stunning force.

Michael.
Rejection.

And anger.

Hey, okay. You didn't like what I was thinking. We'll forget it and start again. But you can't always have it your own way, Michael.

Rejection.

And another searing bolt of emotion.

Wrong. This was wrong, she thought dazedly. She was suddenly cold. She linked her arms about her knees to stop from shivering. What was happening to her?

Rejection.

I heard you, Michael. But now I'm getting scared. Cira? Does it have something to do with Cira?

Rejection.

"Eve?" Cara was standing beside her, her eyes wide. "You look . . . funny. What can I do?"

"Tell Joe . . . I need him. Something's . . . bad."

Cara turned and flew up the hill.

Fear. Anger. Rejection.

We'll take care of it, Michael. Just give us a chance. It will be—

A text. Her phone was pinging a text . . .

Not now.

Now. Now. Now.

She accessed the text.

Some news story . . .

"What's wrong?" Joe was kneeling beside her, taking her in his arms. "God, you're shaking."

"It was crazy." She held on to him with all her strength. "Michael . . ."

"What about Michael?"

"I don't know. I was sitting here and thinking about Cira and her Marcus, and all of a sudden—Michael didn't like it. He was angry. Then this stupid text came in, and I—"

"What text?" He looked down at her phone. "Oh, shit."

He buried her head in his chest as he stared down at the text. "Dammit to hell."

"It's some news story . . ."

"Yes, it is. A bulletin from a TV station in Glasgow. It's set to repeat over and over."

"What?" She pushed him away and looked down at the phone. "What bulletin?"

Then she saw the face on the screen. "Dr. Rampfel?" Only it wasn't the face of the doctor she'd seen this morning. The remaining features on the lower section of his face were the same, but the top of his head was blown off. "No," she whispered. "Dear God, what happened?"

"He was shot and killed an hour after we left the office," Joe said curtly. "He had an appointment to go out to lunch, and he was killed as he left the building."

"Dead." She moistened her lips. "Why?" She shook her head as she remembered how warmly human she'd thought the doctor. "Why, Joe?"

"That's what I want to know." He looked over his shoulder. "Cara, go tell Jock I need him to take a trip back to Glasgow. I don't want to leave Eve right now."

Eve hadn't even realized that Cara had come back with Joe and had been standing in the background. Cara nodded and turned and ran back to the tents.

"You don't have to stay." Eve tried to straighten away from him. "I just needed . . . you. I was confused. I'm still confused."

"Do you think I'm not?" he said harshly. "I checked out that doctor the minute I knew you were going to go to him. Pristine-clean medical reputation. A regular Boy Scout as far as his moral character is concerned. Why would he have been killed the same day you showed up for an exam?"

"Maybe it had nothing to do with me."

"I hope not. I just don't believe in coincidences." He

looked down at the text that was still repeating. "And this is definitely no coincidence."

She had been so upset she had not even made the connection, but, of course, this bold attack could never be a coincidence. "Natalie."

"We were wondering why she was so silent."

"But why my doctor? Is it some kind of warning? She couldn't get to me or Cara, so she killed an innocent man?"

"I imagine we'll know soon. Now that Natalie has put a plan in motion I don't believe she'll let much time pass before she lets us know what she's up to." He got to his feet. "That's why I don't want to leave you right now. You don't need to face her by yourself. I'm just going to go up to talk to Jock. I'll be back in a few minutes. Okay?"

She nodded jerkily. "I'll be fine. It wasn't the news story that was scaring me. It was Michael. I can handle Natalie. Michael is something else. He was . . . strange."

Joe tilted his head. "All right now?"

"Yes. No. Better. I think he wanted me to have support."

"And you will. In just a few minutes." He was striding up the slope. "I'll send Jane."

He was calling out all the troops, she thought ruefully. She shouldn't have panicked and sent Cara running to get him. She should have handled it herself. But Michael was his son, too, and she had been confused and needing someone who loved him to help her understand. So she had to bite the bullet and accept the consequences of that moment of weakness.

"Eve?" It was Cara again. "I told Jock to watch that news story. He thought it was bad . . . stuff. He's talking to Joe for just a minute, then he's going to see what happened."

"Good luck to him. I'm having trouble getting anything clear." She was looking down at the text again. It was ugly and brutal and meant to shock. If she hadn't been already shocked by Michael, it would have had a maximum effect. "What's clear is that a man I liked and respected was killed today. We'll have to find out all the rest."

"It was Natalie."

"We don't know that."

"Yes, we do." She paused. "I told you that she hated you. Maybe she thought this would hurt you."

"There's no use speculating. Joe said we should know soon." Eve saw that Cara was looking at that repeating text, and she instinctively moved to distract her. "Could you get me a cup of coffee? I'm a little shaky."

"Sure." Cara immediately turned away. "I'll have to heat it, but I'll be right back."

"That will be fine. Thank you." She watched her go toward the fire.

I'm getting all the support you could possibly want for me, Michael. I just wish that I knew what you're trying to protect me from.

Her cell phone rang.

She stared down at it.

Natalie.

She didn't want to answer it. That call had come too close to that last thought she'd sent to Michael. She felt if she answered the call, she'd know what other horrors Natalie might have in store for her. Don't be a coward. She'd told Joe she wasn't afraid of Natalie.

She answered the call. "Why, Natalie? That poor man had nothing to do with what's between the two of us."

"That just goes to show that you have no idea how I feel about you, Eve. Everyone that touches your life has something to do with what's between us." Natalie laughed. "I told you that I'd investigated everything about you. Do you think that I wouldn't know about your visit to Dr. Rampfel and what it meant? It didn't really interest me at the time, but when you managed to win our first battle, I went back to my notes and took another look."

"And decided to hurt me by destroying him."

"He was just a piece of the whole. I had to protect myself from his talking after he'd done his job."

Eve stiffened. "His job?"

"Of course. He was the center of the plan. I had to make sure you'd immediately get the message, but not all the details connected to Rampfel. I wanted to share some of those with you myself. In fact, I believe I'll set up a Skype computer link so I can actually see your face when it's time to have our principal discussion. I've been anticipating that."

"And anticipating killing an innocent man."

"No one is really innocent. Your fine doctor certainly wasn't. Oh, he tried to pretend he was one of the good guys, but Ivan only had to dig deep beneath all that bullshit, and he found a way to get to him. He's very fond of his family, and he had a younger brother who likes his cocaine and the casinos. All Ivan had to do was squeeze him. We gave him a choice whether he wanted his brother to die or to cooperate with us."

Eve's heart was beating hard. She felt sick to her stomach. "Cooperate how?"

"But that's part of the surprise. Did Cara tell you how much I like surprises?"

"She told me what a monster you are. What did you ask the doctor to do?"

"I suggest you send your lover, Quinn, to the crime scene and get him to do a little squeezing of his own. Rampfel has a notebook in his jacket pocket with a name and the person who might be able to fill you in on what you're up against. I'll be in touch again after you man-age to absorb just what a big mistake you made to try to make a fool of me."

"And what are you going to ask of me?"

"Everything. My father insists Cara has to be part of the deal." Natalie's voice was laden with malice. "And I want Cira's gold that you cheated me out of. I know you must have it, or you wouldn't have been able to give me that coin that was worth over two million dollars. We know you're still down at that lake, but security is so tight that MacDuff must be making sure no one else knows about that gold."

"Or that we're still looking for it."

"Two million dollars. You found it, all right. You just couldn't convince MacDuff to give it up just to keep a kid alive. So you decided to go after Cara and try to take everything for yourself. It's what I would have done."

"We're not the same."

"No, you have this weird thing about kids. It's already cost you two million. It's going to cost you a hell of a lot more." Her voice lowered to soft malevolence. "And, when I was trying to think of the way to hurt you the most, I naturally came up with your greatest weakness. Oh, yes, it was worth waiting a little longer than I wanted to make sure that I did it this way."

Eve was no longer just afraid, she was terrified. She had trouble getting the next words out. "What did—you—do?"

"I taught you a lesson. I'm going to enjoy watching you try to wriggle your way out of it. I'll be thinking about it all the time until I call you back." She hung up.

So much ugliness, and the nastiest part of it all was that Natalie had been able to instill this panic and fear in Eve. Everything that she had said was leading down a path that was her worst nightmare.

And that was what Natalie had wanted.

She couldn't sit here, frozen, sick, she had to do something. They had to start fighting Natalie. Or at least trying to find out the weapons Natalie was using to fight them.

Joe.

She had to get to Joe.

She jumped to her feet and started to run toward the tents.

CHAPTER
14

"What was in his pocket?" Eve asked jerkily as Joe came out of the magistrate's office four hours later. "Was it the notebook?"

"It was *a* notebook," Joe said as he got in the car. "That's all that they'd tell me. They didn't let me know what was written in it. They only told me that much as a professional courtesy."

"We've got to find out."

"I know. I've let Jock loose on them. He can usually carry the day. He's a Scot, and between that charisma and MacDuff's influence looming in the background, he almost always gets what he wants."

"If he doesn't lose his temper." Her hands clenched. "Remember, Cara's involved in this, too."

"From what you said, Natalie was treating her almost as an afterthought. It was all about you."

"Everything. Natalie said she wanted everything." She

drew a shaky breath. "I have to find out what she's done that she'd think I'd give it to her."

"It could be a bluff," Joe said.

"It wasn't. If you could have heard her voice. She thinks she has me."

"You're shaking." Joe pulled her jacket closer around her. "You should have waited back at the camp."

She shook her head. "No way. It would have driven me crazy."

"I can see it." He kissed her temple. "But it's hell watching you go through this." He was silent a moment. "That son of a bitch, Rampfel, must have done something to you while you were in that office."

"I know," she whispered. "It's the only explanation for everything Natalie has done today. I went over everything he did to me, and it had to be when he was giving me that B-12 shot. I was thinking that I'd have you take me directly to the hospital instead of coming with you here. Natalie might want to kill me, but she has to have something else in mind if she thinks she can use this to get what she wants. We have to know what that is first, Joe."

"Fifteen minutes," he said grimly. "Then I take you to that hospital."

"No, this isn't only me, it's Michael. We have to know what we're dealing with. I won't have anyone blundering around in my body and make a mistake. Natalie would enjoy that enormously if she saw me let that happen."

"Eve . . ."

She could see his pain, but she couldn't let it move her. She had to think of Michael. He had to have his chance. "Michael is fighting, Joe. He has to know what she did to us. That's what first frightened me. We're going to do everything we can to do this thing right."

"Even if it kills you," he said thickly.

"We won't think about that." Except if it came close, she had to prepare him in some way. "We have to keep him alive. Hey, he has your DNA. We're halfway there, Joe."

"Yeah." He held her close. "Halfway . . ."

"It's Iranian," Jock said curtly as he came toward the car an hour later. "Something called *Zaphondan*. Natalie evidently spelled it out in detail in that doctor's notebook. She wanted it very clear. There was even a reference number at the headquarters of MI-6 we could go to for verification."

"And what is *Zaphondan*?" Eve asked.

"One of the ugly little capsules the Iranians created to interrogate prisoners. A ticking clock that keeps them in an agony of suspense. Very innovative, in its way." He gazed at Eve. "And deadly. We should get you to a hospital right away."

"We've already gone down that road," Eve said unsteadily. She had to keep from shaking. Something monstrous and ugly was buried inside her. Dear God . . . Michael. "It can hurt my baby, can't it? It can hurt Michael?"

"Only the doctors can tell you that," Jock said. "We have to get you to—"

"Tell me about this . . . capsule. Is there an antidote?"

"Possibly. There have been cases where a few prisoners survived. But no one but the Iranians have it."

"And maybe Natalie," she said numbly. "How does it work, Jock?"

"It's a microcapsule given generally by a special hypodermic into the muscle tissue. Tiny. It's smaller than a grain of sand. It's set to time-release at a specific time. I believe the Iranians set up a ticking clock so that the prisoners would know exactly how long they had left. It tended to be very effective. But the antidote has to be administered before the release of the capsule, or it won't do any good. The poison works too fast."

"But then the antidote *does* work?" Joe asked.

"Sometimes. It works in the lab. But it depends if any of the poison gets in the bloodstream while the antidote is dissolving it." He added grimly, "The Iranians didn't really give a damn about keeping their promises."

Eve swallowed. "So I have this capsule inside me that's set to go off like a time bomb."

"Presumably," Jock said. "So let's go and find a way to disarm the damn thing."

She nodded. "No more arguments." She was trying to keep calm. "I just had to get a handle on what I was facing." What Michael was facing, she thought in agony. "Take me to the hospital, Joe. I want to know where that damn capsule is located and if there's any chance of a leak to Michael right now. I need to know everything that Natalie knows before she gets in touch with me again."

"You should stay there in that hospital. I'll get specialists over here from the U.S."

"You'd do better to get me one from Iran," she said. "Or at least find one that Natalie imported to Moscow to create that poison. That could be a package deal."

"I'll work on it," Joe said unevenly as he pulled the car away from the curb. "It's going to be okay, Eve. I promise you."

She didn't answer as she leaned back in the seat. It had to be okay. Not for her, because she'd become accustomed to the thought of that other life to come. But Michael had an entire wonderful life on the horizon. She wouldn't let it be taken away from him.

Did you hear him, Michael? We'll find a way . . .
Strength. Warmth. Comfort. Love.
No longer that anger and rejection. That had been for

her, a warning. Now Michael was back to what he had been before. All love. Special. Caring.

And Natalie had wanted to kill this wonder?

SOUTH GLASGOW UNIVERSITY
HOSPITAL
TWO DAYS LATER

"What is going on?" Jane's voice was shaking as she came into Eve's hospital room. "This isn't supposed to happen to you." She came over to the bed and took her hand. "Not you, Eve. The universe is turning upside down."

"She's not going to beat us," Eve said. "We just have to get past this first patch and get some sort of plan together." She paused. "How is Cara?"

"What do you think? In shock."

"Is Jock with her?"

"No, he came back to the camp and gave us the news, then for the last two days, he's been talking to Palik and other contacts he made in Moscow trying to get information." She shook her head. "And I'm not sure he could have helped Cara anyway until she gets through this first trauma. I haven't been able to break through to her."

"I should talk to her."

"Eve, you can't handle everything yourself. Give us a chance. Joe said that those doctors were exploring every possibility about how to save you and Michael." She paused. "How to save you *or* Michael if it comes down to choice. How to delay the time release to give you more time." Her voice was becoming uneven. "Pretty heavy stuff."

"Cara would want to talk to me."

"Okay, she wanted to come, but I told her that they

wouldn't allow too many visitors while they were giving you all these tests." She swallowed hard. "It was the truth. I had trouble getting in myself. It's quite a hospital . . . all those robots and supermodern gadgets. I think I'd prefer a nice, knowledgeable nurse. Someone who would just say that, of course, you were going to be fine."

"I *will* be fine." She looked her in the eye. "Those robots you're scorning have located the capsule, it's fixed itself to the muscles of my right hip. Rampfel didn't give me a shot, he inserted the capsule instead in that special hypodermic he was given by Natalie's people. It's a microcapsule and incredibly tiny." She used Jock's description. "Smaller than a grain of sand." How could something that tiny be the means to kill her Michael? She swallowed hard as she remembered how she and Rampfel had joked as he had done that to her. Why hadn't she seen, sensed, what he was doing? He had been so *damn* plausible. "Conveniently, I couldn't see what he was doing at the time. He must have blocked it from the nurse standing by the door, too. The capsule's contained in a sleeve that's superstrong, and it appears that it's not going to budge or dissolve until it's time for it to do its thing."

"Can they operate? Can't they just cut the damn thing out?"

"Not without risking the capsule's breaking open. Joe called MI-6 and they said they'd tried to do that with a prisoner they'd rescued, and he was dead in two minutes. We have to have the antidote to first neutralize the poison."

"Shit."

"Joe's sentiments exactly."

"And yours."

"Oh, yes, I was hoping for a simpler fix to this particular disaster." Her hand tightened on Jane's. "But there's not a simple fix. We have to deal with Natalie. You're going to have to help me, Jane."

"Anything."

She shook her head. "You won't like it. Joe is going to want me to stay in this hospital and have them wrap me in cotton wool while they try desperately to perform a miracle."

"I'd second that motion."

"I know you would. But I can't do that. There's going to come a time when Natalie is going to pull the strings, and I'm going to have to dance to them." Her lips twisted. "Or at least pretend to dance. I can't take a chance of missing an opportunity to confront her by being too careful."

"I don't like where this is going," she said warily.

"I told you that you wouldn't."

"You can't go running around and risk breaking open that capsule."

"The doctors said that I could leave the hospital and conceivably do anything I would normally do without doing that."

"Conceivably. There's still a danger. They wouldn't want you to do it."

"Of course they wouldn't. They don't know very much about this damn capsule."

"Joe would never permit you to take a chance like that."

She smiled faintly. "I know. And that's when I call you and tell you I need you and that you have to come and spring me from this place."

"Eve, don't ask me to do this."

Eve hated asking her, but she had no choice. She had thought long and hard and knew it was the only solution. "I will ask you," she said steadily. "I'll stay here as long as I can and let them look for their miracle, but I know there will come a time when Natalie is going to want to confront me and rub my face in her victory. She hates me."

"Jock will go after her. So will Joe. Maybe they'll get to her before—"

"She hates me. In the end, I'll have to face her." Her expression hardened. "I *want* to face her. She's trying to kill my son." Her hand tightened on Jane's. "And that's why you'll do as I ask, Jane. Because you understand about family, and Michael is the beginning of something very special in our family. She can't be allowed to destroy him. Can she?"

Jane was silent. "No." She leaned forward and held Eve close. "But Joe may never forgive me. I may never forgive myself." Her eyes were glittering with moisture as she straightened. "You'll keep your word? You'll give those miracle workers their chance?"

"As long as I can." She cleared her throat. "Now get out of here and get back to Cara. She needs you more than I do."

"But we all need you," Jane said. "Don't you forget it." She gave her a kiss on the cheek. "Let me know as soon as Natalie sees fit to call you."

Eve nodded. "It should be soon. She's just letting me see how hopeless my situation is turning out to be. But Natalie will start to be impatient to actually see me suffer."

"I think I might kill her," Jane said fiercely, "I know I will if she hurts you."

"Jane." Eve braced herself. Now she had to say the words she'd been dreading since Jane had walked into the room. But they had to be said. "One of the possibilities the doctors are considering is trying to delay that capsule from breaking until Michael is developed enough to survive without me. To keep me alive for the next few months until he has a chance." She held up her hand as Jane started to speak. "If, by some miracle they manage to save Michael and not me, I know you'll care for him as if he were your own. He *will* be your own. And I'll try my best to be there . . . looking over you."

"Eve." Jane's tears were suddenly overflowing. "Nothing is going to—"

"And Joe. It will be so hard for Joe." She blinked her own tears back. "Big job, Jane. I wouldn't trust anyone but you with it."

"No job at all. A privilege." Her voice broke. "A gift." She headed for the door. "But one I pray I won't . . . have to accept."

The next moment she was gone.

Eve wiped her eyes. She had been hard on Jane. But she didn't know what was going to happen yet, and if hope and determination weren't enough, she had to face the worst that could happen.

Okay, all tears over. Turn down the lights so that Joe wouldn't notice the traces when he came into the room. He was going through enough without seeing her like that. They would talk and she would hold him and for a little while, they'd try to forget that computer on the bedside table.

Skype.

Natalie had wanted Skype so that she could fully enjoy Eve's pain.

Eve wished that the damn computer would ping so that she could know what Natalie had in store for her.

Patience. Natalie was using Skype as she was using that capsule, to try to torture Eve. To make Eve desperate enough to give her the treasure she wanted.

Block it.

It won't work, Natalie.

I have Joe. I have Michael. You don't even know the meaning of treasure.

LOCH GAELKAR

Jock was busy. Cara shouldn't bother him. He was trying to help Eve. They were all trying to help Eve.

Everyone but her.

She *had* to bother him.

Cara stopped outside his tent where he was sitting, dialing his phone. "Could I speak to you, Jock? I won't be long."

"In a minute," he said absently. "I just have to check with Palik about someone he—" He broke off as he saw her face. He hung up the phone. "Be as long as you like. I tried to stop by to see you this morning, but then I had to go talk to MacDuff about—"

"I know you're busy," she interrupted. "I want you to be busy. You're trying to help Eve. I just wanted to tell you something."

"So tell me," he said gently. "I realize this is hard for you, Cara. I'm sorry I didn't have time to really talk to you. I had to leave it up to Jane."

"That was okay. You told me what you had to tell me. What else could you say? I couldn't expect you to treat me—I have to stop being such a kid."

"Jane said you weren't talking. She was a little worried."

"She shouldn't have been—No one should worry about me. Only about Eve." She took a step closer. "That's what I wanted to tell you. It has to be about Eve. You can't think about me. No one can think about me. You said that Natalie told Eve that Kaskov wanted me back. If that's part of what will help get her to save Eve, then you can't—"

"You're giving me too many can'ts," he said roughly. "We'll do whatever we can to get Eve safe and sound through this, but you're not going to be a bargaining chip. Eve wouldn't want that, and I sure as hell don't."

"It doesn't matter what you want. What anyone wants. All that matters is Eve's getting what she needs." She moistened her lips. "Natalie wants the treasure, but there is no treasure yet. But I'm here, maybe you could use me."

"And I'm supposed to send you right back into those claws of hers?" His hands were knotted into fists. "We just got you away from them, dammit."

He was getting angry. She wanted to back away, or to come closer. Anything to stop him from being upset with her in this world where everything else was dark and bewildering. But she couldn't let anything matter but what she had come to say. "You can't just turn me over to her, that wouldn't do any good. I've been thinking about it. Natalie is using me. You've got to do that, too."

"I'm not listening to you, Cara."

"You *have* to listen." Her voice was suddenly passionate. "Because I won't let this go on. All my life, people have given their lives so that I could live. My sister, Jenny, Elena . . . Do you think I'll let Eve do that, too? Only this time it would be Eve and Michael. And I promised to take care of both of them. It has to stop. *I* have to stop it."

"By taking a risk with Natalie? No way."

"Use me. I just wanted you to be prepared, to be able to make plans. Because if you don't do it, I will."

"Are you trying to bluff me, Cara?"

"Oh, no. That would be a lie, and I would never lie to you. You're my dearest friend, and I love you. Friends don't lie to each other. I'd like you to help me, but, if you don't, I want you to know that I'll have to do it by myself."

His jaw tautened. "Cara, Natalie would kill you."

She nodded. "I know that. It doesn't hurt anymore. I believed you when you told me about souls and that she wasn't really my mother. Well, maybe it hurts a little, but only because I don't understand people like her."

"No one could," he said hoarsely. "Except maybe Satan."

"She hates Eve. She hates me. That's why we have to go around her."

"Around her?"

"Kaskov doesn't hate me. I'm not sure exactly what he feels, but it's not hate. When you use me, it should be with Kaskov."

"No one's going to use you."

"Yes they will." She looked him in the eye. "You're so clever, Jock. You told me that this is what you do. I hate it, it hurts me, but you're doing it right now. Only you're trying to keep me out of it."

"I will keep you out of it, Cara."

She shook her head. "You'll just make me do it alone. Remember when we were on that plateau, and you were so angry and frustrated because you said that you could see me standing in your way over and over and not letting you help me? Well, I'm letting you help." She straightened. "Otherwise, I have Kaskov's telephone number. I can call him and set up a meeting. He'd come for me."

"And I'd kill him."

"He's not stupid. Neither am I. I've been running for a long time. I don't want to run toward Kaskov, but I will if I have to do it." She turned away. "Use me. I know you're not going to do it until you think that there's nothing else to do. But I can't wait long, Jock. I'll be thinking and going over everything I learned about Kaskov while I was with him. You do that, too. And make a plan that will give both me and Eve a chance."

"Cara, this is crazy."

She looked over her shoulder. "Yes, it is. And it's crazy that a child that Eve loves and needs almost more than life could be a pawn in Natalie's game. It's crazy that Eve could die." Her eyes were glittering with tears. "We have to stop it, Jock."

She walked away from him.

She had meant every word.

Jock muttered a curse as he watched her disappear into her tent. He had known she was upset, and he should have spent more time with her and not let her work out everything for herself. Now she'd had time to think and come to conclusions. Knowing Cara, those conclusions would now be translated into determination.

He had two solutions to the problem.

Tie her up in that tent until this was all over.

Or get Eve to talk to her and hopefully persuade her to keep out of it and let them do their jobs to save Eve.

He reached into his pocket, pulled out his phone, and dialed Eve.

"I can't talk long, Jock," Eve said when she picked up the phone. "I'm waiting for Natalie to get in touch with me."

"This will be short," he said curtly. "I just want you to call Cara when you get a chance. I need some backup. She's had too much time to think, and she's about to spiral out of control. I think if anyone you can bring her down to earth."

"Talk," she said briefly.

Jock told her swiftly and succinctly of his conversation with Cara. "She'll do it, Eve. No question. Of course

I could knock her out and keep her chloroformed like Natalie did. That would mean she'd hate me for the rest of her life, but at least she'd have a life."

"Easy, Jock. I know you're upset, but there has to be a way to handle this that—" She stopped and was silent a moment. "You do know that Cara is right, don't you? Natalie does hate me, and it will be difficult to deal with her because of that hatred. We do have a better chance with Kaskov."

"Of course I know Cara is right. She's smart as a whip, and, naturally, she came up with the right answer. I've been probing possibilities in that direction myself. Kaskov is intelligent and cool as a cucumber. We might be able to negotiate with him about the antidote. But there's a massive difficulty to find a way to take off his blinders about Natalie."

"Which have been firmly in place since she's been a teenager," Eve murmured. "But, if he's intelligent, there must have been signals that he detected."

"I don't know how much time we'll have to try to persuade him that she's trying to kill his granddaughter." He paused. "On another note, I just heard from Palik that he might have located the Iranian doctor who sold the poison capsule to Natalie. His name is Nasim Feroz and the word is that he was brought to Moscow several days ago and has been put up in a house in the city. We're trying to find out more about him now."

She felt a leap of hope. "That's good news for a change."

"Palik isn't certain. But he has a name, and we didn't have that before. I'll find out more as soon as I can." Jock brought the conversation back to the original subject. "Cara. Will you call her?"

"Yes. And I'll ask Jane to bring her to the hospital tomorrow and talk to her in person . . . If I'm still here."

Jock was silent for a moment. "How are you, Eve?"

"I feel fine. Perfectly normal. The doctors said I would."

"You will be fine," Jock said. "We're all working hard. We're going to get you out of this, Eve."

"I know. I've got quite a team. I have to go now, Jock. I'll call Cara when I can." She hung up.

Eve had sounded a bit absentminded, Jock thought as he hung up. Well, why not? With everything hanging over her head from a death threat to Cara's threatening to run to Kaskov?

Jock's gaze went to Cara's tent. Go and try to talk to her again?

No, she'd been too determined. Better to apply himself to the job at hand and finish the call to Palik he'd been making when Cara had come to him.

Leave it to Eve.

Eve sat there in bed, thinking, after she'd hung up from Jock.

Cara . . .

It was like her to try to persuade Jock that she should be used as a chess piece in this struggle against Natalie. And also like her to come up with what she thought was a way to do it.

Kaskov.

Eve's gaze went to the computer on the bedside table. Natalie was still taking her time. Eve had better brace herself. When she did call, the fact that she'd chosen to make the call Skype was a clear indication she was going to let loose all the venom she'd been storing up.

Just as she'd done when she'd talked to her on the phone . . .

Wait. Why had she . . .

Eve's mind was suddenly racing. Did you make a mistake, Natalie? We're you so angry and outraged that you gave me an out?

She inhaled sharply as a thought came to her. She sat up straighter in the bed. Oh, my God.

Don't call yet, Natalie.

Give me just a little more time.

She quickly reached for her phone.

Hurry.

She had to call Joe.

There was just a chance if it was in time . . .

The signal for the Skype pinged at three thirty the next morning.

Eve was not sleeping. She had known that Natalie wouldn't be able to wait much longer. She was just grateful that she had waited this long. Joe was straightening in his chair across the room, and Eve motioned that she'd get the call. She took a deep breath, swung her feet to the floor, and flipped open the computer.

Natalie's beautiful face smiled at her from the screen. "Did I wake you? I'm certain that all those doctors and nurses haven't let you sleep very much. You look quite haggard."

"I feel fine. I'm getting more rest than usual. You did wake me."

"Liar." Her smile was catlike. "You've been lying there, scared to death, waiting for my call."

"I'm not scared. I'm angry and planning what I'm going to do down the road to punish you for putting my son through this."

"Always the children." She wrinkled her nose distastefully. "That's what's brought you to this point. My daughter Jenny's skull that you meddled with and caused so much trouble. Cara. Now your own child. They've made you weak. So very weak, Eve."

"No, they've made me strong. You're the one who had to come to me, Natalie."

Natalie's complacent smile ebbed slightly. "You're such a fool. I've killed you, Eve. You just don't realize it yet."

"No, you haven't. You've threatened me. But you must be willing to offer me a lifeline, or you wouldn't have set up this little 'surprise' as you called it." She paused. "How long do I have before this capsule inside me releases its poison?"

"My. My. All those fancy doctors who have been studying you like a bug couldn't tell you?"

"Not without removing it, but that would have been too risky. They believe I may have another four or five days."

"That's optimistic. You have three days."

Eve felt as if she'd been kicked in the stomach. "But you have the antidote that will neutralize the poison?"

"Of course I do."

"Prove it."

"I don't have to prove it, do I? You're at a disadvantage. You must feel very desperate to know I have the antidote in my hands. You do what I wish, I give you the antidote."

"You do have to prove it. I won't give you anything until I know we have a chance. And I also want you to give me the name of the Iranian agent who sold you the pill and where I can reach him."

"Why, Eve, you don't trust that I'll keep my bargain?"

"I want his name."

"You might get it. After I get what I want."

"And what exactly do you want?"

"I told you, the treasure."

"And Cara?"

"Well, naturally, but that's not as important."

"I regard it as very important. I won't give you Cara. You tried to kill her in Moscow. You killed her sister, Jenny."

"They were in my way. And Cara might be able to testify against me at some point." She shrugged. "But she might live for a while. My father is being very stubborn about her. He's always been foolish about that stupid music. I managed to deal with it when my brother was taking his attention. But it may take me a while to work around him to get my own way this time."

"I'm sure that's no problem for you," Eve said bitterly.

"None at all." She smiled serenely. "I know exactly what makes him tick. I've always been able to control him." Her smile disappeared. "And in the end, you'll give me what I want. You barely know Cara. Why should you give up a chance to let your own child live to save her? It's a matter of choice, Eve. Your life, your child's life, or Cara, who has been on borrowed time for years anyway." Her voice became ice-cold. "And make no mistake, I will go through with this. I won't lose twice to you. You'll give me everything I want, or you'll never see that antidote."

Eve was silent. She bit down on her lower lip. "Change your mind. She's your daughter. Let her stay with me and live."

"You're begging me." Natalie was almost purring with satisfaction. "That's what I was hoping you'd do. Do you know how much pleasure that gives me?"

"I can imagine. Let her live."

"Choose." Natalie was shaking her head. "Your life and that baby you're carrying or Cara."

Eve looked down and was silent again. Then she raised her head, and said shakily, "You seem to have me over a barrel. You're right, I barely know your daughter. I can't sacrifice my own family." She paused. "Give me your instructions."

"You come here tomorrow night at midnight with the gold. I'll call and give you an address in downtown Moscow when you arrive in the city. You bring no one with you except Cara." Her voice was mocking. "No Joe Quinn. No Jock Gavin, who caused me so much trouble. This time you face me alone."

"I can't trust you."

"Too bad."

"I'll come alone, and I'll bring Cira's gold to Moscow, but I won't give you its location until you hand over the antidote and the name and address of the man who created this particular poison. MI-6 has already given me a list of the Iranian projects' doctors. If I don't recognize the name, you don't get the location of the gold." She grimaced. "Just in case you decide to give me a placebo. Of course, that would never happen."

Natalie smiled sweetly. "I'm glad you realize that it's only a precaution."

"And is this address in the city one of your father's compounds, where I'll be surrounded by his men?"

"No, but I'll have my own men to make sure that you don't slip through my fingers. I prefer not to share the gold with my father, so it's just as well that I only let him know what I need him to know."

"You're being very open about this. Not like you at all. I remember how cautious you were about incriminating yourself when I first talked to you."

"Ivan helped me protect myself. You'll see after I hang up. It's very amusing. Sort of like that old vintage spy series. I couldn't bear not being able to talk freely to you. I deserve it."

"I'm certain that you think you deserve everything. Get back to me with that address. I can't wait to get this . . . *thing* out of my body." Eve hung up.

She sat there, tense, watching the screen.

One minute passed.

Two minutes.

The screen blinked and clicked, and then went dead.

She turned to Joe. "She thinks my hard drive is wiped clean of this call?"

Joe nodded. "That's what her computer will read. What I set up in your computer to tell her."

"And everything is still intact? All we have to do is retrieve it?" She drew a shaky breath. "I realized tonight she wouldn't be able to resist a little malicious bragging when she said she was going to set up Skype. And when I thought back, she'd said things on the other phone call that she wouldn't ordinarily have said. She'd always carefully protected herself before. That meant this time she had to have it stream on protective software. I was only worried that you wouldn't have time to get the right software installed tonight to block it."

"We got it." He sat down and held her close. "Now stop shaking, or Michael will start giving you hell."

"In a minute." She slipped her arms around him and buried her face in his chest. "Just talking to her makes me want to go take a shower. She was at her most venomous tonight, wasn't she? I felt like I was watching a cobra weave back and forth."

"Shh." He was rocking her. "You did a good job. Forget her for now."

"I can't forget her. She's there waiting for me. My mind is zinging around trying to find a way to make this work." She lifted her head. "But we have a chance now. If we can get that computer to Kaskov, there's enough on it to disillusion him with Natalie and maybe get him to bargain about the antidote."

"You led her to boast about everything from child

murder to personal insults at Kaskov himself. Yes, we have a chance." His lips tightened. "But I'm not letting you go anywhere near her alone."

"Yes, you are. If it comes down to it. She's setting the rules. She'd love to kill you in front of me. I won't lose you, Joe. We'll just hope to reach Kaskov and win him over before we have to face Natalie." She sat up straight. "And now we have to call Jock and see what we can do to run that gauntlet. He knows more than anyone else about Kaskov's setup."

CHAPTER
15

"It may work," Jock said slowly. "But it's a big risk, Eve."

"Everything's a big risk now," Eve said. "But Natalie is the biggest risk of all. Can you get me into Kaskov's house or at least the grounds?"

"Probably. I've never made the run, but I memorized the floor plan when I was going after Cara. But I'd have to clear the way for you. Losing a couple men might piss him off."

"We'll worry about that when it happens. I have to try to get to him. Natalie was arrogant as hell on the phone. She's not going to let me get out of Moscow alive." She paused. "She's demanding that I turn over Cara to her. Cara might live for a little while, but I doubt it. Natalie's more likely to forget about what her father wants and kill her immediately."

"You weren't thinking of taking her with you?"

"No, I just have to work out a way that Natalie will

think I am." She didn't know what on earth that would be, she thought wearily. "She's got to believe that I'm doing as she orders, so we can stall until we can get to Kaskov. But I had to make sure that you could get me to him before I did anything else."

"I'll get you to him. And I'll set up a way to get you out if things go wrong." He added, "What about Quinn? He's going with you?"

"Not if I can help it. I've asked him to go to check out Feroz, that Iranian doctor you thought might have created the poison and could have the antidote. The chances are that Natalie won't give me the antidote and will lie about the doctor who created it."

"I was going to check that out for you."

"But I need you to get me to Kaskov. You can't be everywhere, Jock."

"And you want Joe as far away as possible from the action."

"He'll see plenty of action. It's his nature. But I want my baby to have a chance of having a father if he makes it through this, and I don't. God, that sounds terrible. It's not as if I want to put you in danger, Jock. It's just that Michael has to be—"

"Protected," Jock finished for her. "I understand." He added wryly, "I've been telling Cara this is what I do. Now I guess it's time I proved it. When do you leave?"

"No later than tomorrow morning. I have to meet Natalie tomorrow night. It seems I don't have as much time as I thought according to her. Three days."

Silence. "She could be lying."

"She was taking a little too much pleasure in it. I believe she was telling the truth this time."

"Tomorrow night." He was thinking, calculating, setting up the kills to come. "That's not going to give me enough time if we leave tomorrow. I'm heading for Moscow right now. Tell Joe to get Caleb to fly you in tomorrow, and I'll meet you at Skovski Airport."

"I could go now. Just wait until—"

"I don't need you. There are things I have to do. I'll see you in Moscow." He hung up.

Three days, and Eve could be dead.

Jock could feel the anger start to burn within him. Strange that he had never felt anything but icy coldness before at the thought of a kill. But then he had never cared about anything during that period. Certainly not danger to a person he cared about.

Eve . . .

He turned and headed up the slope to his car, which was parked on the road.

"Jock."

He turned to see Cara, outlined by the leaping flames of the campfire, walking toward him.

Dammit. He'd hoped to get away from camp without seeing her. He instinctively tensed, but he stopped and waited for her to reach him.

"Where are you going?" She was gazing up at him. "I saw you talking on the phone for a long time. Is Eve okay?"

"Eve is fine. No change in her condition."

"Then where are you—"

"Cara, stay out of it."

She shook her head. "Where are you going?"

She wouldn't give up.

"Moscow. I'm heading for Edinburgh to catch a flight."

She went rigid. "Natalie?"

"She called Eve, and we're moving. But we have a chance of getting that antidote now."

"Eve's leaving now, too?"

"No, Caleb will take her in the morning. I have some preparations to make."

Her eyes were wide with fear. "What preparations?"

"I'm not going to go into it with you, Cara." He took a step closer to her and grasped her thin shoulders. "You're going to stay here with Jane and MacDuff and let them take care of you." He smiled. "Or you take care of them, whichever way you decide. But it's got to be here and out of the line of fire."

"No!"

"That's how it's going to be." He let her go and stepped back. "But you should be glad to know that you're going to get what you wanted. We've found a way to go after Kaskov. We're going to try that route before Natalie."

"Then I should be going with you," she said eagerly. "I know him. I can talk to him. I can help."

"And you can get yourself caught in the same trap you were in before."

"Then you can do something to get me out of it if I do. But I'd be so careful that it wouldn't happen. Eve needs me." She gazed up at him, her eyes pleading. "Michael needs me. Please, Jock."

Damn, he wished he'd gotten away before he'd seen her. She was tearing him apart. He wanted to give her the world.

"Not possible," he said hoarsely. "Trust me to take care of it for you."

"It has to be me. This is why I was meant to come to Eve. It was because I could help her and Michael."

He couldn't take any more of this. He turned and headed up the slope. "Trust me."

"They *need* me," she called after him. Her voice was agonized. "Take me with you, Jock."

He didn't answer, his pace increased.

When he reached the road, he looked back, and she was still standing there, her hands clenched into fists at her sides, looking up at him.

He turned his head away and strode down the road to his car.

Jane's cell rang at 5:10 the next morning. Her heart jumped when she realized it was Eve. "Are you all right? You're not—"

"Dying?" Eve chuckled. "No, though I can't blame you for thinking that considering what a downer of a conversation we had when you were at the hospital. No, I only called to tell you Joe and I are on our way to the airport to meet Caleb. We should be there in a few minutes. We're heading for Moscow."

"I know. Jock called me last night after he got on the road and told me that Cara was upset and to keep an eye on her. He was right. She stayed by the fire for hours, and all she'd say was that you needed her. She didn't go to her tent until nearly midnight."

"I was afraid of that. Maybe she'll be better today."

"Or maybe she won't," Jane said. "I'm feeling a bit abandoned myself. I much preferred the scenario where I was to come and break you out of the hospital. I want to be with you, too."

"We need protection for Cara and MacDuff. There's no one I trust more."

"Sorry. I'll stop complaining and do my job. But you do your job and take care of yourself."

"That's what I intend to do." Eve was silent an instant. "You know when we came back from Moscow, I was so happy. I thought that it might be almost over. But Natalie had other ideas. So here I am on my way back to face her again. It seems as if it goes on and on."

"Maybe it will be the last time." Jane paused. "This could really work? Kaskov is a dangerous criminal. Even if you convince him his daughter isn't what he thinks she is, he might still prefer her to you. He might not give a damn what happens to you."

"That's true. But there's a chance, and I have to take every possible chance for Michael." She paused. "And for all the rest of my family. I love you, Jane. Watch over Cara and MacDuff." She hung up.

Jane blinked away tears as she hung up. These good-byes were beginning to have a frightening finality about them. She wanted it over, Eve healthy and safe, the baby normal and on his way to a happy life. It was going to seem like a long time until Eve called her to tell her whether Kaskov had given her what she needed to stay alive.

She envied Caleb that he was going to be with her, helping them, bringing them home.

Caleb hadn't even told her that he was taking them to Moscow. She'd had to hear it from Jock. Not that it should have surprised her. Caleb hadn't been very communicative since that morning in the mist. She had been grateful that she hadn't had to deal with him and the tumult of her emotions when he was around. But he could have let her know that he was going away.

And she was being completely unreasonable, she thought impatiently. She couldn't have it all ways. He had gone too far. Or not far enough. Whenever she let her guard down enough to think of him, her body still readied, burned. Her heart would start to pound, and she still remembered him lying there naked in the mist. Because he had been different during those last moments, his attitude, not threatening, but darkly decisive. It was better that she had a chance to get over that memory before she let herself think of Caleb again.

So stop thinking about him.

Her body was becoming flushed, her breathing rapid. All of this nonsense because she had envied that he had been able to go with Eve and Joe and she'd had to stay at the camp.

Well, she was here, and she'd make the best of it. She'd help MacDuff all she could. Spend as much time with Cara as the girl would let her. Last night by the fire, she'd been completely despondent. Okay, let her sleep a couple more hours, then go cook breakfast, wake her, and try to get her to talk.

But Jane knew she wouldn't go back to sleep now. She was too on edge.

Be safe, Eve.

I'm praying for you.

And, dammit, you bring her back to me, Seth Caleb.

"Coffee?" Caleb came out of the cockpit. "You look as if you could use it." His gaze raked Eve's face. "A little tense."

"Maybe she'd be less tense if you were back in the cockpit flying the plane," Joe said dryly. "I think I can handle anything else."

"It's on autopilot. Just thought I'd pop back to make sure that you were comfortable." He smiled mockingly. "I always like to be a good host."

"We're fine, Caleb," Eve said quickly. "When will we arrive in Moscow?"

"Another couple hours. We're making good time though." He turned back to the cockpit. "But Quinn is right, I'd better get back. Autopilots are a wonderful invention, but mountains can be so troublesome . . ."

Eve shook her head as she saw Joe about to say something. "He's just being Caleb. And I'm grateful he was there for us when we needed him."

"So am I." He grimaced. "But if I didn't know he was such a good pilot, and if this Gulfstream 650 plane wasn't the fastest aircraft around and required special checking

out, I'd be in that cockpit flying the damn plane myself."
He laced his fingers through hers on the leather arm of the
seat. "Do you want that coffee? I'll go get you some from
the dispenser in the back."

She shook her head. "I'm trying to cut down on caffeine. It's not good for Michael." Then she smiled ruefully.
"And that's totally bizarre. I have this megadose of poison
inside me, and I'm worried about caffeine."

"I believe Michael would forgive you." He lifted her
hand to his lips. "And we'll take care of that poison soon,"
he said thickly. "I promise you that I'll get that antidote
from that Iranian son of a bitch. It will be in your hands
long before you have to meet with Natalie. You'll be able
to tell her to go to hell."

"I know you'll do your best," she said quietly. "But if
something goes wrong, if everything isn't what we hope
it will be, don't blame yourself. That's the only promise I
want from you, Joe." She met his eyes. "It's going to be
a strange night, isn't it? After all, we have two other options we can tap before we have to show up at Natalie's
place at midnight. You have a chance to get the antidote
from Feroz. We might be able to bargain with Kaskov if
we can persuade him to look at this disc I have in my
handbag." She moistened her lips, "And, as a last resort,
we'll deal with Natalie. Three chances, Joe. Better odds
than we had before."

"I'll get the antidote from Nasim Feroz," Joe repeated
grimly. "We won't need another option."

She didn't doubt that he had a good chance. When Joe
was at his most deadly, he could intimidate the devil
himself. He was way past that point now. "It may take
longer than you—"

Her cell phone rang, and she instinctively tensed.
Natalie? Another report from one of those specialists
who'd been running tests on her? Jock?

Jane.

She put it on speaker, and answered. "We're fine, Jane. We haven't reached—"

"She's gone," Jane interrupted. "I've been looking for the last hour, and I can't find Cara anywhere. I went into her tent to wake her for breakfast, and she wasn't there."

"Gone." Eve's hand tightened on the phone. Had Natalie's demand that she bring Cara just been a ploy to hide the fact that she was sending someone to take her? "Did any of the guards see anyone who might have—"

"Nobody took her," Jane said. "I checked with the perimeter guards, and they didn't see anyone. MacDuff doubled the guards when he knew that Jock and Caleb wouldn't be at the camp. Security was supertight." She drew a shaky breath. "I've looked everywhere. I even went about a mile into the mist. She's not here, Eve. I'm scared to death. She was so worried about you. I kept remembering that she told Jock that if we didn't let her go to Kaskov, she'd call him and arrange for him to pick her up."

Eve was remembering that, too. "How much time did she have?"

"Midnight to about eight in the morning."

And Cara was used to being on the run. That was a sizeable head start.

"I'm sorry, Eve," Jane said unevenly. "After I hang up, I'm going to get in the car and start driving around and asking questions at the villages. I just thought that you should know what to expect when you try to talk to Kaskov."

"I should probably turn around and come back and help you."

"No!" Jane said. "You don't have time. Less than three days now, Eve. I'll do everything you could do. I have MacDuff, and he'll pressure the police until they find some sign of her. Besides, if she contacted Kaskov, she might be heading in the same direction you are."

Everything Jane was saying made sense, but it still didn't halt the shock and fear Eve was feeling.

"I'm hanging up," Jane said. "I'll let you know if I find out anything." She broke the connection.

Joe was swearing softly. "You didn't need this. When I see Cara, I'm going to—"

"Do what? She's just doing what the rest of you are doing. She's trying to save me. Only maybe she's a little more desperate because the person she's trying to save me from is her mother." She ran her fingers through her hair. "But we're not alone, Joe. She thought she had to do it alone because none of us would listen to her. How can I blame her?"

"Did I miss something?" Caleb was standing in the door of the cockpit. He was gazing at Eve's face. "Yes, I see I did. A telephone call?"

Eve swallowed. "Jane."

He nodded. "I expected it before this. She must have been concerned that she'd worry you."

Joe got slowly to his feet. "Caleb."

"I think it's time you had that coffee." He moved down the aisle toward the back of the plane. "You might keep an eye on the instruments, Quinn. I think it's okay, but you can never tell."

Joe didn't move, his gaze narrowed on Caleb.

Caleb shrugged. "Suit yourself."

He opened the door to the small lounge in the rear. But instead of going to the coffee machine, he went beyond it to the storage compartment. He threw open the door. "Time to face the music, Cara. Too bad you didn't bring your violin." He reached down and helped the girl to her feet. "Little stiff? I would have brought you out earlier, but Jane was being stubborn about admitting that you couldn't be found. But then, that's Jane."

"Cara?" Eve was staring at her in disbelief. Cara's face was pale and pinched, and her jeans and chambray shirt were rumpled. But she was alive. She was not in Natalie's hands, nor Kaskov's. They could keep her safe.

Then the anger came. "I want to *murder* you," Eve said. "How could you do this?"

"You need me." She moistened her lips. "I can help you. I'm supposed to help you. Why else would Jenny send me to you?"

"Duty calls," Caleb murmured. "I believe it's time I went back to the cockpit. But feel free to join me at any time, Eve."

"Don't worry, I will," she said grimly, as the cockpit door closed behind him. She whirled to face Cara. "This is *my* life. My son's life. I'm in charge here. I don't want to have to worry about you, too. You shouldn't have taken the decision out of my hands. I won't—"

"There has to be a reason." Cara's face was paler than before and her voice was unsteady. "It all fits together. Can't you see that? My mother, Kaskov . . . I have to be the one."

"No, I can't see that. I won't risk you to—"

"Eve." Joe put his hand on her shoulder. "What did you say to me just before Caleb exploded his little surprise? At least she didn't go to Kaskov."

"You're defending her? It's going to be twice as hard to deal with Natalie if—" She met Cara's eyes and forgot what she'd been going to say. Desperation. Determination. Love. Everything Cara had done had been done for love. Love was a precious gift in this world. "Come here." She pulled Cara into her arms. "You were wrong. But we'll try to find a way to make it right."

"No, I'm right," Cara whispered. "I tried to tell Jock, but he was too scared to believe me. Don't you be afraid, Eve. I think that whatever happens is meant to be. That maybe Jenny knew all this was going to happen, and that's why I had to be the one."

"I *am* afraid." She pushed her back. "And I don't like this one bit, and I'm going to try to keep you as safe as possible. We have plans, and we're keeping to them. We'll just try to find a way to keep you out of them."

Cara shook her head. "I'm here. If I wasn't meant to be with you, I wouldn't have been able to persuade Caleb to bring me."

"Oh, yes, Caleb." Eve turned toward the cockpit. "I have a few words to say to him. Totally irresponsible. What possessed you to go to him?"

"Jock mentioned that he was going. I thought . . . Caleb is . . . different. He doesn't seem to think like other people."

"Absolutely."

"And he doesn't care what anyone else thinks . . . except maybe Jane."

"Evidently not this time. Jane is going to kill him." She glanced at Joe. "Will you get her a soft drink and something to eat? She looks like she's going to fade away any minute. I want to talk to Caleb."

He was reaching for his phone. "Right after I call Jane and tell her that Cara's not been hijacked by Natalie or Kaskov."

Cara's eyes were fixed on the cockpit door. "He was only trying to help me, Eve. Don't be angry with him."

"There's no telling what Caleb's agenda is at any given time," Eve said as she opened the cockpit door. "And I don't promise that I'll be as easy on him as I was with you. You're a child, he's supposed to be mature."

"I heard that," Caleb said, as the cockpit door closed

behind her. "I take it that you're a little irritated with me?
Sit down. You might as well be comfortable while you're
taking me to task."

"More than a little." She dropped down in the copilot's
seat. "Whatever possessed you to let Cara talk you into
smuggling her onto this plane? You know that it put her
in danger, that it's the last thing we all wanted for her."

He nodded. "She made that clear. She didn't lie or try
to convince me that it would be all right with anyone in
camp. She told me that she was out on a limb all by herself. I respected that honesty."

"I would rather that you'd respected our wishes in the
matter. She's only twelve years old."

"Twelve?" He smiled. "Age is only a number. Remind
me to tell you all the wickedness I was up to when I was
twelve. I like Cara. I felt obligated to listen and judge for
myself if you should have tossed her out on that limb."

"And you decided?"

"I brought her, didn't I?"

"Why?"

"She's right," he said simply. "If anyone can move
Kaskov, it could be her. Since the situation is so critical,
she should have the opportunity. And something else occurred to me. You were worrying about not having Cara
with you when you arrived as Natalie demanded. Now
anyone watching at the airport will see Cara and believe
you're complying." He glanced at her. "If Cara wasn't so
young, you'd probably admit that she has a better chance
than you or anyone else to save you and your son."

"She *is* that young. And she's a target."

"We've already discussed my attitude toward unnecessary sheltering of the young. And she has you and
Quinn and Jock to protect her. I might even join in if it
became necessary. Though I rather doubt it. Cara is very
intelligent."

She was silent. "Joe is calling Jane right now. She's going to want to kill you."

"More than likely. But that's no loss. She was in the mood to do that anyway."

"Why?"

He shrugged. "I got a little impatient. When that happens, my true colors tend to come to the forefront. She has a conflict with whether she wants to accept them."

"Is this bit with Cara an example?"

"Perhaps. If I'd had something to lose, I might have done the conventional thing instead of following my instincts."

"You have incredibly bad instincts."

"No, they're excellent, they're just not like anyone else's."

"That's what Cara said about you."

He chuckled. "I told you that she was intelligent. How can I regret going along with a girl who has judgment like that?"

"Why don't you ask Jock that question when he meets our plane and finds Cara on board?"

"Jock," Caleb murmured. "I admit I had a few apprehensions about his attitude regarding the wisdom of my decision. But that may be interesting, too."

KASKOV ESTATE
MOSCOW

"They're here." Ivan turned away from the phone to Natalie. "I just received a report from Kaskov's man at Skovski Airport. Duncan disobeyed you and brought Quinn . . ." He smiled. "But she also brought your daughter. Kaskov will be pleased."

"I'm not certain we should tell him Cara's here yet. It might be better to wait until we see how things go . . ."

Ivan shook his head. "I know what you're planning, and I went along with you before when Kaskov wasn't in the city. But now he's back on home turf, and it's too dangerous. He was actively involved in getting her back this time. He doesn't like to lose."

She smiled sweetly. "Neither do I."

"Give the kid to him for a little while. I'll take her out for you later. Maybe an accident . . ."

"And in the meantime, I'd have to worry if she's telling him things that would cause him to doubt me."

"I won't risk having Kaskov doubt *me*," he said flatly. "I've been there when he's decided that one of his men had broken his damn rules. It's not pretty. We're going to wait until it's safe for me."

She was tempted to argue, but they were too close to getting the treasure. Agree now and take care of Cara herself.

Along with Ivan Sabak. He was proving entirely too troublesome. It was frustrating that she couldn't control him with sex, and he wouldn't take orders.

"Whatever you say. I wouldn't want to cause you problems." She moved toward the door. "Now I have to go and make sure that my father is still planning to go to that violin concert at the Novako Opera House tonight. I don't want questions about where I'm going when I head for the apartment we rented."

"When are you calling Duncan?"

"I might not call her until the last hour or so before she comes to meet us." She smiled at him over her shoulder. "Now that we know that she's here and ready to give me what I want, it won't hurt her to wait a little longer." Her voice became laced with pure malice. "Do you realize that the entire purpose of that capsule I had inserted in her was meant to bring excruciating tension and fear? Nasim Feroz said he'd seen soldiers weep and beg for mercy. Oh, I do hope that Eve Duncan is prepared to do that."

SKOVSKI AIRPORT

Jock was standing, waiting, near the hangar where Caleb had parked the jet.

Cara tensed as she saw him from the window of the terminal building, where she was standing after she'd gotten off the plane with Eve. Fair hair shimmering in the cold sunlight, his features just as wonderfully perfect as always. But now they looked as if they were carved out of ice. "He's angry."

"What did you expect?" Eve asked. "Do you want me to run interference?"

"No." She jumped to her feet and headed for the door. "I did it. I'll face it."

That was easy to say, but her heart was beating hard as she walked toward Jock. He didn't move. He just waited until she was standing before him.

She braced herself. "I had to do it, Jock."

"Obviously."

She moistened her lips. "Caleb understood that it had to be me. Kaskov likes me. Or the idea of me . . . or something. That means he might listen to me. Caleb could see that could be valuable."

"I may kill him."

She shook her head. "It was all me, Jock. You wouldn't take me, and I had to come here." She took a step closer. "But I don't want to fight you anymore. I have to go to see Kaskov."

"The hell you do."

"I believe I can make him listen. He's used to having his own way. Eve will have trouble if I don't sort of pave the way."

"And what are you going to say that will pave the way with a criminal whose kill record is probably even higher than mine?"

She flinched. "I don't know. I'm hoping it will come to me," she said simply. "Because I have to do this. I can't let you stop me. No matter what you do, I'll find a way to get to him. It will just mean I'll have to run away from you and do it alone. I don't want to be alone, Jock." She swallowed to ease the tightness of her throat. "You promised me I wouldn't have to be alone any longer."

He stared at her for a long moment. "That was below the belt, Cara."

But the ice was breaking, she realized with relief. "Yeah, I know. But it's the truth, and ever since you said it, you've been trying to push me away. Being with someone doesn't mean only in the good times." She looked pleadingly up at him. "You keep telling me that this stuff is what you do. Well, do it, and find a way for me to help Eve. I'll do anything you say. But I have to go with Eve to see Kaskov."

He was gazing down at her. Then he reached down and gently touched her hair. "Shit."

Relief soared through her. "You'll do it."

He nodded. "But I may still kill Caleb."

She hugged him, then stepped back with a luminous smile. "I won't be any trouble. You'll see, Jock."

"Just like you weren't any trouble on that plateau when the helicopter landed." But he was smiling. "And Eve won't be any more pleased than I am about this. You'd better have Caleb convince her to his way of thinking."

"I'm so glad you're not angry any longer. When I saw you standing there, I was so scared."

"I was more terrified than angry. You'll have to learn to tell the difference." His lips twisted. "Or maybe not. I'll need every weapon in my arsenal with you." He turned to Eve as she came out of the terminal. "It appears we have a problem. I may have to make a few adjustments to what I was planning."

"Cara is entirely too happy." Eve was frowning. "I don't like that. You're not planning on giving in to her on this?"

"She offered me an ultimatum. I've gotten to know her well enough to realize that she doesn't bluff. So I'll just have to work around it and keep her safe. She's promised to do everything I tell her to do." He paused. "As long as she goes with you to see Kaskov."

"No."

"Yes. I'll set it up." He was watching Joe and Caleb coming out of the terminal. "And now we'd all better get to the hotel room I rented and go over the plans for tonight. The scheduling may be very tight." He moved forward. "But first I believe I'll have a word or two with Caleb . . ."

CHAPTER
16

BAROZ HOTEL
5:45 P.M.

In spite of Cara's protests Eve deposited her in a hotel room next door to the one where Jock had arranged for their meeting. "You got your way with Jock, but I'm not going to let you be present for the rest of the planning," she said grimly. "You're out of this except for talking to Kaskov."

"But, Eve, what difference—" Cara broke off and nodded her head. "Okay, whatever you say." She opened the door and went into the hotel room. "I did promise Jock."

"Congratulations, you won that battle," Jock said as he unlocked the room next door. "She's twelve. She shouldn't be hearing all this."

"Nasim Feroz," Joe said as soon as the door of the room shut behind them. "You know the address, Jock? You said you'd have it for me."

"I have it." Jock took a small notebook from his jacket

pocket. "And I had Palik scout the area. It's a brick house with a wrought-iron fence in the Arbat section of the city. Feroz has a fellow countryman, Hassan Mehnar, acting as his bodyguard. We're not sure if he's protecting Feroz from us or from Natalie and Kaskov. Palik said that there are two of Kaskov's men on guard there, too."

"So Kaskov is fully involved in this?" Eve asked.

"At least to the extent of providing Natalie with the Iranian doctor who could give her that damn capsule. And I'd bet that those two guards are insurance that Feroz gave Natalie the right poison and antidote for Kaskov's money." His lips twisted. "But you told me yourself that Natalie is trying to keep him in the dark about Cira's gold. She still thinks she can have it all her own way."

"MI-6 told Joe that those Iranian agents often had more than one antidote in their possession," Eve said. "At times, they sold the extra ones to the highest bidder."

Jock nodded. "It's possible." He turned to Joe. "But it's not a sure thing. That's why we have to explore the other two options. Kaskov or Natalie. We try to convince Kaskov that we can offer him whatever he wants for the antidote. If that doesn't work, we follow through with getting Natalie to give it to us. Though God knows I hope we don't get down to having to trust Natalie to do anything but betray us."

"That won't matter," Joe said coldly. "She'll give it to us, or she won't live through the night. She may not anyway." He bent down and was scrawling Feroz's address down. "But first things first. If we get the antidote from Feroz, we can forget about Natalie and Kaskov and get the hell out of Moscow and rush Eve back into that Glasgow hospital." His lips tightened. "We don't have much time."

Jock nodded. "I know. It's going to be close even if—"

"Forget about Natalie." Caleb suddenly straightened from where he'd been leaning against the wall. "You just said she was the last resort. But you'll have to hit Kaskov and Feroz at approximately the same time if you don't want either faction to be on the phone yelling for help from the other."

"No," Joe said instantly. "I need to be with Eve when she goes to Kaskov."

"No, you don't," Eve said. She had known how difficult this was going to be for Joe and had hoped to avoid it. "You have to do what you were planning and let us do what we have to do."

"I won't let you go alone."

"Jock isn't exactly a nonentity." She met his eyes. "And we've got to cover all the bases if we're going to protect Michael. Cara's managed to talk me into risking her neck, and I'll be damned if I'll hesitate about risking my own. You don't think about me right now, Joe. You think about Michael."

"I can't let—" He drew a deep breath and whirled on Jock. "Where are you taking her to meet with Kaskov? His estate? That's too far away from town. It will take me too long to get there after I finish with Feroz."

"No. Not his estate," Jock said. "Kaskov's going to go to a violin concert at the Novako Opera House this evening. That's probably why Natalie set up your meeting for tonight. She wanted to pick a night when she knew he'd be busy and not get in her way." He smiled. "I have a few more details to arrange, but Kaskov may get more than his price of admission tonight at the opera house."

"He'll have bodyguards."

"Yes, but not as many as he'd have at the estate. Leave it to me. I'll take care of them, Quinn." He glanced at Caleb. "But Caleb's right, we should coordinate our efforts. I'll call you when we reach the opera house. You'll be glad to know that it's no more than thirty minutes from Feroz's house. Do you need Palik to arrange for extra firepower for you, Quinn?"

"I don't believe that will be necessary," Caleb answered for Joe. "Strangers so often get in the way of the fun. I think I'll tag along and lend a hand. Between the two of us, I think we can handle it."

"Why are you being so accommodating?" Joe asked dryly.

"It's just a balancing act. I gave you Cara, whom you didn't want. Now I'm giving you my inimitable services, which will make up for anything I've done to put me in your bad books." He smiled at Eve. "And Eve will like the idea of your not being alone to face those guards surrounding Feroz. Isn't that right?"

She couldn't deny it. Caleb was a force to be reckoned with, and she wanted Joe to have every advantage. "I'm still angry with you, Caleb."

"But you'll get over it." He turned back to Joe. "And you know how persuasive I can be when I want something. It may save us a good deal of time." He added softly, "And the more time we save, the sooner you can get to that opera house."

"You don't have to push it. I'd take the help of Satan himself if it got me to Eve sooner tonight." He turned to Jock. "What time?"

"The concert starts at eight. Nine should give me enough time to set up Kaskov. If you can get rid of Feroz's guards, so that I have time to work and not have anyone calling Kaskov to set off an alarm."

"Nine it is. Come on, Caleb. Let's go and see about reconnoitering that area around Feroz's house." Joe turned back to Eve. He kissed her long and hard. "I hate this," he said hoarsely. "And if Jock doesn't take care of you, I'll—"

"Hush." Her fingers covered his lips. "We'll take care

of each other. And we'll all take care of Michael." She kissed him again. "Stay safe, Joe."

He nodded jerkily and turned away. "I'll see you later. I'll be there as quick as I can."

The door closed behind him and Caleb.

Eve drew a shaky breath and, with an effort, tore her gaze away from that door. Don't think of what Joe and Caleb might be facing. Just think about what she and Cara had to face in just a few hours.

"Cara." She turned back to Jock. "I'm so scared for her. Isn't there any way we can keep her out of it?"

"You think I'm not scared?" he said roughly. "If it makes you feel any better, I'll kill anyone in that opera house who even hints at being a threat to her."

"It doesn't make me feel any better." She closed her eyes for an instant. Keep Cara safe. Keep my Michael safe. Maybe the rest of us can take care of ourselves.

Her eyes opened, and she straightened. "We'd better go and get Cara. I hated leaving her alone, but it didn't seem right to have her in the room while we were talking about disposing of Natalie and Kaskov and the others."

"I was just glad that you didn't leave it to me to be the bad guy again. There may be a lot of that tonight." He took her elbow and pushed her gently toward the door. "But now we have to move quickly. I want to have you at the opera house and settled by eight when Kaskov arrives."

"We have over two hours."

He smiled. "But you and Cara have to dress for the occasion in order not to look out of place. These concerts are very formal. Palik sent gowns up for you and Cara. But I'm not sure his taste will be appropriate for a kid of Cara's age."

"Formal?" She made a face. "Oh, for goodness' sake."

"A slight disadvantage but better than facing him at his estate that would be bristling with automatic rifles."

She nodded as she opened the door. "Whatever you say. Let's just get out of here."

"Very nice." Jock's gaze ran over Eve in the elegant bronze-silk gown with the square neckline that displayed a simple gold necklace. "Attractive but not too showy. What about Cara?"

"I only caught a glimpse of her before she disappeared into the bathroom, but I think it's not as inappropriate as you thought it might be." She tucked a small computer and the disc into her brocade evening bag. Then she was quickly running a comb through her hair. "It's sort of ivory, and the neckline isn't low like mine. Maybe Palik has a young girl in his family."

"I never inquired." Jock was checking his watch. "But we'll have to get her out of there. It's time we—" He stopped as Cara came out of the bathroom.

"Am I okay?" she asked breathlessly. "I'm sorry I'm late. I'm not used to dresses, and I couldn't get the zipper in the back to fasten."

Jock didn't speak for a moment, but his expression said it all. "What do you say, Eve? Is she okay?"

Cara looked like a young Juliet, Eve thought. The bateau neckline and empire waist of the ivory-velvet gown that fell to her feet was wonderful on her. Her shiny dark hair was held back by a black, sequined ribbon that matched the sequins on her ballet flats.

"Beautiful," Eve said. "You look lovely, Cara. It's perfect. It reminds me of—" She inhaled sharply as that memory came flooding back to her.

But Cara had seen the hesitation, and she nodded slowly. "Jenny," she said softly. "I saw it, too. Jenny wore a long white dress like this the night she died in the forest, the night she saved me."

"Not quite like that, but similar. She was beautiful, too. But I didn't mean to make you sad by reminding you."

"You didn't make me sad. When I saw it, I thought it was like a sign that I was doing what I should be doing. It was as if Jenny were standing there behind me and telling me that." She suddenly giggled. "But I wish she could have helped me with the zipper."

"You did fine on your own," Jock said gruffly as he grabbed their black-velvet theater cloaks. "Now let's get you to that opera house and see if all this finery helps to scoot us under the wire and into Kaskov's august presence."

NASIM FEROZ RESIDENCE
ARBAT, MOSCOW
8:10 P.M.

"Two guards on the perimeter," Caleb said. "Do you take them out or do I?"

"You're giving me a choice?"

"I thought it would be polite. After all, you have a greater commitment, and there's a certain satisfaction to—"

"I'll take them out."

"Then I'll go in and get rid of Hassan Mehnar, Feroz's personal bodyguard. If that's all right with you? I'd hate to step on your toes."

"Fine." He turned and moved toward the wrought-iron back-garden gate. He was on edge. Sometimes Caleb's mockery grated on him but there was no one that he'd rather have in his corner in a situation like this.

Forget about Caleb.

Concentrate on the man at the gate.

NOVAKO OPERA HOUSE

Crowds of elegantly dressed people milled around the huge lobby of the nineteenth-century opera house.

An enormous crystal chandelier cast a mellow amber glow over the crimson-carpeted grand staircase that dominated the lobby.

The strains of the Mendelssohn violin concerto poured out of speakers on either side of the arched, twenty-foot entrances.

"That's Hans Finster playing tonight." Cara's eyes were suddenly shining with excitement. "I heard him play on PBS last year. He's only twenty-two, but everyone thinks he's wonderful. You didn't tell me he was the one who—"

"I don't think Jock regarded it as a detail on which he had to focus," Eve said. "Though, of course, you would, Cara."

"Straight up the stairs," Jock murmured. "Kaskov has a huge box with velvet-cushioned seats and privacy curtains. It even has an adjoining lounge, where he's served drinks during intermission. Nothing but the best for him . . ."

"He probably doesn't even notice all that stuff once the music starts," Cara said. "It means too much to him."

"Let's hope he doesn't notice anything but the music tonight," Jock said grimly. "Because I'm going to furnish a few distractions." They had reached the top of the staircase, and he nodded toward two gold-leafed doors a few feet away. "That's Kaskov's box." Then he nudged them toward a huge, jade-colored malachite column several yards from the entrance of the box. "Stay here behind the column. There are enough people around so that Kaskov shouldn't notice you."

Eve could see that was true. This level was also filled

with elegantly dressed patrons, and there were waiters moving among them, serving wine from ornate silver trays. "Very posh."

"Kaskov could care less. He always goes straight to his box and ignores all of this. I'll come for you as soon as the performance begins, and Kaskov is settled."

"Where are you going?" Eve asked as she pulled Cara behind the column. "You told me that this place is safer than Kaskov's estate, but a man like him will have bodyguards surrounding him. Some of those guards must have seen Cara while she was staying at the estate. All it would take is one of his men to recognize Cara and drop a word to Kaskov."

"That's why you're staying away from the box until I'm ready. I guarantee that none of Kaskov's guards will be strolling around the theater once he's ensconced in that box. He'll be their first priority."

"Where will they be?" Eve asked.

"You want their usual locations?" He shrugged and rattled them off. "According to Palik, one man stands outside the door to prevent attacks from the rear. One is inside in the lounge, waiting for Kaskov to come out during intermission in case he needs something. Kaskov never goes to the downstairs public bar. It's too dangerous for him to be in a crowd. There's a guard who waits by his car in front of the theater and another who acts as his chauffeur."

"Nikolai," Cara said. "I think he's been with Kaskov longer than any of his other men. He often uses him as a driver. He sent him to get Natalie and me when she brought me from Gaelkar."

"Four men," Eve whispered. "And you're supposed to take care of all four of them before I'll be able to reach Kaskov?"

"I *will* take care of them," Jock said. "You'll get your

chance." He looked at Cara. "And she'll get her chance. I just hope Quinn will be able to make my efforts totally unnecessary. If I get a call from him that he—" His phone rang. "Palik." He picked up. "Has he arrived? Same number of guards?" He hung up. "Kaskov is here. He'll be coming in the front entrance in a few minutes. Move a little farther behind that column."

"Not yet. I want to see him," Eve said suddenly. "I've never even seen the man, and I'm supposed to persuade him to abandon his daughter to save my life? Could I just get a glimpse of him?"

"A glimpse." Jock shook his head at Cara. "Not you. Get behind the column. Eve's right, you could be recognized."

Cara opened her lips and turned and walked toward the column.

"She's keeping her word to you." Eve moved close to the elaborate gold barricade at the side of the steps but kept discreetly behind a couple who were laughing and drinking as they looked down into the lobby. "Point him out to me."

"You have thirty seconds," Jock said. "I can't risk being seen either. Palik said that my photo was being circulated among Kaskov's men after I snatched Cara the last time. He's probably put a price on my head."

Her gaze flew to his face. "You didn't tell me that."

"It didn't matter. This had to be done. It just means I have to be careful and move very fast." His gaze was fastened on the front entrance. "Thirty seconds."

"I don't have to see him if it means—"

"There he is."

Eve's gaze flew to where he was nodding.

A tall, powerful man in an elegant black tuxedo moving through the doorway with a man who was also formally dressed on either side of him. They were all heading for the staircase with single-minded purpose.

"Go!" Jock took Eve's arm and moved her away from the staircase toward the malachite column. "No one looked up, so I think we're safe. So what did you think of him?"

"Powerful. Hard. So hard. But he doesn't look anything like Natalie. I don't know what to think of him except that he appeared as if he were made of stone."

"Maybe he is. You're going to get the opportunity to find out." He grabbed a wineglass from the tray of a passing waiter and handed it to Eve. "Look like you're enjoying yourself." They had reached the column, and he moved behind it and gazed down at Cara. "The action is about to start. Change your mind? Eve and I can do this."

She shook her head. "It has to be me, Jock." She drew a shaky breath. "But it's kind of scary. This place is so beautiful, and I know the music will be beautiful, too. But it can't matter, can it? I have to close it all out."

He nodded. "You have to do what you have to do. And, since you think you have a handle on this, I'd do it the way you think you should." He smiled. "It can't hurt, Cara. I'll see that nothing hurts you." He turned to Eve. "I'm going to move you both into Kaskov's private lounge just before the intermission. Stay here until then."

"The guards?"

"They won't be there." He glanced behind him. "Kaskov has gone into his box. His guard's standing there at the door and looking very grim and efficient. So I'd better leave and mix with the crowd who are starting to head downstairs for their seats."

"Downstairs?" Eve asked.

"Two of Kaskov's men are down the street by his car," he reminded her. "They'll be the easiest. Don't move. I need to be able to find you when I'm ready for you."

The next moment he was gone.

Don't move to watch him leave, Eve told herself. She had to stay here with Cara and take care of her. But it was hard not to make sure that guard outside Kaskov's box hadn't noticed Jock.

There's probably a price on my head.

"You're worried." Cara's hand slipped into hers. "Me, too. I hate his having to do this. But it's you, and it's Michael."

Michael.

Eve felt a rush of warmth that didn't stop the fear, but it helped.

We're doing everything we can, Michael. Jock is having to do some things that are hurting him. Bonnie says you're extraordinary, and I think you are. So if you have any kind of clout, it would be nice if you could find a way to help him.

"Yes, it's Michael." Her hand tightened on Cara's. "And sometimes the innocents of the world are given guardian angels to protect them. We've just got to hope that Jock is given one, too."

NASIM FEROZ'S RESIDENCE

Joe dragged the man who had guarded the front gate deep into the bushes and quickly covered him with brush.

Good enough.

He'd already disposed of the other guard Kaskov had sent to protect Feroz. Now to head for the library and see if Caleb had disposed of Mehnar, Feroz's personal bodyguard, yet.

It was dark in the library. He warily slipped over the windowsill and stood there in the dark, listening.

"It took you long enough," Caleb said from the darkness across the room. "I grant you that you had two to
take care of, but I—"

"Where's Mehnar?"

"About three feet from you. Unfortunately, he fell
down and broke his neck. Don't stumble on him as you
come toward me."

"I'll be sure and watch out." He moved across the
room. "And why am I coming toward you?"

"Because the door in back of me opens to a hall that
leads to the lab where Feroz is working. He's there right
now."

"Are you sure?"

"Relatively. Mehnar told me he was there before he
fell down and broke his neck."

"And did you ask Mehnar about the antidote?"

"He didn't know anything about it. He said that he was
paid to guard Feroz, not help him in the lab." He opened
the door. "I thought we'd go ask the son of a bitch himself. This time I'm not going to be polite. I really don't
like what Feroz did to Eve. Very ugly. You'll have to fight
to keep me from doing something equally ugly to him."

"You don't do anything to him until we know whether
he has an antidote other than the one he gave to Natalie." He strode quickly but silently down the hall. "And,
if he doesn't, how long it will take him to create another
one. After that, you can do what you want to him while
I get to Eve at that opera house." He stopped a few yards
from the laboratory door. "I don't hear anything. Are you
sure you didn't—"

"No, I'm totally innocent," Caleb whispered. "I waited
for you. Not that I wouldn't have—"

The laboratory door was thrown open, and Joe
glimpsed the barrel of an AK-47; he hit the floor. "Down!"

He rolled forward into Feroz's knees, knocking him sideways as the Iranian let loose a spate of bullets that nearly tore apart the wall where Joe had been standing.

He saw Caleb moving with gun drawn out of the corner of his eye. "Don't shoot the bastard. I told you that he has to—"

His hand closed on Feroz's wrist holding the weapon, and he twisted it, then he butted his head into his stomach, knocked him down and wrestled the weapon away from him. He savagely struck Feroz's jaw with the butt of the gun. Feroz took one look at his face and stopped fighting, his dark eyes wide with fear. "Don't hurt me," he said frantically. "I have money. I will share—"

"And I wonder where you got that money?" Caleb said as he strolled into the lab. "And you're speaking English. Have you been expecting us?"

"Perhaps." He moistened his lips. "She said that I might have a visitor."

"Natalie?"

"I don't know her name."

"Not a good answer."

"I hardly saw her."

"But you were on intimate enough terms that she told you that you should shoot anyone who tried to talk to you."

"You startled me." He was suddenly defiant. "You don't know whom you're dealing with. I have powerful friends. You hurt me, and you won't live another day. In fact, I have men to protect me outside this house. I expect them to rush in here at any minute."

"You'll be disappointed," Joe said.

"You're bluffing," Feroz said. "Who do you think gave me that gun? I'm important to them. I'm not going to let you tell me what to do."

"Yes, you are," Caleb said softly. He turned to Joe.

"You don't have time for this, do you? He appears to have gotten a small injection of courage, and it may be difficult to filter the truth from lies. We have to call Jock and tell him what he has to deal with." He paused. "And it has to be the truth."

"It will be my pleasure to make certain," Joe said.

"Yes, but I'll be quicker." Caleb gazed appraisingly down at Feroz's face. "Five. Ten minutes tops. You may need those minutes."

Joe gazed down at Feroz, the rage pounding through him. This was the man who had deliberately created the poison that had put Eve and his child at risk. In the past, the man had been not only a conscienceless torturer but also a killer. Now that killer for hire had targeted Eve.

Never in his life had he wanted more to kill a man.

"No time," Caleb said. "Leave it to me."

And Caleb was angry, too, and would not be easy on Feroz.

Joe got to his feet and picked up Feroz's gun.

"Get those questions answered," he said harshly. "And make it five minutes, Caleb."

"I'd prefer to stretch it out as he did with his victims. But if you insist." He dropped to his knees beside Feroz and put his hand on Feroz's chest. "Your chest a little tight? Yes, your heart is starting to beat harder. I can feel it."

"Get your hand—off me." Feroz's eyes were bulging, his lips drawn with agony. "What are you doing to me?"

"We're going to have a little talk. I'm going to ask you questions, and you're going to answer . . . And, if you tell me the truth, it won't hurt . . . excruciatingly. No, that was a lie. I really do want you to suffer. But you might live a few minutes longer. Or I might be kinder and let you die. Now let's talk about the antidote . . ."

NOVAKO OPERA HOUSE
9:20 P.M.

"Now!" Jock was suddenly beside Eve and Cara behind the column. "Intermission is in five minutes. I want you in that lounge anteroom when Kaskov leaves the box." He took Cara's hand and was pulling her across the luxurious stretch of crimson carpet toward the door of the box. "Eve, intermission is only twenty minutes. We have our best chance of leaving this place undetected if we mix with the audience before they return to their seats. I have an exit strategy through the rear of the bar on the first floor. But try to make that twenty minutes work for you."

"Nothing like a little pressure," Eve said. "Have you heard from Joe yet?"

"Not yet. It's just as well. I've been a little busy."

She stiffened. There was no guard in front of Kaskov's box. "I can see that. Would you like to tell me where that guard is now?"

"In a stall in the men's restroom. He became suddenly ill, and I had to get him there very quickly."

"And the guard in the anteroom?"

"He's behind the bar in the lounge." He glanced at Cara, whose gaze had flown to his face. "Just peacefully sleeping. I didn't believe you'd like anything more permanent at close quarters." He opened the door. "Sit down, and I'll go get your host."

Eve put her arm around Cara's shoulders and shepherded her toward the elaborately curved beige-velvet couch that looked like it might have originated at the turn of the last century. "It's going to be all right, Cara. No matter what happens, you're not responsible for anything or anyone."

"Yes, I am." Cara's voice was a little breathless. "Because I chose to do this. Jock told me once that I had my own soul that had nothing to do with Natalie, and I was responsible for my choices. I think . . . this is a big one." She tilted her head as she heard applause break out. "I think it's intermission. Kaskov will be here soon. I'm a little scared to face him." She took Eve's hand. "But I won't be for long. It's like playing the violin. You're a little afraid to break the silence, but then everything comes together."

"I'm a little afraid, too." Eve smiled. "But only for Michael. It will be—"

"Eve Duncan, I presume?" Sergai Kaskov was standing in the doorway of the box with Jock close behind him, a gun in his hand. Kaskov's cheeks were faintly flushed, his eyes glittering. "You do know that you'll be a dead woman even sooner than my daughter planned after this little scenario." His gaze shifted to Cara. "Or are you trying to trade your life for Cara? It's too late. You've caused both me and my daughter, Natalie, a good deal of trouble. Plus threatening to kill my granddaughter. No one takes anything from me without paying for it." He looked over his shoulder at Jock. "You're Jock Gavin. You have to be very talented to take out my men and corner me like this. She must have paid you well. I'll pay you double to point that gun at Eve Duncan and pull the trigger."

"No." Jock gestured for Kaskov to enter the lounge. "But if she'd asked me to point the gun at you and pull the trigger, I would have done it. It appears that Eve just wants to have a talk with you . . . about the antidote."

"I'm not interested," Kaskov said curtly. "Natalie said that we'd get Cara back if we held that capsule over Duncan's head. It appears that she was right." He turned back to Cara. "You're safe now. Natalie told me all about how Duncan is trying to hurt you. She can't hurt you any longer."

"Eve was never trying to hurt me," Cara said. "She just wanted to keep me safe from Natalie."

Kaskov's brows rose, and he glanced at Eve. "A little selected brainwashing? I don't like that. I may not let Natalie negotiate for that antidote. Now that Cara is back in Moscow, the power is all on my side."

"I never brainwashed Cara," Eve said. "I just wanted to keep Natalie from killing her . . . as she did her sister, Jenny."

"Liar."

"I'm not a liar," Eve said. "I can prove it, if you'll listen to me. If you'll listen to *her*."

"I'm not interested in your lies. You've done everything you can to hurt Natalie and her daughter. That means you've tried to hurt me. I won't tolerate anyone who does that to me or my family."

"Because it's all you have?" Eve asked. "I understand about families and how you have to protect them. I'm carrying a child that Natalie is trying to destroy as she did her own children. I have to protect my son." She held his gaze. "Please, let me protect my child. All you have to do is listen to this disc I have in my evening bag."

He didn't speak for a moment. "You're very convincing. Natalie said you were clever." He shook his head. "But I won't waste my time. I think you'd better call my daughter and tell her that you're in town and ready to negotiate."

"I'm sure she already knows. You're the only one who didn't know that I was coming to Moscow tonight," Eve said. "Ask yourself why."

"More lies." His lips tightened. "I'm finished talking with you. You think you have me? Your Jock Gavin may be lethal, but at occasions such as this, I always have an arrangement with a friend in the local police department. If my personal guards don't check in every thirty minutes, they send someone to make sure that I'm not having problems. You could kill me, but you can't force me to do anything. And no one will give you that antidote if I'm dead. Now I'm going to take my granddaughter home, and, if you try to stop me, there will be no antidote coming from any source." He smiled coldly at Eve. "Tell me, how much time do you have left?"

"No!" Cara was suddenly on her feet and running across the room to him. "You *listen* to her." She stood before him, her eyes blazing, her hands clenched into fists. "All she wants is for you to listen. You're blind where Natalie is concerned, and you have to see her as she is."

He frowned. "Don't be disloyal. She's your mother."

"No, she isn't. A mother doesn't kill her children like she did Jenny."

"Brainwashing."

"I'm not the one who was brainwashed." She was gazing up at him, frantically trying to make him understand. "It's you. She's always used you. I think you know that, but you won't admit it. Sometimes I'd watch the two of you together, and I could see it. You had no one but her, and that's the way she liked it. You had Jenny. Jenny died. You had your son, Alex. Alex died. How long do you think I'd last if you made me come with you tonight?"

He was silent. "Such passion. You're quite a surprise. You've not spoken more than a few sentences to me since the first day Natalie brought you to me."

"I had my orders from Natalie. I *had* to protect Eve. She didn't want me interfering with her relationship with you." She took a step closer. "I was a danger because of the music. Like Alex, your son, was a danger. She killed Alex. I was supposed to die that day in the park." She moistened her lips. "But Jock and Eve saved me."

He shook his head. "You have to be confused. Natalie loves me. She's my family."

"She's *not* your family. She doesn't . . . feel like other people. You want family? I'll be your family. I think you feel something for me. Though it may just be the music. I'll do anything you want if you just look at that disc that Eve wants to show you."

Jock took at step forward. "I don't like where this is going," he said harshly.

"And I like very much where it's going," Kaskov said, his gaze holding Cara's. "It's all probably lies and nonsense, but I've always been one to hedge my bets."

Cara nodded. "Like when that guard broke your hands and you had to go in another direction?"

"Very clever for you to compare and make that connection. The violin may not be your only talent."

"*Please.*" Cara's desperation and intensity were almost frantic. "Just watch the disc. Listen to what Natalie is saying."

He was silent. Then he nodded slowly. "I'll watch it." He held out his hand to Eve for the computer and disc, his eyes still holding Cara's. "And we'll talk later, Cara." He took the small laptop to the bar and plugged it in. He gazed quizzically down at the guard slumped behind the bar. "Dead, Gavin?"

"No. I had Cara to think about."

"I appreciate you considering her delicate feelings, but I'm beginning to believe she might be tougher than either of us guess. She has my genes."

"No," Cara said. "That doesn't mean anything. I belong to myself." She turned to Eve again. "And I make my own choices, don't I, Eve?"

She smiled. "Yes, you do. And some of them are not—"

Jock's phone rang. He glanced down at the ID. "Quinn. Let's hope he'll tell us something that will make all this completely nonessential." He answered the phone. "Are you on your way? What did you find out?" He listened for

a moment. "We're secure. I'll see you when you get here."
He looked at Kaskov. "I hope that you don't convince
yourself that disc is a forgery because you're going to be in
a very tight corner in about twenty minutes."

"What did Joe say?" Eve asked.

"That Feroz couldn't duplicate that antidote in less
than four days." He met Kaskov's eyes. "But Feroz never
turned over the first antidote to Natalie. She never autho-
rized Feroz to make one. She wasn't interested in anything but the poison capsule. She never meant to give Eve
a chance."

"Natalie appeared to be very angry," Kaskov said.
"But, then, so was I."

"But Feroz *did* create an antidote," Jock said. "Since
Kaskov paid the money, he called the shots."

Kaskov shrugged. "As I said, I always believe in hedg-
ing my bets. You can never tell when you have to initiate
an alternative plan."

"That's why you demanded that Feroz create and give
you an antidote . . . just in case."

"As you said, I was paying; therefore, I was in control."

"So *you* have the antidote?" Eve asked.

He nodded. "And you will never see it if you stand in
the way of Natalie's getting Cara."

"She *will* see it," Jock said. "I'd make sure of that myself, but Quinn's right. As I said, he'll be here in about
twenty minutes and—"

"Jock, just let him see that disc," Cara said. "Stop all
this talk. You can't make him afraid. Can't you see that
threats aren't going to do any good with him?"

"Very wise," Kaskov said. "I'm more and more impressed. I can see how much I missed if it's true that Natalie was suppressing all that fire."

"It's all true. Everything I've told you is true."

He gazed at her for a long moment. "Then perhaps I'd

better look at this disc and judge for myself." He sat down at the bar and punched the PLAY button.

Eve studied Kaskov's face as he watched and listened to Natalie during that last phone conversation. She had almost forgotten how ugly and incriminating those words had been. Yet she could see no change in his expression as he heard both the insulting arrogance and the revelations that Natalie was spitting out. Hard. She had never met a harder man. It was clear that Natalie had manipulated the death of his son, but he wasn't showing pain or anger. Did it matter to him? Would it be enough to save Michael?

Finally, he turned off the machine and sat there staring at the blank screen. "Interesting."

"It's the truth," Eve said. "No forgery."

"No, I'd know the difference." He was silent again. "It seems I'm faced with a decision I never thought I'd have to make." He closed the lid of the computer. "But that's been my life since I was a boy. I should be accustomed to it by now, but it seems that I haven't reached that point yet. Not with Natalie."

Cara was suddenly standing before him again. "Forget about Natalie," she said fiercely. "Now that you know what she is, you'll be able to control her as you do everyone else. But you have to stop her from trying to hurt Eve. If you have that antidote, you have to give it to her right now. Tonight."

"Do I?" He tilted his head. "Tell me why?"

"I don't know why you'd do it. Sometimes I think I know you. Sometimes I don't. But I know that Eve has to live. Her child has to live. And you can make it happen. So do it."

His lips twisted. "Are you giving me orders? I thought I'd made it clear that I'm always the one in control. I'd hardly accept orders from a child."

"Cara," Eve said. "Let it go. I told you that whatever happened, you weren't responsible. We'll find another—"

"Give her the antidote," Cara said. "You're angry at Natalie? Punish her by making her lose what she wants this time."

"Excellent thought. But what about what I want? You were an asset I didn't want to do without. I looked forward to those evenings when you played for me."

"Back off, Kaskov," Jock said. "The conversation is over."

"Is it?" His gaze was fastened on Cara's face. "I'm not a generous man, but I do keep to my bargains. Perhaps we could come to an agreement."

"Give Eve the antidote," Cara repeated. "You *have* to do it. She has to live. Her son has to live."

He was silent again, staring speculatively at her. Then he shrugged. "Perhaps this isn't the time for negotiations. I have too many other things on my agenda at present." He glanced at Eve. "This appears to be your lucky day. My granddaughter is determined, and I find myself reluctant to disappoint her. Very strange." He turned away from the bar and looked at Jock. "The antidote is in the safe at the library of my estate. Suppose you and I go and retrieve it, then I'll drop you off at the airport to meet with the rest of your party."

"Don't do it, Jock," Eve said. "You'd be walking into a trap. Directly into the lion's mouth."

Jock was studying Kaskov's face. "I think I can find a way around it. I know that estate."

"Jock has to live, too," Cara said quickly to Kaskov. "Nothing can happen to him."

"You're very demanding," Kaskov said. "I'll have to work on that. But I'm willing to be accommodating and oblige this time." He looked at Jock. "Do I still have a chauffeur and guard at my car?"

"No guard. He's in the alley. The chauffeur is unconscious and in the trunk. You'll have to drive. He'll stay there until I pick up the antidote."

"I'm glad you didn't dispose of Nikolai. He's been with me a long time. That would have upset me."

"I wouldn't have given a damn, but Cara said something that made me reconsider."

"You're as exceptional as I heard you were." Kaskov smiled faintly. "You wouldn't care to work for me? I admire efficiency."

"No, I would not."

"Too bad." He headed for the door. "Deadly, and you don't look bad in a tuxedo. You'd fit my lifestyle admirably. Perhaps you'll change your mind." He looked over his shoulder at Cara. "Stop worrying. I believe we both understand each other, don't we? You wanted your Eve and the child to live. It's going to happen. I just have to handle the details." He nodded at Eve. "But I want you out of Moscow within the next four hours. I have things to do, and you'll get in my way. And I'm not going to go to the trouble of giving you a chance to live, then have you blow it by not acting quickly enough. Cara might be upset."

"I'm touched by your concern," she said dryly. "I assure you that if you give me that antidote, I'll make good use of it." She paused. "I suppose I should say thank you. But it doesn't seem appropriate, does it? You did this for some purpose of your own."

"Quite true," Kaskov said. "I'll see you at the airport." He stopped once again, and said to Cara, "By the way, I'm not sorry to have this concert interrupted even by such traumatic events. That violinist wasn't really worth my time. You're much better, Cara." He strode out of the box with Jock beside him.

Eve felt dizzy with relief. Was it over? Had they won?

Kaskov was an enigma, and there was no way she could read him. "Jock . . ."

"I think he'll be okay." Cara was staring at the door. "If Kaskov really has the antidote, and Jock doesn't have to—" She swallowed. "I don't know. I'm just guessing. But I'm guessing that Kaskov is going to give you the antidote."

"And he wants us out of Moscow." Eve was reaching for her phone. "We'll definitely give him what he wants. Come on. We'll go down to the front entrance to meet Joe and Caleb. I'll call Joe and see how close he is . . ."

CHAPTER

17

SKOVSKI AIRPORT

"It's been over two hours." Cara drew her velvet wrap around her to block out the cold as she moved closer to Eve by the hangar. The wind was sharp, but that wasn't why she was chilled.

Jock.

The lion's mouth.

Why had she thought that she knew Kaskov well enough to be able to know what he would do, what she could make him do?

Because that's why she'd been sent to help Eve and Michael, she thought desperately.

This had to be the reason.

I did what you wanted, Jenny. But you have to help bring Jock back safely. Let Kaskov have kept his word and given Jock the antidote. Let everything go right. I know what's coming. I'll do the rest. Just let Jock come back safe.

Eve's hand touched her arm. "Get on the plane, Cara. There's no use standing out here in the cold."

"He should be here."

"If he doesn't come soon, I'll go after him," Joe said grimly. "And that antidote."

"It's not been that long," Eve said. "We're just—"

Headlights pierced the darkness.

A sleek black limousine was coming toward them.

Cara took an eager step toward the approaching car. "Jock."

Eve grabbed her arm. "Wait, we *hope* it's Jock."

The limousine came to a stop a few yards away, and Kaskov got out of the driver's seat. "Hello, Eve. Are you a little nervous perhaps?"

"Of course. I—" She stopped as she saw Jock getting out of the passenger seat. "Jock, did everything go—"

"I have the antidote," Jock said as he handed her a small black cylinder. "Kaskov was very cooperative."

"But he still made me drive to make sure that he could keep his eye on me," Kaskov said with a smile. "I would have done the same thing." He turned to Joe. "You're Quinn? You'd better have a very good doctor to administer that antidote. Feroz was too afraid of me not to give me what I asked for, but he didn't expect me to use it. I would trust Feroz to make a poison, but he could have been careless with the antidote."

"Eve has an entire hospital of good doctors," Joe said. "Nothing is going to go wrong if you've given me the right thing. If you haven't, I'll come back for you."

"Oh, I've done what I promised." He looked at Cara, who had drawn closer to Jock. "You were concerned about him? I'm learning more about you all the time. You seem to have an entire circle you care about."

Jock went still. "Get on the plane, Cara."

She shook her head, and said to Kaskov, "He's my friend. All of these people are my friends. I do care about them. We're like a family." She paused. "We take care of each other."

"A family . . ." He stared at her for a moment. "I understand about families, but I suppose sometimes family members aren't so loyal . . . or loving." He turned away. "I'll be in touch soon, Cara."

"I know you will," she said quietly.

Jock's hand was on her elbow and pushing her toward the plane. "What the hell was that about?" he muttered.

She was looking over her shoulder as Kaskov got in the driver's seat and started the car. "He gave Eve what she needed. Everything she and Michael needed. He could have made it difficult. He didn't do it."

"You're not answering me."

"He's not like us. Nothing is free in his world. Someone always has to pay. But this time it's not going to be Eve, and it's not going to be Michael."

"And it's not going to be you," Jock said harshly.

"Not now. I don't have to worry about it now. I can have time to make certain Eve is well."

"It's not going to be you," he repeated.

She smiled at him as she started up the steps behind Eve and Joe. The moonlight was shining on his fair hair and those wonderful features, and he was safe, and she would treasure every minute with him. "Maybe it won't be. Kaskov said he had a lot on his agenda. Why would he want a kid around to get in his way?" She went down the aisle. "Come on, Jock. Sit down and buckle up. We're going to take Eve back to that hospital in Glasgow, and she's going to come out of it as shining as Cira's gold."

11:25 P.M.

Eve's phone rang as she watched Caleb go up the aisle toward the cockpit.

"Natalie," she said to Joe as she glanced down at the ID. "She must be getting impatient. What a pity."

"It's almost eleven thirty," Joe said. "Another thirty minutes before we were supposed to walk into the trap."

Eve's phone was still ringing.

"Are you going to answer it?" Joe asked.

She had been thinking about it. She would have loved to do a little taunting of her own now that they had the antidote. Natalie had caused them all so much suffering during these last weeks.

But Michael wasn't safe yet. It wasn't the time for spite or malice. It was time for hope and prayers until that capsule in her body was safely dissolved.

"No." She turned off the ringer. "I want to concentrate on Michael's future, not revenge." She leaned her head against his shoulder. "I'm going to try not to think of Natalie again. I believe Michael will help me out there. He's usually all for serenity and happiness. Though he did get pretty upset when he knew that she'd slipped me that capsule."

"He wasn't the only one," Joe said as he pulled out his phone. "I'm going to call the specialists and see if we can get that antidote in to be examined the minute we land."

"Okay." She leaned there against his shoulder, listening as he made the calls. She was full of hope, but there was still that element of sheer terror at the thought that something could still go wrong.

We're on our way, Michael. I don't know what those doctors are going to do to us, but Joe will make sure that we'll be safe.

There was a vibrating on the phone in her lap.

Natalie was calling again.

"She's not answering." Natalie's voice was shaking with rage and incredulity. "That bitch, Duncan, is ignoring me. How does she think she can get away with that? She's going to die. I've beaten her. Anyone else would be desperate to get me to give her that antidote." Her finger was stabbing the numbers on the phone again. "I'll make her beg. Do you hear me, Ivan? I'll make her *beg* to give me that treasure."

"I hear you." Ivan hung up his own phone. "But we may have to chase after her to get her to give you anything. I didn't like that she wasn't answering and just called Nasim Feroz. He's not answering his phone either. She may already have what she wants."

She shook her head. "I told him I didn't want him to create an antidote."

"And Feroz would do it anyway if he thought he could sell it to a higher bidder." His phone rang again, and he picked up and listened. "Yes, I want you to head for the airport, you fool. You have to stop them." He cursed and hung up the phone. "Feroz is dead. Duncan won't be coming to give us that gold." He headed for the door. "But we might be able to stop them at the airport. Since they brought that gold to negotiate, then it may be on that plane going back to Scotland. Coming?"

"Of course, I'm coming. Do you think I'd trust you to share that gold with me if I let you go alone?" She was running down the steps of the flat after him. "We can still do this. I'll call Daddy from the car, and he'll phone one of his government people and stop them from taking off." She was trying desperately to think of a reason to give her father. She might pull the Cara card . . . Oh, well, she'd find some reason and make him believe it. "Do you have any men close to the airport? Call them. Get Duncan off that plane."

Ivan nodded. "I'll do it. But you'd do better to get Kaskov to pull his strings. They're much more effective." He got in the driver's seat of the black Mercedes at the curb. "Get in and let's go."

Her hand went to the handle of the passenger door.

"Not there," Ivan said. "Backseat."

"What?"

"Backseat," Kaskov repeated as he leaned forward to look at her from the rear seat. "With me, Natalie."

She stiffened in shock. "Daddy?"

He reached over and opened the rear door for her. "Come along. We have to hurry."

She was completely confused, but she didn't like this. "What are you—"

"Get in, Natalie."

She knew from that steely note in his voice that she was going to have to deal with something. It would have to happen now, when she had no time for it. She got in the car, trying to put the pieces together. "What are you doing here, Daddy? We have a small problem, but I can—" Ivan had lied to her, and he must be involved in this nightmare with her father in some way. "It's just as well you're here. You should know that Ivan isn't as loyal as you think he is."

"I'm aware of that. But I'm going to give him a chance to make reparations." He looked at Ivan's reflection in the rearview mirror. "He's always been a person who knew what was in his best interest. When I called him tonight, he realized that he really didn't want to go out on his own when I furnish him with everything he could ever want. Drive, Ivan."

Ivan started the car and pulled away from the curb.

Betrayal. "He lied to you," she said quickly. "Did he

tell you about that treasure Duncan was supposed to have found? I would have mentioned it to you, but I knew it was lies. All she wanted to do was hurt me and Cara." She put her hand on his arm. "But we can see if there's any truth in it, if you like." She smiled. "We could do it together."

"Do you know, Natalie, I'm not particularly enthralled at the idea of that gold." He smiled back at her. "I have more than enough in my accounts to give me anything I could conceivably want. These days, I'm more interested in control and power."

She couldn't believe he could be that stupid. It was so clear to her. "But power would come with that kind of treasure," she said gently. "Surely, you can see that, Daddy."

"I see many things, Natalie." He leaned back in the seat. "A few that I've been ignoring because I didn't want to admit that they might be true." He took her hand and looked down at it. "Such a beautiful hand. You've always been exquisite. You really take after my mother, you know. Her face was almost as beautiful as the music she played. Did I ever mention that?"

"You never talked much about her."

"Because you never seemed interested. Your brother, Alex, was more intrigued about family matters." He paused. "He even had an affection for you, Natalie."

"He betrayed you."

"No," he said gently. "He did not. You found Alex expendable, and you framed him."

She inhaled sharply. Bad. This was bad. How had he—"That's not true." Tears. There had to be tears. But she was so shocked, she was having trouble bringing them to her eyes. "How could you ever believe something so terrible?"

"Because you told me." He dropped her hand. "As you told me about Jenny and Cara."

"You're crazy, I would never have told you—it was Ivan, wasn't it?"

"I suppose you might say he had a part in it." He added, "But it was you. And Eve Duncan."

"That bitch," she said viciously. "Lies. All of it lies."

"No, the truth. I can separate the truth from lies. It just takes me longer when my family is involved." He looked out the window. "It's one of my idiosyncrasies, that the idea of family is important to me. I've been alone most of my life, and I truly like the concept."

"You have a family. *I'm* your family."

"No, I've heard a recent description of what a family should be, and you're nowhere near it, Natalie. I'm afraid I'll have to look elsewhere. And, if you're not family, then all my rules of conduct apply. Unfortunately, you've broken quite a few of them." He leaned forward. "Pull over when you find a place, Ivan."

"Right ahead, sir."

Natalie's heart was beating hard. "It was all lies, Daddy. What do you think you're going to do?" She smiled shakily. "You love me. You have to believe me."

"Do I? I don't think so. I'm not the fool you thought me." He looked at her. "And I don't know if I still love you or just the memory of what I wanted you to be. I might never know."

He was sounding frighteningly final. "If you think I did something bad, you *have* to forgive me. We'll give it a little time. We'll talk about it. I'll make it up to you."

"Forgive you?" He was silent, thinking about it. "I might have done it. As I said, family is important to me. Do you know that my mother sat watching and did nothing when that guard was breaking my hands at the work camp? She was too afraid." His lips twisted. "I forgave her. Later, I gave her a good life until the day she died."

"Then forgive *me*." Her hand clenched on his arm as Ivan pulled the car to the side of the road. "Please, Daddy."

He shook his head. "Alex. Jenny. Cara. It's such very bad form to kill family, Natalie." He opened the car door. "I can't tolerate that kind of mistake."

He was actually going to do it. She couldn't believe it. "You fool! What did any of them matter? I did everything right. Just give me another chance, and I can make you see how right I was."

"Good-bye, Natalie." He slammed the car door and started walking down the side of the road. He called back over his shoulder at Ivan, "Don't indulge yourself. You may be angry with her, but I want it quick."

"Yes, sir." Ivan was out of the driver's seat and coming around to the rear door.

She still had a chance. The gun in her handbag . . .

She dug frantically through the bag.

She couldn't find the gun.

It wasn't there!

Ivan opened the door. "I had twenty minutes after Kaskov called me to get rid of it." He took out his Magnum. "I'm sorry he isn't going to let me enjoy myself. You've caused me a good deal of trouble, and now I'll be scrambling to get back in his good graces."

"Don't." She screamed, "The treasure! Think of the gold. You can have it all. Just let me—"

He blew her head off.

Nikolai pulled up beside Kaskov in the limousine. He jumped out and ran around the car to open the rear door for him. "Home, sir?"

Kaskov nodded as he got into the limousine. "It's been a long night, Nikolai."

Nikolai gazed back at the Mercedes still parked at the side of the road a few hundred yards back. "Ivan Sabak? He did break your rules."

"Yes. Let it go. Not right now." He could still hear the sound of that shot. Would he always hear it? No, he was stronger than that. Block it out. "Tomorrow will be soon enough."

Nikolai nodded as he got back into the driver's seat. He hesitated before he started the car. "May I say that I'm . . . sorry about your daughter, sir."

"Daughter?" Kaskov leaned wearily back on the seat. "I have no daughter, Nikolai."

SOUTH GLASGOW UNIVERSITY HOSPITAL

"What was the report? Was the antidote Kaskov gave you the right thing?" Jane asked as she hurried down the hall toward Joe. "Did the doctors say that it will work?" She stopped in front of him, trying to read his expression. "We're so close to saving her. Give me some good news, Joe."

"Slow down. They think it will work," Joe said. "But there are still problems. They want to do some more testing, but Eve's run out of time. If they don't administer that antidote in the next six hours, the capsule will release its dose." His jaw was set. "And it's not only the capsule; they have to keep the blood flow from picking up micrograms of the poison after it's dissolved and carrying it to her vital organs." He paused. "And Michael. A complete blood transfusion would be safest, but controlling and isolating the poison in the bloodstream while that's going on could be a nightmare."

"Six hours? Then they can do some more tests, can't

they? They've got all these high-powered doctors and specialists here. They can find something to make it safer for her."

"Eve's made it a little more difficult for them," he said huskily. "She's already told them that if it comes down to choosing one of them, it's going to be Michael."

Jane inhaled sharply and closed her eyes. Of course that would be Eve's choice. They were so close to saving her, and she wouldn't be saved if it meant Michael was going to die. She opened her eyes and went into Joe's arms. She could feel his pain as well as her own.

It will be so hard for him, Eve had told her.

She had given Jane the task of taking care of both Michael and Joe that day in the hospital.

But only if Eve wasn't around to do it herself.

Eve *had* to be around, dammit.

She pushed Joe away and gave him a quick kiss on the cheek. "They're both going to live, Joe. We're going to see to it." She turned away. "Talk to those doctors and see what you can do."

She walked away from him.

And she would see what she could do.

LOCH GAELKAR

"I need to talk to you, Caleb," she said jerkily as she walked toward him across the bank of the lake. "It would have helped if you'd been at the hospital with the rest of us instead of making me track you down."

"I was expecting you to be too busy to notice the lack of my humble presence at the family gathering." He tilted his head. "Much less have you come to find me. What do you need?"

"Need?"

"Yes, I'm the outsider here. No one generally seeks me out unless they need something."

How could she argue? He was right. He was too dangerous, too . . . different. "But there have been times when you've offered to help. We didn't have to ask."

"When it suited me." His gaze was narrowed on her face. "What are you trying to say, Jane?"

"Eve may have trouble when they administer that antidote. They're afraid the blood will still transfer some of the poison to her vital organs or to Michael." She moistened her lips. "You know all about blood. Could you keep that from happening until they manage to do a complete blood transfusion?"

"It would be difficult." He thought about it. "But possible. It would be a matter of regulating, filtering, and blocking the blood flow at the same time. Difficult balance, but I believe I could do it."

Thank God. She had been terribly afraid that even with Caleb it couldn't happen. "How certain are you that no poison would get to them?"

"No promises. As I said, difficult."

"I *have* to have a promise." She took a step closer to him. "They have to live, Caleb. I know you told me from now on that there would always be a price. I'm okay with that. I'll do anything you want. Anything."

He went still, then stood there, gazing at her. "Motivation? Not just assuming I'd do it anyway to help Eve?" His lips twisted and then he smiled recklessly. "No, of course not. That would be what you'd expect of someone like Trevor. Not me."

There was something in his expression . . . Had she hurt him? She could never tell with Caleb.

"Anything I want?" He savored the words. "That's too tempting to pass up. True motivation." He turned and started up the slope to the road. "If it's at all possible, I'll

save your Eve and her child. Call Quinn and tell him I
have to be in the operating room during the entire pro-
cedure. He may have trouble convincing her doctors that
I have any business there." He glanced at her over his
shoulder. "And you might stay away from me while I'm
taking care of doing this. You're a distraction. All that
motivation . . ."

SOUTH GLASGOW UNIVERSITY HOSPITAL GLASGOW

The first thing Eve saw when she opened her eyes after
the transfusion was Joe looking down at her. His face was
pale, but there was no pain. "Michael?" she whispered.

"The doctors think you both made it through with no
bad effects." He took her hand. "They won't commit to
the long haul. We'll have to wait until Michael is born
before we know for certain that no poison reached him."

"Months . . . That's a long time." She smiled unsteadily.
"But maybe Michael will let me know before that. I've got
a good feeling about this, Joe."

"Me, too." He bent down and kissed her cheek. She
could feel a faint moisture on her cheekbone when he
raised his head. "I've got to go to the waiting room and
tell Jane and Cara that you're going to make it. There
were a few doubts floating around."

"I had a few myself." She looked at the chair across the
room, where Caleb had been sitting during the entire
transfusion. "But not after Caleb showed up. Where is he?"

"He stepped out a few minutes ago and told me to
come in and see you."

"I think Michael owes him, Joe."

His hand tightened on hers. "I think *I* owe him. Hey,

how about hopping on a plane and going home to wait for Michael's arrival?"

Home. The lake cottage. Her work. Her life.

"That sounds wonderful." She frowned. "But what about Toller?"

"We'll still have to deal with him about Cara." He paused. "But Palik says that there's been no sign of Natalie since yesterday. No one is even talking about her. It's as if she didn't exist. Cara may be missing an acceptable legal guardian in the eyes of the Justice Department. I don't believe Kaskov would qualify."

"Missing." Eve had been too busy with worries about keeping Michael alive to even think about Natalie. "I can't believe she's out of our lives. I wasn't sure that Kaskov would forgive and forget. Maybe he did, and she'll show up later."

"I don't think she will. Palik said that Ivan Sabak was found dead in a wrecked car on a railway crossing a few hours ago." He kissed her again and turned to the door. "Stop thinking about Natalie. I believe she may be history."

Eve watched the door close behind him.

No more Natalie.

She could feel the tension gradually leaving her.

Home.

Michael.

We're going home, Michael. You're going to like it there. You'll have Joe and Cara and sometimes Jane. And me, always me. Family. None of the conflict and problems that you've been going through lately. Smooth sailing.

Warmth. Strength. Love.

And laughter, she realized. Michael was laughing at her words of comfort as if he knew that smooth sailing would not happen. Maybe he didn't want it to happen.

"We'll see." She closed her eyes. "Right now, just

concentrate on keeping well and kicking any stray ugliness away from you. We'll settle the rest when we get home . . ."

"It's done," Caleb stopped in front of the chair where Jane was sitting in the waiting room. "Quinn will give you the details, but I did my part. They want to keep an eye on Michael when she delivers him. But the chances are that they'll both live with no harmful effects."

"Thank God," she said fervently. "And thank you, Caleb."

He shrugged. "No thanks necessary. You chose to take this out of the realm of a favor. I kept my word, and I know you'll keep yours." He smiled. "I look forward to it. You promised me anything, and my interpretation of that is both intricate and erotic."

She stiffened in her chair. "You're right, I won't break my word. When?"

He shook his head. "It would be a pity to hurry things when anticipation can be so exquisite. I think that I'll trade it for an IOU that I can redeem at any time. Perhaps when we're absolutely sure that Michael is completely fine." He smiled. "Or before. Or afterward. My choice."

"Caleb."

"You may get to like the anticipation. I'll make it very intriguing." He turned and headed down the hall. "But now I have to get back to Eve to make sure everything is going well. I'll see you later, Jane."

She watched him walk away from her. Sleek, graceful, totally sexual, completely dangerous. She was aware that she had made him angry, and there was no telling how he intended to punish her.

Or maybe she did know.

Only time would tell.

"Jane." Cara had left Jock across the room and come to stand beside her. "Is Eve okay?"

"She's very okay." Jane stood up and put her arm around Cara. "Caleb said he thought they would both be fine. They're going to watch closely when Michael is born, but Caleb's not worried. And he probably knows more than those doctors about what's happening with her blood supply. You can trust Caleb about things like that."

"I knew it!" Cara hugged Jane exuberantly. "See, everything is going the way it should. All it took was a little help from us. Where's Caleb now? I've got to go thank him."

"He's with Eve."

"Then I'll wait for a while." Her gaze flew to Jane's face. "But you thanked him, didn't you?"

You saw fit to take this out of the realm of a favor.

"Yes, I thanked him."

"That's good. Sometimes you don't seem to—He likes Eve. He saved her. He helped all of us."

"He also smuggled you onto his plane and put you in danger. And still you're prejudiced in his favor."

She nodded. "Because I wanted him to do it. Because he sees things differently than other people. I don't know why. Do you? Has he told you? Did you ask him?"

She shook her head. "My relationship with Caleb doesn't lend itself to confidences."

"I'd ask him. Maybe I will. But right now, all I want to do is thank him." She looked past Jane down the hall. "There's Joe. He looks so happy." She started down the hall toward him. "I told you that everything was going to be all right. We all just have to help a little . . ."

"I take it that Eve is out of the proverbial woods." Jock was standing beside Jane and gazing after Cara, who was now looking up at Joe with a glowing smile. "Cara kept telling me that she would be, that all Eve and Michael needed was help. It appeared she was right."

"You don't seem too happy about it."

"I'm happy about Eve. I'm just a bit wary about Cara's attitude." He shrugged. "But I'll just keep an eye on her and make sure that she's safely ensconced with Eve and Joe in Atlanta."

"And then where will you be?"

"I'll come back here and help MacDuff find that treasure." His lips twisted. "Cara will be better off without me for a while. She has a new family, and she'll be making friends her own age. I won't be needed. The healthiest thing would be for her to forget about me."

"Maybe," Jane said bluntly. "But this is Cara. That's not going to happen. The bond is too strong. You abandon her, and she'll come after you to make sure that you're all right."

"I won't abandon her."

"Then don't make her think you are. Strike a balance. Just let her know that you'll be there for her."

He was silent. "I always knew you were very wise, Jane." He smiled. "Or maybe I just want you to be right about this."

"Wise?" She made a face. "Wrong. It's easy to see things when you're not involved. I tend to make a hell of a lot of mistakes when emotion rears its head." She smiled ruefully at him. "So when I'm not needed in Atlanta with Eve, I believe I'll join you and MacDuff back at Gaelkar. Perhaps I'll be better dealing with Cira and her ancient treasure than anything more current." She took a deep breath and straightened her shoulders. "But right now, we have Eve to think about. That's all that's important until she delivers her Michael." She started down the hall toward Joe and Cara. "And I'm going to think like Cara. Everything is going to be fine with Eve as long as she has help from her friends . . ."

EPILOGUE

EMORY HOSPITAL
ATLANTA, GEORGIA
SEVEN MONTHS LATER

"How is she?" Jock asked Cara as he strode into the waiting room. "Where's Quinn?"

"With Eve. He hasn't left her since she went into labor. They wouldn't let me be there." She jumped to her feet and went to the door to look down the hall at the delivery room. "It's that kid thing again."

"Imagine that," Jock said. "Or it might be that this is an experience they don't want to share."

She nodded. "I thought of that. But what if she needs me, and I'm not there?"

"Whenever I've dropped in on you and Eve and Joe in the last months, she's seemed perfectly healthy, and you were waiting on her hand and foot. I believe Joe and Eve can handle it from here."

"She wouldn't let me do very much." She looked away from the delivery room. "You got here awfully fast. I only phoned you and Jane a couple hours ago when we left the lake cottage. Jane said that she wouldn't be able to get here for six or seven hours."

"I was a little closer. The last time I was at the cottage, I thought that you might need me sooner rather than later."

"How close?"

"I checked in at a hotel in downtown Atlanta three weeks ago."

"But you didn't come to see me."

"You were busy. School and your practice and Eve."

"Not that busy. I'm never that busy. Didn't you want to see me?"

He touched her hair. "I always want to see you. But do you remember, I told you once that sometimes we wouldn't be able to be together?"

"Yes. I thought it was stupid."

He chuckled. "I got that impression. But you're in the minority, Cara. You need all the experiences these years will bring you. But I'll always be here when you need me."

She gazed at him. "Like now?"

"Aye. Like now." He smiled. "Now, may I get you a cold drink or something to eat?"

She shook her head. "I just want you." She plopped down on a chair. "I've been telling myself that everything's going to be okay with Michael. But I'm a little scared."

"I'm not." He took her hand. "You convinced me, and I'm going to stay convinced."

She looked at him. "See, that's why you're being stupid. You always make me feel better. Would I ever be too busy for that?"

"I hope not."

"Never," she repeated emphatically. She restlessly jumped to her feet again. "They thought Michael was going to come right away. What's keeping him?"

"You'll have to discuss that with him when he appears on the scene."

"He seems to have his own way of doing things. I just want Eve to be done with the—" She broke off as her phone rang. She glanced down at the ID impatiently. Then she stiffened, hesitated, and pressed the access. "It's not done," she said quickly into the phone. "It's not finished. I'll call you after Michael is born." She hung up.

"Who was that?" Jock was gazing at her with narrowed eyes. "You're upset."

"No, I'm not. I just didn't want to think about it yet."

"Think about what? Who was that?"

He wasn't going to give up. She knew Jock too well to believe that. "It was Kaskov."

He stiffened. "Kaskov? What the hell is he doing calling you?"

"He just wanted to know if Michael and Eve are all right."

"He knows she's in labor? Did you call him?"

"No, he's been concerned and probably had someone check."

"Why?"

"The antidote. He wanted to make sure that what he'd given us had good value."

"And when did he tell you that? Has he been phoning you?"

"Only twice. And then tonight."

"Did Eve and Quinn know?"

"No, it would only have upset Eve."

"I can see that," he said grimly. "It's upsetting me. Would you like to tell me what your discussions with him were about?"

It was the last thing she wanted. "I think you know. I told you that Kaskov doesn't think anything is free. He gave me Eve and Michael. We both knew that I'd have to pay eventually."

"The *hell* you will."

"I *will* pay, Jock. I was sent to save Eve and Michael, and I did it. I think I'm the only one who could have done it. For some reason, Kaskov wants me to be with him and, if that's the price, then it was worth it."

"I'll *kill* him."

"No, you won't. You said I had a soul and choices, and this is one of the choices." She smiled shakily. "But Kaskov isn't going to have it all his own way. Why do you think I've been talking to him? He'll only have me with him for one month a year, and I get to choose the place. Anything else is only open to negotiation."

"And you actually believe he'll keep his word?"

"Yes, if I keep mine."

"You're crazy. Do you know how dangerous he is?"

She didn't answer directly. "He won't hurt me. He wouldn't damage anything he values. If he wants me with him, he must value me." She took a step closer to him. She had to make him understand. "Eve might be dead if he hadn't given her that antidote. There was a reason that I had to be the one to go to him and persuade him to do it. Maybe there's a reason I have to be the one to go to him now."

"Bullshit. You don't have to do this. I won't allow it. Eve won't allow it."

"Then I'll go to Kaskov anyway. It will just make it more difficult for all of us. One month, Jock." She tried to smile. "Hey, some of my school friends go away from home to summer camp for that long."

"Some summer camp," he said through his teeth.

"It will be what I make it," she said quietly. "Choices, Jock."

"It's not going to happen."

"Not for a while. I'll make Kaskov understand I have to be with Eve during these next few months. As long as he knows I'll keep my word, he'll be patient."

"And you think I'll just let you go off with him?" His gray eyes were shimmering with intensity, his jaw tense. "Think again, Cara. For God's sake, you're happy, you love your life with Eve and Quinn. Nothing's going to destroy that."

"Only you, if you don't let me work this out to suit myself." She reached up and put her hand on his lips as he opened them to speak. "And I'm not going to talk about this any longer. You don't talk about it either, not to me, not to anyone else. This is the day that Eve has been waiting for, and nothing is going to spoil it or worry her. Do you understand, Jock?"

He stared down into her eyes for a long time. Then he reached up and took her hand from his lips. "Oh, I understand. You'll have your grace period, Cara." He lifted her palm to his lips. "Because, when you're not being totally irrational, you're full of grace yourself, and this day is important to you, too. I came here to share it with you, and I'll even promise that I'll try to handle this particular insanity without involving Eve." He smiled. "Let's call it a birthday gift to Michael."

He might still be upset with her but there was no anger, she realized with relief. There was only warmth and affection and that closeness that had always been there between them. "Michael will like that. He's always very protective of Eve." Her hand tightened on Jock's as she looked impatiently down the long hall. "But I wish he'd get here. Where on earth is he?"

"Where is he?" Eve asked in panic, reaching out for Joe's hand. "Where are they taking him?"

"Shh. Everything is fine."

"No, it's not." She was empty. Michael was gone from her body, and she was feeling a terrible loss. She wanted him back. "Not if he's not here with me."

"Hey, you're just exhausted and not thinking clearly. You had a pretty rough labor. You should have a long talk with Michael about putting you through it." Joe smiled down at her. "The doctors told you that they'd take the baby right away to examine and make sure there was nothing wrong with him."

She remembered, but it didn't stop the panic. "So when do I get him back?"

"Fifteen minutes, Eve. Give them a chance."

"I barely got a glimpse of him before they whisked him away."

"He looked pretty good to me. I think you did a stellar job, Eve."

"Michael wouldn't agree." She swallowed to ease the tightness of her throat. "He believed he was running the show, and I was just along for the ride."

"I'll have to teach him more respect. You're never just along for the ride." He bent and kissed her, slowly, deeply. "Thank you for my son, Eve." His arms were suddenly around her, and he held her tight. "It's . . . fantastic. A miracle."

"You *did* contribute, Joe." She chuckled, but she held him even closer. "Thank *you*." This was a precious moment that she wanted to cherish. When she had given birth to Bonnie, she had been almost alone, and there had been no one like Joe to hold and share the wonder.

But she wasn't sharing the wonder yet. She didn't have Michael.

He let her go and looked down at her with a quizzical expression. "You want me to go and hurry those doctors along?"

"Please."

He laughed and straightened away from her bed. "No problem. On my way, I'll stop and give Cara the good news." He moved across the hospital room and out the door.

Cara. Yes, they had to tell Cara, who had become such an integral part of their family during the last months.

Jane. Eve should call her and tell her that Michael had been in too much of a hurry to wait for her. But she would be here soon anyway.

Lord, Eve was lucky to have people around her who were loving and loyal and totally unique. She had never felt that gratitude more than after what she had gone through during the last months.

But where was Michael? She could feel her tension growing as the minutes passed. Those doctors wouldn't have said there could be a possible problem at birth if they hadn't had reason.

Caleb had not been worried. Trust Caleb.

But where was Michael?

Joe wouldn't leave her alone to worry when he knew that she was on edge. She just wanted to see her son and know that he was well. She would ring for the nurse if Joe didn't come back soon. Or, dammit, she would get up from this bed and go get Michael herself. It had been too long for—

"Here he is." Joe was holding the door open for a nurse carrying a small blue-blanket-wrapped bundle. "I had to commandeer Nurse Carey here to bring him back to you."

The nurse smiled and carefully put the soft bundle in Eve's arms. "And maybe I wanted to keep him a little longer. He's pretty wonderful."

"I know." Michael's softness was against her instead of in her body. It felt strange but wonderfully right. Don't look at him yet. Stretch out this moment she was going to remember forever. She looked at Joe. "What did the doctors say?"

"Eight pounds, two ounces. Twenty-one inches." He crossed the room and stood beside the bed. "And absolutely healthy."

She closed her eyes for an instant. "Thank God. No effect from the capsule?"

"Evidently nothing nasty touched him during the transfusion. I believe I'm going to have trouble being annoyed with Caleb whatever he does from now on."

Her eyes opened. "You'll get over it." But she wasn't sure that she would. Anything or anyone that kept her son safe was a gift beyond price. "They're certain?"

"Positive."

"Don't you want to see him?" The nurse was gently shifting the folds of the blanket. "He's one cool dude. He's going to be a heartbreaker when he grows up. He didn't cry at all when he was born. We had to make him do it while we were cleaning him up. Then he looked at us as if we'd insulted him. But then I swear he smiled at us. *Really* smiled. I know they say that babies don't smile before six weeks but he—" She shrugged. "Anyway, all the nurses are crazy about him."

"I bet they are. Michael has a talent in that direction." Eve felt Joe's hand on her shoulder as she moved the blankets away from her son's face. "Someone I love very much once told me that he was special."

Eve could see his face now. So small . . . Bright blue

eyes, pale satin skin, dark tufts of hair on that tiny head.
He was staring solemnly up at her.

"Hi," she said softly. "How are you doing? Glad to
meet you at last. We made it through, didn't we? Now
we'll just concentrate on all the good things." She reached
down and touched his cheek with a gentle finger.

He became still, alert, as if he was trying to hear her,
understand her.

It's a new way for us, isn't it? But we'll get used to it,
and it will be just fine.

Everything was fine in this moment. The waves of
love were overpowering in their intensity, and she was
having trouble keeping back the tears.

I told you he was extraordinary, Mama.
Bonnie.
She looked up, expecting to see her.
*No. Later. It's his time now. I just wanted to be with
you.*

And Bonnie *was* with her, and it made this time all
the more golden.

Bonnie . . . Michael . . . Part of her, the very best part.
Perfect.

She couldn't take her gaze from Michael's brilliant
blue eyes. They seemed to be holding her, talking to her,
telling her wonderful secrets about Cara . . . Jane . . .
Joe . . .

Oh, maybe those secrets were not as wonderfully
perfect as this moment, because they were all human
and so would change and grow through the years as Michael was going to grow and change. Still, pretty darn
wonderful, and all the more so because of that very hu-
manity.

And *he* was wonderful and that was all that was important right now. "Isn't he beautiful? He reminds me of

someone, Joe," she said softly. "But I just can't place who . . ."

"Well, it's not me. I'm definitely not beautiful."

"Yes, you are." But it wasn't Joe, and the baby didn't have her features either. "Maybe he's a throwback." She looked down at him again, and she felt an enormous rush of sheer love that filled all her mind and heart. "Welcome to our world, Michael."

Warmth. Comfort. Love.

All flowing toward her in an eternal stream from this tiny individual she was holding in her arms.

And then Michael smiled at her.

Read on for an excerpt from

NO EASY TARGET

by Iris Johansen

Available in April 2017 in hardcover from St. Martin's Press

CHAPTER
1

SAN DIEGO ZOO

Not mine!

Don't get angry. Margaret Douglas tried to make the thought soothing. But there was little you could do to soothe a female tiger as bad-tempered as Zaran. Margaret had only just forged the link between them and it would take time and patience to influence her. Even now the Sumatran tigress was baring those sharp white teeth and glaring menacingly at her. She was probably not going to listen. *I'm just asking you to consider that the cub might be your own. Everyone here at the zoo appears to think so.*

Stupid. Not mine.

Margaret tried something else. *Let me try to help you remember when the cub was born. It might—*

NOT MINE!

The thought was immediately followed by a roar. The tigress's green eyes were blazing as she gathered the muscles in her powerful body and then bounded at top speed across the cage toward Margaret!

Zaran's lunge just missed Margaret as she dove out of the cage and slammed the gate behind her.

Margaret drew a deep breath as she got to her feet and stared back at the roaring tiger through the bars.

Close. Very close.

Not polite, Zaran. I'm just trying to help.

The tigress was still pawing through the bars at her. *Stupid!*

"What the hell are you doing?" One of the zookeepers was striding toward Margaret. "You volunteers are supposed to feed and water the animals, not get them all upset."

He evidently hadn't seen her in the cage, thank heavens. "The tigers are a little testy, aren't they?" She smiled. "I wasn't feeding her. I was just thinking about cleaning her cage. Maybe I'll wait for a while."

"You shouldn't be near her anyway. Why do you think she's not in the habitat? The vets are having problems with her. She's not been accepting her cub."

"Right. Sorry." She started to walk toward the road. "I'll go help out at the vets clinic instead."

She glanced back over her shoulder at the tigress. *But think about it, Zaran. I'll get back to you later.*

Not mine!

We'll see. . . .

Not exactly a successful session with the tigress, she thought ruefully as she paused to get a Coke at a refreshment stand. But no one else at the zoo had gotten any response at all and they might give up soon. She couldn't let that happen. It would have a lifetime of consequences for that cub. She would just have to let Zaran settle down and then go back later and try again.

Her phone was vibrating in her pocket and she vaguely remembered it also doing that when she'd been in the cage with the tigress. Not surprising that she hadn't paid any attention to it.

She pulled it out and checked it.

A text from Eve Duncan.

CALL ME.

She smiled as she dropped down on one of the green park benches at the side of the road. She hadn't talked to Eve in too long a time. Eve could be demanding, too, when it suited her, but she was one of Margaret's few friends. And she'd much rather try to soothe Eve than that tigress. She started to dial Eve's number at the lake house.

"No arguments, Margaret," Eve Duncan said firmly after making her wishes known. "I want you here at the lake cottage by the end of the week. I'm going to prepay an airline ticket to Atlanta for you, and Joe will pick you up at the airport. I'd do it, but I don't want to expose Michael to some of those germs floating around airports."

"And you can't bear to leave the baby yet," Margaret Douglas teased. "How old is he? Six months?"

"Six months going on six years," Eve said softly. "He's totally amazing, Margaret. You'll see when you get here. Yes, I'm besotted, but at least I'm trying to expose him to other people and experiences. That's why I'm demanding your presence. He should get to know my friend Margaret, who helped saved both my life and his big sister Cara's. How soon can you get here? What are you doing now?"

"I'm working at the San Diego Zoo. But it's mostly volunteer." She thought about it. "Four days' notice. But you don't have to buy me a ticket. I know a pilot for a movie company who has a studio in Atlanta whom I can hitch a ride—"

"No," Eve said immediately. "No hitching rides with anyone. Not safe. Joe lectured you about that the last time." She paused. "Is it that you don't have ID in your own name to get on a commercial plane?"

"Don't worry about it. This pilot is a good guy and he owes me for—"

"Hush, Margaret," Eve said resignedly. "What name should I pay this ticket under? And don't give me any bull about it not being necessary. Someday I'm going to persuade you to tell me what's going on with you, but I owe you too much to force it right now. I just want you here to meet my son. What name?"

Eve wasn't going to be dissuaded. Oh, well, she really wanted to see Eve's baby. She'd find a way to reimburse her later for the airline ticket. "I've always liked the name Margaret Rawlins."

"You've got it," Eve said. "It will be at Delta Airlines in four days." She was silent an instant. "Everything okay with you, Margaret?"

"Everything's always okay with me. What could be wrong?"

"That's what I want to know. You're the closest thing to a Gypsy that I've ever met and you're always operating under the radar. Put those two things together and it usually spells trouble."

"Not for me. It's all in the attitude. I'll see you in a few days, Eve."

"Yeah, take care, Margaret." She hung up.

And I'll probably be bombarded with subtle and not-so-subtle questions when I reach the lake cottage, she thought as she hung up. No problem. She was used to fielding questions, and Eve would be so involved with that new baby and her career as a top forensic sculptor that she wouldn't press it too far.

Baby.

That reminded Margaret of Zaran and the brand-new tiger cub. She needed to find a solution on how to make the tigress accept the cub before she left for Atlanta. Which meant she should get working on it right now. If she couldn't work out the problem with a few suggestions to the vet about the way to handle it, she might have to pull an all-nighter on her own. Tigers were never easy. Females were twice as difficult when they were as unstable as Zaran.

So get moving so that she could finish her job before she left to go to see Eve and her son, Michael. She finished her Coke, got to her feet, and headed for the clinic. She could feel the happiness zinging through her at the thought of all the new things on the horizon. Babies and tiger cubs and friends she could love and trust. She wished she could explain to Eve that, in the end, nothing else was really important. All the fear and the running could be handled as long as she kept one truth in mind.

Life is good.

SUMMER ISLAND
CARIBBEAN

"Yes, I see him now, Officer Craig. He's near the exercise fields, talking to one of the techs." Dr. Devon Brady's narrowed gaze was fixed on the tall man in khakis and a black shirt, who was talking to Judy Wong beside the high white wooden fence. His back was to her, but she knew a great deal about body language, and she relaxed a little. "No sign of aggression that I can tell, but you were right to let me know he was on the island. I don't know how the hell he got this far without a security escort."

"I don't know, either," Craig said grimly. "He flew in early this morning and just slipped under the radar. Johnson was on duty at the airport terminal and said he seemed to be a nice guy and that the Gulfstream he was flying was pretty awesome. He didn't seem a threat to the clinic."

"That's not good enough," Devon said sternly. "He could be anyone from a rival researcher to a journalist. The Logan Institute doesn't want publicity about our work here. We're doing terrifically well and we want to keep it that way. How did he slip away from Johnson?"

"He doesn't know. Johnson turned his back for a minute and he was gone. We've been looking for him ever since."

Devon didn't like that, either. People who just flitted away from experienced security personnel could be either very clever or exceptionally well trained. This man had evaded the hunt of the island's very efficient security team for the past few hours, so he might be both. "Then you'd better have a few refresher training sessions with your men. And get some people down here right away."

"I'll come myself." He hung up the phone.

He knows his job is on the line, Devon thought. Craig was a good man, but this breach should never have happened. Just because they weren't dealing with biological agents or weapons on this island, everyone tended to let down their guard occasionally. They thought that just because the people here were working with very special dogs and documenting their unique, sometimes almost incredible abilities, there was no real threat. But industrial espionage was entirely possible with the groundbreaking results they were getting working with the dogs these days.

And men like the one she was approaching now managed to take advantage of that carelessness. She studied that body language again.

No aggression, but something else . . .

Persuasion. He was bent toward Judy Wong and every line of his body was focused and aimed on her. He could not have been more intent or interested.

And Judy was responding. Oh, yes, she was definitely responding to that persuasion. She was looking up at him and she was smiling, her cheeks flushed, and she appeared a little starstruck. No, more than a little.

Not good.

She increased her pace. "Judy, do you need me?" she called. "Do we have a problem?"

"No." Judy looked startled. "Everything is fine, Dr. Brady. I was just explaining to Mr. Lassiter what my job is with the dogs. He was interested in how I—"

"I'm sure he was," Devon said dryly. "But suppose I explain it to—is it Mr. Lassiter? You need to get back to the morning exercises, Judy."

The man turned, and for the first time she saw his face. "John Lassiter. And you must be Dr. Brady, who is in charge of the clinic and research facility. Judy is a great fan of yours." He smiled. "Did I step on toes?" He turned back to Judy. "I didn't mean to get you in trouble. I was just so interested. Forgive me?"

"Sure." Judy grinned and turned back to the exercise field. "Anytime."

No doubt she would have forgiven him if he'd nailed her to a cross, Devon thought sourly. Lassiter wasn't movie-star handsome, but that was a fascinating face. Pale green eyes, high cheekbones, and wonderfully shaped lips, not more than thirty-something, but he had a few threads of silver in that dark hair. But it wasn't that face so much as the powerful charisma he exuded. She found herself being drawn as Judy had been.

"Please don't be hard on her," Lassiter said gently. "She's a nice girl. I'm sure you're lucky to have her."

"Yes, I am. And I don't appreciate your taking up her time with your questions. What are you doing on this island, Mr. Lassiter?"

He smiled. "Not trying to weed out research secrets. I'm sure you do fascinating humanitarian work here, but I have no interest in it. Actually, I'm here to try to locate a former employee of your clinic. I should probably have gone to your office in the beginning, but I thought I'd amble around and see if I could find out a little on my own."

"We don't encourage 'ambling,'" she said coolly. "We work very hard here and strangers tend to be a disturbing influence."

"Oh, sorry, then I won't waste your time. Suppose we go to your office and I'll ask my questions and then get out of your hair." His smile remained, but Devon was aware of a subtle change in attitude. He had seen that she wasn't responding to that personal magnetism and had discarded it and gone on to the next stage of getting what he wanted. "I'm sure you've sent for security by now. But you don't really want them to get in our way when it would be so easy to end this by answering a few questions."

"I don't mind them getting in my way."

"But I do," he said softly. "So please accommodate me. Only a few questions."

There was just a hint of steel beneath that velvet softness, and she stiffened. "What questions? What employee?"

"Margaret Douglas."

She tried to keep her face expressionless. "I haven't seen Margaret in a couple years. I believe she's left the area. However, I don't know. She's never requested a reference."

"And you haven't been in contact with her? Strange. Judy was telling me that you were good friends when she worked here."

"Once someone leaves a job, they often cut off relationships. Why do you want to know where she is?"

"I may want to offer her a position." He tilted his head. "You see, we both have questions. We should really go up to your office at the clinic and discuss it."

She hesitated, gazing at him. Cool. Very cool. The threat was subtle, but she could sense its presence. He appeared to be as many-faceted as a glittering kaleidoscope. And who was to say that he wouldn't discover another way to find Margaret if Devon didn't satisfy him?

And the last thing Margaret needed was to have to deal with a threat like John Lassiter.

So maybe she should expose herself to the threat and try to find out more to tell Margaret when she warned her.

"Whatever," Devon said casually as she turned away. "I can give you an hour or so before my next appointment. But I can tell you now that I'm not going to prove very helpful to you."

"I appreciate your time, Dr. Brady." He fell into step with her and that smile had returned. "And you can never tell. I've found when it concerns Margaret Douglas, I always need to make it a practice of taking what I can get."

SAN DIEGO
THREE DAYS LATER

Margaret's phone rang as she was walking out the door to go for her shift at the zoo. She glanced at it casually and then stiffened warily.

Devon Brady.

It might be nothing, but she never liked to get a call from Summer Island. They were too close to what she considered ground zero, only several hundred miles from the place where all the nightmares had begun. And that made the threat not only to Margaret but to everyone on the island itself.

And this was Devon Brady. Margaret considered her a friend, but as head veterinarian at a cutting-edge experimental station that dealt not only with taking gigantic steps in improving health but actually extending the life of the dogs in her care, Devon was far too busy for casual chitchat.

Well, then don't waste her time.

She accessed the call. "Hi, Devon. How are things down there? I've been thinking about going back to the island for a month or two, if I'm still welcome. How are the goldens doing? Still as much—"

"Don't come," Devon said curtly. "Don't come anywhere near here, Margaret. We had a visitor three days ago."

"Visitor." Her hand tightened on her phone. "Who?"

"John Lassiter. Do you know him?"

Relief. "I've never heard of him. Maybe it will be okay."

"He doesn't look okay to me," she said grimly. "He looks like big-time trouble. He talked to a few of the techs before I even knew he was on the island and managed to dazzle them a bit. Then he went on the offensive from the minute he sat down in my office. He's sharp as a stiletto and he's used to getting his way. He moves from strength to strength. Tough. Very tough. I had a few problems fending him off."

Margaret had trouble believing that and it made her nervous. She knew that Devon was a powerhouse of both efficiency and skill. "What kinds of questions?"

"All about you. He gave me some bull about wanting to hire you for a job on his property in Texas. Where you are now. Where you came from. Who you associated with while you were on the island. Whether you had any off-island visitors. It went on and on." She paused. "I didn't tell him anything and I got rid of him as soon as I could. But that wasn't the end of it. He evidently doesn't like being frustrated. Because we had a security break-in the next night."

"What?"

"Only the file cabinet containing your records. Not that there was much in them anyway. You made sure that they were pretty scanty before you left the island. But he must have wanted to know every single detail about Margaret Douglas." She paused. "One other thing. I think he managed to hack my phone. Which means that he has your phone number. And if he's as sharp as I think he is, he might be able to trace your phone location. I thought you should know."

"Yes, I should." She could feel her heart start to pound. Calm down. John Lassiter. As she'd told Devon, she didn't know the name. He didn't have to be connected to Stan Nicos, the monster who had tormented and almost broken her. "Thanks for calling me, Devon. I'm sorry you had to go through this."

"Don't be ridiculous," Devon said bluntly. "Besides your being the best tech I've ever had, or ever hope to have, I don't want you to end up in the same shape we found you when we stumbled over you on that beach. I didn't think you were going to make it."

"I wouldn't have if it hadn't been for you. I've told you how grateful I am."

"Not grateful enough to tell me who did that to you."

"It's my problem, Devon." That had been such a close call. One of many since she had escaped from Nicos. It seemed as if he had been on her heels forever. "I wasn't going to involve you or anyone at the clinic. You got me well again; you gave me a job. I wasn't going to repay you by heaping that kind of ugliness on you." She added dryly, "But it seems I may have done it anyway. I was hoping that he'd give up the search. It's been over three years."

"'He'?" Devon didn't wait for an answer that she knew wouldn't be forthcoming. "Look, if you don't want to talk to me about it, that's fine. But I'm going to give you the same advice I gave you two years ago when you came to us. Talk to the police. Or I'll do it for you."

"Not an option. But you might make sure that island security is doubled for a while. I don't believe they'll bother you again if they think they've found out everything you know, but don't take chances."

"You're the one who shouldn't take chances. Look, I'm sending you a photo of Lassiter that I managed to take before he took off after grilling me. We ran down the name that Gulfstream he was flying was registered under. It was a corporate registration in California. Still under Lassiter. And I notified our security chief, Craig, to run a check on him after he left my office that first day. I wanted to be able to give you the entire background before I called you. I'll let you know what he finds out."

"That's good." She had a sudden thought. "But I'm getting rid of this phone. I'll call you with a different number as soon as I buy a new one. How long ago did you find out you were hacked?"

"I just discovered it this afternoon, but I think it must have happened sometime after the break-in. It was very slick. Lassiter didn't want me to know that he'd managed to do it."

And that meant that this Lassiter had had more than

twenty-four hours to trace her cell phone location. He could be listening now. "I'll call you," she said quickly. "Thanks, Devon." She hung up and drew a deep breath. She could feel her palms damp with sweat.

Close. Nicos hadn't been this close to her since Santo Domingo. How had he traced her to Summer Island? She'd thought she'd left everyone safe when she'd hopped that flight off the island. She hadn't even let Devon take her to that hospital in San Juan after she had found her. And she had been very careful not to leave any paperwork that might lead anyone to her since then.

It had happened. Nicos had evidently sent a particularly efficient bloodhound and tracked her down.

Stop worrying about how it happened. Accept it. Do what's necessary.

Her phone was pinging and she accessed the photo Devon had sent her.

John Lassiter.

He was half turned away, but he was gazing with a faint mocking smile at the camera, as if he'd known Devon was taking the photo.

As if he'd wanted her to take it.

And he appeared to be everything that Devon had said he was.

But she didn't recognize him, she realized with relief. It wasn't that he was traveling under a false name; he hadn't been on Nicos's island when she'd been there. The relief lasted for only the briefest moment.

That didn't mean Nicos might not have hired Lassiter after she had escaped from Vadaz Island. Since she had never set eyes on him, he had no other reason that she could see to go after her.

It had to be Stan Nicos. Nicos, with his fat wallet and hideous soul, had found a man as talented and corrupt as himself to hunt her down. Nicos, who controlled the major percentage of drugs and arms that made their way from South America to the rest of the world, wouldn't have found it that difficult. Just a small job in the scheme of his crime network, but he'd given the order to go and find her.

To bring her back to that house on the hill, as he'd told her he would.

Blood on the black-and-white tiles of the guest house.

"Too late." Nicos met Margaret's eyes. "Remember this, Margaret."

His gun pointed execution-style at Rosa's head.

"Please, Margaret." Tears running down the young girl's cheeks. "Make him stop. I'm begging you. I don't want to die. He'll listen to you."

Blood on the tiles. Blood on the tiles.

Don't think of that day. It had taken her years to move beyond it and come to terms. No, that was a lie. She had never come to terms with anything connected to that day or Stan Nicos. It still haunted her dreams and it only took a chilling threat like this to bring the memories flooding back to her.

She swallowed hard. Okay, Lassiter represented a threat and she had to deal with it. It wasn't as if she hadn't had to run from Nicos before. But that had been during the early years, when she had been skipping from island to island in the Caribbean, just trying to stay one step ahead of him. Once she'd managed to come back to the United States, it had been merely a question of, as Eve had said, staying under the radar.

So that's what she had to do again. Just get out of here and lose herself as she'd done so many times before. Stay away from the friends she had made over these last years to protect them. After a while, maybe she could afford to make contact again.

So text Eve and tell her that she wouldn't be able to meet her Michael yet. If she didn't, Eve would start to worry, and that would mean that she would be likely to start a hunt of her own. But not with this phone. She just hoped Lassiter hadn't been able to tap her calls for the last two days.

Get moving. Time to get out of here.

She turned and headed for her closet across the room. She could be out of here and on the road within thirty minutes. She pulled out her backpack and started stuffing it with clothes from the paper grocery sacks on the floor beside the backpack. It took her only a few moments and then she headed for the bathroom. Toothbrush, comb, hairbrush, soap, washcloth. Anything else she could do without or pick up later. It was amazing what you could live without if you were forced to do it. She had found that out when she had lived those years in the woods. Sometimes it was even emancipating not to be dependent on—

She stopped.

She had caught sight of her face in the mirror as she turned to leave the bathroom. Good God, she was a mess. Her lips were tight and the blue eyes looking back at her were wide with strain. She looked pale, tense, and on edge.

No, be honest, she looked scared.

Nicos has made me look like this, she thought with self-disgust. Three years and he could still cause her to feel this fear. She wasn't that kid any longer; she was over twenty. He shouldn't still have this effect on her. Three years and he could cause her to run like a rabbit because he'd sent some creep after her who had even been able to intimidate Devon.

Okay, she would run because it was smart to do it. But she was no rabbit and she would not abandon the things

she had to do before she had to leave. It shouldn't take
that long. Her duties at the zoo could be done by someone else, except for that tiger cub. It had become clear
that no one else could do that adjustment but her. She'd
stop on the way out of town and spend enough time to
try to reconcile the tigress to her cub.

She was already feeling better because of the decision,
and the woman in the mirror was no longer looking like
someone she wouldn't want to know.

She tilted her head and made a face at her reflection.
Hey, you've had it too easy lately. We can get through
this. Just stick with me, kid.

She opened the bathroom vanity drawer and took out
the small wallet photo album and stuffed it in her pocket.
You could do without most things, but memories were
important and photos helped. Same for music. She took
out her iPod and earphones and jammed them in her
other pocket. Then she took the SIM card from her phone
and smashed the phone against the porcelain bathroom
sink until it was in pieces. She'd pick up her new phone
at that shopping center near the zoo. She slipped on her
backpack and headed for the door.

As usual, she had left nothing behind that meant anything to her, nothing that could show anyone who she was
or where she would go next.

A broken phone, a few dishes in the cabinet, a couple
paperback books.

Try to put that together and find me, Lassiter.

She didn't look back as she slammed the door behind her.

Lassiter isn't going to like this, Neal Cambry thought,
as he looked around Margaret Douglas's one-room studio flat. He had orders to locate the woman and not let

her get away. But she had clearly abandoned this place. Bite the bullet. Call Lassiter and let him know that Margaret Douglas was in the wind again. He reached for his phone.

"We have a problem," he said when Lassiter answered. "She's not here. I talked to her landlord and she slipped an envelope in his mailbox with this week's rent this morning. No forwarding address."

Lassiter was cursing. "Of course there's no forwarding address. She never leaves one. Did you search her apartment?"

"I'm there now. There's not much to search. It's pretty basic, a minimum studio apartment. I can't find any leads."

"Look harder. I'm on my way there from the airport now. I'll be there in fifteen minutes. Find something by the time I get there." He hung up.

Cambry flinched. When Lassiter gave an order, he expected it to be obeyed and the impossible to become possible. And he had only fifteen minutes to make that happen. Ordinarily, he looked upon working for Lassiter as a challenge; the money was excellent and his employer was usually not unreasonable. Besides, they were friends, and he owed him big-time. But *usually* wasn't in Lassiter's vocabulary where this woman was concerned. He was totally committed to finding her and nothing was allowed to get in his way. Lately, Cambry had actually found himself feeling sorry for Margaret Douglas.

But not sorry enough to pit himself against Lassiter unless it was absolutely necessary. They went back a long way and in Afghanistan he'd become fully aware of both his potential and ruthlessness. No way that Cambry would take his money and not turn in full value. That would be most unwise.

So find something that would make Lassiter believe he was earning that money.

Fifteen minutes.

"She smashed her phone." Cambry handed Lassiter the remains when he walked into the apartment. "She did a good job. It'll be hell checking her directory history."

"I managed to get a lot of info from the tap I put on it after Summer Island. I'll get my San Francisco office to put it on priority," Lassiter said. "What else?"

"Just a few paperbacks." He handed them to Lassiter. "Two mysteries and a how-to manual on how to set up a Wi-Fi system. She bought them at a used-book store in the Gaslamp Quarter." He hesitated. "That's how the entire apartment is set up. Everything cheap and second-hand. Her landlord said that she never had visitors and he had no idea where she worked. I asked if he'd made a copy of her driver's license, so we could at least get her photo, but she told him that she'd lost it and hadn't gotten her replacement."

"I have her photo now." Lassiter handed him a copy of a small faded photo. "I got it from one of the people she worked with on Summer Island. I suppose her landlord didn't even make her fill out a reference or credit application?"

"How did you know?" Cambry shook his head. "He said that he usually did that, but he kept putting it off. He said he knew that she would pay her rent." He met Lassiter's eyes. "He trusted her. He liked her. He said he was sorry to see her go. Kind of a surprise."

Not to Lassiter. It was the first time Cambry had been directly involved in the hunt, but this was old news to Lassiter. "She manages a great con wherever she goes. I ran into the same thing down in the Caribbean. I couldn't break through that protective wall she builds around herself." His lips tightened. "I was forced to take alternate steps."

"I won't ask you what they were," Cambry said with a grimace. "But any con she's working evidently isn't bringing her any money." He was looking down at the photo of the fair-haired girl in jeans, sandals, and blue chambray shirt. "This is Margaret Douglas? She's not much more than a kid. She looks like some fresh-faced college girl. She kind of . . . glows, doesn't she?"

That had been Lassiter's first thought, too, and he had tried to dismiss it immediately. He'd been having enough trouble keeping his perspective in the past months. He'd seen photos of Margaret before while he'd been on the hunt for her, but they'd all been scratchy, out of focus, and faded. He knew Margaret Douglas didn't like her photo taken. This one that he'd talked Judy Wong into giving him was . . . different. As Cambry had said, her blue eyes were shining with humor and she looked tanned and glowing, as if lit from within. Her smile was luminous. Even her pale brown hair was sun-streaked and seemed to glow. "It was taken three years ago."

"She doesn't look more than eighteen or nineteen. That means she was even younger when she was living with Stan Nicos."

"He has a reputation for liking them young. The son of a bitch has whores imported from bordellos in Bogotá who are much younger than that. And she must have been very satisfying. He kept her for nine months and he's been searching for her ever since she left him."

Cambry slowly shook his head. "If she was only a kid, maybe she had a reason to want to start a new life. Why else would she have been running all this time?"

"I don't know and I can't let it matter. He wants her

back. That's what I have to concentrate on. She's the key, the only one I've found. That's what *you* have to concentrate on."

"I believe in new starts, Lassiter. You gave me one."

It wasn't the first time he'd said something like that. "Drop it, Cambry," he said. "The circumstances were different with you. In this life we have to pick and choose. And I can't afford to choose Margaret Douglas this time. Decisions always have repercussions. She'll have to live with the decision she made when she went to live with Nicos all those years ago. He probably dangled a few expensive baubles and she—"

" 'Expensive baubles'?" Cambry chuckled. "Look at this place. I've seen better apartments in the L.A. housing development where I grew up. She sure isn't into luxury."

"No?" Lassiter's lips twisted. "You should have seen the guesthouse where Nicos was putting her up before she decided to part company with him. It was very impressive." He looked around the flat. Cambry was right. It was clean but shabby and completely without personality. That very lack of comfort made him more frustrated. He had spent the last year trying to track down Margaret Douglas, but she had been like a ghost. She had carefully erased her presence wherever she had traveled. In a world that ran on bureaucracy and documents, he had been able to find only the flimsiest of paperwork pertaining to Douglas. A few photos. No fingerprints. He had traced her movements through five towns in the Caribbean, and it was only when he reached Summer Island that he'd found anything concrete to use to find her. "Okay, I admit she's clearly trying not to do anything that will draw Nicos's attention to her again."

"Then why not try something else?" Cambry said quietly. "I've never seen you like this before. I thought you'd give up when you couldn't locate Margaret Douglas after you checked out Santo Domingo and Curaçao. But you just went on and on, until it became an obsession. Why, Lassiter?"

"You know why."

"I thought I did when it started. Somehow I became lost along the way."

"Too bad. Because I can't afford to stop now. Time's running out and she's the only card I have left to play. Do you think I've been focusing solely on Margaret Douglas while I've been searching for her? I've contacted everyone I could, pulled every string, but I've come up zero. It *has* to be her." He looked him in the eye. "Do you want to back out?"

Cambry shook his head. "I wouldn't do that. I owe you too much. I just don't want anyone hurt who shouldn't be hurt."

"It will be up to her. I'll work with her, if she'll work with me."

"But you don't think she'll agree to work with you?"

After months of hunting and investigating everything about her, Lassiter knew that she wouldn't. "Maybe you can change her mind. I'll let you try, Cambry. She's been on the run for over three years. It's not likely she'll stop." He went to the window and looked down at the street. "And, as I said, time's running out."

"I know." Cambry sighed. "I might give it a whirl, but you'd have a better chance." He suddenly grinned. "And you were talking about cons? Who's better at it or has more experience than you? Besides, you seem to know her inside and out."

Inside and out, Lassiter thought wryly. Sometimes he thought that was true. After all the people he'd talked to about her, all the apartments and flats where he'd searched and tried to build a picture of the person who was Margaret Douglas. He knew her favorite pieces of music, he knew she liked comedy and adventure movies and shied away from anything sad. He knew she could drive a car but seldom did because she needed a license, and that required documents. He knew that she drew people to her but was wary about taking lovers.

And he knew a few other rather bizarre and interesting things about her that he had not shared with Cambry.

He knew all those things, but he'd never heard her voice and only recently had seen a decent photo of what she actually looked like.

"It won't work," he said. "I want it too much and I've waited too long. I'm past the point of persuasion where she's concerned." He shook his head. "And if she doesn't agree, then I'll use her anyway. I've gotten this close and I'm not letting her skip away into the sunset again." He turned and strode toward the door. "She's *mine*."

"Not if we've lost her again," Cambry said.

"I haven't lost her yet," Lassiter said over his shoulder. "She was in this apartment only a few hours ago, before her friend Devon sent her flying away in panic. I have a few more places to search before I give up. I believe I found out more about her on Summer Island than she'd want me to know. . . ."